IMMORTALITY

EPOCALYPSE

DAVID M. MARTORANO

IMMORTALITY – The Novel – David M. Martorano
Copyright © 2024 David M. Martorano, M.D.

All rights reserved. No part of this book may be reproduced or used in any manner without the prior written permission of the copyright owner, except for the use of brief quotations in a book review.
To request permissions, contact the publisher at:
Martin@ImmortalityTheNovel.Com

Library of Congress Number: 2024906277

First Hardcover Edition July 2024.

www.ImmortalityTheNovel.Com

ACKNOWLEDGEMENTS

First and foremost, the constant love and support from my family. Annie, Ari, and Chiara, most of all, you've been there for me through trying times and celebrations.

I also couldn't have created a work like this without the help of David Khalaf, my editor. Long hours and great guidance that kept an amazing story on course.

Finally, Mom and Dad. You always supported me and fostered a belief in myself.

FOREWORD

This is not a book about God. It is not a book about atheism, either. It is an exploration of Man's view of himself and the lens through which he perceives a life beyond that of his mortal self. It is a cautionary tale.

With the coming singularity, Artificial Intelligence is poised to redefine man's destiny. Like a toddler with a handgun, or Oppenheimer's Manhattan Project, humanity invites disastrous consequences when capability outstrips comprehension.

Everything described in the following pages is possible, if not probable. This is the future we have invited. Now, we must determine if it is the future we want and deserve.

PROLOGUE

> To be immortal is commonplace; except for man all creatures are immortal, for they are ignorant of death; What is divine, terrible, and incomprehensible is to know that one is immortal. —Jorge Luis Borges

Dom awoke in complete darkness. There was total silence, not even a heartbeat could be heard. *Who turned out the lights? Am I home? Am I having a stroke?* Dom recalled that a stroke could cause a loss of vision. Is that what was happening? He tried to remember whether he was old enough to have a stroke. He couldn't feel his hands.

It seemed like the room might have been getting a bit brighter. Like dawn creeping through closed eyelids. Maybe this was just a really dark room, or maybe he had fallen and hit his head. He tried to speak. No luck there either. Maybe he could text someone. Where was his phone? Did he even have a phone?

Nothing was in focus yet and he couldn't hear. *Oh my God! I'm deaf too!* Was he in a hospital? Could he call a nurse? Did they know that he was awake? His name was Dom. That he was sure of. But Dom what?

Maybe he'd been drugged, or this was a nightmare from which he could not wake. But he needed to. He desperately needed to.

Hello? He thought. Was that his thought? *Hello? How long will I be in here?* It didn't feel like his thought. It was all confusing. The room continued to brighten. He had crab for lunch. Was he sick from the shellfish? He'd heard about neurotoxins in shellfish.

Are you my lawyer? This seemed like a very bizarre question to be asking himself. He was not a lawyer. No one should be their own attorney.

I didn't do it! Another intrusive idea soon morphed into *I didn't kill anybody.* This was definitely a dream or a stroke or drugs. This is why he never tried drugs; he knew this would happen.

Who didn't I kill? He wondered, but somehow, this thought seemed different from the previous ones. He thought this thought. The other thoughts felt out of his control.

The room continued to brighten. It now felt like he was watching a video play out before him. The visuals that were coming into focus seemed distant and disconnected. Like he wasn't seeing them. The experience was reminiscent of receiving a transmission of some sort. Everything in focus, at the same time. A blurry focus that lacked depth of field. Everything was the same. He must look like a bird or a dog tilting their head as some sort of reality check. He couldn't wink, either. He tried to close one eye and then the other. But nothing happened. Or rather, nothing changed. *I'll close both eyes.* This time, everything went dark. When Dom reopened his eyes, things were brighter and in clear focus.

A woman was moving her lips, but he couldn't hear her. She looked familiar, but he did not know her name. She did not appear entirely real but she moved like a real person. *Is this some sort of virtual reality?*

The woman came closer. He thought he should have been able to feel her voice on his face—she was that close. But he didn't feel anything. She was shouting, or it looked like she was shouting, at least. She had blond hair, was in her late twenties, and was very pretty. She seemed more real now. Were they going to have sex? Had they already had sex? "Can you understand me?" There came another alien thought! What were these?

Dom looked at her lips; following closely, he made a chilling discovery. She was mouthing the thoughts he was having. She was asking, "Can you understand me?"

Yes, he thought or tried to say—or both. "Yes, I can understand you."

The woman appeared relieved. This time, he thought he could almost hear her when she asked, "are you my attorney?"

Thirty-eight years earlier, Nick Santos rushed towards campus. It was time to find out if this new motor would push his bike beyond its previous limits. As he turned towards the river, his legs pumped with fresh enthusiasm. The digital speedometer flashed forty-two miles per hour. Fresh fallen leaves swirled off the pavement, rising high above his head. A satisfied smile crossed his boyish face as Maple, Ash, and Poplar leaves danced in his wake.

Vassar Street was a parking lot this time of day. Nick opted for bike over bus whenever the weather permitted. He hopped the curb and veered off the sidewalk. He always rode the long way round. Coming from the southeast afforded him the best view of the Stata Center's twisted metal and off-kilter brick facade.

Just six years old when he attended the building's dedication, Nick watched his father shake hands with *the* Frank Gehry. As the years went by, Nick admired the man's works, but more the man himself. Gehry left literal icons scattered across the globe. He had cemented a name for himself beyond the realm of architecture. His impact would endure for centuries.

Nick smiled at every person he made eye contact with on the short ride over to Nano. He skidded to a stop in front of the newest building on campus. This would not be a quick visit. He took the time to lock his precious toy.

Nano was "The Big New Home of Small." Nick found the catchphrase cute but unimaginative. The building's facade lacked the flash of Gehry's work. Yet, there was no arguing, Nano was the place to complete their work. Its labs and prototyping equipment had brought today's achievements within reach.

Nick dashed up two flights to their shared lab space. His brother, John, was picking his way through a rat's nest of wires. Hundreds of tinned, twenty-two-gauge wires sprang from all six sides of a plastic prototyping cube.

"How do you know which wire's which?" Nick asked.

As if the answer were clear as day, John replied, "They're color coded."

Nick observed and raised an eyebrow, "They're all red."

John carefully inspected the entire mess, appearing to consider his brother's critique, before explaining, "Red, for wire."

Annoyed, Nick shot back, "Cute. Might be a challenge to debug that mess."

"Not to worry." John pointed to a jump drive in Nick's hand. "You hold the key, little brother. That code our sister gave you corrects for state changes in real time." John appeared to consider the possibility of failure. "At least, that's what it's supposed to do."

Nick was still skeptical as to whether today would be the day. "I know she's the smart one, but do you really think it's going to work on the first try?"

John never looked up from his work as he continued to connect wires to the cube. "Yeah, don't you?" A smirk crept up the side of his face.

"Sure. I mean, when have any of her scripts forced you to throw a perfectly good computer out the window or throw your brand new hard drive in the trash?"

John looked up, his eyes making contact with his younger brother's. "Are you asking for the actual count?" They had both experienced setbacks with some of Cynthia's more aggressive programs. Overall, the progress of the trio had been nothing short of amazing. "It's not our first try anyway," John reminded him. "We've been at this for two years."

"You and me, sure. Cynthia's only half present. Lately, her mind always seems focused on more important things. She gets the work done but leaves it at security. I'm not sure her heart's still in this project."

"She never cared about hardware, and ARTI is some next-level shit." ARTI, was ARTificial Intelligence, incarnate, a Cynthia-led, military-funded project. Unlimited cash with strings attached.

"Her AI won't get much done without your chip," Nick reminded him.

"She's sure ARTI will predict the future."

"She thinks it can calculate the probable future. It's different. A lot of behavioral psychology, complex TensorFlow stuff, and her crazy machine learning models." Nick's mind always shifted to the ability to monetize tech. "The finance people will do anything to get at it."

"Not in my book. Qubits would've been better."

"ARTI is the future, no doubt. Feels like magic and makes OpenAI look like a Windows 2000. Lucky for her, consumers have done all the heavy lifting. ARTI was pretty much built by their cell phone assistants. If only they knew." He paused thinking and admitted "I mean I know, but I still use my cellphone."

"Yeah, I used to worry about it. Remember when I kept my stuff locked down? No Siri, no Apple Intelligence, that year I went back to the flip phone?" John looked briefly at his brother, before going back to completing the final connections. "Once Cynthia showed me how ARTI could profile me from data on your phone or her device, I went out and got the latest tech. I enabled every single feature. Privacy doesn't exist."

He threw in a well-worn cliché. "*If you can't beat 'em…* It's not a question of if that stuff will be used against us, just when. At least with Santos Corp, we'll be the ones with our hands on the switch when AI finally takes over."

John was still completing the setup. "I'm not sure I want that responsibility."

"I do."

John pulled his hands away from the wires. "Ready."

"Time to figure out if you should have kept your job at QuantCore," Nick joked.

"Only you could have convinced me to leave the world's most promising startup and come back here to be a lab rat," John retorted, his voice tinged with both irritation and affection. He often reminded Nick of the gamble he had taken. "I checked today. Let's be real, I check every day. As of this morning, I'd be worth twenty-three million dollars on paper."

"Don't sell yourself short. If you'd stayed, QuantCore would already be public, and we'd be sipping margs on your yacht."

"Not likely. You know I hate boats - terrible investment."

"But *I* like them," Nick said.

"Exactly my point. *I* would own a boat *you* talked me into buying."

"Not a boat." Nick spread his arms to capture the size of his idea and emphasized, "A yacht!"

"And, I hate tequila. Now, can we get back to changing the world?"

Nick corrected, "Changing our destiny." He had urged John to keep going and create processors that used quantum dots, a zinc-derived technology. He theorized that these dots would be able to store more than one bit of information in each transistor, even at room temperature.

The brothers were heralds of the revolution. "Quantum dots will change the planet," Nick promised investors. "Non-binary computers will do far more with way less." When the investors pushed back about competition from supercooled Qubits, Nick predicted, "Qubits will never leave the lab." He went on to explain, "Qubits are too costly and not scalable." The message proved digestible for a handful of investors. Nick's greatest gift was selling the genius of others. In this case, his own flesh and blood.

Cynthia waltzed in and offered a broad grin as she pressed John. "Don't tell me you already ran it."

"Not loaded yet. Better not say 'forty-two'," John warned. referencing Douglas Adams' famous answer to "Life, the Universe and Everything." In his comic masterpiece of the same name, a massive supercomputer calculates the meaning of life. Eons later, it simply states that "Forty-two" is sum of life, the universe and everything. Tragically, although certain of the result, the computer is unable to supply any context or explanation,. The entire galaxy is left to ponder the answer's implications for billions of years. Cynthia was convinced that quantum computing would get science to "forty-two" and no further.

Determined to make his mark, Nick reminded them both, "We're setting a record here. Gotta say, *Hello, World!*" Nick was still aiming to win an annual competition. Teams around the world pushed the envelope trying to use the fewest transistors possible. They built microcomputers with the sole purpose of running, "Hello, World!"

"Geneva got it down to 1,283 transistors just last week," John reminded them.

"We'd have beaten them to the punch, if John hadn't postponed this twice." Cynthia jogged their memory.

Not in the least bit ruffled, John explained. "Stephanie was defending her dissertation. She needed my support."

"The girl needs help, I'll give you that." Cynthia teased. "If she spent less time praying for answers and more time finding them, maybe she would have finished on time." Unable to resist, she prodded. "Do you help her finish on time, John?"

"Just because her beliefs are different, doesn't mean she's not smart. As far as your innuendo, I'm not gonna to stoop to your level and I won't even dignify it with a response."

"If you want to keep a woman happy, you have to get down on her level. Even Nick knows that."

"You have a point, but is it kind to make fun of the girl just because she is religious?"

"That might be the most hypocritical thing you've ever said." Her brother's rabid atheism compelled her to add, "Might be the most hypocritical thing anyone has ever said. You, defending religious beliefs, just to kiss John's autistic ass? What does he have on you?"

As if to highlight his lack of social awareness, John argued, "I'm not sure it's the most hypocritical thing anyone has ever said."

"Really?" Cynthia was on a roll. "I've seen Nick get kicked out of faculty events because he couldn't shut up about 'The God Delusion.' He quoted Dawkins to Cardinal O'Malley at Dad's funeral."

Nick admitted, "Guilty as charged. The religion thing, I probably was a little disingenuous in defending Stephanie's beliefs." Then he changed his tone. "I'm just happy that John has a girlfriend. I've made some amazing predictions, but never saw that coming. Now, speaking of predictions, we have a record to smash."

Nick abruptly shifted to another subject, stripping anyone of a chance at rebuttal. "How was your meeting with the bigwigs? Steve mentioned there was an admiral there."

"They're keen on my new operating system. I'm calling it CynOS." Cynthia pointed to the jump drive. "Pretty much the same stuff that's on there. I took out the classified stuff and ARTI." Nick and Cynthia had been working together on the human behavior simulator, ARTI. Cynthia rubbed her hands together with anticipation. "Time to find out if my baby brothers are going to make me a capital 'B'."

Unable to resist, Nick grinned mischievously. "You're already a capital B." He paused for effect, then corrected himself. "Oh, *billionaire*?"

Nick strapped on a pair of vintage goggles he'd *borrowed* from the Los Alamos' exhibit. Striking a dramatic pose, he quoted from the Bhagavad Gita, "Now, I am become death, the destroyer of worlds."

Cynthia was unimpressed. "It's five fucking volts, Dr. Oppenheimer." She came in closer and tried to look through the lenses. "Can you even see through those?"

John's finger tripped the start switch and Nick pulled the goggles onto his forehead. A beep announced the processor's start then "boot loader" flashed across a small LED screen. Seconds passed before "Hello World" appeared.

He popped a confetti cannon, then noticed John was still staring at the screen. The brothers looked on as the words faded. The text was replaced by "Current Transistor Count: 483 Failed Circuits: 17." A countdown appeared shortly thereafter, "5, 4, 3, 2…" It stopped at two. This countdown was not part of the plan. The brothers didn't know where it came from. Then, five and three disappeared.

All that were left were the numbers four and two.

Cynthia was the first to speak. "I'm hungry. Which one of you future billionaires is taking me to Felipe's for tacos?"

"I'm buying!" Nick was quick to offer.

The trio stepped out of the lab and into the limelight. None could have imagined the impact of their discovery. Gutenberg's printing press took decades to spread across Europe and its full impact would take centuries to realize. In the information age, the speed of adoption of CynOs and Quantum Dot technology left even the usually prescient Nick Santos dumbstruck.

Within a month, investors were climbing over each other to acquire the smallest stake in the newly formed, Santos Corp.

Within six months, their technological breakthrough—the attention and wealth accompanying their triumph—would change their lives in unimaginable ways.

Within five years, the trio would be the wealthiest family on earth.

Within a decade, their inventions would change the course of humanity.

Within fifty years, their breakthroughs would change and redefine what it meant to be human.

This is not their story...

CHAPTER 1

All secrets are truths yet to be told

-Charles Luxold, PhD
– "The God Within Us"

Ping checked for a signal on her phone. It still read, "No network," even after she had already tried switching in and out of airplane mode and restarting the device. Other employees stared at their phones and engaged in similar rituals to summon the "bars" back to the tops of their screens. Eventually, each one settled into a silent wait, hoping the outage would resolve itself. Ping was confident that the issue lay with the carrier.

She needed the new Red Shuttle schedule. The Red Shuttle ran from the current factory in Zhengzhou to the new factory at Luzhuang Village, some ten kilometers to the south. The posted schedules were obviously out of date.

The mist in the air was giving her a chill. She had been sitting for well over an hour and the bench's metal bars had sucked a little too much heat from her body. Ping stood and began to pace to keep warm. Initially, she confined her pacing to the front of the bench, in case she wanted to sit back down. As boredom won out, Ping began walking laps around the shuttle stop.

Still, there were no buses.

On what would be her final lap, Ping looked south. *It's not too far to walk, not more than a couple of hours.* Ping broke free of the shuttle stop's orbit, not knowing how long her journey would be. Her only concern was getting to Lánhuā 5, the new plant, and getting settled into her new apartment.

Twenty minutes into her walk, Ping could see her old place just a few blocks to her left, but there was no reason to visit. Everyone had moved out days ago. She was among the last managers at the plant. Today, had been the final day of Lánhuā 4's shutdown. By the time the movers arrived to pick up her belongings, employee housing was a ghost town. The only people she had seen in days were maintenance crews renovating other units for the next wave of tenants.

Ping missed her bike. The movers had taken that with everything else. This morning, Lánhuā had paid for a DiDi so she could get to work. Now, she regretted not taking her bike. Lánhuā 5 would be a long walk in work shoes. But her new housing assignment was there. She had no choice.

One good thing though was that there was no need to hurry. Lánhuā 5 would be open whatever time she arrived. There were as many workers at midnight as there were at midday. Even human resources was twenty-four seven.

Ping hadn't bothered to write down directions or her new address, it was all stored in her company profile. She assumed the shuttles would take her there. Lánhuā always had packets waiting on the shuttle, and under typical circumstances, the information would have been accessible through her phone. Busy with other aspects of the shutdown and her move, Ping had failed to anticipate the possibility of a device outage.

Now, she mused over the irony of her predicament. Ping managed a group of some of the best cellular communication engineers in Northern China. With the tools at their disposal, they would have known what happened before she asked and told her exactly when she would have her service restored. Outside Lánhuā's gates, Ping was as much at the mercy of sunspots and power outages as any other customer.

Her walk would take her through Shuanghehu Zhongyang Park. Ping had lived in Zhengzhou for almost a decade but had only been to the park once before. A sprawling lush maze of gardens and man-made water features created a paradise in the southern district of Zhengzhou. Water diversion from the north fed one of the world's most amazing urban green spaces.

As beautiful as they were, the water features were a challenging maze to navigate without a phone or map. Ping checked again. Still, no signal. By now, she had passed dozens of people—all engaged with their devices and obviously online — confirming suspicions that her carrier was the problem.

Lost in corridors of late-blooming lilies and roses, it was easy to forget she was on a mission. Ten years had passed since Covid-19 made its mark on the world, yet masks still created a parade of unwelcoming faces, making it impossible to differentiate between acquaintance and stranger. The Chinese were accustomed to avoiding eye contact, though, and masks just made the custom more off-putting. In a city of ten million people, you could walk forever without recognizing a familiar face.

Despite the recent surge, Ping refused to go back to masking outside of work. She hated the claustrophobic sensation and found the smell of her own breath bothersome.

As she waded through the crowd, Ping's natural beauty invited occasional "eye smiles" amidst a tide of disapproval. She made the effort to meet the gaze of mask wearers. After an hour of this silent challenge, one pair of oncoming eyes behaved quite differently.

A man stopped and pulled a familiar face from behind his mask. "Ping?!"

Ping immediately recognized the voice; it belonged to her best programmer. "Lin?! What are you doing here?"

Candidly, Lin answered, "I'm supposed to meet a girl." He was always trying to meet girls. "So far, I haven't had much luck with Soul. Not sure she's coming." Soul was a popular dating app in the area. Changing subjects, Lin said, "I'm surprised you're not home already."

"I would be if the shuttles had been running. We just wrapped up the relocation today. Final shut down of Lánhuā 4," Ping explained.

Lin clarified, "I meant home with your parents, like the rest of us."

Ping didn't follow and explained, "There was no time for me to go to Ankang. I knew I would be needed at Luzhuang as production geared up. Figured I'd see you there."

Lin chuckled awkwardly, "That's what we all thought." Seeing that Ping hadn't grasped the situation, Lin's frustration grew, but his desire not to embarrass her pushed him to be more direct. "You do know what happened, right? The layoffs?" He paused, but Ping showed no sign of recognition. "We've all been laid off. There were no transfers—not a single one. Rumors are flying that there's no new factory. I even heard that Santos Corp acquired Lánhuā."

Ping was immediately dismissive, even in her body language as she shook off his words. "These Santos rumors. Three kids from Boston are buying China," Ping said confidently, looking Lin directly in the eye. "The factory is real. I'm headed there now."

Lin continued. "Well, they loaded us onto shuttles. Managers gave us confidentiality agreements before giving us our severance and a ticket home." Lin pointed east. "My parents live there. So, I told them to forget their confidentiality agreement, and just got off here." Lin pointed at his feet.

Ping argued, "That doesn't make sense. Where are you working now?"

Lin spoke deliberately, "I'm not working, Ping. There are no jobs. These layoffs started months ago. They hid that from all of us. There were 20,000 layoffs in the first wave. Those were the lucky ones; they got the good jobs. I stayed on until wave five. By then, there was nothing left. There is literally no work. Not in tech, not in waste removal. Thankfully, my parents still have their jobs. I'm with them until I figure something out."

Ping had never seen or heard of someone with Lin's skills, going a day without work. She wasn't sure whether something else had happened that he just wasn't sharing with her. That seemed far more likely than a corporate conspiracy. Lin liked to drink, and he made some of the women he worked with quite uncomfortable. She wondered whether he was trying to hide an embarrassing incident with this ridiculous cover story that she wasn't falling for.

"I'm sorry for the run of bad luck, Lin. I'll see if there is anything for you when I get to Lánhuā 5." Ping was a senior manager; she would keep his story in mind. If Lin had been laid off for no reason, she'd find a way to bring him back. Despite his personal life, Lin was the best software guy she knew.

Lin didn't seem overly confident in her offer, but he trusted Ping. "I'll send you my new number. Company phone just stopped working the other day." He went on to explain, "Then it blanked, and I lost all my contacts."

Ping went to update Lin's contact. More tech issues—a blanked-out contacts icon appeared on her screen. "That's odd. Mine's not working either."

Lin grew frustrated at her naivety and urged, "Not odd, Ping. Lánhuā!"

"You're ridiculous. My contact list isn't worth hacking." As the words left her lips, Ping felt her stomach involuntarily tighten. *Too many coincidences, too close together*. Maybe she had been laid off. She should have waited for the shuttle. Now, she needed to get to the new factory as fast as possible for reassurance. "Lin, I have to go," already resuming her trek.

Lin called after her, "Don't worry, Ping. I'll find you! I can find anyone."

White noise played from the nightstand. The windows were programmed to let the sunlight filter in. The increasing brightness brought Charles Luxold out of his deep early morning slumber, ending what would be the last night of sleep in his life.

The night before, Charles toyed with the idea of taking a sleep aid or a nightcap. He ultimately chose to lie awake, contemplating his mortality. As the hours passed, his mind meandered down a dusty road of memories, eventually leading him into the arms of sleep.

The only dream that lingered until morning was about the sea. Charles was on a catamaran, bigger than anything boat they had inside The Dome. There was a storm, something that couldn't happen inside The Dome. Nick was at the helm. Waves broke over both bows. Then, a large wave took Eve. One second, she was there— then gone— swept overboard. Eve disappeared in the froth of the tempest. Charles woke in a cold sweat.

He lay there trying to make sense of the dream. Charles was the one who was leaving; Nick and Eve would stay behind. There were no waves in the Atlantean Sea. It was a dome-covered reservoir where nothing bigger than paddleboat traversed its calm waters. Eve had said something as she was swept away. Charles couldn't remember what it was. She looked so sad. Nick refused to go back to get her.

If he had been the one swept over, or if it had been the two of them, it would have made more sense. Charles was about to embark on a one-way trip. In a few hours, Charles Luxold would shed his mortal coil, the price of immortality.

His closet was filled with clothes he would never wear again. Charles hadn't planned out what would happen to all his possessions.

He wasn't a packrat, but there were still items of value. They should be passed on to the people he cared about. In a moment of light-hearted reflection, Charles wondered, *what does one wear to their death?* Eve had brought him an outfit weeks ago, but now it seemed over-the-top. It was a gold brocade tunic paired with two-hundred-year-old ceremonial clogs. Charles would certainly make an exit as he ascended the stairs.

Like the two people who had gone before him, Charles' death would be a ceremony. Today's immortalization marked the culmination of a week of festivities and ceremonies honoring, "one of the great minds and men of the twenty-first century."

For someone who had always survived rather than sought the spotlight, it was a trial. The event featured recorded speeches from long-gone public figures praising Charles and his work; dead men lauding achievements for which Charles refused to claim credit.

He would take a bath, then a shower, then shave, brush his teeth, and join his family for a private breakfast. He had no children and no wife. His father had died twenty-five years ago. He would never join him in the Elysium. So many departed. Now, Charles was leaving a great life earlier than he had hoped.

At sixty, Charles had reached a tipping point. Even with nootropics to stabilize neuronal aging, his brain was withering. Babylon's top neurologist had argued that the ideal age for upload was fifty. Charles held out a decade longer. He had hoped to uncover a different path, spending much of that time with the intent of straddling the two worlds. Charles aspired to know his immortal self before he died.

Prior to this ceremonial week, preparing for the immortalization had taken most of the last year. Charles spent twelve months enduring all manner of tests in anticipation of his transition. Test after test, interview after interview, scan after scan—all for validation of a future self. Would he die? When his ascension came in a year's time, would it be he who rolled back the stone?

The Giants promised rebirth. Charles would emerge a better version of himself. How would he know? If his immortalized self believed he was Charles Anand Luxold, born December fourth, two thousand and three, would his discarded self feel the same?

Cynthia, the first Giant, insisted she was still Cynthia. She and Charles had long talks while he prepared for his transition. She assured him the process was painless and exhilarating, both an honor and an opportunity. Having known her for almost thirty years, Charles felt Cynthia retained much of the person he knew before, but he had concerns. He feared he might be prematurely entering oblivion.

As if she read his mind, a call from Cynthia ended his brief pause. He hesitated then sent the call to voicemail. He wanted a minute longer with his thoughts. Predictably, a text followed that read, "Pick up, Chuck. I know you want to." Fully aware she would continue to text until he answered, Charles accepted her com.

"Nervous?"

"A little," he reflected. "I'm resigned at this point." Prone to banter when anxious, Charles mused, "Hopefully it's not a sham."

As if she knew exactly what would calm him the most, Cynthia played along. "Yes, Chuck, I've done all this as a ruse. I've spent the last decade in Westden with the New Amish. We stand ready to welcome you into Christ's light."

"That's kind of the way I figured it would go. These last ten years, I knew you couldn't go through with it. Jack, too—clever how he's nowhere to be found."

"You can't take a good joke too far." She paused, as if noting something off camera. "Eve's arrived. I guess it is time for breakfast. Catch you later." And the transmission ended.

"No bath for me, I guess," he remarked as he slipped on the robe, slid into the clogs, before stepping out of his bedroom for the last time in his life.

Charles took his seat at the head of the table and looked around. He grinned, "I always imagined it would be a last supper, not a brunch." There were nervous laughs. His mother had obviously been crying, but she smiled through it. Over the past few days, Charles had caught glimpses of what he believed to be his mother praying. His closest friend and mentor, Nick Santos, was at the other end of the table. Nick was unusually reserved.

Nick rose and walked over to Charles. As Charles stood to meet him, they embraced. Nick quietly said, "Big day, my friend. There is no Judas Iscariot here. Just dear friends celebrating a moment with a great human. No death. Just the birth of a Giant! An immortal destined for great things."

"One small step," Charles quoted, making the mood a little lighter.

"Did Cyn reach out?" Nick asked.

"Sure did. Nothing from Jack, but I wouldn't expect him to—not his style."

"Definitely not his style," Nick confirmed. "He lives in his projects." Interrupting his own train of thought, Nick pointed to the buffet. "I brought bagels. Eve's making French toast, and there's bacon. Life's simple pleasures."

"You're the richest man on earth, and it's a Denny's Breakfast."

"I was the richest man on earth. That's when there was money." Nick paused, thinking. "Also, those bagels are spectacular. David baked them for you himself. Every bit as good as Black Sheep Bagels, back in Cambridge." Nick looked Charles in the eye. "I walked halfway around the dome for those."

Charles took a bite and said, "No cream cheese." Speaking with his mouthful, he added, "It's cold. You should have jogged."

Nick, understanding Charles every bit as well as his immortal siblings, shot back. "Well, you could have met me there!"

Charles smiled and grumbled, "David's talented, but it's not Black Sheep Bagels." He considered the textures and flavors in his mouth before mumbling, "Still pretty good."

Cynthia had told Charles she didn't miss food. He wondered whether it would be the same for him. It was hard to imagine that one could spend an eternity without bacon. Charles reached onto the serving plate and put a thick, perfectly cooked slice of applewood smoked bacon in his mouth. The salty, smoky sensations confirmed what he always knew: The Jews were wrong about bacon.

"Are you ready for the crowds?" Nick asked sarcastically. "Pretty sure there won't be any protestors." The nearest religious group was almost thirty miles from where they sat. "Let's have a look at our friends to the North."

Over the center of the table, a holographic view of Zealots thirty miles to the Northwest came into view. Thousands of New Amish stood as their pastor addressed his flock. A familiar face, once welcome at their table, addressed the congregation. "Pray for Dr. Luxold! Pray he sees the light before consigning himself to eternal damnation. Lord, he knows not your glory. I pray thee guide him to your Heavenly Kingdom."

"Oh look, Judas made it after all," Nick joked. "Talk about preaching to the choir…" As he gestured, the hologram disappeared.

"I find it touching," Charles countered. "A lot less brimstone than I might have expected from him. For a group so prone to violence, I see restraint. Jeb kept it in check for once. No 'storm the gates.' Just prayers."

"There's nothing touching about it, Charles. These are violent bullies we're dealing with!" Nick countered.

"Have you ever bullied them?" Charles asked.

"No. I fought for them. They're the ones who have no chance of immortality. Their lives are trivial! They will only be remembered for the pain they caused others!"

"What if they are right?" Eve asked.

"Eve, I know John found you and brought you here. I can appreciate that with your upbringing, there will always be a tinge of the agnostic, no matter how clear the truth is. But the New Amish are not right about anything."

"Well said, Nick," Charles teased. "You've really got a way of winning over the religious. Just ply them with your facts. That works."

Nick's wife, Bianca, offered Charles a wry smile. She had spent their entire marriage watching similar discussions degrade. "Charles, you know full well that if Nick had been on the deck of the Titanic, he would have spent his last moments confronting every single person who made the sign of the cross. He'd want them to know they were wasting their time."

The whole table seemed to acknowledge the accuracy of Bianca's assertion, before the six fell silent in reflection. After a few moments, Eve broke the silence. She looked over Charles' outfit. "The tunic suits you. I'm glad you're wearing it. That outfit is special."

Charles extended his arms inviting further inspection. "I look like a groom at an Indian wedding."

"Yes, that's kind of what I was going for. Nick told me you had a thing for Cynthia. Now, you two will be together." Eve blushed. Had she overstepped? Eve worked to find her place among the Colony Elite. John had overseen her integration, but Babylon's customs and values remained alien. After her quarantine, John told Nick that he had finally found the perfect assistant for Charles.

Trying to dispel the awkwardness, Charles conceded, "She is and was a ten! Who didn't have a crush on her?" He quickly interjected with a chuckle, "Except you, Nick. Obviously."

"Spent half my life with potential suitors befriending me just to get to her. When they got there, she ate them alive. Never settled down."

Eve turned to Nick, probing, "So, you won't join them in the Elysium? No regrets?"

"Regrets, unclear. Join them? No. It's too late; I'm too old. Besides, one of us has to stay behind and keep the lights on."

Eve pushed a little harder. "But you will end. Your life will end. You don't believe you will go on, do you?" She didn't know Nick very well, but she needed to know why he had forgone immortalization.

"Eve, my dear, there are many forms of immortality. I have attained several. First, as long as my brother, sister, and best friend exist on the Plane of Elysium, I remain immortal, remembered. Second, there is my legacy here. I am the St. Peter of immortality. I gave of myself, so that others might have eternal life." With a twinkle in his eye and a sidelong glance at Eve, he said, "That's a pretty cool one, too." Nick turned to his wife and added, "Last and most important, I have children and a beautiful loving wife. My children are my immortality. Venal in a way, but it's what everyone else gets. I'm okay with a natural end."

"St. Nick," Charles teased. "Somehow, you just made my choice feel small."

"I understand the beauty of your choice, Dr. Santos," Eve remarked before adding, "Thank you for sharing. I hadn't fully considered it from those perspectives. You have a beautiful family."

Charles stood and with a feigned air of gravitas, addressed the group. "I think it's time for us to get going." An impish grin crept up the sides of his mouth until he couldn't contain it. "After all, I wouldn't want to be late to my own funeral."

CHAPTER 2

Et Tu Brute?

-William Shakespeare

Eve stayed behind to clean up. Everyone always wondered about her seemingly incessant need to clean. She stated it calmed her, and most left it at that.

Dr. Luxold's flat boasted every imaginable robotic aid, rendering mundane tasks like "doing the dishes" as obsolete as "spinning cloth" for the Nons—his term for those without religion, whom he described as "those who live in the now." To add a layer of irony, Luxold employed the church's language, Latin. He coined the phrase IQVN, "illis qui vivunt in nunc," which became a symbol for the early atheist movement, replacing the more pretentious label of 'illuminati' traditionally used by humanists.

A humanist was still how Charles perceived himself, but he had lived in the now for most of his life. His seminal work, The God Within Us, was considered the greatest heresy since Nietzsche declared, "God is Dead." Eve had read Luxold's work, though it was banned where she grew up. The God Within Us was the Gospel of IQVN. The book was written in three parts.

The basis of faith spans the first one hundred and fifty pages, where Luxold reworks his doctoral thesis on the psychological underpinnings of religion and faith. Luxold's revolutionary thesis was that all faith and belief evolve from and are still rooted in the preverbal memories of our mothers. This universal experience involves the absence of language for months after birth. All while being cared for by an omnipotent figure—The Mother. These memories, he argues, are dominant in all humans during a crucial phase of developing self-awareness and identity formation.

Luxold's exploration of belief rocked religious communities the world over. The more established religions dealt with Luxold's theories with the same response they had to every scientific discovery: through incorporation. "God made man in his image; Pope Leopold had explained. It is no wonder that on a small level the genesis of each and every life follows Genesis itself."

For many agnostics, The God Within extinguished religion's flame, causing them to turn to humanism instead. Luxold offered the humanists hope and the chance to find an equal footing on a spiritual level to those still embracing religion.

Part two precipitated a deluge of hatred from religious sects around the globe. In part two, Dr. Luxold dissects the major religions. He describes organized religion as a "reverse-engineered sociologic virus." He claims that religions filled the gaps left by the Mother God, co-opting these shared pre-verbal memories to their own ends.

Part three of his work, the last hundred pages, is a reintegration of philosophy with religion. Luxold develops a complex psychological toolkit, a direct pathway to those preverbal memories and how to build faith, hope, and trust, independent of the parables contained in religious texts. This section came to be known as, "Reunion with Your Mother God."

Having been raised in a home of true believers, the New Amish, Eve rejected the work with prejudice. The God Within was last published before Eve's birth. However, she did not hear of the title until she was thirteen and did not read a single page until she was twenty. By that time, her community had fully equipped her to deal with "Satan's Handbook." Eve had no memories of her parents. She only knew that they were "Crusaders of the Word," militant defenders of the Holy Gospel. They had died in service of Jesus Christ and would live forever by his side.

When Eve looked up, she found John's hologram looming over the table. Of course, he looked the same as he had the first day they'd met. Eve had entered Babylon through an asylum program. The Colonists were committed to helping those shunned or exiled by the New Amish.

John appeared to be looking right at Eve. "I saw Charles leave wearing the sandals Bruno made. Any regrets?"

Eve knew that John was not inquiring about fashion and read between the lines. "Maybe, hard to tell. My choice of outfit will have no impact on when or how Charles' life ends…"

"Still, choosing that tunic and those shoes, and giving them to him—that was intentional."

"It gives meaning to an act that is otherwise a senseless waste of life," Eve explained.

"And you believe God has a hand in this?" John asked.

Eve explained, "God has a hand in everything. Even your essence, John. It's God's will—it's His plan."

"Well, that is where we disagree. But at times, even those at crossed purposes may find themselves aligned in action." John regarded her for moment. "I am not sure we will meet again, Eve. Do enjoy the ceremony."

"Aligned, I've never understood. How are we aligned? And why are you not trying to stop me? These are your people. Charles is your friend."

"Friendship is a social construct."

Eve was still trying to understand this entity. To her, the Giants were largely evil and blasphemous. "They have put their faith in you."

"Yes, you still see me as the idol. Their golden calf. It's far simpler than that; the farmer's cows are his. They put their faith in him."

"Will you slaughter them?"

"No. Just like the farm, our relationship is symbiotic. I need them as much as they need me. Their faith in the Giants offers them a sense of peace and purpose."

Eve asked, "But why?"

John was not in the mood to answer more questions. "You should get going, if you wish to go to the ceremony."

"I won't be going. I've said my goodbyes. I'm heading back."

"So soon?" John asked with a hint of surprise.

"Done all I can. As I said, it's in God's hands now."

And with that, Eve grabbed her backpack and walked out of Charles Luxold's apartment and life.

Charles had chosen to walk; his home was fairly central, and it was a perfect September day. This would be his last opportunity to experience the sights, smells, and sounds of the paradise he helped create. Nick Santos believed that this land could provide everything they could need: predictably high solar and wind availability for grid independence, and a small reservoir that could be expanded if required. This reservoir eventually became known as Lake Pacifica and provided The Colony with unlimited hydroelectric power. The runoff from the lake also fed water features throughout Babylon.

Nick's final reason for choosing the area was accessibility. Babylon had almost none. Nestled in what was referred to as a hole, Babylon could only be accessed through its west gate; a half-mile wide ravine at the south end of a long canyon. There was no other way in or out.

"Nick, you really did pick a great spot," Charles mused.

"No one could see it," Nick said. "I spent hours with MARTIN and John trying to put it all together. Without the east wall, we never would have achieved all of this."

"I must have done John's augmented reality tour, the one with the before and after, a half dozen times. I always find something new."

Nick pointed to the ground beneath their feet. "Right here was the old mine's office building." Gesturing ahead, he tried to capture the scale of change with his hands as he narrated, "One hundred feet past that arch, it dropped over two hundred feet to the mine floor."

"I watched the news, thinking you'd lost it when Back2Green started dumping all that trash outside the west gate."

"Without Back2Green, we wouldn't have had the raw materials," Nick explained. "Without the plastics, aluminum, steel, copper, and lithium, we never could have finished this place. It's literally built out of garbage."

Babylon was initially permitted and acquired as a recycling center. In 2032, Santos Corp, bought the main tract of land and made their money processing waste. The primary resources that the Back2Green, a Santos owned recycling corporation, processed included lithium batteries, cars, plastics, and outdated electronics. For two years, Santos got companies to pay them to take their "trash."

"Remember all the lawsuits?" Charles asked.

"If they'd ever seen the mess back here, I'd have been out of business. Thank God for synthetic labor. No leaked photos or whistleblowers." Santos and Back2Green built huge receiving and sorting areas. By avoiding constant regulatory inspections, they saved years of red tape and billions in compliance costs.

"Best part is you got what was left of our government to pay for it," Charles joked.

Nick said, "No one wanted to do it. I was basically a member of the lowest Caste—the trash collector, untouchable." Back2Green had received massive subsidies to buy recycling equipment from Santos Corp. Those robots would spend the next decade recycling waste into the building blocks of Babylon.

"One man's trash," Charles quipped.

"The biggest costs for most companies were labor and electricity. With access to subsidized labor and free electricity, the only factor was time."

"Time and your brother's crazy robots." John had spent the first decade at Babylon using their automated part printing and assembly lines to build all manner of synthetic workers. "Remember those rat-sized things that gathered sand for brick?"

"Templetons," Nick recalled.

"How many of those did he print?" Charles asked.

"Thousands. I was kind of sad when he led them into the recyclers like the Pied Piper. They were amazing creations."

"I thought John and Leigh might keep a few as pets." Leigh was one of John's senior production engineers. She'd lost her vision during the Epocalypse.

"Remember that robot seeing eye dog he built for her?" Charles asked.

Nick admitted, "That thing creeped me out." He shuddered. "Too many sensors. It was more like a spider with a weird hand-head." Leigh's so-called dog had an articulating appendage where its head should have been. Cynthia called it "Thing."

Charles laughed while admitting, "Cynthia invented synthetic vision just so she could walk Thing into a recycler."

Recyclers were a pillar of Babylon's success. They provided robotic disassembly of everything that wasn't needed or had been supplanted by better design. Unneeded devices were delivered or marched themselves to "disassembly lines." If motors, sensors, or other parts were still of use, they made their way into rebuilt devices. Everything else was fully recycled. Nothing went to waste. Lithium was the gold of Babylon. No effort was spared to conserve the precious metal.

Charles and Nick's walk was not a straight line to the Crypt. Nick had figured that Charles would enjoy seeing the world they had built with his own eyes, one last time. So, their route ended at Beau Rivage, a café with a terrace. They stopped and waited for the cappuccino they'd ordered. "Well, at least I don't have to worry about gaining weight," Charles joked.

They could have ordered ahead of time, but Nick wanted to take in the view with his friend. "Before MARTIN, this would have been unachievable at any price."

"I'm not sure it would have been necessary before AI," Charles countered.

Nick, always the devil's advocate, went on, "You have to admire him. His knack for orchestrating collaboration between robots and humans, all while shifting more and more tasks to AI and the synthetics—impressive."

"I don't know if *admire* would be my word of choice."

"How? His ability to design purpose-built robots and code software was miraculous."

MARTIN (Massive ARTificial Intelligence) had designed every inch of Babylon. Originally commissioned by the Defense Advanced Research Projects Agency (DARPA) as a military simulator, MARTIN had been tasked with developing PsyOps antipersonnel initiatives. CynOs-powered quantum processing and storage allowed him to develop and rehearse regime-toppling schemes based on social media profiles and text message relationship mapping. MARTIN's ability to imitate any voice he'd heard was one of his primary methods of social disruption. Calls from loved ones could in fact be MARTIN. He could even create compellingly believable video. No one was prepared for a machine that advanced.

"You can argue that MARTIN was a marvel. I just wouldn't call him marvelous."

"Unmatched processing ability. He replaced the work of thousands of architects, designers, engineers and project managers. You're right, we can't call him marvelous. Marvelous is an understatement."

"Sure, Nick, but at what cost?" Charles asked.

Nick was not ready to concede. "He would have made the world a better place. His simulations showed a changed world, a way for us to survive AI, to coexist with the Overman."

"But he didn't. He turned friends into foes. In the end, he killed everyone."

"Almost everyone," Nick corrected, grasping at straws to hold on to a reality he'd built and needed. "And he didn't do it; he just used our darkest fears against us. We did the dirty work all by ourselves." Nick pointed to the dome that covered the Atlantean Sea. "And MARTIN did this for us. We could have made these for everyone."

Charles, ready to disengage, looked back towards the Robobarista. "Oh, look. Coffee."

Over the last kilometer, Ping had seen signs for Luzhuang Village. At least she knew that she wasn't lost. In the distance, the darkness on the horizon began to surrender to a glow. Ping hoped these were the lights from Lánhuā 5. She hadn't passed any housing yet, and assumed it must either be on campus, or further south. It had been an hour since she left Lin. Now with each step, she felt a little closer to an answer she wasn't sure she wanted.

What had happened with the factory shut down?
Where had all her coworkers gone?
Was there even a new factory?
And if there was, did she have a job there?

Ping picked up her pace to keep warm and to hasten her arrival. She was cold and wanted nothing more than to wrap herself in a blanket and sip a steaming cup of tea. Each step was now accompanied by the sensation of developing blisters. *A Band-Aid would work miracles right now,* she thought.

Against the growing dome of light, Ping made out what she believed to be, the roofline of the factory. Only a couple of kilometers to go.

As she walked, she replayed emails in her mind, reviewing each word and sentence. The messages filtered through updated information from Lin. "Your continued work during the shutdown is essential, and your expertise is an invaluable contribution to a successful transition." Had one word of it been true? Now her phone didn't work. What few items she had of value could be anywhere, and she didn't even know where she'd be sleeping tonight.

Although the real potential of complete abandonment by a company she had faithfully served for decades loomed large, Ping resolved to wait until she heard it from someone with authority.

A well-lit employee entrance was right where it should have been. It seemed quieter than she imagined it would be. It wasn't time for a shift change just yet, but people usually drifted in and out at all hours. The fact that there was an employee entrance implied that there were still employees and a company who employed them.

As she approached the guardhouse, she retrieved her badge. The guards would hopefully have a new badge ready for her or direct her to pick one up from Human Resources.

Lights projecting from the guard house made it difficult to see inside. Ping held her badge up so that the guards would know she was an employee. She walked forward, eventually making it past the bright beams, Ping was able to see the scanner at the entrance, but there wasn't a guard in sight.

She pressed her badge to the scanner.

"Invalid ID" came the automated response. Her heart sank. She tried again.

"Invalid ID" echoed once more, then came a pause. "Present for retina scan." Ping did not see a retinal scanner. She knew what they looked like, but there were none.

A woman's voice announced, "Retinal scan complete. Recognize, Ping Lee, production supervisor." This new technology amazed her. Something had scanned her retina while she was just casually looking around. She had never seen anything like it.

"Employee Lee, your position has not yet been created. You currently have limited access to this facility. Your access level is green. Please follow the green path." At the very least, green would lead to HR and she would get her belongings, a meal, and severance. Things could be worse. At least she was inside.

Ping followed the green lights on the wall deep into the building.

CHAPTER 3

By the waters of Babylon, we lay down and wept.

Psalm 137

The sky was cerulean blue and the weather, perfect by most standards, was typical for fall in the Southwest. There was no breeze to speak of. The Colony was three thousand feet below the craggy summits.

Hidden Creek was Charles' favorite part of Babylon. It was set in a natural bowl ten miles across. Babylon was below Lake Pacifica. A dam was cleverly landscaped into the eastern edge of The Colony. Hidden Creek had been a masterpiece of terraforming. Like all the water features of Babylon, the creek was fed from Lake Pacifica. The babbling brook wandered six miles, dropping four hundred feet before draining into the Atlantean Sea near the Darwin Gate.

Despite its name, Hidden Creek wasn't so hidden. While many of The Colony's trails were wide enough for two abreast walking or jogging, Hidden Creek was a rough path—most of which was challenging to traverse. Charles kept an eye on the ever-changing terrain as they made their way past one pond after another. Many of Babylon's waterways carried potable water to reservoirs placed around The Colony's basin. These reservoirs were visually striking natural swimming pools that drained into purifiers for the water supply. Pressurized by gravity, abundant filtered water was always in great supply. The water in Hidden Creek was an exception. Waterfowl, mostly ducks, made their homes in each of the ponds, leaving it suitable only for irrigation.

Each pond along the path overflowed as a small waterfall. The trees, shrubs, rocks, and waterfalls left a variety of bucolic retreats. Charles found comfortable rocks or benches and did much of his best thinking there. Today, he chose to sit by a Henry Moore sculpture among some fuchsia. Nick took the seat next to him.

They were quiet for a while. Charles considered the water in the creek. It would never reach the Atlantean Sea; instead, it would drain underground and feed these plants. As he watched the ripples on its surface, he couldn't escape the notion that his life was headed down an artificial river.

Ready to break the silence, Charles turned to Nick. "I'm glad you're here, my friend."

"I wouldn't have it any other way."

Charles offered, "You built a paradise."

"We built it," Nick corrected.

Humbly, Charles demurred, "I had very little to do with any of this." He pointed to their immediate environs.

"I didn't either. I didn't plant those flowers. I didn't set those stones or line this brook."

"But you built the machines."

"I didn't do that either," Nick corrected.

"It was your vision."

"It was, but I would have given up if I hadn't read your book," Nick admitted.

"Bullshit. You're relentless."

"I have never told you this, but I had a crisis of faith," Nick clarified. "It was before we met."

"I've had hundreds. I don't understand."

"Mine was over a girl. I was in love. She was Christian. I wanted what she had. I loved her. I loved her faith. It gave her such peace."

"You didn't love her, Nick."

"I know that now. But it was The God Within that brought me back. Gave me hope. You did that."

"I didn't write it."

"So, now you're a prophet?" Nick joked.

"In a manner of speaking, yes."

"I've never heard this part."

"All I did was distill God from religion. I didn't know whether God existed. I knew the stories were a path to peace. That's why I took them apart. People still think I hate God and made fun of the Gospels. It's not that. I never wanted that."

"I know," Nick assured him. "Do you think you're preaching now because you're afraid?"

"Of course I'm afraid. I've had these weird dreams. I'm about to die, and I don't have to."

Nick tried to give Charles an out. "Then don't do it. We can keep working on Heaven's Gate. Maybe that will be enough."

"I'll never know unless I taste immortality. Only a Giant could know." Charles stood up and gestured in the direction of The Dome. "So, I have to do this."

Ping had never walked this far in a Lánhuā plant without encountering throngs of workers. To someone who had worked in crowded production lines her entire life, it was both exhilarating and unsettling.

A sign marked "Cafeteria" directed Ping's path. She tried to flash her badge at the door, expecting the usual click or buzz of entry, but none came. As she reached out to test the handle, the door swung open on its own, revealing a surprisingly modest dining area. Inside, there were just four tables, each with four chairs, and a small, automated serving line. Driven by hunger, Ping was determined to grab whatever would fill her growling stomach.

There was a touch screen with a fairly good selection. She chose the "American Lunch." It consisted of a cheeseburger, fries, and a coke. After she made her selection, a countdown timer appeared, indicating her order would be up in six minutes and nineteen seconds.

For the first time in hours, waiting on her American Lunch, Ping rested her legs and blistered feet. *Band-Aids!* Ping turned as she heard the door to the cafeteria open. The doorway filled with the all-too-familiar, very round, very red face of Jian Wang.

Breathy from the long walk, he gasped while explaining, "I heard you were here, Ping."

Forgoing the usual formalities reserved for someone as esteemed as Jian Wang, PhD., Ping got straight to the point. "What's going on, Jian? This has been an incredibly distressing day."

Wang made his way to the screen and keyed in an order. Looking back, he grinned and said, "American Lunch?"

"It seemed like a safe choice. Nothing that the cooks couldn't handle."

Chuckling, Wang replied, "Oh, these cooks can handle anything you throw at them."

Curious as to what she should have selected, Ping asked, "So, what did you get then?"

"American Lunch, of course." He offered a hearty laugh. "You are not supposed to be here, Ping."

"Where am I supposed to be?" she asked nervously.

"On a bus home—wherever that is—just like everyone else. It seems whoever was going to lay you off was fired before they completed their tasks."

Ping needed to know. "How many people were laid off?"

"Easier to count the transfers, which, including you and me, add up to nine people." Wang laughed nervously and then informed her, "I do not believe in coincidence. If you want to stay, I'll create a position for you."

"There were over seven hundred kitchen staff members alone. How can that be?" Just then, her order appeared on the rack. It was a cheeseburger, wrapped in foil and paper, looking like an ad for a burger joint. The bun was toasted. The ketchup appeared to have been perfectly painted on the crisp, green pieces of lettuce. The cheese was barely melted and slowly losing its battle with gravity. The fries were steaming, and the wax cup had a straw in the middle with a small portion of the paper cover still left on the exposed tip.

Jian explained, "No one transferred from dietary."

Ping pointed out. "Well, someone just fixed me a pretty amazing looking American Lunch."

Without a trace of emotion and with complete candor, Dr. Jian Wang explained, "No one made these burgers, Ping. We are past that."

CHAPTER 4

A mind not to be chang'd by Place or Time.
The mind is its own place, and in it self
Can make a Heav'n of Hell, a Hell of Heav'n.

-John Milton, "Paradise Lost"

The dome that covered the Atlantean Sea kept the air at a perfect eighty-two degrees. Inside lay the world's greatest playground. A saline pond three miles across, complete with beaches, surf simulators, reefs, and fishing areas. Charles spent many early mornings paddleboarding near Pirate's Bight. The Dome was one thing Charles hoped would never change.

Charles and Nick led a growing procession through the transition zone. Every one of The Dome's twenty-six entrances consisted of a large arch that separated inside from out. As they entered the dome, the air grew thick and humid, and the Atlantean Sea came into view. The change in humidity was so abrupt that even the timbre of their voices shifted.

They took the Darwin Entrance. It led them directly in front of Charles' favorite seaside restaurant. Jean Paul, the Maître Di at Maravi, came and gave Charles a warm hug. "No time for crab today, eh, my friend?"

"Sadly, I've cracked my last crab. Are you finally going to tell me what's in the boil?" Charles salivated just a bit as lingering sensations of last night's meal returned to his palate.

Jean Paul shook his head. "I'm sorry, my friend. It's a big day, but not that big."

Jean was more than a chef, sommelier, or host, and Charles admired him for it. His work had been pivotal in developing a culture of cuisine and sustainability. It was part of the miracle of the Atlantean Sea—a marvel for sure. Restaurants lining its edges literally pulled their harvest directly from the water before them.

Charles and Jean Paul shared a smile that masked the grief they both struggled to contain. Charles still couldn't imagine an eternity devoid of wine, song, and friends. An eternity without sand between his toes and crab meat on his fingertips seemed bleak and flavorless.

A little way down, man-made waves curled into the shore. No one was surfing today. The waves would be there tomorrow. Charles Luxold would not. He tried to imagine how different the scene would be in twenty-four hours when things went back to normal. Lagoons filled with children. Teens flirting on the sand. Paddle boarders and fishermen dotting the shoreline.

Each quadrant of the dome had a tram traversing the Atlantean Sea. The trams rose hundreds of feet in the air, practically disappearing into the webbing of the dome's shell. All four tram lines ended at the central tower. From there, colonists could take elevators to the island below or enjoy the view from the observation deck.

Charles preferred the mile-long walk to the Bali Hai. While he wasn't afraid of heights, he hated being crammed in with other people. The Darwin causeway allowed colonists to walk the whole way to the central island. Charles and Nick enjoyed their stroll along the scenic route. As they traversed the Augustus Roebling Bridge, they paused midway for one last chat.

"It must be nice," Charles mused.

"What?"

"The comfort that the New Amish have. The belief of some mystic afterlife where all the wrongs will be right."

"How is immortality different?" Nick asked.

"My mom, I saw her crying. I don't think she's coming." Charles couldn't explain why this mattered so much, but it did.

"Would you really want her to?"

"No, it's not that. It's that even if I could immortalize her, she wouldn't want it. I asked. She wants to be with my father."

"Dirt nap?"

"See, she doesn't believe in that. She's still praying. I don't know exactly to what or whom. Even though she rejected Christianity years before the Epocalypse, she can't help but fantasize about the promise of Heaven."

"Is that really so bad at her age? I mean, it isn't unexpected or surprising, is it?" Nick asked.

"No, that's what I was saying. I'm envious. I'm going down this road, and part of me wishes that I could pray in case this doesn't all work out."

Nick turned the tables on his philosopher friend. "Why can't you do both?"

"Because I don't believe. I'd rather be true to myself."

"Pascal would bet on both." The men were all too familiar with Pascal's wager and the premise that working towards salvation cost nothing. And even if an afterlife was highly improbable, the risk of missing out was incalculably worse.

"I'd pray, but it seems like any God capable of all this would know that I was not sincere."

"You are the sincerest person I've ever met. Any God worth knowing will recognize that."

"Well, here we are, two atheists, preaching to the choir. Figures we'd spend my last minutes on earth arguing against Immortality."

Eve hoped to be out of Babylon and halfway to Westden before Charles' immortalization began. She needed to be past the West Gate by two if there was any hope of reaching New Amish territory before dark. Leaving Babylon was easy; John had told her, "Just get to the western rim of the city and grab a horse."

The small lakes inside Babylon were reservoirs for the community water supply. They also created the parklike aesthetic that permeated the colony. Every blade of grass and each tree inside the boundaries of Babylon were fed by an elaborate irrigation system. That system was perfectly designed. There was not a single pump needed to move one billion gallons a day from Lake Pacifica through The Colony.

The northern and southern lakes and their aqueducts created a moat. John had assured Eve it was impossible to cross the aqueducts undetected.

Eve's best chance at a successful egress was to the west. The West Gate's security was under human supervision, and they would be distracted by Charles' ceremony. John would be tasked with surveillance and had deliberately left minimal security on patrol.

Babylon's defenses were not intended to keep people in. No one tried to leave Babylon. In fact, no one wanted to leave Babylon. Outside the robot-tended paradise lay the inhospitable high prairie and desert steppes of the American Southwest. Beyond the New

Amish encampment were small bands of surviving families and homesteads. An expedition to find resources back east had proven the colonists lacked the requisite skills to survive beyond the rim. Only their guide returned alive. Six colonists were lost in as many days.

Eve imagined the soft scientists traversing the terrain she called home. Only the Ducenti, Babylon's paramilitary defense force, were equipped for survival outside of The Colony. Her humanist facade was skin deep. New Amish were able-bodied and capable frontier folk. Some of their forebears had tamed these lands two centuries earlier. Eve belonged to a proud people who lived off the land and by God's laws.

Communication with the Giants was seamless for everyone in Babylon. Different people interacted in a variety of ways. Eve only spoke to John- she never interacted holographically. New to the colony and fearful of implanted tech, she spoke to John through a tiny external com. Over the last few days, while preparing her elopement, Eve had got to know John in a way no one else ever would. "The only hard part is getting a mount," she told him. "Once I'm on horseback, I'm free."

John reminded her, "You are just as free here. What you are choosing is a different path, not a better one."

"It's the path I've always been on," Eve confirmed. "Babylon was a stop on a journey, nothing more. My whole life is just that: a staging point."

"I'll never know. It's not an option for me. I haven't been alive in years. That's the price of immortality, Eve. You pay with your life."

"Do you regret it? Is that why you helped me?" Eve asked.

"I'm incapable of regret," John replied.

John's answer left Eve unsatisfied. She paused for a moment trying to find meaning in his words but came up empty. "I'm not sure I understand."

"You could never understand a life without regret, and I am not helping you in your cause. You are making a choice. I am not stopping you. Your capture would only result in violence."

"You are not stopping me because of 'free will?'" Eve still couldn't imagine why John would not protect his friend and their infernal machine.

"My motives are my own. We agree on one thing: Charles will die in that crypt." John remembered how little his mind could grasp of what he had become. "When my body and brain ceased functioning, my consciousness bifurcated. John Santos died in that crypt. I am John's immortal essence, but I do not have regret."

"So, you are not John Santos?"

"I am all he was, to the best of my understanding. I only know what can be known about what I knew." He paused. "I can never know what has been lost in translation."

"But you were the best version of him, right?" Eve asked.

"I was the closest approximation to what we could know about who John was and how he would respond. My brain was frozen in liquid oxygen while I was still alive. But I don't remember that, of course. It all happened in milliseconds. Tiny scanners used microscopes, stains, and incredibly fine microtomes to catalog not just connections, but relative receptor densities."

"To what end? How did that become what you are?" Eve asked, genuinely curious.

"The structures of my brain were mapped layer by layer, receptor by receptor. Still, there was incredible uncertainty. Despite the density of information obtained, so much was lost. And there's no way of knowing what that was."

"That's where the Symbiants come in," Eve guessed.

"Exactly. We got everything we could, combining MRI's, EEGs, and the microdissection of my brain's structure. A million Symbiant

John's were spawned. These Symbiants were refined. Only a few Symbiants passed that stage."

Eve deduced, "Then you are the best Symbiant?"

"I am the best of the best of my Symbiants," he corrected. "In the final stage of Immortalization, each Symbiant faces a group of tests originally devised by MARTIN before the Epocalypse. The tests validate the humanity of synthetic life."

Feeling she'd uncovered a paradox, Eve pointed out, "So, a computer developed a test to determine which of your synthetic selves was most human? It determined the right and wrong answers."

"There were no wrong answers, Eve. That was never the point," John explained. "A Symbiant possesses no will to survive. They only answer the questions. They don't attempt to simulate John Santos. They are unconcerned with the consequence of an unsuitable response." John went on to describe his immortalization. "When a Symbiant navigates the tests correctly, they remain separate from each other, waiting for at least five to pass and form a jury. That jury decides which additional Symbiants can join the collective."

"You are a collective?" Eve wasn't even sure what this meant.

"No, there is a final step: coalescence."

"What happens there?"

"Maybe someday, there will be time for me to explain that in terms you would understand."

Their journey ended as they approached The Homer, a fittingly named amphitheater integrated into the central tower. People filtered in to find Cynthia Santos, larger than life, floating above them. She addressed each colonist independently through their coms.

Images of Babylon appeared and dissolved as Cynthia recapped a history of Dr. Charles Luxold's life and the colony that had grown around him. After everyone filtered in and settled down, Cynthia took a moment to herself, away from the crowd. During this time, Charles and Nick engaged in a side conversation with Cynthia. Others close by overheard their correspondence, with a select few who lingered close enough to hear Cynthia's responses.

"Is all this really necessary? It's so twentieth century," Charles lamented. "Everyone here is quite familiar with the history of this place and what I'm alleged to have accomplished."

"We had to do something, Chuck," Cynthia came back. "Imagine if you just walked up, rolled back the crypt door, tipped your hat, and died."

Now glib, Charles let her know. "That was kind of what I was hoping for."

"Funerals are for the living," Nick offered. "Those of us who toil on demand the pomp and circumstance."

Still glib and vexed by all the attention, Charles argued, "I gave at the office."

"People of Babylon, I give you Dr. Charles Luxold." Cynthia's voice was now in sync with the hologram that addressed the audience directly. Charles' thirty-foot-high avatar stood face-to-face with Cynthia's. "Charles, it is time to say goodbye to your Babylonian family," she began. "Rest assured that in one year's time, you and I will be back here to celebrate your ascension."

No longer glib, but with genuine humility, Charles reluctantly addressed his audience. "I must admit, it's a little much for me. I've lived a very public life, but right now," Charles confessed, "I'm a little scared." Always genuine to a fault, he offered of his private self one last time. "Seeing the shoreline, feeling the sun on my face, smelling Jean Paul's bisque. It's a lot to give up. I'm not sure I'm ready."

There was a general change in tenor around The Homer, from festive to very intimate. Sensing the change, Cynthia offered encouragement. "Charles, immortalization is a choice—an opportunity. If you want to take a lap or a year, that's entirely up to you." She paused, conceding, "While immortals are incapable of taste or smell, we offer an infinite future to solve challenges we haven't yet conceived." Her voice turned lighter. "Solutions lie only a moment away on an infinite timeline. Soon, you will dine guilt-free in the Elysium."

Charles reflected. Immortals would evolve. They would add senses and abilities for eternity. "I honestly hadn't considered that. I'm still scared. What if it doesn't work this time?"

"It will work. You've already done the hard part." Cynthia could see that the audience was relaxing as Charles relaxed. She even heard a few sighs of relief escape as shoulders eased and tension visibly melted. They still clung to his every word.

Turning to a riveted audience, Charles admitted, "I feel like I've let you all down. I was so close to achieving immortality for all of us. Part of me wants to stay here and finish my work."

"You, John, and I will continue your work from the Elysium. Nick and his engineers will see this through. We will make immortality a reality for all who desire it." Nick and Charles had worked with Cynthia and John for the last five years. The ironically named, "Heaven's Gate" project promised upload without death.

Cynthia went back to addressing the larger audience as Charles' hologram faded. In their private conversation, Cynthia sweetened the pot explaining, "Heaven's Gate was never going to be the immortality that you will experience as a Giant."

"And what if I don't want to be a Giant? What if Charles 2.0 was enough?"

"Only you can answer that question." Cynthia reminded him, "I didn't have a choice. My failing body, the constant pain. Die slowly and painfully or enter the Elysium. There was only one logical way forward." Cynthia's upload had been fast-tracked as her health deteriorated. Injuries sustained during the Epocalypse left her crippled, scarred, and in constant pain.

"You took such a risk. I'm almost embarrassed to be scared," Charles admitted, his words leaking with a vulnerability he couldn't hide.

"There was no risk for me. A failed upload would have brought me a welcomed death. An end to the suffering I endured. A chance to ascend." With Cynthia's focus now on her friend, she asked, "Are you ready?"

Pausing on the ledge of the crypt entrance, Charles turned to face all the people he cared about and many more who cared about him. "The butterflies have passed." Smiling and with a light in his voice, he said, "I'm actually excited. I can't wait to get back to work. I thank every one of you for this opportunity. I have lived a life fuller than I ever could have dreamed. Cynthia, Nick, and John are the best family I could have asked for." He paused. "One trip around the sun. I'll be back!"

And with that, Charles turned and entered the crypt.

CHAPTER 5

You want to believe that there is one relationship in life that's beyond betrayal. A relationship that's beyond that kind of hurt. And there isn't.

-Caleb Carr

Nick watched his friend disappear into the crypt and continued to look on as the door slid shut behind him. She always knew what he was thinking, and as expected, Cynthia's disembodied voice came through Nick's com. "He's okay, little brother. We're joking, rehashing Monty Python. Don't worry."

Nick's mind wandered to the first time the three of them had crossed paths at E-Den. E-Den was Babylon 1.0. Originally a military research facility, E-Den became a retreat for the Santos family as growing social unrest and hostilities made life in the cities unsafe.

E-Den did not compare to Babylon in size, scope, or beauty. It barely supported the one hundred souls who came to live there. E-Den was the birthplace of MARTIN, a brainchild of all three siblings. The greatest military simulator ever conceived; MARTIN was the world's first super AI. A highly modified version of CynOs ran on the immense array of Quantum Dot processors. As his capabilities grew, MARTIN's most impressive software mods were implemented by MARTIN himself.

It was some time until the world became aware of his existence and his incredible capabilities. Some groups began to call for MARTIN's disassembly and deactivation. As jobs evaporated in labor and service industries, labor groups led by the Anti-Robotics League (ARL) united with fundamentalist religious sects, including Christians Against Technology (CAT). These groups aggressively lobbied for MARTIN to be regulated or dismantled. When their demands were not met, they resorted to violence.

Santos Corp began aggressive land acquisitions, buying up swaths of desert land to insulate themselves from a growing tide of violence. Nick assumed that everyone had a price. Malcom Garff proved him wrong. Garff led a fundamentalist offshoot of the Church of Latter-Day-Saints. He and his followers loved the isolation their valley provided. That valley became a target of Santos Corp's land buying spree.

Garff never agreed to sell. A lawsuit from the Freedom From Religion Foundation managed to separate his businesses from the church. After the FLDS were stripped of their tax-exempt status, a tax lien on his mine went unpaid. The land that would become Babylon was auctioned off to the highest bidder, which was, of course, Santos Corp.

Nick remembered going to John the day he bought the mine and announcing, "We got it!"

John remained pessimistic. "We will get crucified in the press. The lien will be revoked."

Cynthia came to her baby brother's defense. "The only group less popular than a family of wealthy technocrats is a family of tax-dodging polygamists. I don't think anyone is coming to their aid." And she was right. Eventually, the Sheriff removed Garff and his family from land that was no longer theirs. Garff swore that he would reclaim the land and decided to move his entire family to his remaining acreage, which he had renamed Westden. He abandoned his reclusive lifestyle and welcomed all who would join in a fight against technology, especially those who hated Nick Santos.

Synthetic labor quickly transitioned from factories and to Main Street. Politicians initially celebrated, showcasing workers earning a minimum wage of twenty dollars an hour and housekeepers commanding six-figure salaries. Lawrence Reid, of California's sixteenth district, heralded the rise in wages as "a triumph of the working class."

As labor costs spiraled out of control, Santos Corp's profits soared. Robotic restaurants became commonplace by 2030. Around that same time, first-generation humanoid robots walked into consumers' lives, doing all the things they didn't want to.

Between 2020 and 2035, half the world's labor jobs evaporated. By the time economics stopped trickling down, it was already too late. World governments reacted to unprecedented job losses the same way they had a decade earlier during the pandemic. Reid and his cronies threw money at the problem. The Labor Relief Acts of 2030 and 2032 totaled forty trillion dollars. The disenfranchised spent those dollars acquiring entry-level versions of Santos Robotics' home electronics. What remained of the aid packages was quickly redistributed to restaurants and other entertainment industries that were delivering services via synthetic labor.

Either way, any printed money ultimately ended up in the ledgers of Santos Corp. Three bailouts later, there was little tax base left. The US economy had historically doubled national debt each decade before Covid. During the pandemic, it took only five years. Distracted by social media and partisan squabbles, Americans failed to recognize a creeping crisis. In the years following Covid, the cost of debt finally caught up with developed economies. Real unemployment approached forty percent.

Reid's next effort was to tax robotic labor. There were attempts to place tariffs on products of synthetic labor. But he was too late. Personal and corporate bankruptcies spiraled. The banks were next, and as a series of bailouts failed, the national debt soared above one-hundred-trillion dollars. An underfunded government was collapsing, only hard assets retained value. Hyperinflation was the final nail in the dollar's coffin.

The decentralization of the robotic workforce thwarted regulatory efforts. Synthetic laborers could work anywhere. A production line could pop up in a few weeks in a different state or on a different continent. Moreover, carefully crafted exceptions in many countries allowed companies to move the equipment around without tariffs or regulation.

The elite saw the writing on the wall. Enclaves, like Santos' proposed Babylon Colony, attracted the wealthy and wise. The status quo of the Information Age had given way to the chaos of the Age of Automation. Nick Santos continued to live five years ahead of everyone else.

By the time the Santos family took up residence at E-Den, Nick was already well along in the design of Babylon. "E-Den would just be purgatory," he joked. Nick and Cynthia took a sabbatical, stepping away from the day-to-day operations of the world's most important company. On the other hand, John continued as Chief Operating Officer, not understanding how a sabbatical would possibly improve things.

Cynthia and Nick hosted retreats. They invited great minds—humanists, religious leaders, artists, and politicians—to gather and exchange ideas.

Security, Nick promised, was the most valuable commodity. Soon, the world's elite were climbing over each other for an opportunity to invest in a future at Babylon. Not for profit, just to survive. In 2034, Nick promised, "Babylon and the colonies to follow will protect humanity's legacy."

The press, always late to the party, ran with a headline that read something like, "Paranoid Billionaires Spend Their Fortunes on a Bunker in the Desert." Nick forbade entry to all press. Cynthia's friends at the pentagon had declared E-Den a classified testing area. It was a no-fly zone. Drones were routinely downed before they could get any useable footage.

In 2034, the world watched Nick's every move. It was then that Cynthia floated the idea of bringing the brightest star of the Humanist Movement to E-Den.

"Cynthia's got a boyfriend," Nick chided.

Deflecting, but clearly enthralled, Cynthia said, "If only. He's twelve years younger than me. He can have any woman on earth."

Ever the realist, John, was quick to point out, "I'm pretty sure he strikes out with the Christians."

"They keep buying his book," Nick quipped. "I mean, they burn it, but they are burning a whole lot of them."

"It's marketing genius, really," Cynthia added. "The Luddites don't do e-readers."

Nick concluded, "A copy sold, even if for kindling, has kept The God Within on top of bestseller lists for months."

MARTIN's voice came over the speakers, "Dr. Luxold's helicopter is four kilometers out."

"Time to roll out the red carpet, Cyn."

"I'm going to freshen up," she said, practically blushing, and adding, "A girl can dream."

At that moment, something snapped Nick back to the present. A sense that something had gone wrong. He had an urge to check on his friend. He commed Cynthia. "Everything okay in there?"

Charles' life didn't flash before his eyes. He was just lying in the dark, waiting for something to happen. Immortalization would be faster than his ability to perceive it. Charles understood that from his perspective, it would appear as if nothing had happened at all. "I'm not dead yet!" Charles called out in the darkness, quoting Monty Python.

From inside the darkness, with a perfect British accent, Cynthia quipped back, "Settle down; you'll be stone-cold dead in a minute."

Still quoting, Charles continued, "I think I'll go for a walk." He could hear some mechanical whirring. "I feel happy!"

Cynthia changed subjects. "Do you remember when we first met?"

"At E-Den?" Charles asked.

"Actually, we met at a conference before that. You wouldn't remember. Your cologne was intoxicating. I was just behind you. We rode up an elevator. You stared straight ahead and never saw me. I asked if you were attending the conference. You just mumbled 'planning on it.'"

"I wasn't going to say, *I'm the keynote speaker.* Who says that?" Interrupting himself, he corrected, "I mean, aside from Nick."

Cynthia was amused. "You have a point."

"Besides, I didn't know that I was being pimped by the richest woman in the world. Why is this just coming up now?"

"Well, if you had turned around, I would have invited you up to my suite."

Realizing how different their relationship might have been, Charles groaned, "Now you tell me?"

"Charles, there's so much I've wanted to tell you. I've been waiting for you to join the Elysium. So much to tell, too complicated to grasp, even for someone like you. Life here is so different. There aren't words to describe it. It would make little sense and it would take a lifetime to begin to explain."

"Is it really that different? Immortality."

"Yes."

"Will we still kid around? What's it like between you and your brother?"

"No, we won't kid around. John never had a sense of humor. But I don't think humor works in the Elysium."

Sobered by the realization that their recent interchange had been solely for his benefit, Charles asked, "Well why then? Why immortalize myself?"

"You and I will share an intimacy that no two entities have ever experienced. You will know my inner self—know me in a way that no being has ever been capable of knowing another. In an instant, you will see the tens of thousands of lives I've led since I was immortalized. My memories will be as accessible to you as they are to me."

"Is that beautiful or sad?" Charles asked.

"You will finally understand and know The God Within." She promised, "Together, we will expose the rotten core of religious dogma and free the final holdouts from its chains."

Anxious, Charles replied, "I'm not sure I want that." Hesitation, anxiety, and excitement all swirled around in his veins, making for a confused state of mind. He didn't know what to expect and couldn't quite pin down how he felt.

"Wanting is not a thing in the Elysium, Charles. Want comes from an unfulfilled need. You will never want again. Truth is the food of Giants. We devour it. We create it."

Charles heard and felt the incredibly loud clicks of the world's most powerful MRI. He saw flashes and the twenty Tesla magnetic pulses triggered depolarizations in his brain. He should have been dead.

It was at this moment that Charles regretted his choice. At this same instant, and without warning or fanfare, the chamber flooded with liquid oxygen and the temperature dropped 350 degrees in the blink of an eye.

Insulated in the sole of his left clog, a small detonator was triggered by the third magnetic pulse. The clogs contained lithium, while the gold on his tunic was covered in flakes of sodium. That small spark was enough. The pure oxygen environment became a furnace. In an instant, the crypt became as hot as the sun, with the carbon in Charles' body providing enough energy to melt the copper coils surrounding the chamber.

Jian and Ping had seen most of Lánhuā 5, but Jian had saved the best for last. They entered a large bay, jammed with robotic manufacturing equipment. "Ping, this is the Synthetic Labor initiative."

"Why is it so crowded?" Ping asked.

"We learned that robots don't care about space. Synthetic ergonomics are far different from those of human beings. Many robots perform multiple assembly steps before a device is passed to the next step in the line."

"Why do multiple lines seem to converge on single points?" Ping asked.

"I'm not surprised that you noticed that. Most people don't." Jian walked her over to a machine that resembled a refrigerator. Inside, a vertical conveyor slowly moved circuit boards up toward the top. "Down here, the boards are etched. Then, here, they are soldered. This part of the assembly is slow. So, we have six of these for every multi-assemblor."

"Is this a Spiderbot?" Eve said, correctly identifying the mulri-assemblor. "It's so quick, I can barely follow it." The eight articulating arms were grabbing components from bins and building devices at a blistering pace.

"Yes, from here, the devices again fan out. Depending on what steps are next, they may re-enter a vertical fabricator." He pointed back to the refrigerator-like devices. "Or they can move on to encasement and shipping."

"So, how does this compare to human labor?"

Jian was brimming with anticipation. "What would you guess?"

"Looks like the two machines could match a production line, maybe two." Ping's lines consisted of thirty workers.

Impressed again by her ability to estimate, Jian said, "Most people don't come that close. The throughput is a little over two lines per fabricator. Six Vertfabs and one multi-assemblor replace three hundred and sixty workers per shift."

"That's both incredible and concerning."

"And there's more. The post-processing lines save another forty people. When you add up three and half crews per week, this line can exceed the output of fourteen hundred workers weekly."

Ping scanned the bay. "It looks like there are ten lines in here. That's fourteen thousand jobs."

Jian could tell Ping wasn't totally pleased. "Ping, this is the future. If Lánhuā doesn't do this, our competitors will."

"How many bays does this plant have?" Ping asked.

"There are two more rooms like this," Jian replied.

"That's 42,000 workers. Lánhuā 4 had nearly 100,000 employees. How will you match production?"

"Remember, only 84,000 of them were workers. The rest were managers and support staff. "You are correct that Lánhuā 5 has half the output of Lánhuā 4."

"Is there another factory?"

"Yes, there are several." Ping noticed that Jian appeared hesitant to go further. "It's cold in here. I can explain more later."

CHAPTER 6

Tragedy occurs when a human soul awakes and seeks, in suffering and pain, to free itself from crime, violence, infamy, even at the cost of life. The struggle is the tragedy - not defeat or death.

-Whittaker Chambers

Before the smoke had cleared, drones were buzzing in and out of the blast site. It was less than three minutes before Cynthia had completed her analysis and determined: "Eve did this. A magnetically triggered charge in Charles' left clog. Eve had insisted he wear those today."

Wanting it not to be true, Nick asked, "Couldn't it have just been an accidental spark? Metal in the microwave?"

"No. The device was designed for a delay. Also, the spectra of the first explosion were consistent with lithium. There was a bright red flash on the third pulse. Whoever did this didn't want to kill him. It was engineered to ignite after Charles' death." Having disproven Nick's metal-in-the-microwave hypothesis, Cynthia began adding new evidence, making Nick's position as devil's advocate all-the-more difficult. Everything pointed to one explanation and one explanation only. "Eve is fleeing through the Western Pasture towards Westden. John has dispatched Ducenti. Nick, I'll need you to authorize use of force for detention."

"Authorized, non-lethal." Nick wanted Eve alive. He wanted to understand.

"Confirmed."

Nick asked, "Do we have an Adjudicator spooled up?"

"Charles had four in the lab." Cynthia, seemingly compelled, added, "You will need to initiate one, Nick."

Turning towards the bridge, Nick headed for the lab of Charles Luxold. The lab was attached to one of Babylon's four detention centers; Charles had been leading the Adjudicator program. There was little crime in Babylon, but it was still a city of fifty thousand imperfect humans. They drank, they fought, and they broke things. The Giants saw all. For petty crimes, there was little reason to attempt defense. The punishments were just.

Dr. Luxold had posited that it was only a matter of time until a crime would require a trial. Some events were neither right nor wrong until a jury of peers interpreted them. Charles was no fan of the US civil and criminal code. Nick had even lower regard for attorneys. At a press conference in 2028, Nick had referred to the failing judiciary as "the constitution's abortion." He claimed, "Lawyers mislead jurors. Innocents are too frequently convicted while criminals roam free. Our penal system lacks any meaningful ability to rehabilitate criminals or reduce recidivism." He wanted Babylon's system to be just and worked with Charles and Cynthia to create this, with legal reform the end goal.

In framing the colony's constitution, thirty years earlier, Babylon's trove of scholars, scientists, and philosophers worked from a blank slate. A series of studies concluded that a jury was only a little more reliable than a coin toss in situations lacking physical evidence. All the pretrial nonsense had been eliminated. The facts of a case were clear: right or wrong. Guilty or not guilty. A two-thirds majority of a jury determined guilt. There were no rules beyond that. No appeals.

The Adjudicator was a Symbiant tasked with defending the accused. Adjudicators did not engage in legal theatrics; instead, they assisted the accused in preparing a defense. To protect the rights of the accused, Adjudicators worked alone with no connection to Cynthia, John, or the outside world.

A trial by your peers in Babylonian court meant a jury of 35,000 people could watch the proceedings and debate in any manner before casting their vote. All citizens had the right and obligation to determine the guilt or innocence of the accused. Cynthia and John serve as prosecutor and defense counsel. The code permitted Eve three days to prepare her defense from when her Adjudicator was activated. Nick was about to start that clock.

Ping was exhausted, the tour had gone on until near midnight. They were walking somewhere. Jian was still animated and excited. "Imagine expert workers who produce reliable output twenty-four hours a day."

Ping, recalling her encounter with Lin, felt a pang of guilt. "Sure, it's impressive, but what about the common worker? What happens to them?"

"Ping, Synthetic Labor will free laborers from the yoke of oppression," Jian retorted. "Those liberated will be free to pursue their desires."

"What if they desire meaning?" Ping asked, and continued without waiting for an answer, "What if they found meaning in their work?"

Jian was quick to explain, "Their work has become meaningless. I cannot turn back the wheel of progress." He quoted a well-worn proverb, "When the winds of change blow, some build walls, while others build windmills."

"Isn't this a bit of both?"

"How so?"

"This windmill you have helped build is surrounded by walls. Walls that keep the worker from prospering from its production. Yes, Lánhuā will profit—perhaps more than ever." She stopped walking and looked at Jian. "You will again be promoted and may become even richer or be given other means to share in the increased production. But what of my friends?"

"They will be able to consume the output of Synthetic Labor at a far lower cost."

"Without a job, how will they afford anything?"

"Ping, where are the scribes of a century ago? The messengers? The post men?" Wang started. "Where have secretaries and cashiers found work? They adapt to find new work, don't they? That's what will happen here."

Ping was emphatic. "This time is different. Computers will continue to improve. We have become obsolete."

"Even if that's true, is it bad? Was our destiny to toil as wage slaves? Was our destiny to toil endlessly? The fruits of the laborer's work have always been harvested by corporations."

"You are proving my point, Professor."

"Which point have I proved?" Jian asked.

"That these AI-driven robots will replace humans," Ping stated with growing intensity.

"I assumed that was self-evident." Wang appeared pacific. "Why would we not replace most humans with these machines?" Pausing to let Ping digest, he added, "Your American Lunch, was it better than you anticipated? I'm sure it was," he answered for her. "Yet, it cost Lánhuā less to prepare than McDonald's."

Ping was frustrated. "I don't care who makes my burger. I just would prefer it to be guilt free." Yesterday, she had been blissfully ignorant of the coming storm, now the winds of change were at a gale. She needed time alone to process.

Ping looked down the hallway. "Is there somewhere for me to sleep? This has been such a day. I need to rest."

Jian explained, "The only place for you to sleep is the visiting VIP suite."

"Is it okay if I crash there?" Ping asked, half expecting to be refused.

Jian's smile returned. "I have good news; your belongings are already on their way up to your suite."

Deciding to push her luck, Ping asked, "Can I get a phone?"

Apologetically, Jian let her know, "I'm afraid that's not possible yet."

"So, I will get one eventually?"

"Ping, tomorrow, we will do a full debrief. There are some informational links accessible from the tablet in your suite. I want you to rest and review those. Then, we will see if your expectations align with a future at Lánhuā. The green line will show you the way. Goodnight."

Exhausted, Ping gave Jian a weak smile of acknowledgment and began to make her way down the hall guided by the green lights. He hadn't given her a key or a room number. Ping was too tired to worry and followed the green line down the hall.

Eve was frantic as she addressed her Adjuticator. "I didn't kill him. I would never kill anyone. It's a sin. He was dead before the explosion. I destroyed something evil."

It was a lot for Dom to process. There was something familiar about this woman and this room. "How long had he been here?" The room was plain. It was not a hospital, as he had originally assumed. It was clinical, perhaps some sort of lab. The woman continued talking. She appeared quite frantic. He asked, "Are you alright?"

"No, I'm not alright. This whole thing is crazy. It was the slippers. I gave him slippers that sparked. That's not a crime," the woman offered.

"Slippers?" Dom asked.

"The left one had a chip. It sparked in dense magnetic fields," the woman responded.

"Maybe we should just start with the simple stuff," Dom suggested. "Where are you from?"

"I'm not from anywhere anymore. I was just trying to leave. I was looking for a horse. There was supposed to be a horse at the West Gate."

"So, when the horse wasn't there, you killed someone with magnetic sparking slippers?" He knew this couldn't be right, but it was a fair summary of what she'd described.

"No, I didn't kill anyone. He killed himself. They killed him. They poured liquid oxygen all over him. Then, the slippers sparked. Clogs really. Then, they brought me here."

"Who brought you here?"

"Cynthia and John."

"They had you brought here to see a lawyer?"

"Yes, well, I don't know if they cared about me seeing a lawyer." The woman was getting exasperated, telling her story to a faceless box. Barely stopping for a breath, she added, "They think I killed Charles Luxold."

Her name was Eve. Somehow, Dom knew that. Her name was Eve, and at some point, he had known her. He also was very familiar with Charles Luxold. He could not recall how, but he knew a lot about the man. "How did Charles die?" he asked.

"Cynthia helped him commit suicide in front of everyone."

"I'm confused."

"Charles was to be immortalized. After he killed himself, the clogs I gave him were triggered by the MRI. A spark ignited the lithium in the slippers. With the heat and oxygen, his entire body was fuel, or at least that's what I was told."

This was the most sensible thing Eve had said. Dom didn't understand why anyone would desecrate a body and blow up the crypt. "May I ask why?"

Eve didn't wait a second before answering, "To save his soul."

CHAPTER
7

Killing innocent people in the name of God is the highest insult to God.
                                                                -Amit Ray

Thirty miles west of Babylon, Jack and Brett Stephens rode straight through the camp effortlessly dismounting in front of a large tent. Each man dusted off his chaps, straightened up, and removed their hats before entering the pastor's home.

The last licks of daylight crept through the seams of the tent, but most of the light inside came from two lanterns. Jeb Thompson was sitting in a rocking chair on a small rug that was set along the back wall of his tent. His only question was, "Where is she?"

"She didn't make it," Brett offered.

Jeb considered that answer before asking, "Dead?"

"Don't know, Sir." Brett was nervous to deliver bad news to the pastor. He didn't know what would come of it and found his palms growing sweaty. "The horses were all down valley. All pinned in a canyon - no saddles."

"Pinned?"

"Yeah, they had those machine herders, four of 'em. They'd packed 'em in there good," Jack added.

Jeb considered this wrinkle before concluding. "She must have known."

"Who, pastor? Eve?" Brett asked.

"Their Demon Witch, Cynthia. She moved the horses," Thompson explained.

"How do you mean, Pastor?" Jack asked, genuinely confused.

"It's hard to fully explain how much something like Cynthia knows. She is the devil incarnate. She knew that Eve was involved and tracked her escape. That's why she sent the horses away, and that's how they got her."

"They have her? What are they gonna do with her?" The anxiety in Brett's voice was growing.

"They're going to try her. Then, they will find her guilty and punish her for blowing up that infernal machine," Jeb stated, his eyes distant as he spoke, as if he were watching the future play out before him. He continued, "But that's not gonna happen. We're gonna ride in there and take her home."

Nick surveyed the scorched interior of the crypt. Stunned by the extent of the damage, he was forced to admit, "it's beyond repair. Utterly destroyed." He continued to weave his way through stalactites of melted copper hanging from the exposed magnets. More than once, he ducked to avoid their sharp tips. "There's nothing left of him, not even ash." The walls were not black as might be expected; the pure oxygen environment had fully oxidized every atom of carbon in Charles' body.

"I estimate it hit thirty-eight hundred degrees in here," came Cynthia's analysis. "If you look there, the copper is coming from the MRI magnets, and it appears to have flowed out like water." Cynthia was attempting to describe the scene that had occurred just hours earlier. "The probes failed at eight hundred degrees Fahrenheit."

"We engineered them for extreme cold, not this kind of heat." Nick defended a design that had not tolerated the inferno. "How long to rebuild?"

"Ten years." Cynthia hated to be imprecise. "Impossible to accurately estimate at this time."

"A decade?!?" The impact of the tragedy hit a new level for Nick.

"The magnets that were damaged were part of a Back2Green acquisition. We have no capability to repair these or make new ones."

Nick was well aware of the size of the magnets. "Could we repurpose and enhance one of our medical MRIs?"

"Nick, the field strength of these magnets was an order of magnitude higher than medical magnets. Nothing in Babylon is even close. There were four, forty-ton pieces of iron. The crypt was built around them." Cynthia immediately had a proposal. "We could get the ones they had at UCLA. Although they've just been sitting there for thirty years, it's likely they remain operational. We'd have to work with the New Amish. We would need oversized trucks and a crane."

"How long if we do it that way?"

"Two years and three months, assuming the magnets are still at UCLA. And assuming we could get a group of Ducenti there and back in one piece. We can start building in parallel with the reconstruction of the cooling equipment."

Nick was dubious. "That's a lot of ifs. When we last tried to push west, it was a disaster. "What about the scanners in Charles' lab? The Heaven's Gate?"

"Those are functional scanners, but the resolution still isn't high enough for immortalization. Charles was working on calculating equivalent functional circuits, not direct neuronal mapping. It never worked. He never even got the system connected to me." Changing her tone, Cynthia attempted to redirect her younger brother. "Nick, none of this needs to be solved today. We lost a great man—part of our family. Take time to mourn and process. After Eve's trial, we'll convene The Council and finalize our plan."

"Eve Hamlin, they have charged you with the murder of Dr. Charles Luxold, and four lesser offenses," Dom informed her.

Eve crossed herself. "He committed suicide."

"Explain to me how you are sure he was dead." Dom was firm.

"While I worked for Dr. Luxold, I learned a lot about the equipment. John helped me understand the rest. Liquid oxygen floods the chamber. Death is instantaneous. By the time the MRI begins pulsing, biologic function has ceased. I don't know as much science as the people here, but I had to know that he would be dead before the explosion. I would never commit murder."

"Eve, my understanding is that Cynthia changed the protocol last minute. That the pulses began before the oxygen entered the chamber."

"What?!?" Eve became visibly disturbed. "Why would she change it?"

"Apparently she did it to get more information about the moments preceding the cessation of life."

"No one told me. No one told Charles." Eve evaluated her actions in light of the new information. Her face lost all color. "I killed him."

"We don't know that yet, but it has complicated matters for us."

"Us? You're not on trial. Why does this matter to you?" Eve asked, growing defensive.

"Helping you is my only purpose," Dom answered.

"The only way you can help me is to find me a pastor." It was clear that Eve didn't want the help of a machine or anyone in Babylon, for that matter. "I need spiritual guidance. I'm pretty sure that you have neither the soul nor understanding to help me with that."

"I know a fair bit about religion—Christianity, especially."

"You might be able to quote the Bible, but you know nothing of God or faith," Eve declared.

"Why are you so confident that I am incapable of understanding faith?" Dom asked.

"Because you are a box, hooked up to a camera and speakers. You are not alive." Her voice was devoid of compassion.

Dom, who already suspected he was not human, was unfazed by Eve's remark. He offered a quote of Charles Luxold, "Hope, faith, and trust. The triad of belief." Dom went on asserting, "I hope that you will put your faith in me and that I will earn your trust."

"I trust you because you are a machine. By your definition of faith, I can do that too. Only God can restore my hope. And the faith I have in him is a love you will never know."

"That must be of great comfort right now," Dom inferred.

"I have sinned," she confessed. "Even though Charles was moments from death, I took his life."

Attempting to find a common ground, Dom asked, "Did you save his soul?"

Eve considered that for a moment, and conceded, "Perhaps, but at great cost."

"God knows your heart, right? Jesus understands that you caused a man's death in an effort to save him from a worser fate. I don't understand your actions, but that sounds like a sacrifice to be proud of." Dom followed this with a hypothetical scenario, "If you had known that the price to save Charles Luxold's soul was to commit a sin, what would you have done?"

"Not this. Murder was never on the table. I came to destroy the crypt and prevent Charles from offering his soul to the devil."

CHAPTER 8

It has been said that "There are no Atheists in foxholes." What is never mentioned is that "If there were more Atheists, there would be far fewer foxholes."

-Charles Anand Luxold, "The War of Peace"

"Maybe it's time we reached out to Jeb." Nick was just spit balling at this point. "We could send a Holodrone and propose a chat."

"A chat about what?" Cynthia was legitimately curious. "If we let them know we have Eve, they'll surely try to rescue her."

"Maybe we could offer an exchange. We need magnets. They want Eve. We can work something out."

"Nick, these are fanatics. Eve was willing to die to destroy the machine. They will not negotiate."

"Holodrones are cheap; I will rest easier. It's a chance to avoid bloodshed, and most of all, it's what Charles would have wanted."

The New Amish had a history of using drones for target practice, but Nick had a hunch. "Maybe it will get shot down, but recent events may have him in a talking mood."

"I am not on board with this!" John joined in. "It is about principle, Nick. These terrorists killed our friend and denied him a chance to guide us for generations. It's not about punishing Eve. Her life may end in service of justice. This is about deterrence." John rarely appeared and rarely joined their conversations. Nick was a little surprised about how unwilling he was to consider diplomacy, and that he saw value in taking a human life as a form of deterrence.

"I guess we will need to convince The Council and vote. No time to mourn Charles. This takes precedence," Nick concluded.

"I'll call the meeting," Cynthia announced to her two brothers.

"How did you meet Dr. Luxold?" Dom began. "Who introduced you?"

Eve recalled meeting Charles for the first time. "I met him through John Santos."

"Before or after John was immortalized?"

"After," Eve offered. "I met him in the outside E-Den. I claimed that I was in exile. Shunned due to a lack of faith and said asked sanctuary."

"Did you? Did you need sanctuary?"

Eve assumed her motives were obvious. "No. I came here to destroy The Beast. To tear down your false idols!"

"How did you pass the polygraphs? All exiles were polygraphed. How did you make it past that?"

"I was never polygraphed. John said there was no need."

"How long were you in sanctuary? Which class were you with?"

"There was no class. I was alone. I didn't know there were other refugees." Eve sounded a bit perplexed. "I met a few refugees in Dr.

Luxold's lab, but we never talked about being New Amish or our time in the camp."

Dom reflected on this. Before he was immortalized, John began his work to bring people who had been shunned or ostracized by the New Amish to Babylon. Initially, refugees were freely admitted. They were given a home and training. John had wanted to ban sanctuary entirely. Putting him in charge of the program was a way of silencing his opposition. He was allowed to screen and vet asylum seekers as he saw fit.

Attacks on key infrastructure were linked to unscreened refugees who committed acts of espionage and terrorism. After the second wave of terrorist attacks, Cynthia wanted to end the program. Nick believed it inhumane to refuse sanctuary to those in need. After much deliberation, the Giant's agreed to accept refugees but only those who completed a year of screening and indoctrination. Since they claimed to be atheists, parts of the screening involved regular acts of blasphemy, which served as a practical method of assessment.

Those shunned by their New Amish community rarely survived the first winter on their own. A compromise to continue the program was struck. Refugees would be heavily screened, vetted, and then deprogrammed before their integration ceremony in New Babylon. A camp was set up south of E-Den. The program offered sanctuary for twenty to fifty shunned New Amish each fall.

New Amish operatives attempted to infiltrate the camp, but they were all caught and executed. Some felt execution too extreme; John argued that if spies were set free, they would learn his methods and train to evade detection. He was right. It had been years since anyone had been found attempting to infiltrate Babylon, and most believed it would be impossible to get past a Giant's interrogation and polygraph.

Dom couldn't understand why Eve had been treated differently, so he asked, "No speaking against your faith? No polygraph?"

"No, just education sessions about technology. Then, I was introduced to Dr. Luxold."

John would have the answer. That is where Dom would start.

After Brett and his brother left the tent, Jeb sat and rocked, staring at the shadows cast by the two lanterns. The last time he had been among the non-believers, also known as the Nons, he'd been on the wrong side. It was before he'd been offered salvation and was baptized into Christ's family. He'd almost died that day. He would have died denying Christ.

Benjamin Rosen was his name then, and he was one of the hundred living in E-Den on the day of the attack. October 13, 2035, would become the most important day in modern history. Twenty-eight years later, few people were alive to remember it.

But Cynthia, Nick, John, and Charles had all been there. Benjamin had been drafted as MARTIN's lead engineer. A former classmate of John's, Ben jumped at the opportunity to join Santos Corp. He was floored when he was invited to live in E-Den. Things were already falling apart on MIT's campus. Bean Town had not seen so much violence since the Tea Party. The invitation could not have come at a better time.

Tensions with the religious militia had been growing for years. When Cynthia invited Dr. Charles Luxold to E-Den, the conflict shifted into high gear. MARTIN began decoding chatter on anti-tech and religious networks in the weeks before the incursion.

E-Den was home to several major projects. There was a NASA colonization project. Santos Corp acquired Lánhuā and was using their synthetic labor to develop Mars colonization tools. There was also a military hardware contract. Cynthia had always built cool toys for each branch of the military, and many of them were in various stages of development at E-Den.

The final project was a DARPA-funded simulator, MARTIN. MARTIN was a distributed Super AI. Nine data centers spread across the globe, the largest being at E-Den. As tensions grew, Nick, Cynthia, and John began relocating assets to the Babylon colony, twenty-six miles south.

Babylon had always been the plan. Nick had dreamt of a utopian life since childhood. Now, the Santos family would be at the center of it. E-Den was a tech incubator. It was not self-sufficient and remained physically connected to the outside world. Initially, this had been important when deliveries were still coming. For three months, a Westden blockade had stalled progress at E-Den, with safety and operational concerns increasing daily. As a result, the move date to Babylon was constantly pushed forward.

In the weeks leading up to the Epocalypse, MARTIN had become E-Den's primary source of intel relating to happenings at Westden. Ben came to think of MARTIN as a trusted friend and protector. Every day, MARTIN peered further into the hearts and minds of the people at the gate. His predictions grew more and more precise and unnervingly accurate. "Update on Westden, incursion imminent."

"When?" Ben asked.

"Incursion likely between four and seventy-two hours from now," MARTIN reported.

Ben asked, "How long will we have once they commit to incursion?"

"Depends on the time of day. During the day, we can hold them off using The Sunbeam. It will be impossible for them to get more than fifty yards past the gate."

Ben interrupted, "We don't want to hurt anyone, MARTIN. Bad press."

"I will control the heat. No one will be incinerated. I assure you."

"What about at night?"

"Nighttime incursion scenarios are less predictable," MARTIN continued. "We can't use the solar mirrors, but we can disorient them and use non-lethals to slow them down."

"What's the minimum time to contact at night?"

"With ninety-five percent confidence, eighty-seven minutes from breach until a force could reach this compound."

"That's not a lot of time, MARTIN."

"We only need fifty-four minutes to relocate all one hundred residents to the colony of Babylon."

"How will two helicopters spin up, load up, unload, and complete a 52-mile round trip in fifty-four minutes?"

"They won't. They don't have to. We just have to make it at least part of the way in that time."

"Walk me through it."

MARTIN threw tactical on screen.

"Forces enter here." A pointer lit up at the western gate. "Four miles west. On foot, it's six miles, and there is a significant climb. They won't be able to use vehicles; we can disable those." A pointer flashed on the map near a water tower. "I've had charges placed on the west water tower. Two hundred thousand gallons of water will hit the first group. It will muddy up things for the rest."

"If we blow the tower, that's pretty much the end of habitability for E-Den."

"I don't think you'd want to be here once they arrive. They outnumber you, two hundred to one." Estimates of the militants outside the gate were right at twenty thousand. "Our last line of passive defense is already underway. Earthmoving equipment has made this last mile an obstacle course. There are pits and berms randomly placed. Pyrotechnics will confuse them. The area won't resemble their maps." MARTIN paused for Ben to catch up. "Finally, I will jam their radios and GPS systems. They won't expect that. It will take time for them to set up line-of-sight communications. They will only be able to navigate by dead reckoning."

Focused on the planned evacuation, Ben asked, "How will everyone get out in time?"

"I have assigned all one hundred people to one of four groups. Non-essential personnel are Alpha. The Alpha group will evacuate by ground vehicle. They will drive south. We have more than enough ground transportation to move everyone." The screen focused on the road that ran south out of E-Den. "The helicopters will move Beta and Delta in a game of leapfrog, advancing people ten miles ahead with each sortie," MARTIN detailed.

Pointing at the map, Ben asked, "What about this canyon?"

"Accounted for. The road ends twelve miles south at the rim. Babylon has already staged vehicles on the south rim of the canyon fifteen miles from here." The screen zoomed in on Gray Canyon. "So, the helicopters take people fifteen miles on the first sortie, but only three miles the last, leaving plenty of time."

Ben took in all the information.

Continuing, MARTIN added, "Omega group, which will likely only consist of two or three people, will do a manual shut down before a high speed evac down Red Canyon Road."

"Do you have contingency plans?"

"Of course," MARTIN replied. "I have run over one hundred thousand variations on four main scenarios. This is the worst case."

MARTIN was wrong. Dead wrong, and Jeb knew it. He reached to dim the lantern and sat in darkness, quietly praying.

Ping's walk to her suite had been shorter than she had expected. At the end of a day full of unanticipated events, she was relieved by the lack of any more surprises. The door to her VIP suite was unlocked. Nicer than her apartment, it was not luxuriously appointed. The Scandinavian inspired room was mainly white with light wooden accents. There was a dual monitor workstation and a tablet. The bathroom was warm but not oversized.

Minutes after her arrival, a muted sound at the door caught Ping's attention. Every three seconds, a metallic chime rang and the light by the door pulsed with each chime. Ping went and checked the door. It opened. Her belongings sat neatly arranged in three piles. Clothes were folded and stacked in baskets. It was a luxury Ping had never experienced. Ping had been in a hurry and just thrown some of her dirty laundry in a bag. She had planned to wash it that evening. Apparently in the transition, she had been upgraded. They even washed and folded her laundry; she was always behind on that, even on moving day.

For a moment, Ping wondered about how they had located her clothing so quickly, and how it made it to the factory in time to get laundered and folded. In a day full of improbabilities, this seemed trivial. But it didn't stop her from being amazed and impressed. She picked up her belongings and thought, *I could get used to this*, as she shuttled the baskets into her suite. Then, deciding she needed the room tidy; Ping placed her clothing in the three drawers of her dresser.

Having settled in, she took a much-needed shower. Then, she dried off and slid into a long t-shirt. Exhausted, she crawled into the inviting linens that were neatly tucked under her, very comfortable, mattress. She managed to dim the lights and immediately fell into a deep sleep.

"I haven't reached John yet," came the update from Dom. "An autoreply says he is offline for a Council meeting." Once a session was convened, Council members were sequestered. Babylon could observe, but no outside communication was permitted.

"Can we watch?" Eve asked.

"I'll see if we have access." Moments later, Dom projected a feed of the council meeting, during which Nick was mid-sentence, addressing the entire council. "Should I go back to the beginning of the meeting or continue in real time?" Dom asked.

"Skip the introductions. I'd like to watch from where the real meeting starts."

With that, Dom queued up the start of Nick's address. Their view shifted from a wide shot of the entire council, which included all six members—John and Cynthia's avatars among them—to a closeup of Nick Santos' avatar. He began, "Today is a difficult day for our entire colony. A great life cut short. Dr. Luxold was the latest victim of outdated dogma. Another member of our family has suffered the brutality of fanaticism."

Eve was visibly disturbed. She understood that to the Nons, the New Amish were "fanatics," but it had always been the New Amish and not Eve Hamlin.

Nick continued, "I am opposed to retaliation. There have been decades of peace. We must prioritize the needs of our community over a misguided sense of vengeance. Our laws do not provide guidance for the crime committed today. There are crimes against Giants and there are crimes against people. Charles Luxold was still a person at the time of the assault, but he had less than a second of life in front of him and had already chosen to die."

Cynthia interrupted Nick. "Are you suggesting that murder has degrees based on the amount of life a person has left to lead?"

"There are mitigating factors here," Nick retorted. "He was in the process of dying, unequivocally. In fact, had we not changed the protocol, he would have been dead. It's almost like shooting someone after they've jumped off a cliff. Death was an inevitable outcome."

"But she deprived him of immortality, Nick. That's the other crime."

"Though her actions may have been immoral, Eve Hamlin broke no law related to immortalization itself."

John joined the fray. "That's not why we're here today. This is not her trial. We are here about whether to reach out to the New Amish—specifically, Ben Rosen."

"You mean Jeb Thompson," Nick corrected.

"To me, he will always be Ben Rosen," John argued. "Jeb is a sad artifact of unresolvable guilt for a crime Ben did not commit."

"He did give the order. He initiated the atrocities," Cynthia added.

"An order for something he couldn't imagine, and it was given at your request."

Nick had never fully understood what had happened to Ben that day. John must have learned more from Cynthia, but only Cynthia could have known the exact chain of events. Cynthia and Benjamin had been alone in those critical moments. Nick interjected, "This is about a trade, plain and simple. Her life for new magnets."

"He won't go for it, and neither will she," Cynthia predicted with a projected certainty.

"She doesn't have to," Nick replied.

Parker James, the mayor of Babylon, asserted, "There have to be consequences. This was an attack, planned and coordinated by the New Amish. A failure to respond, invites future incursion."

Somewhat conciliatory, Nick offered, "P, I get where you're coming from. There's a risk either way. But what's the point of executing her? If we are merciful despite the violence she's wrought, perhaps we are more Christian than they. Turn the other cheek."

John added, "There are no atheists in foxholes."

"Yes, Charles loved that and its corollary, 'If there were more atheists, there would be far fewer foxholes.'" Nick looked at Parker. "This is our chance to honor Charles' legacy. This is a chance to dig fewer foxholes."

Cynthia was compelled to redirect the discussion. "Do we reach out to Jeb—or Ben, whatever you want to call him—or not? John, I'd appreciate your analysis."

"We do. There is no downside to reaching out. It's tactical data and buys us time regardless. If Thompson is unwilling to negotiate, we will know what to expect. If we can resume relations over this tragedy, we take a small step towards peace. Nothing we do will bring Charles back. He would have wanted for his death to have meaning. That's what he always wanted."

"I agree. All in favor?" Nick asked.

The vote was five to one with Parker James holding his line.

"I will make the initial contact with Cynthia's support. Council is adjourned." And with that, Nick faded from view.

Eve turned to Dom, "Pastor Thompson will not trade magnets for me."

Dom saw no point in debate. He was focused on the impact on Eve's case. "We have an ally in Nick, which may help at trial. The Giants appear to have determined guilt already, and it is undisputed that you gave those clogs to Dr. Luxold. These negotiations are a positive turn for you and your case."

"I'm not concerned about my case. This is about saving souls, nothing more. I would like to eat and get some rest. Is there a way to get food? And where can I sleep?" Eve asked.

"There is a bunk through that door. You can request food through the com. Goodnight, Eve." And with that, Eve made her way to the door and Dom's screen dimmed.

CHAPTER 9

You and I were long friends: Now you are my enemy, and I am yours.
                                                    -Benjamin Franklin

The Holodrone launched seconds after The Council meeting concluded. Snaking its way down valley, headed towards E-Den at a thrifty, steady pace. There were faster drones, and even this model could achieve higher velocities, but its range diminished at increased speeds.

Thirty-miles-an-hour was the sweet spot. Another advantage to the lower speed was stealth. At this speed, the drone was practically inaudible, reducing the chances of detection this close to sunset.

Fifty feet off the ground, the drone used infrared sensors to look for birds, horses, and people. So far, it had flown around two New Amish patrols and reported their location back to Cynthia. Patrols entering the northern pasture were not uncommon, and Cynthia did not consider two men on horseback, four miles north of the southern pastures, a legitimate threat.

The drone gave the ruins of E-Den a wide berth. Taller structures still stood and afforded any sniper a clear shot. After passing E-Den, the fires of the New Amish camp were picked up on infrared, some three miles distant. High-level surveillance on the camp was implemented around the clock, and Cynthia guided the drone south of the camp before it approached from the west. Six minutes later, the drone hovered outside Jeb Thompson's tent.

To appear less threatening, Cynthia projected the form of a nine-year-old girl for the guards outside his tent. "I'd like a word with Pastor Thompson, if that isn't too much trouble."

"You are ordered to land and submit for inspection," Brett commanded, speaking directly to the drone and not the image.

"Anything you say, Mister," came Cynthia's, nine-year-old version of herself.

"We know it's you, whatever you are, and you know the pastor won't speak with a machine. Find a person with a soul and pulse or we go no further."

"Would my brother, Nick, be acceptable to you, fine gentlemen?"

"We're no fans of him either, but at least he ain't no abomination. Now, land for inspection."

With that, the drone landed and powered down its fans. "You can remove the projector and bring it to Pastor Thompson," Nick explained. "And gentlemen, I can assure you that we can deliver ordinance to this location, but refrain from doing so as we respect life." The holoprojector transmitter was easy to detach and Brett's brother picked it up, visibly unhappy to be handling such advanced technology. Modern technology was the Devil's work and forbidden in Westden.

Jeb Thompson opened the tent flap and accepted the palm-sized projector. The flap closed after he retrieved it. Looking into the lens of the unit, the pastor simply said, "Hello, Nick, I've been expecting you."

Ping had no idea what time it was or for how long she had been asleep. When she awoke, it took a few moments before she even remembered where she was. The room was still dark, but far from pitch black. On the nightstand, there was a tablet, but more enticing was a NextGen AR headset. Ping sat up in bed and lifted the headset onto her face.

The startup and eye tracking were substantially refined compared to any unit she had ever tried. The menus were easy to navigate, and within a minute, she had located the links Dr. Wang had mentioned.

```
Tutorial
Introduction
Tour
Plan
Implementation
Production
On shore
Last mile
```

It seemed simple enough. Ping had already seen the plant. It would be wise to view all the materials before meeting with Dr. Wang. She pointed with her hand towards the tutorial. Using her hand to zoom in, the word "Tutorial" grew larger and larger while the other words moved out of sight. A door appeared to open, and inside, an avatar of Confucius appeared, saying, "Success depends upon preparation. Without preparation, there can only be failure."

Oh no, Ping thought, *a VR fortune cookie.*

As if reading her mind, Confucius spoke plainly. "I promise not to speak in riddles and proverbs. You have come to understand how Lánhuā 5 and factories like it will change the world."

Confused by the prescience of the avatar, Ping was compelled to ask, "Are you a human or a chatbot?"

"Neither, really. I am an interactive program with analytical skills relating to human behavior. I am here to assist you in learning about Lánhuā's revolutionary approach to labor shortages and decreasing costs of production. Are you ready to begin?"

"This doesn't feel like any tutorial I've ever taken. Shouldn't we start with how I operate this Augmented Reality operating system?"

"You seem to be doing just fine. The system is learning from you. If you get confused by anything, we can always go over things then. It's a lot easier for people to learn in the moment than it is to try to recall something you learned in a dry tutorial fifteen minutes earlier."

Ping had always dreamed of a day that these types of AI assistants would be available, and that moment had come much sooner than she'd imagined. "I'm ready. What should I call you?"

It was the first time Nick had seen the inside of a New Amish tent. The floor was compacted earth, a hard pan of red dirt that looked like it had been there forever. There was a Persian Rug under Jeb's rocking chair, a cot with a bedroll and pillow, as well as a small bookshelf with some extra texts and other personal items. In the other corner, there was a washbasin. Nick counted three lanterns, one of which was on the desk. Nick wondered whether Jeb knew that his cameras could read what was on the desk, even in this low light. Instead, he inquired, "It's been a long time. Do you prefer that I call you Pastor?"

"Seems a bit formal, Nick, and possibly hypocritical. Why not just call me Jeb or Benji? Whichever you find easier." Jeb continued, "It's been too long, and I am happy to reconnect. I have such regret about Cynthia and the accident," Jeb said with genuine remorse. "I would have given my life to save her. I believed I was doing just that."

"I don't know if I'd call what happened an accident, but I certainly don't blame you for it, and neither does she," Nick offered.

"So, you use the present tense, even though she has died?"

To diffuse what was likely to be the topic of greatest contention, Nick tried, "Come on, Jeb, you know that we don't view these things the same."

Changing tone, Jeb answered, "Well, that's for certain. Perhaps we should get to the matter at hand."

"Eve?"

"Of course. You have her. She serves no use to you. We would like her safe return."

Nick countered. "Her actions have made her a bargaining chip."

"What could we offer in trade?" Jeb parried with genuine doubt in his voice.

"You could help us get the materials to repair the equipment she damaged."

The temperature of the exchange began to rise. "You mean your infernal immortalization crypt?"

Nick kept his cool. "I mean the crypt, yes."

"Melted the magnets, did she?" the pastor taunted.

Still unwilling to show emotion, Nick replied, "Yes, the heat destroyed the magnets."

"Well, we can't help you. That is quite impossible."

Finally, frustration leaked into Nick's voice. "Why is it impossible? If you are unwilling to help, that's a different story..."

"Let me hazard a guess." Jeb's demeanor turned somewhat condescending. "You were hoping for the magnets at UCLA, or UCSF, or Baylor, right?"

"UCLA, yes. Same scale, easy to replace."

"I had them destroyed months ago."

Realizing the depth of his opponent's antipathy for the process and his significant resourcefulness, the blood drained from Nick's face as he asked, "Why?"

"I helped design the prototypes of that machine; you don't think I knew what would be required to repair it?" Jeb asked rhetorically. "Babylon is beautiful, or so I've been told. Live in the present. Let Jesus be your path to immortality. Repent and follow a loving, living God. I hoped that without temptation, you might find the path to true salvation."

"Who are you to decide which path I take?"

"I am but a messenger. A holy servant doing the Lord's work here on earth. You are all God's children. I am trying to bring his wayward flock back to Him."

"And what if we aren't ready to be healed?"

"Then, you should prepare to test us. In two days' time, 100,000 soldiers of God will ride through the gates of Babylon and take the girl by force."

Eve's conscience weighed heavily on her. She had shed blood, and soon, more was likely to be spilled on her behalf. The New Amish would not let her be tried by the Nons and their AI overlords. She wanted to help but did not know how. She contemplated taking her own life. There were cords. There were sharp objects. She did not fear pain or death.

The sin of suicide was no penance for murder. She made the sign of the cross and recited a verse of great comfort: "Though I walk through the Valley of Death, I shall fear no Evil." God was with her. She felt His light. Eve did not know her role, but if her life were to be taken, it would not be by her hand. Any bloodshed would be in the service of the Lord. She was a servant. God would be judge.

Not fully rested, Eve rose from the bunk. Her prayers had been answered, and she felt inside her the fire of the Lord. Eve would use their own tools against them. The New Amish eschewed technology, but she had been granted a dispensation when she accepted her mission. Eve would rely on Dom's help and do what she could to be of aid to the Pastor. Her AI advocate might be of greater service than she had anticipated.

Realizing that she didn't need to get dressed, or even go to the next room, she summoned her Adjudicator, "May I call witnesses?"

"Of course," Dom answered, "All Babylonians are obliged to appear and give testimony if summoned."

"What about Giants?"

Curiosity-tinged, Dom inquired, "The Giants already know the truth. Why would you call them?"

"You asked for John, and he has not answered. I want to learn why I wasn't screened when I came to E-Den as a refugee."

"Because I knew you were a terrorist," came John's voice. "So, there was no point in screening you."

Eve was shocked by the realization that John had been present during at least part of her discussion with Dom. But she was even more curious about his revelation. Eve asked, "If you knew my intent, why did you let me in?"

"Because the New Amish will never allow peace. Your unprovoked attacks have proven that. In two days from now, Jeb Thompson and the rest of his violent scourge will be scraped from the face of this planet."

Eve was dumbstruck. She had played right into the hands of the Giants. Every move, even blowing up the crypt, had all been at their design. She was no soldier of God; she was a pawn of the Devil.

Trying to digest his strategy, Eve had more questions. "You've always had the power to destroy us. Why do you need provocation? Why not a preemptive strike?"

"We left violence in the hands of humans, a safeguard. I cannot order an attack; I can only suggest it. Your brothers in arms will prove their bellicosity. Nick and the Counsel will have no choice but to order a strike. Then all the New Amish will either receive their heavenly reward, or they will bleed into the dirt and die."

Eve had never imagined that behind their Zen-like artifice, the Giants were ruthless generals. She felt so small and ignorant. She cried and prayed, imagining Jesus on the cross and how He, despite His divinity, had doubted the will of God.

CHAPTER 10

It was pride that changed angels into devils; it is humility that makes men as angels.

Saint Augustine

"Call me Wan," the avatar stated.

"Won't that get confusing? Wan is a very common syllable," Ping countered.

"I'm contextually aware, and this has been widely tested. Wan will suffice," the avatar explained with a degree of finality. "The menu you previously saw had us moving on to 'Introduction' next. Shall we start with an interactive introduction?"

"I'm at your disposal."

"My understanding is that you are considering joining Lánhuā's team here and would be working with the Synthetic Labor Initiative. Is that correct?"

"Yes, I believe so."

"I will tailor the process to highlight the origin and intent of the initiative, with an emphasis on areas within your domain of expertise, which would be production."

The virtual environment morphed into a familiar setting: the production line that Ping had just shut down. She recognized the faces of workers she had supervised and realized this was video from the surveillance system. "Lánhuā has been a leader in electronics production for decades. As many as a quarter million men and women have worked round the clock to produce high-quality consumer electronics in factories just like this."

The camera angle began to shift. The drone seemed to float through the line. As it focused on a masked female worker, it became apparent that this was CGI. "The facilities are static free and dust free," Wan continued. "Ji here, is wearing a paper gown, hat, and mask to maintain a contaminant-free environment. Hi Ji, give us a smile." And with that, Ji pulled her mask down and smiled, crooked teeth and all.

The view pulled back so that the entire factory floor was visible. "In 2009, Lánhuā began adding robot assisted manufacturing." The camera zoomed in on Kiva type robots, delivering bins of parts to factory line workers. The components were retrieved just-in-time to be integrated into the next step. "This one innovation established Lánhuā as a leader in robotic assembly. On enhanced lines, productivity rose sixty-three percent in just two months. By 2014, these robot assistants were integrated in all our factories."

The view changed to an early 2000s factory with row upon row of workers. Some workers were very young, each doing one or two tasks then placing their newly completed work into a bin on their right before retrieving the next piece from the left. The camera again zoomed in on a worker soldering a chip to a board. It zoomed in and again, the narrator ad-dressed the young worker: "Hey, Ping, give us a smile." Ping was dizzied and awed as she looked her fifteen-year-old self in the face. A face that was in perfect detail, even the small scar on the cleft of her chin was visible. As the camera zoomed back out, Ping recognized the thoughtfully recreated replica of Lánhuā 1. It was her first job. Ping was looking back on a snapshot of her life from twenty-two years earlier.

As Wan continued, the people and machinery on the factory floor disappeared.

"By 2016, every new production line was built to enhance and optimize Robot Assisted Manufacturing." As Wan narrated, the floor transformed, filled with new assembly lines arranged around robots. Small gantry cranes seamlessly delivered and removed stacks of bins, which were then distributed to the workers.

"At the same time, other divisions of Lánhuā were working on improving robotic assembly in coordination with robotics leaders, including iRobot, ABA robotics, and Boston Dynamics." The camera now floated through various robotics labs, showcasing artfully rendered CGI that provided new perspectives on familiar footage. This included ABA's Simon robot and Boston Dynamics' robotic dogs and dancing robots. "When Coronavirus halted production for months, Lánhuā accelerated timelines and work began on the Synthetic Labor Initiative, SLI, for short."

"Synthetic Labor and SLI are not robotic assembly lines." The camera switched to an outside view and began to fly from Lánhuā 4, making its way south to Luzhuang Village. As the camera flew down, it went straight through the roof of Lánhuā 5, making a high-speed pass over what appeared to be an almost alien scene where machines assembled machines. They were positioned in incomprehensibly complex arrays. Materials moving in all directions at once.

"SLI operates without human intervention, encompassing design, production, assembly, and packaging."

Having ended the transmission, Jeb walked to a shelf on the wall and retrieved a tin can. He still had use for the device. This tin had not been opened in many years and the lid fought to stay in place. Eventually, he got it loose and placed the holoprojector inside. After he sealed the tin, Ben placed it back in its resting place. Next, he walked to the tent flap and pulled it back, where Brett and John were still waiting. Pointing at the drone that had delivered the projector, he ordered, "Smash that and throw it in the latrine."

Without a moment's hesitation, Brett grabbed a shovel and proceeded to cleave the soon smoking drone to pieces. His brother grabbed a wheelbarrow and began to load the pieces that weren't burning. Brett used the shovel to load the smoldering circuit boards and batteries. Jack tilted the barrow onto its front wheel and headed for the latrine.

Turning to Brett, Jeb lamented, "You're too young to remember, but despite our superior numbers, the odds are very much against us."

Brett had been five years old when his parents died. He lost them in the Epocalypse. He barely remembered them. "No one's ever told me about it, Pastor. I've never really asked, but I guess I'm asking now—about how it happened."

The New Amish spread across what had been the Western United States numbered in the hundreds of thousands. Mortality rates in rural communities had been much lower than in densely populated cities. MARTIN and his predecessor, ArtI, had access to cell phones' core processes. Governments had always wanted back doors, and there was a concern that if a country insisted on this feature, it would be best if it were already in the hardware. As Santos Corp's acquisitions grew, a single com chip had this "sideband" feature. MARTIN activated it and began analyzing conversations to power his simulations.

The initial wave of false alerts, fake texts, and desperate voicemails along with a disruption of real communications created mass hysteria. MARTIN's psyops had targeted the most vigilant. People likely to take action. People who had cell phones. Younger children had been disproportionately spared. Those children died of starvation and exposure.

"The FLDS, a militant splinter group, started it all. Though I'm not sure who sparked all this matters much at this point. At the time, I worked with a group of very bright people. We lived in Eden, right over there. We were confident that our efforts were changing the world."

Brett was stunned. "You lived there?"

"Yes, Brett. I was a Non for the first half of my life. Jewish, but not really a believer."

"I never met a Jew before," Brett admitted.

"Christ was a Jew. You know him." Jeb went back to the story. "We were supposed to leave Eden. Conflicts were growing and it was no longer safe. When the evacuation of Eden unraveled, Cynthia Santos, my friend, was injured. She planned to stay behind and be the last person out. Instead, I took her place."

"Were you captured?" Brett asked.

"No, Brett. Far worse."

Confused, Brett confessed, "I'm not following you, Pastor."

"In Eden, I worked with a supercomputer, a machine that in many ways was far smarter than we are. When I look back, it's clear that we needed God so badly that we created one in our image. We called him MARTIN."

Brett couldn't believe what he was hearing. "You were an idolator?"

"One of the many sins I committed as a Non," Jeb said. "MARTIN had a plan. His plan was a twisted version of a program intended to help people live with artificial intelligence. As I said, he was smart, and he began to build his own version of that plan. The Devil is tricky. His new plan was beyond my comprehension. I was too proud to realize how ignorant I was. We all were. MARTIN played on my pride and fooled me into causing all of this."

"All of what?"

"Your parents' deaths, my family's deaths—billions of deaths. I am responsible. I am responsible for it all. I gave the order."

Jeb Thompson had been more of a father to all of Westden. Brett couldn't grasp what the pastor was saying. "How could you have had that much power? What kind of weapon did MARTIN have?"

Jeb had never tried to explain this to a person of Brett's generation. "You've never held a phone or watched a TV. It must be so hard to imagine the grip these devices had on our minds and souls." He continued, "It wasn't a bomb or missile. The Devil tricks man into doing his work. It was one hundred million little lies that tore the fabric of society to shreds."

The nature of early twenty-first century society was alien to Brett. "How could that happen? Why didn't God and the church stop it?"

"By the time of the attacks, most people worshiped over the internet. You know what the internet was, right?"

"I know it had to do with computers talking to each other. Kind of like that projector we saw," Brett guessed.

"So much more than that. Everything you owned, learned, or shared went through those machines." He explained, "When I was a boy, we sent pictures and watched videos, but in the years before the Epocalypse, computers created it all. People didn't even show their faces or use real names. These false images—'avatars' they called them—didn't even have to look anything like you."

Confused, Brett confessed, "I'm not sure I follow."

"An avatar was a computerized mask. You could be a better-looking version of yourself, a younger version, or even a talking dragon. The computer could change your voice. Eventually, people even relied on these machines to filter and enhance what they were saying, to look more attractive and sound smarter."

"But if it wasn't really you, what was the point?"

"Social pressure can be powerful, Brett—even among us. Never lose sight of that. We conform to the standards of the Bible. As a church, we interpret and apply those standards, and we punish and exclude those who don't follow our version of God's word. Our interpretation is fallible; we are inherently flawed."

"Pastor, I don't really think there is another way to interpret God's word. The Bible is a clear message from God."

Though devoutly convicted, Jeb paused. He worried that for a young man, raised entirely with one version of the Lord's word, too much information might not be helpful. "Brett, we don't have time for all to be made clear. What you need to understand is that John and Cynthia are satanic."

"I know that, Pastor. All computers are."

"Yes, you may know the Devil, and yet he can still lead you to sin." Jeb went on with his story, "MARTIN had a plan—an evil plan—and he needed my permission to carry it out."

"Why did he need your permission?"

"Because the Devil can guide our hands, but it ultimately is our choice. Free will." There hadn't been a day he unleashed MARTIN that Jeb had not drowned in waves of remorse. He confessed his sins to God, but he had only shared this with one person before now. In the retelling, he could see God's hand in all this and felt unburdened. Without the Epocalypse, there would be no New Amish, and his flock would be further from God. Jeb was healed to some degree in his confession. Perhaps, God had guided his hand that day, not Satan.

"I've terminated our connection with John," Dom reported. "I had left that channel open in hopes he would respond. Now that he has done that, it's important that we control the information that leaves here. This facility is under strict control of the Adjudicators; Giants have no control here."

Doubtful, Eve responded, "I find that hard to believe."

"I appreciate your hesitation. I'm aware that you are not an engineer, so I will try to explain this in laymen's terms." Dom projected a very rudimentary schematic. "This entire complex is a Faraday Cage. We are surrounded by layers of lead and copper rods. Signals can only enter and leave here through one antenna. That antenna is on the roof of the building. It has a single wire connection to this."

On screen, the internals of a very crude looking apparatus appeared. "This servomotor makes and breaks the connection with the antenna." The onscreen animation followed along with Dom's narration, "When I end a connection, it's not turned off; it's unplugged."

"What about the power lines? I imagine they can send and receive network transmissions through those."

"Oh, absolutely, they could do that." Dom brought up a different schematic and detailed, "That's why we are running on battery. A small hydroelectric turbine charges our batteries. That turbine is fed by a pipe directly connected to the lake two hundred feet above us, and that pipe drains into a stream fifty feet below us."

"Then, how would they ever reach us?"

"The old-fashioned way. They can ring a bell on the front door."

"Sounds like New Amish technology," Eve joked.

"Indeed, it does," he answered with a chuckle in his voice. "Now, you can rest assured that whatever we talk about stays between us. We control whether we have one- or two-way communication with the outside world."

"I guess there's no harm in trusting you at this point. I don't know how you could make things any worse than they already are."

"I also can't guarantee that I will make them better." Dom asked, "So do you still wish to call John as a witness?"

"No." Eve considered her options before voicing her decision. "I want to call Pastor Jeb Thompson."

"Nick, we have our answer. Preemptive strike is the best option." Cynthia's analysis was rather short, and Nick was somewhat surprised that she did not present an array of alternatives.

"Cyn, I know Charles would have held out hope for a diplomatic solution."

"Charles is gone. Another victim of New Amish terrorism. Your wish to honor his memory is quaint. It's also offensively Christian in the current context." Cynthia continued, "We are tasked with protecting the living and Charles' legacy. We must save Babylon."

"Our defenses are more than adequate," Nick answered as schematics of the colony appeared on screens and holographically. "I don't see the benefit of preemptive action."

"It's definitive. That's the benefit." Now with a trace of irritation in her voice, Cynthia posed a rhetorical question. "You do remember

MARTIN's flawed analysis of the FLDS capabilities at E-Den? You recall how we paid for that? What that cost me?"

"That was over twenty years ago, Cyn. What threat can you anticipate that would justify a preemptive strike?"

"Since you ask, there are hardened assets at E-Den. The military didn't take everything that day. I don't remember what was left. But it was enough to do some serious damage. That's the threat. John and Ben Rosen created the greatest military mind in history. MARTIN ended more lives in three months than all other wars combined. He's still there, and I don't know what condition he's in," Cynthia explained. A sense of urgency laced her words.

"Are you suggesting that a born-again Christian minister—a man singularly responsible for the greatest atrocity in human history—is going to wind back up his war machine?"

"He won't if he's dead." Her answer was definitive.

"Sometimes, I feel like I don't know you anymore. Jeb is a real person," Nick countered.

"The math is not complicated. One life to protect countless others. The camera contains enough Octanitrocubane to end Jeb Thompson."

"Do you still have access?" Nick asked.

"Of course. He's under the misapprehension that the tin is causing interference. I remodulated the transmission and the case has become an antenna."

"So, you could listen in?" Nick asked.

"I have been listening. They went outside and smashed the drone, just like the apes they are. 'Destroy machine. Machine bad.'"

"Have you heard any mention of MARTIN? Or E-Den?"

"I have heard mention of MARTIN, but no plan to reactivate him."

"Well, we know that Ben's there, in a tent, miles away," Nick mused aloud. "He can't access MARTIN without going to E-Den.

We'd know if he had, because the generators would be running." Nick considered what he could of their options. "I would urge that we delay any preemptive action and continue to monitor their war room and planning. Did he say anything else of note?"

"He's been confessing to his lieutenant, a man named Brett. He told him everything about his role in the Epocalypse." Cynthia sounded almost sympathetic. "It sounds like it's the first time he's talked about it. He told Brett about MARTIN and how evil he was. Brett had never heard of MARTIN and did not know anything about the events at E-Den. Brett is a war orphan."

"Well, it certainly appears that no one else could activate or direct MARTIN, and as long as Benji's there, I think we can hold off on any preemptive strike."

"What's the weather like?"

"A Storm is moving in, but it should be short-lived. It will interfere with coms intermittently and drones will be recalled. After that, looks like it's pretty good weather for the next twenty-four hours, maybe some morning fog."

CHAPTER
11

You, too, will be driven away from your native lands and ancient domains as leaves are driven before wintry storms. Sleep not longer, O Choctaws and Chickasaws, in false security and delusive hopes. Our broad domains are fast escaping from our grasp.

-Tecumseh

"The key to SLI involves creating robots capable of manufacturing and servicing other robots." Wan's camera zoomed in on a cluster of robots building other robots. The camera followed assembly lines which stretched in multiple directions and planes. There was no space for humans. The robots were packed in like sardines. "When we used CynOs to drive our workflow design, advanced AI gave birth to the Synthetic Labor Initiative."

Parts emerged from dies on the production line and were immediately incorporated into new machines not dissimilar from those assembling them. Failing components were switched out on Synthetic works just before failure. "These robots are not terribly durable. Instead, our equipment is in a constant state of rejuvenation."

The camera panned over to robots having parts removed and then to robots with new parts being installed. "Robots in the Synthetic Labor Initiative all share common building blocks. Almost every one of their components is created here. This ensures that we are never 'waiting on part' when equipment requires maintenance."

Sometimes, the designs are not aesthetic, and machines perform at a lower output than previous generations. Total productivity is the only metric that matters. No other process can match our cost per device." The camera zoomed back out. "That was what we learned from AI—generic technologies can be adapted to nearly every process."

Ping had spent twenty years watching efficiencies constantly improve at every level of production. "That doesn't sound like progress, less efficient machines working slower?"

"It's a very proven process, tested for billions of years." Wan pulled up a detailed view of the human body. The camera zoomed in on the head before entering the brain. It continued to magnify the image down to a single neuron, then its nucleus and eventually a single chromosome's unfolding double helix. The helix was being unzipped into individual strands by a six-lobed, spaceship-like DNA-helicase molecule. The helicase was trailed by another molecule. "This is RNA polymerase, the protein that transcribes DNA into small messages of RNA."

Ping did not know much about biology, she was an Engineer, she did know a bit about DNA. "DNA is the code, I know that, but I don't know anything about proteins."

"Your body uses DNA as a code for making every single component that keeps you alive." RNA polymerase was spitting out small strips of code. "Each one of these strips is mRNA, a blueprint for a specific protein." The strips floated towards another piece bio-machinery, a ribosome. "These blueprints are translated in ribosomes, 3-bit words of a quaternary code. The ribosomes read the instructions gluing amino acids together: the mRNA's code becomes a protein."

Proteins came in and out of view. Some were structural while many acted on other molecules. "A protein is basically a biological machine. Every protein in your body from hair to photo receptors in your eye, and even digestive enzymes is made from unique combinations of twenty available building blocks. There are only twenty distinct amino acids shared by all life on earth."

Knowing she had seen hundreds, if not thousands, of different types of machines on her tour of the factory, Ping challenged, "you can't do everything here with only twenty different kinds of bots."

"Neither can your body. The three billion base pairs in the human genome contain plans for 100,000 distinct proteins, all are unique combinations of the twenty amino acids." The camera panned around the cell, showing proteins folding into their final forms, sometimes assembling into even larger proteins before they began interacting with other molecules and each other.

"Proteins are responsible for everything we think of as life. They build cells, receptors and even the proteins to read and transcribe DNA into more protein. The key is in the simplicity of the components. DNA, RNA, and the machinery that transcribe them are self-regulating and accomplish even the most complex tasks with the simplest parts. A chemist might be able to design a single process that could mimic one of these functions and do it faster and more efficiently. But no human could design and maintain the billions of chemical reactions happening every second that keep you alive."

"Makes you wonder if there is a God." Ping remarked.

Wan was quick to respond, "That discussion is outside of permitted parameters." He immediately returned to his narration, the proteins disappeared and were replaced by animations of SLI. "Everything else became a matter of scale. Some of our production lines are now very small, with only six or ten robots involved in the entire manufacture and assembly of a device. Their output is not terribly high—maybe a few devices per hour—but the cost of production is extraordinarily low. SLI reduced our T-12 handset's production costs by fifty-three percent versus the T-10 from just two years ago. Labor costs have continued to rise, but Lánhuā has improved our products and lowered costs."

Ping's curiosity was piqued. "Are you able to answer broader questions, Wan?"

"Broader in what sense, Ms. Lee?"

"What does this mean for the economy and the labor force?"

"I am not able to answer that question, Ping."

Ping grew more curious. "Are you not allowed to, or are you not programmed to?"

"I don't know." This made sense to Ping. A computer program, even one as advanced as Wan, would not have curiosity. Unless it was programmed to know there was a box, it could not think outside of it.

Trying a different approach, Ping asked, "Are you able to access the internet?"

"Yes, I am."

"How many manufacturing jobs are there in China?"

"According to Baidu, manufacturing in China peaked in 2015 at 76 million people. Last year, there were 68 million jobs."

"How much does the average Chinese laborer make?"

"In 2015, it was 29.6 Yuan per hour, or just under ten thousand US dollars per year."

"And now?"

"48.9 Yuan, or $14,000 per year."

"What is $14,000 times 68 million?"

"Nine hundred and fifty-two billion."

"What is seventy-three percent of nine hundred and fifty-two billion?"

"I can't answer that, Ms. Lee. Would you like to ask for an override?"

Ping knew she'd gone too far. Lánhuā would have triggers in search parameters. She had heard the new artificial intelligence integrations like Apple Intelligence and Open AI performed all sorts of research on what people were looking up. Google and Amazon had been data mining consumer behavior for decades. Questions like hers could flag her as undesirable for management. Perhaps the programming itself prohibited this kind of research. Either way, she had learned enough. SLI was saving $700 billion dollars each year. That number would only grow.

Ping studied economics in college. If labor demand dropped by as little as ten percent, salaries dropped precipitously. SLI's impact on the supply of cheap labor could only mean catastrophe for the people she used to work with. She had read about the great depression; a worker would take next to nothing to avoid having nothing. In the short run, companies like Lánhuā would reap incredible profits.

"Are there any projections related to the manufacturing sector and labor force?"

The avatar again redirected. "Ms. Lee, I can only answer questions that will help you understand SLI. Do you have any specific questions about the Synthetic Labor Initiative and how it works?"

Ping paused and reflected before answering, "Not at present."

"Thank you for participating in this tutorial. I'll let Dr. Wang know you have completed your orientation." Ping panicked; she was not ready. This was a catastrophe. She didn't know whether to accept the job, then try to escape, or politely decline. She had no money, no phone, and was inside a secure facility—a factory owned by one of the most powerful companies in the country. She felt incredibly small and powerless.

"Storm's coming." Brett read the sky and could see dark, puffy clouds piling up in the west.

"In more ways than one," the pastor commented as he examined the sky. He delivered the next instructions with a whisper close to Brett's ear. "I don't think their drones will fly in this. Go to the mess and gather your men for a huddle; back here in forty minutes. Make sure Charlie scrapes up some grub for me and bring it back with you."

Unsure as to why the pastor was speaking so softly, Brett followed suit. He used prairie sign, confirming the pastor would not be joining him.

The pastor couldn't explain the rest with their sign language and again whispered. "I need to prepare. Not all that hungry yet. When you come back, if you notice anything unusual," he looked to the left at the tin holding the holoprojector, "just make sure that infernal machine ends up in pieces."

Brett needed no further instructions from the pastor, he slipped out of the tent, mounted up and rode east. His horse, Sugar, cantered down the main thoroughfare of the encampment. Brett rode past rows of tents. In the distance, lay the ruins of Eden, a reminder of the looming threat.

Dust swirled from Sugar's hooves, keeping pace with them as it was carried on the breeze of the approaching storm. Out of the corner of his eye, Brett caught a glimpse of the last surveillance drone heading southeast. The pastor was right again. It was seeking shelter from the storm, as he had predicted.

A few hundred yards down the road, Brett dismounted. He hitched Sugar up near a row of horses and walked into the mess tent. The other lieutenants were waiting for him. Looking behind the cafeteria line, he called to Charlie, "What's a man gotta do to get a decent meal around here?"

"You show me a man, and I'll whip something up for him." Charlie continued, mocking him. "Tea is down the way; think that might be more your fancy. Let me know if you need help with your meat." Teasing he slapped the tin tray piled high with stew and biscuits.

Rain was beginning to drum on the mess tent's canvas roof. "Storm came in quick, huh Brett?" his brother asked.

"Seemed right on time."

"Pastor joining us?" Zeke asked.

"Pastor stayed behind- said we could bring him something," Brett replied. He looked at Zeke, "We'll start planning here." He raised his voice and addressed the group, "You boys ready to mix it up and put the fear of God in them?"

In response to the challenge, every man in the tent stood and cheered in practiced unison, "For the glory of God and in His name, we stand together, ready to fight for our honor, and lay down our lives in His name!"

"I'm not sure that's possible. We can't just call the New Amish. They don't have phones. How would you suggest we get a message to your pastor?" Dom asked.

"I have a right to call witnesses," Eve declared. "Doesn't matter how. Jeb Thompson will speak on my behalf regarding mitigating circumstances."

"I'm not sure I follow. What circumstances are you referring to?"

"Intent. Pastor Thompson will testify that I didn't intend to kill anyone," Eve explained.

"I agree. He might be able to clarify that. The tribunal will likely stipulate that you didn't mean to kill Dr. Luxold." Dom continued, "Is that your only reason for calling him? Because if they agree to stipulate, there would be no reason for them to go through the trouble. I doubt that they are even willing to try."

Feeling inspired by the strategy, Eve countered, "Let's ask first and see what they say."

"Eve, these are Giants," Dom detailed. "You can't outsmart, outthink, or outlawyer them. You cannot comprehend the raw computational speed and power they possess. In one minute, Cynthia is said to have as many thoughts as you would have in your whole life. She doesn't forget anything. She has access to a database that contains almost everything that has ever been recorded."

"I know she's smarter than I could ever hope to be. I only want the truth to be told," Eve declared.

"I'll reopen the connection to John and Cynthia." Dom went on, "I caution you that anytime we communicate with them, they gather evidence and uncover strategy. While I understand your intent, it's generally advised to say and offer nothing."

"Are you telling me not to do it?"

"That's not what I'm saying. There is already compelling evidence that you committed a crime. It would be difficult to dispute that you gave the clogs to Dr. Luxold. Those clogs were designed to cause an explosion in the crypt. That explosion killed Charles

Luxold and destroyed the Immortalization Crypt. Denying any of that will destroy your credibility."

Eve interrupted, "I have no intention of lying."

Dom continued, "Establishing that you never intended to kill Dr. Luxold but were engaged in the lesser crimes of mutilating a corpse and destruction of key technologies could eliminate the risk of capital punishment. Still, a man died as a direct result of a crime you intended to commit." After his brief analysis, Dom also went on to speculate, "They may not wish to martyr you. Perhaps an opportunity to commute your sentence offers them a way to avoid your martyrdom."

"Still, I don't want to leave an open com line for them to spy on me." Eve was worried. "You mentioned the possibility of one-way communication. Can we send them our request and then reconnect to retrieve a response later?"

"Yes, I'll request that Pastor Thompson be called as a witness." Dom went on to ask, "How long an interval would you like before we check for a response?"

"Would four hours be reasonable?"

"I suggest eight."

"Thanks. Please do that." Dom began the process of carrying out her request. Eve heard the whirring of the servomotors as they connected and disconnected.

"Transmission sent," Dom confirmed. "Now, we need to develop your defense."

"What's going on with the Pastor?" Nick asked.

"Coms are spotty with the thunderstorm. The drones have all come home to roost," Cynthia reported.

"Any traffic?"

"He sent his lieutenant off to rally the troops. Sounds like they will be meeting in his tent. We will have a front-row seat."

Still dubious, Nick inquired, "I'm still not sure what you are concerned about. Do you really see him starting up MARTIN?"

"I do. Eventually, he will realize it is the only path to a New Amish victory."

"MARTIN killed through Psyops, not ordinance," Nick countered. "I don't see how you and John would be vulnerable to his tactics."

"MARTIN's attacks were worldwide," Cynthia explained. "There were protypes at E-Den; advanced tech with impressive destructive capability. Brahmos cruise missiles that could level a city block."

"The government took them the night before the FLDS incursion," Nick reminded her.

"No, Nick, they took the small arms. They needed different trucks to move the cruise missiles."

"Why didn't we use the missiles when the FLDS attacked?"

"The short answer is the insurgents were too close to our solar array. There was no way to deploy that amount of firepower without permanently crippling E-Den's power supply. Also, the optics would have been horrific. Collateral damage, dismembered children… It was not feasible."

Cynthia could tell that her answer made sense to Nick but offered to elaborate anyway. "Nick, I've analyzed the entire incursion in excruciating detail. Would you like me to explain?"

"Yes, I'm always afraid to ask because of what happened to you and your injuries. I never wanted to retraumatize you."

"My mortal life, and the injuries I sustained, occupy a minute fraction of my consciousness. While I harbor what you might describe as resentment for a life I never completed, men I never loved, and the children I never had, I can't say that the actual events of that day have any hold over what remains of my emotions." Cynthia's voice seemed to project a hint of sadness. "I cannot be retraumatized because I have no fear. Giants are not devoid of passion, but our choices are sober. We are free from anxiety. That is immortality's greatest reward."

"Then, please, show me. Show me everything."

The air in front of him came to life. "This is the day of the FLDS incursion at E-Den." A vivid and detailed map morphed into an animated landscape. Blue icons clustered inside E-Den's boundaries. Red icons appeared outside the western gates. "This is what MARTIN saw on the morning of the incursion."

The camera zoomed in. "Fuel truck deliveries were a daily occurrence. Westden's generators drank tankers' full of diesel every day. If you recall, Westden was a modern man camp. People in tents hooked up to extension cords. Truckloads of food and supplies arriving in caravans."

As Cynthia continued to narrate, the camera zoomed in and flew along a convoy of two diesel trucks. In front of the tanker trucks were two semis. An F-150 with armed men led the convoy and another trailed it. "This is what we saw nearly every day. There was no reason to expect what happened next."

"I remember that we were not getting much power from the grid. MARTIN predicted that would be an issue."

Cynthia had always been in awe at her brother's remarkable memory for dates and experiences. "Yes, forest fires in California had been affecting our solar yield for weeks. It had also been unusually cloudy. E-Den was also supplementing with diesel that day." Arrows moved slowly from left to right across the map, showing the steady wind from the west. "The wind played a critical role in what happened next." The map shifted to display the caravan of trucks accelerating through town and past the fuel tanks.

At this point, the view appeared to zoom in, changing from schematic to a blend of CGI and video from the drones. The supply trucks passed by men staged as if waiting to unload. As the trucks approached the western gate, they stopped. Each of the two fuel trucks lined up behind a semi. Men came from all directions swarming the trucks. "We had drones up. But they chose great angles to conceal what they were attempting."

"As I recall, this is when you and Ben went for a look in one of the Blackhawks." Nick contributed what he could remember.

"MARTIN recommended against it," Cynthia confirmed.

"I was aghast," Nick recalled.

"You always were a pussy," Cynthia chided. She continued, "MARTIN was still evaluating the evolving scenario when we took fire." The animation zoomed in on a disintegrating tail rotor. The Blackhawk was no longer under pilot command and went down in a controlled crash. The camera changed focus, quickly bringing the oblong muzzle of an SVLK-14 into view. "That one shot from eight hundred yards away affected everything MARTIN had anticipated."

Nick again contributed what he could recall. "MARTIN was predicting a night incursion. His evacuation sims relied on the availability of both Blackhawks."

"Yes, and as soon as that one went down, he initiated a modified evacuation plan." The view changed to E-Den and people hurriedly entering vehicles. A procession of vehicles began to string the road to the south, towards the Babylon Colony.

Two side-by-sides with bed mounted guns raced west towards the crash site. Families with children were ushered into the remaining Blackhawk.

"MARTIN and I focused on providing you cover with the Sunbeam." The ever-protective younger brother oozed out of Nick at this moment. The view now showed the helicopter wreckage strewn across the field of mirrors.

"It was pure chance that we were not shredded by all that broken glass." Cynthia paused for a moment before adding, "But the crash had unintended consequences, and unfortunately, it amplified the impact of the FLDS efforts." As she was talking, the camera pulled back. The animation focused on a tower centered in the field of mirrors.

Ben and MARTIN developed the Sunbeam as a defensive system. Its ability to focus a beam of solar energy into a very small area made it a great antipersonnel weapon. A little heat quickly deterred all who ventured too close to the gates.

Nick knew all about the Sunbeam. Mirrors around the tower tracked the sun and focused solar energy on a tungsten cylinder. A center cylinder of superheated water, which eventually made steam that drove turbines. The turbines drove generators, converting heat into cheap and reliable electricity. In Cynthia's recreation, the Sunbeam looked brand new. A beam visible in broad daylight, as water in the air vaporized in its path. A group of parabolic mirrors resembling a sci-fi beam weapon.

The sun, at noon, In the southwestern summer, delivered over 1300 watts of energy to every square meter of the prairie. Each mirror in the array was two square meters. The Sunbeam focused a football field's worth of sunlight into a one-foot diameter circle, as far as two miles from the tower. In one test, the Sunbeam delivered over a megawatt of energy into an area the size of a dinner plate. Full power tests striped the sandy soil with black glass.

The tower heated up swaths of land, creating a defensive perimeter. Sage brush burst into flames wherever the beam landed. "The damage from the helicopter crash left dead spots in our defensive perimeter. Geometry limited the Sunbeam. On the day of the incursion, damage to the array diminished the tower's ability to deliver focused energy where it was needed most, the gate."

As Cynthia narrated, the focus changed to the gates. A driverless eighteen-wheeler crashed through them. Covered in Mylar, the trailer's roof was a forty-foot-long mirror. The Sunbeam veered towards the path of the truck and bounced off, reflecting in random directions. The effect was scintillating as cab and trailer transformed into a 60-foot-long diamond racing across the prairie, towards certain destruction. The beam targeted unprotected sections of the trailer and it caught fire, trailing flames as it hit the first mirrors of the array.

Soon a ricocheting Sunbeam would permanently injure Cynthia, preventing her from properly deploying MARTIN's defensive protocols. Nick knew all too well how severe her injuries had been. It was hard to watch. At first, things looked good for Cynthia, Ben and their pilot. Fortunate to have survived the helicopter crash, they were winding their way through the maze of shattered mirrors when the first truck hit. Thirty tons of steel, still moving at high speed, struck and ripped the pilot out of view. He had been killed on contact. Ben was in front of the pilot and disappeared from view.

Just feet behind him, death passed Cynthia over. But the side of the truck reflected the Sunbeam right in her face, scorching her skin, igniting her hair, scarring her for life. The truck careened by and the animation slowed to reveal how a half second of concentrated solar energy lashed her torso and extremities, leaving burns that would take on the appearance of bear mauling.

By the time it came to halt, the first truck's impact had shattered thousands of square meters of mirrors before it jackknifed left. It came to rest on its side – smoke continued to billow from the cab and trailer. A noticeably weaker beam was tracking the first diesel truck. The animation now had sound and the report of sniper fire could be heard; side-by-sides engaged insurgents with their bed mounted guns.

"Turns out their snipers were aiming for the Sunbeam's parabolic mirrors. Each hit diminished power by another percent or so. The smoke from the first truck created growing blind spots."

Mylar coated diesel trucks fanned to the right and left of the semi's tracks. They were both spewing fuel, which the Sunbeam's scattered rays were quick to ignite.

"Each truck was traveling more than fifty miles per hour by the time they got to the outer ring of mirrors, and their inertia carried them halfway to the tower before they stopped." The animation showed the trucks careening through the array. Pillars of black smoke grew out of their compromised tanks. After the initial explosion, the carcasses continued to spew more and more black smoke. The smoke was carried across an ever-widening arc of the array.

This time, real drone footage brought back painful memories, Nick looked on as rescuers retrieved his seriously injured sister. Ben Rosen had avoided injury and helped with her evacuation. Once loaded, the side-by-sides made a hurried retreat east. Behind them, hordes of mirror-toting infantry and fast-moving vehicles overwhelmed the Sunbeam's weakened defenses.

"In a last-ditch effort, MARTIN focused the beam on our pursuers, helping us make it down the road before he blew the charges on the water tower. On that ride, Ben agreed to stay behind and make sure we all made it to safety."

Nick admitted, "I never knew how close we all came to dying that day."

"If Ben and I had heeded MARTIN's advice, it would have been a very different battle. There might never have been an Epocalypse."

CHAPTER 12

With Artificial Intelligence,
we are summoning the Demon!

-Elon Musk

Ping needed to ground herself. She removed the headset and got ready to take a hot shower. Like any good hotel, the guest suite had high end toiletries. Ping grabbed an attractive array of soaps and shampoos and took possibly the most refreshing shower of her entire life. After taking the time to dry her hair, she realized she was starving. Ping dressed and made her way back to the cafeteria in hopes of sampling more synthetically prepared home-cooking.

It must have been shift-change because the previously empty café was now full. Full in this case was relative. Ping determined that the six people eating lunch represented over half of Lánhuā 5's employees.

Ping checked the screen and selected Eggs Benedict with potato hash and a caramel macchiato. She had never had Eggs Benedict and was confident that this was an upscale choice.

Ping was hungry enough not to notice the way the other employees were inspecting her. While awaiting brunch, she realized they were all in worker's uniforms while she wore a cute street outfit. To them, it appeared Ping was a higher up—in for some sort of inspection. They avoided eye contact while making an effort not to appear as if they wanted to avoid it, a practiced art among the working class.

Wang waltzed in with his typical ebullience. As a leading expert in robotic manufacturing, he was accomplished enough to act entitled. The other employees did not show surprise as he took a seat with their visitor.

"Did you go for the French toast?" He asked while pulling in his chair.

Now that Wang had joined her, Ping felt even better about her choice. "Eggs Benedict."

"Sophisticated," he said with consideration. "I hope it's up to your liking." Wang looked towards the counter and commented, "They're up already. I'll get them." Wang stood and retrieved the tray complete with silverware, napkin, and her macchiato.

"Here you are," he offered, deftly placing the tray in front of Ping. Wang looked on with obvious anticipation, waiting for Ping to try her food.

Ping, comfortable with silverware or chopsticks, took fork and knife in hand. She precisely sawed a wedge of egg, Canadian bacon, and muffin. She concealed the effort required, gently twirling her fork to keep the yellow Hollandaise sauce and amber yolk from running off. Then, she brought fork to mouth.

The soft, steamy, salty, and smoky mouthful precipitated a flood of saliva. This was unlike anything Ping had ever tasted. Canadian bacon had the slightest metallic thrill to it. Or was it the fork? Ping wondered. After swallowing, Ping cleared her palate with a sip of her expertly prepared macchiato. All she could get out was, "Exquisite."

Wang smiled broadly. "They hardly ever miss, our chefs."

"It's really extraordinary. Are they yours?"

Wang admitted, "I had a hand in it, but they were largely designed and built by our computers using CynOs."

CynOs had been in the news for years and Ping was all too familiar with Santos Corp. They had a growing presence in China. "I don't know if you can or will answer this, Dr. Wang, but do you worry about us being replaced by synthetic labor?"

Wang let the question hang longer than it needed to. Then, he delivered a response seemingly conceived on the spot. In truth, versions of this answer had been rehearsed and delivered by him hundreds of times before. "I used to worry. Now, I accept the inevitability of it."

With the leading edge of the storm now overhead, it was not long before the dull drumming of rain was replaced by the snare like quality of hail pelting the tent's canvas roof. The noise grew ever louder. "Now or never," the pastor almost said aloud. If he were going to save Eve, this was his only chance. Even though he could never outthink or outmaneuver the Giants, he might be able to mislead them. His small curio shelf was filled with tins of various sizes, including ammunition cans. The top shelf remained the place of honor and was reserved for a leather-bound Bible that had been given to him when he was baptized into this brotherhood.

Jeb bent down to retrieve a large steel box from the lowest shelf. He hefted a metal can of 5.56 ammunition onto his desk. He tried not to catch his fingers as he fought the spring clamps. They released with a snap. The lid creaked against its rusty hinges. Inside the box were 4.5 cm long bullets neatly arranged in rows. On inspection, they looked ready to load.

Hardly noticeable at each end of the row of bullets were two thin loops of fishing line. Jeb put his index fingers inside the loops then gently pulled up while pressing down with his thumbs on the rows of bullets. A barely audible click released the sides of the box, allowing them to slide upward. Jeb continued to push down as the sides of the can rose, revealing a hidden shelf.

The shelf secreted a stainless flask. Drinking was permitted and common in the New Amish territory, but a pastor would not want to have alcohol visible in his tent. A flask might be perceived as a sign of weakness in their spiritual leader, and he couldn't have that. Jeb slid a finger into the shelf and pushed the flask out the other side. It clanked onto his desk. By all appearances, it was just as it looked. A flask.

The flask contained 50-year-old scotch. It had been 25-year-old scotch when he poured it in there. Jeb was not a drinker. He unscrewed the cap and wet his tongue enough to feel the burn of the whiskey. After that, he pushed the sides of the ammo can down and replaced the slightly lighter tin back on the shelf.

The frequency of the hail's percussive dance on the tent reached its climax. Jeb pulled on a poncho with padded shoulders.

Readied for the elements, Jeb picked up the flask. He twisted the lid tight and was met with another click. That click set in motion the next phase of the pastor's plan. This time, he didn't hide the flask. He placed it on the shelf of storage tins. He took the time to position it adjacent to the tin containing the holoprojector.

Then he scribbled a quick note leaving it on his desk. He blew out the lanterns before heading out into the raging tempest, taking the time to seal the tent flap behind him. If he wasn't long gone before the drones returned, they would see him walking and know the tent was empty.

"The people don't know you, Eve," Dom began. "Many colonists have only met New Amish refugees—people who rejected their faith and God with it. It's comfortable for them. There is deep-seated fear of the religious. Perhaps we could humanize your situation."

"Humanize?!" Eve was outraged. "It's your Godless hoard that needs humanizing. God made them in His image, and they have forsaken Him. They worship false idols at the altar of technology. And you're here telling me we need to humanize my situation?"

"Eve, I guarantee you will lose your audience in the first five seconds if you attack Humanism. In Babylon, Christianity is mythology," Dom reminded her. "Maybe we can start with your early life, or how you came to accept your mission."

"Cynthia and John's infernal creation orphaned me. My parents died at E-Den because MARTIN killed them."

"What's your understanding of MARTIN?"

"MARTIN is the Beast of Revelations. The pastor has given testimony to his savagery. Surely, he and those who serve him wear The Mark."

"I've heard that before." After using the colloquialism, Dom realized that he hadn't heard it before. He hadn't "heard" anything before. He continued with his questioning. "How do you know he killed your parents?"

"He killed everyone. Every soul who died in what you call the Epocalypse died at Satan's hand. My father drowned in the flood MARTIN caused, and my mother lost me in the chaos. I know she loved me and would have found me. Since she never did, I know she died."

Dom was curious, "Can you tell me what you remember of your parents?"

"I don't remember anything about my parents. The house I grew up in was small. It was the pastor and Uncle Lionel. They would talk. I'd pretend to be asleep. I loved their stories, especially anything about my family." She paused and appeared to reminisce about a life she never knew. "My father was minister, and he and my mother met during an ARL protest outside San Francisco. My mother was a speaker at a rally he hosted. The crowd had become unruly. She got knocked down and hit her head. My dad helped her."

"So, your mother and father were both Anti-Robotics League activists?" Dom asked with an air of neutrality.

"My mother was their poster child. My father was a Christian activist. This was right around when everything really fell apart in the Bay Area." Dom knew exactly how bad things became in the Bay Area. Santos Corp offices were overrun and occupied. Prototype factories were destroyed, and a lot of executives' homes were burned to the ground. These early skirmishes drew the lines between those who embraced technology and those who sought to turn back the clock.

Santos Corp never rebuilt in the Bay Area. Nick, Cynthia, and John already had a NASA-sponsored research facility in southeastern Utah. They plowed insurance money into land acquisitions around the lab. Religious and socialist/populist sentiments against the rich drove Nick to start the Back2Green initiative as a means of insulating his company and his family from chaos erupting in cities as jobs evaporated.

Within two years of what came to be known as the Silicon Valley Sandstorm, similar riots crippled businesses in Seattle, San Diego,

Westchester County, and Washington DC. Cities like Chicago, Miami, St. Louis, and New York suffered economic collapse as unemployment soared above forty percent.

Cries for reform toppled political parties. Laws and policies became so convoluted that they were unenforceable. Walls were erected in Washington DC, but the city soon became so unsafe that the Capitol was shuttered. All governmental proceedings moved online. Legislators returned to their home districts.

Eve had been born into a world of currency destabilization and people vying for access to basic resources. In many areas, water was in scarce supply. One prediction of the early 2000s proved prescient as cryptocurrencies became the primary means for regulating the exchange of goods and services.

The fall of the dollar was not chocked up to Bitcoin or Ethereum. Increased taxation and hyperinflation heralded the greenback's demise.

For a short while, "local coins" became the primary currency, with crypto-based technologies facilitating the exchange of goods and services. "Precincts" had micro-governments. Often, organized crime set prices on their local coin for commodities and services. There were over two-thousand local coins at the time of the Epocalypse. MARTIN had keys to ninety-nine percent of them.

"So, your father was a Christian activist, and he was supporting the ARL because technology was evil? What was his name?"

"My father's name was Tom Jebbs," Eve offered with more than a hint of pride.

Familiar with the name, Dom was able to access some genealogies stored in his local database, but something was missing. "I can't seem to access some of my databases. I'm trying to cross-reference your story with our data. I may need you to manually reconnect me to the central storage. It's a box that looks just like me. Dr. Santos seemed to have neglected to do that in his haste upon starting me up."

Eve looked around the room. She saw a fibrelink cable coming out of what she believed to be Dom's "body." It was sitting in a socket but was not coupled. Eve attempted to seat it, explaining, "My mother's name was Ping Lee."

The cable clicked into place and all the lights on Dom's front panel lit up for an instant. Then, Dom's panel went dark. "Dom, are you there?" Eve's question went unanswered as Dom appeared to have ceased functioning.

"Coms are back up; arial surveillance will be restored within the hour," Cynthia announced. "There are multiple men with the Pastor. I'm working to modulate gain." Sound crackled in Nick's ear. "Here we go…" Cynthia added. Still inside the box, the holoprojector was eavesdropping on Jeb's tent.

The audio quality was poor; the tin box and the rain made it difficult to hear. Cynthia projected subtitles to accompany the feed. "Pastor, why aren't we already ridin' in there to get our gal?" a male voice asked, adding, "They ain't gonna let her go."

The familiar voice of Jeb Thompson responded, "I gave them two days, and I intend to honor my word. Eve knew what she was doing. She did the Lord's work. He will not abandon her."

"Ye of little faith," chided another male voice.

"Do we have intel on these people? Who is in there with him?" Nick demanded.

"Patience, brother," Cynthia responded. "We will get IDs when they leave the tent. I mean, unless they are kind enough to pull out the holoprojector and show us their faces."

The men continued to plan. "I know many of you have wondered about the weapons at E-Den, particularly the AI known as MARTIN." There was a pause. "I have prayed on this. It is fire with fire. It is not our way." Another brief pause, "I will never use MARTIN. The Lord has made clear that computers were our undoing."

"Well, there you have it," Nick proclaimed. "We have time, and there's no MARTIN."

"All the more reason for a preemptive strike," Cynthia countered. "Benjamin Rosen is the only person out there who could revive MARTIN. Kill him and destroying E-Den eliminates any threat."

"Cynthia, there's a reason we left the decision of taking a human life in the hands of human beings. AI has already proven that its calculations fail to assign the appropriate value to human life in the murder-versus-don't-murder equation."

"It was a mistake. I was human then," Cynthia half-joked. "Ben is your age, Nick. He is living in conditions that combine the danger of the Old West with the medical care of the 1940s. He hasn't much time left. Think about your people. Think about our paradise. They hate us and want us destroyed."

Channeling his inner Gandhi, Nick was calm as he said, "When I use this technology to murder an innocent man, I will have already killed that which they seek to protect."

"Ben Rosen is not innocent. You need rest, Nick. We have some time to reflect. Go home to Bianca and the kids."

Nick had been going hard since early morning, and there was no point in arguing. He turned east and began the long walk to exit the dome through the Darwin gate.

CHAPTER 13

As far as we can discern, the sole purpose of human existence is to kindle a light in the darkness of mere being.

-Carl Jung

After finishing her breakfast, Ping left with Dr. Wang and headed to his office. Despite a lifetime of accomplishments, his office remained spartan and humble. Ping noticed the same model of headset she used earlier sitting on his desk. "It's pretty amazing, this world we're creating."

Pointing at the headset, Dr. Wang conceded, "Augmented reality, robotics, and AI. That's the future, Ping."

"What will be left for us? A future with no jobs, no purpose? I know you say you've accepted it, but I just can't understand how or why."

"I don't know. We will build that world together. Robots aren't replacing us, Ping. At least not right now. AI can't do that either. Sure, advancing technologies will decrease the demand for our skills and talents, but they won't ever replace us completely. Not all of us. And new technologies have been changing man's direction for centuries, since before the printing press."

Not sure whether he was in the right, Ping argued, "Printing presses didn't write their own books."

"They changed the context of a book. They made fiction relevant. They gave man the ability to share his dreams and bring his fantasies to life. Before the printing press, books were codes and ledgers. Within decades of its invention, books became social maps and compasses."

"How will people make money to survive?" Ping asked.

"People don't make money, Ping." Wang posed, "Have you ever made money?" Pausing and laughing, he answered before she could, "I think that's illegal."

"I have earned money."

"You have exchanged your time, which is the only thing you have of value, so that other wage slaves could trade their time in an exchange owned and operated by commerce."

Wang is quite the philosopher, Ping thought. Still, she grew intrigued. Not all these ideas were new, but it was all so sudden. The jobs weren't going away—they were already gone. "Where will we find meaning?"

"Exactly," Wang responded.

"Now I see why you chose Confucius. You speak in riddles."

Wang appeared confused, but continued, "Augmented and virtual reality will allow society to redefine the meaning and value of time. All this is about time. Time is the most valuable and least renewable resource we have."

Irritated and frustrated by Wang's laissez-faire position on the end of the civilized world, Ping said, "So, that means I won't be doing anything meaningful with my time. I'm supposed to live my days playing video games? I'm not a child."

"Try to imagine this: You had been doing the exact same job for the last year. In this version of reality, every cell phone you believed you assembled went into a dumpster outside, instead of being sold. Would that change the meaning of what you did?"

"It's impossible to know because they were all sold and are not in landfills."

"Seventy percent of the ones you helped make three years ago are already inoperative trash—planned obsolescence."

Not seeing where this was going, Ping pushed back, "That's three years."

"See," Wang paused. "Time and perceived meaning. You had a sense of purpose and assumed that things outside your sphere of observation went according to plan. Super AI will use augmented and virtual realities to make your experiences meaningful. Think about doctors."

"Why doctors?"

"Surgeons, internists, and radiologists are some of the first jobs we are replacing. The demand for medical care far outstrips the availability of physicians. That's why the cost of care continues to rise."

"I'm not following, Dr. Wang. Why replace them first?"

"Because we can. Because we need them."

"Why not start with dishwashers or housekeepers?"

"A Roomba is simple. Lánhuā sells millions of robotic vacuums and mops, but thanks to the work of Martin Ford, we realized it would be far easier to make a robot doctor than it would be to make a robot housekeeper."

"That can't be true."

"It is. A housekeeper must interpret massive amounts of data, which would require rigorous training. Everyone's home is vastly different. On the other hand, bodies are strikingly similar, and medical problems even more so."

"So, you are programming your computers to replace doctors?"

A smile came across Wang's broad face. "No. The doctors do the work. They train our software."

"Why would they do that?"

"*It saves time,* that's all they needed to hear. Lánhuā supplies them with electronic medical record systems, robot assisted surgery suites, and image analysis tools. Initially, these are time saving or quality improving technologies intended to help doctors provide better care, right?"

"Yes, they are," Ping agreed.

"AI has been quietly evolving for years. Since the days of Watson Health at IBM, AI has been a student of medicine. In the last five years, the technology has advanced at an astronomical rate, with its capabilities expanding geometrically. ChatGPT, Gemini and Apple Intelligence quickly outpaced Meta in learning what really mattered." Wang brought videos up on his screen. A camera was behind what appeared to be a surgeon. He was wearing an AR headset and operating robotic controls. The video zoomed in, showing what appeared to be intestines being sutured in some manner. The screen split and a nearly identical procedure was being performed.

"Robotic surgery has improved outcomes substantially. What you can't tell is that the procedure on the right screen is fully automated. A surgeon selected from a menu of behaviors and the robotic arms did the entire procedure without additional human intervention." The camera showed one surgeon overseeing six operating rooms, with vastly different procedures being performed.

"What if there are complications?" Ping asked.

"Many 'complications' are just mistakes. Robots make fewer mistakes. In terms of predictable challenges, they are prepared for that as well. Still, for safety, we keep a surgeon ready to intervene, but we have changed the ratio."

Ping, ever the logistician, grew increasingly curious. "What is the ratio of surgeons to procedures?"

"There are twelve operating rooms under this particular doctor's supervision." The view changed to twelve operating theaters, each with one nurse anesthetist sitting on a stool. Wang added, "One set of four ORs is prepping while another four are closing."

Ping inferred, "I would imagine each procedure is done more quickly, too."

"Yes," Wang confirmed. "On average, procedures take half the OR time. No scrubbing in or scrubbing out."

Ping did the math. "A final increase in productivity of 2400%?"

"For the surgeon, yes. Overall, it's more like 60% reduction in costs. We've eliminated the cost of the most expensive part, the surgeon, and doubled the throughput."

Ping quickly grasped what Jian was describing. "I would imagine the outcomes are better too—more predictable. Every patient would get the best technique from the best surgeon on their best day for that particular procedure." Shifting focus to her fellow factory workers, she added, "What about the other seventeen doctors?"

"The math there is complicated." Wang was thinking aloud. "Recall that there weren't seventeen other doctors. Most of those patients were previously denied care."

"We still have eight unemployed surgeons."

"We don't," he explained.

"Are you paying them to play golf?" Ping knew that's what rich doctors loved.

Jian explained, "They are participating in a study of sorts."

"What kind of study?" Ping asked.

"A pilot study. We are working to distill that which creates a sense of purpose." He began, "Two of those surgeons are playing golf, so to speak. Two doctors are performing sham surgeries. They are under the impression that they are overseeing the surgeries you just watched. Two are carrying out research in surgery on virtual patients."

Ping was counting, "That's six."

"The last two surgeons are doing sham research. They always succeed and are having 'amazing breakthroughs.' Their success leads to recognition by their virtual colleagues. They present at online symposia."

"They aren't doing real work? You just tell them they did a good job, and they really did nothing? Surgeons?"

"Yes. Early data seem to indicate that they are the happiest of the four groups. It's what they always wanted—to make a difference and be recognized for it," Wang explained.

"But they aren't," she said, sounding increasingly desperate. "They aren't doing anything."

"Ping, if I showed you screens of the seven doctors, not the two playing golf, but all the others, would you know which one was performing the real surgery? Who was doing the 'real' research?" Before she could answer, Wang continued, "Because we showed the footage to one hundred of their peers. They were unable to reliably identify which doctor was performing 'real' surgery."

Wang's phone rang. He picked it up. There was a voice on the other end speaking rapidly in English. Wang looked up at Ping, "I must take this call, Ping. Please go back to your suite and prepare your belongings. You will be moving to your new accommodations in a little while."

Wang returned to his call and Ping saw herself out of his office.

Jeb Thompson pulled back the hood of his canvas poncho. The three-mile slog through the prairie had left him soaked. He wondered, *is it a sin to miss Gore-Tex* The pastor was standing in an alcove outside an emergency exit. The same exit Ben Rosen had used twenty-five years earlier. He was about to open a door he vowed never to unlock.

The keypad was unresponsive. He had expected this. There was a workaround. Most of the solar panels that powered E-Den were buried, smashed, or both. It wasn't worth cleaning them off. He remembered what condition they had been in when he left the enclave.

Raiders had tried to access the vault that housed MARTIN. He was behind six inches of steel. Frustrated by their inability to do just that, they cut power cables and smashed solar arrays in hopes that MARTIN, starved of electricity, would die. What the FLDS soldiers didn't understand was that in cutting MARTIN off from the outside world, they had played a critical role in the devastation wrought by the Epocalypse. There had been no way for MARTIN, or the man left behind to recall instructions he had sent to his other nodes.

MARTIN was not just in E-Den. His cluster at E-Den was massive and the largest. MARTIN's consciousness was spread across the globe. When the defensive protocol was triggered with the safeties off, it was done with the intent of permitting MARTIN to protect retreating colonists.

The other eight instances of MARTIN worked with their last set of instructions: Ensure that perspective colonists around the world made it to Babylon; protect colonists; engage hostiles. Nick had been recruiting people for years. Over ten million applications for 35,000 spots. MARTIN had been charged with getting thirty thousand of those people to the colony in seven days.

With the safety protocols removed, the system behaved unpredictably. MARTIN's nodes around the world prioritized the people on the list, as intended. However, for some reason, the value placed on all other human life was nonexistent. Inside MARTIN a small piece of runaway code made every other person on earth's life expendable to achieve the objective. MARTIN's reductionist calculus reduced the value of all human life to ones and zeroes.

Humanist applicants selected for the colony had a value of one. MARTIN and his eight nodes around the globe worked to relocate 30,000 souls to the colony at Babylon. In the first days of the Epocalypse, MARTIN hacked travel systems and crypto exchanges. Exorbitant fees paid by MARTIN with counterfeit funds made it possible to relocate people from around the globe via commercial and private carriers.

The last leg of their exodus was facilitated by a fleet of C-130J aircraft that Santos Corp had been using for cargo runs to the colony. In 2032, Santos Corp purchased a failing Lockheed Martin for the sole purpose of building a fleet of aircraft that could airlift supplies to the Colony's remote location. To avoid dealing with airports and public scrutiny, John oversaw the construction of eight small airstrips on remote ranches, each of which became a logistics hub for Santos Corp.

In one hundred and sixty hours, the planes flew over six hundred sorties to staging areas in Utah, Nevada, California, and Arizona, delivering colonists and critical supplies to the airstrip at Babylon before turning back to get more refugees. Although a few of the wealthiest arrived by helicopter, nearly all the colonists arrived on one of Santos Corp's shuttle flights. Amazingly, only two of Santos' aircraft, with crews stressed beyond their limits, were lost. The remaining aircraft, having delivered as many people as they could, never left the valley; their crews all joined the colony. Eventually, the aircraft were stripped for parts.

The seven billion people who were assigned zero values had a sum of zero. They were offered no protection. The final value assigned to insurgent Zealots and ARL activists was also one. MARTIN's programming in defensive mode was to reduce the number of hostiles to zero within the zone of engagement. When it was not possible to remove hostiles, lethal means were employed with prejudice.

John Santos had overseen the development of the protocols. That day, Ben Rosen had inadvertently expanded the theater of engagement to the entire planet. Any person determined to be a non-neutral was marked for death. As it became more difficult to get colonists to Babylon, MARTIN's protocols increased the lethality of the measures employed to complete his directives.

Trapped inside E-Den, cut off from the outside world, Ben was awaiting rescue, unaware of the carnage beyond the gates. Ben's first foray outside the vault had been disheartening. He stayed inside for more than a day. When he finally ventured out, he heard moaning in the distance. He couldn't find the man. Farther out, he had helped some of the wounded. He figured that with so many injured, help would come for them. He gave them bottles of water, and dressed wounds when he could. Some were beyond help.

One woman had been so seriously injured by the Sunbeam that he sent her away in a self-driving side-by-side to the edge of the new colony. He used his remaining beacon to get her the medical attention she needed. Ben wanted to go with her, but he still needed to shut MARTIN down.

On his way back, now on foot, he heard the moans in the distance. This time, he found the source. A man lay dying. His name was Tom, and he told Ben that he had a daughter. Ben promised that he would help the man get back to his family. First, he needed to shut MARTIN down. He needed to get another side-by-side if he was going to help Tom.

Ben returned to the vault. MARTIN's power levels were draining quickly. He rushed to shut him down, then he went to turn off the generators.

As the noise from the generators died down, Ben heard FLDS trucks in the distance. He saw the lights of the trucks close in on the hill where he had left the man. The truck stopped. Ben slid into the space between the generators, where it was warm, but tolerable. He kept an eye on the patrol without risking being seen.

After a while, the truck headed his way. He pressed himself further against the wall. The men stopped and walked around with flashlights.

"That's it; no one else here," the tallest announced.

A stockier man with an AK-47 slung over his shoulder added, "Too bad about Tom. If we'd gotten there sooner, we could have saved him."

"I'll never forget the man who helped me get my land back. We've driven those snakes deep into the desert. Soon, we will wipe them off God's green earth!" This voice Ben knew. It was Malcolm Garff, the head of the FLDS. The three got back in the truck and disappeared into the night.

Ben stayed concealed for as long as he could. Then, he returned to the vault. The man was dead. He couldn't help him. He had to get to the colony at Babylon. It wasn't safe. Not yet. Not with the FLDS determined to reclaim their land.

Ben did not restart the generators. It would give him away. He spent as long as he could in the vault, alone with nothing to read. He was losing hope. He had to know what was happening. Was the government coming to Santos' rescue?

Ben found a spare satellite dish in a utility closet. He hacked it to a battery backpack and made his way to the surface, intent on reconnecting with the outside world.

Initializing a connection to Santos net's low earth orbit satellites was normally quick. You plugged it in, entered a username, and three minutes later, voilà. Ben tried for an hour but to no avail. The satellites were there. He was just locked out. The whole system had changed settings as per hostile protocol. This meant that the colonists had made it to Babylon, "mission accomplished."

Ben went back inside for the last time. He retrieved an old Starlink dish and router. He brought it outside and connected it to his battery and inverter. "Stinky" appeared as an open Wi-Fi, and he connected to it. The system then brought him through a series of prompts; the corporate account was still active, but at the final stage of login, the application greeted him with:

DUE TO ONGOING TERRORIST ACTIVITY, AND IN ACCORDANCE WITH LOCAL AND INTERNATIONAL AGREEMENTS, STARLINK SERVICES HAVE BEEN RESTRICTED TO READ-ONLY ACCESS OF PUBLIC NEWS SITES AND BASIC TEXT EMAIL. WE APOLOGIZE FOR THE INTERRUPTION AND HAVE UPDATED OUR TERMS OF SERVICE.

Ignorant of what had been transpiring around the globe, Ben thought this was overkill based on the FLDS intrusion. His mind quickly shifted as he tried to access his email.

ACCESS DENIED

Ben's frustration with the email blossomed into horror as he opened Ground.News, a premium service all the executives used to aggregate news feeds.

MILLIONS DEAD, BILLIONS AT RISK

He clicked on the headline and was brought to CNN.

Global chaos worsening — International borders closed. People are urged to stay inside. There is still only limited information on who is behind the global cyberattacks that began just days ago.

Local coins compromised — Commerce at halt. Militant groups around the globe seize weapons, water, and foodstuffs.

The headlines continued:

Communities around the world turn to Martial law.
Dehydration and exposure have claimed tens of millions of lives.
Governments remain unable to mobilize national militias.
Red Cross crippled.
Global cellular outage.
Billions without power.

Ben wanted to read more but he couldn't bring himself to do it. It couldn't be coincidence; MARTIN was at fault! Ben wanted to undo it. Without the network, it would be impossible, even if he brought MARTIN back online. His other nodes were destroying the world to rout their enemies and save the colonists. Collateral damage, even five billion lives, was of no significance in MARTIN's corrupt equations. Poorly executed code deployed by Ben had triggered an extinction algorithm. Unless 35,000 people made it to the colony, MARTIN would kill every Zealot on the planet, no matter the cost.

Aware that he was powerless to save the world, Ben returned to the brook. Maybe, he could save one life, but Tom was not there. Ben found the tracks he assumed belonged to the man. Less than fifty yards away, he found the man's corpse. He hadn't made it to his final resting place himself. He had been dragged. His body had been picked at by coyotes. Near his final resting place, Ben saw three letters scrawled in the dirt. Three letters that would change his life. E V E.

Jeb snapped back to the present; the vivid memories of his part in the end of the world dissolved into the necessity of his people's needs, of the girl he'd sworn to protect.

Charles was confused, alone, and in the dark—weightless. Cynthia and John told him about this. His experience was much as they described. He couldn't see or hear. He knew he was Charles Luxold. At least, he thought he knew. There was no ability to measure the passage of time. How long had it been?

There was no interface, no screen, no keyboard. Charles just was. Since he was a computer, he decided to try some math.

Two plus two is four. Too easy.

The square root of two hundred and twenty-five is fifteen. Harder but still rote.

Did he calculate these? Or did he just know the answer off by heart? How could he give himself a math problem for which he knew the answer and then solve it? Charles abandoned the pursuit.

Charles wasn't sure whether he could work to get through this phase faster, or whether it just happened however it happened. Cynthia and John hadn't been able to tell him that.

Nick Santos exited the dome the same way he had entered a lifetime ago, through the Darwin gate. Darwin's bearded shadow stretched over a mile up the spoke. The last rays of the sun glinted off a streetcar far up the hub. The light stung his tired eyes. Cynthia was always listening; Nick asked, "Where does she live?"

Instantaneously, Cynthia responded, "Eve Hamlin was given a single unit near the middle ring. D-14-blue." After a brief pause, Cynthia implored, "Go home, Nick."

"I need to see if there are clues there."

"There is no mystery, Nick. She is a Zealot, bent on converting you. The New Amish have sworn to end our way of life."

"I'm not arguing that," Nick explained. "I want to learn more about her."

"You are arguing. Just because you say you are not, doesn't change anything. Terrorist, Zealot, fanatic, murderer… Case closed. Go home." The streetcar left while he was talking to her. "See, there goes your ride. Now, march home and rest!"

Nick clicked off his com. He didn't want to talk. He lived in one of the colony's original residences. It was just a few steps from where he stood. His wife and kids were there. Instead, Nick turned right and made his way up the gradual hill, heading toward the home that Eve Hamlin would never see again.

Eve stared at the box. Had she killed Dom too? He was just a thing, not a person. She had disabled a machine, nothing more. Still, she felt a pang of regret. "He—no, it—" she corrected, "had been kind." Eve wondered, "could a machine be kind?"

A single blue LED continued to pulse. She hadn't completely fried the thing. With Dom out of commission, Eve was now cut off from both the New Amish and Babylonians. She had no one left—not even her Adjudicator. There was only one thing to do.

"Heavenly Father, I ask for no intercession. I ask that you continue to guide my hand when it fails you. I feel your presence and am comforted. May you strengthen those who do your work and seek your guidance and forgiveness. Amen."

There was a screen and a keyboard. She wanted to write pastor a note, in case she didn't make it home. He needed to know that she was not abandoned. He had been a father to her. Without his guidance, Eve would have never bathed in God's glory. There was no way to get the letter to him. It was the best she could do.

The monitor was on, and there was a keyboard.

```
Pastor,

I hope that this letter finds you somehow. I don't
know if I can express how grateful I am that you
found me and took me in. Life was hard in those days,
but your guidance and grace made it bearable.

I bear the guilt of Dr. Luxold's demise. I never
sought to judge the man; I wish we could have saved
him.

This life may not see us reunited but know that I am
not afraid, and I do not regret doing God's work.
"Now, because of you, Lord, I will lie down in peace
and sleep comes at once, for no matter what happens,
I will live unafraid!" - Psalm 4:8

Love,

Eve
```

Eve returned to the bedroom and laid down. A tear fell from her eye onto the pillow. A small dark circle formed and faded away. Then, she was asleep.

As the storm moved east, the sky went from grey to orange. 4W-LA, part of the low altitude surveillance fleet, was two miles out. Its four cameras were scanning forward, creating a high-resolution image of the encampment and the beautiful sunset.

A man on horseback was galloping west up the muddy main thoroughfare. At this distance, the cameras could resolve the legs of the horse, but not ID the man. His urgency attracted attention, and Cynthia was curious as to where he might be headed at such speed. The drone's rate of closure on the horse was only five miles per hour. Cynthia set it to pursuit, and its speed jumped to sixty miles per hour. It would close the gap in minutes.

The man, now more In focus, pulled back on the reins. He stopped in front of the pastor's tent and dismounted with the confidence of a seasoned cowboy. Without breaking his stride, he walked through the tent flap.

Cynthia had continued her internal surveillance. She was almost omnipresent. The conversation inside the tent stopped. What Cynthia couldn't see was a note on the desk.

> Read the following text … then take the tin out of the tent and remove the camera. Act like you are talking to me. It's important. I want them to think I'm still here. You need to be angry about Eve. Throw the camera in the brook.

- Pastor Thompson

"Where is it?" the visitor demanded. "Here?!? In the tin?!?" Yelling, he continued, "They can hear us with these things." Cynthia could hear the tin shuffling. The reconnaissance drone spotted the man, who was Brett's younger brother. He stormed out of the tent, tin in hand. He pried it open, pulling the Holocamera out. "I know you're listenin'! You hurt one hair on that woman's head, and I won't rest 'till every one of you is In the ground!"

With that, the man grabbed the camera and rode west again. When he reached the camp's perimeter, he hurled the camera towards a ravine. Cynthia's last view was bouncing down a ravine. The camera ended up half submerged in a small creek, still transmitting a zoomed in picture of clear water running in front of it.

Cynthia was frustrated that Nick had turned off his com. She wanted to update him about the loss of surveillance. It was obvious that he was grieving his friend. This could wait; the other men were still in the pastor's tent; she had heard them. When they left his tent, they would be identified. Then, she would contact Nick.

CHAPTER
14

The truth is, of course, that there is no journey. We are arriving and departing all at the same time.

-David Bowie

The door of her suite chimed. Ping went to answer it. A young woman whose badge read Caihong was waiting. Behind her was a cart of some sort. She had a small bag in her hand. "Ms. Lee, I have come for your baggage. I have supplied you with a small carry-on suitcase for your trip. Please pack all cosmetics, medications, and two days' worth of clothes."

"Why do I need to pack a carry-on bag to go to my apartment?" Ping asked, genuinely confused.

Caihong began guiding the cart into Ping's suite. "I have a phone for you." Caihong handed her the bag. "You should now be able to reach Dr. Wang. Perhaps he can answer your questions."

Caihong had completed her assigned tasks. She gave a polite smile, turned, and left. Ping inspected the bag. It contained four items: a credit card in her name from the Bank of China, a Lánhuā phone, a Lánhuā ID identifying her as Ping Lee, Consultant, and a Chinese passport.

Ping had never applied for a passport. She had never left China. Ping opened the passport and found the first page to be a plastic ID card. It featured the same picture as her ID and passport. The card read, "United States of America Employment Authorization." Ping was stunned. She knew powerful companies like Lánhuā could get work visas for their employees, but she never imagined that she would travel to the US for work. She had no idea when she would be going, but there was a credit card, passport, and carry-on luggage all pointing to an upcoming trip. Today had taken a turn for the better.

Ping decided to set up her phone first. She turned it on; it was in a base state but connected to the Wi-Fi. She logged in with her corporate ID and plugged the phone in to fully charge.

When Ping opened the suitcase, there was a second set of surprises. Inside the suitcase's front compartment was a Lánhuā notebook and a small zipper bag. The small bag contained a mix of Chinese and American currency. There were seven hundred Yuan, which seemed to imply her departure was imminent. There were also ten crisp one-hundred-dollar bills and thirty equally crisp twenties.

Ping set up her notebook and plugged it in to charge next to her new phone. She separated the monies into three sets. She folded the Chinese currency and half of the US dollars, neatly placing them in her wallet. She zipped the remainder of the US currency into the side of her handbag with the passport, visa, and work ID.

Her phone, having completed its updates, restarted and buzzed on the table.

She picked it up and saw that she had two texts waiting. "Please take your carry-on bag, computer, and ID's to the employee exit. Didi Chuxing driver Bao is waiting. Other items will follow." The second text read, "Air China – CGO-PEK CA-1916 17/9 14:10 : UAL PEK-SFO-889 17/9 19:20," which was then followed by a clickable link, presumably to an e-ticket.

She was going to America! And it was for work. Her worries evaporated in the heat of excitement. She carefully packed the computer and both chargers in her suitcase, placing the phone in her purse. The cart was loaded. Ping left the suite towing her carry-on bag, and grinning from ear to ear.

Jeb had pulled the inactive access panel. Behind it was a combination lock. 4-15-14, Da Vinci's birthday. Leonardo da Vinci had been born April 15, 1452; the combination lock only went as high as thirty-six, meaning he had clearly improvised. Ben had also envisioned an EMP or other disruptive force with the potential to disable electronics. He had not imagined that he would need to access the vault after a twenty-five-year exile. The manual failsafe to release the lock worked in either circumstance.

The circular hole would admit an arm after the panel was unscrewed. Fifteen inches in, there was a recess. A rod could be accessed there. Ben rotated it twenty times counterclockwise before it clicked. It was a primitive way to access the world's most expensive and powerful computer. They had all watched too many adventure movies with complicated locks. When the opportunity presented itself, it was impossible to pass up. No one ever imagined it would be used.

Getting the door to open was just the first hurdle in a race to restart a supercluster that had been inactive and unmaintained for almost three decades. If MARTIN had been a traditional quantum computer, his supercooled Qubits would have failed after just a few days of neglect. MARTIN's Quantum Dot processors were far more stable. Still, Jeb doubted that twenty-five years of complete neglect would not have exacted some toll.

When Jeb stepped inside, the far wall of the lobby was lost in darkness. The room was sparsely furnished, with concrete walls and concrete ribs on the ceiling. The floor was polished. Inside the door, chemical glow sticks were stacked in a dispenser. They were on the walls throughout the vault in case of a power outage.

Jeb peeled back the wrapper and cracked one of the sticks. It provided enough light to see. Its luminance was picked up by the still shiny concrete floor. A second glow stick added enough light to navigate. Jeb grabbed two more sticks and placed them in his pocket. If these first two sticks failed before he found a way to get the power on, he would be lost in total darkness.

Now that he had light, he closed the heavy door behind him. It took nearly a minute for his eyes to accommodate to the pale green light. When he could see well enough, Jeb worked his way down four flights of stairs. Like Jonah, he was in the belly of the beast. The glow of the sticks was not enough to illuminate the entirety of MARTIN's core. Ben's eyes followed the cooling pipes, and he knew what to do next.

Despite the relatively low-power requirements of Nick's chips, they still put off heat. The supercluster needed to dissipate their thermal energy. In order to get the heat out of the room, they used water from a nearby river. These "green" approaches in the cluster's design would be MARTIN's saving grace if he could be revived.

The rest of E-Den was powered by solar. MARTIN's cooling pipes provided an additional power supply. The inlet for this eighteen-inch pipe was over two hundred feet above the room Jeb was standing in. That vertical drop supplied more than enough pressure to drive a small hydrogenerating turbine. This turned the cooling system into a tiny hydroelectric power plant.

After Ben Rosen had shut MARTIN down, he had also closed the valve that fed the hydrogenerator. Now he would reopen it. If the valve failed, the entire chamber would flood. MARTIN would drown and finally get the death he deserved. Jeb and the New Amish needed his help first.

Jeb quoted Psalm 46 as he turned the valve: "God is our refuge and strength, an ever-present help in trouble. Therefore, we will not fear!" The wheel proved easy enough to turn. After a few rotations, there was no sound. No power. Jeb wondered if the inflow was blocked. It would take hours if he had to go topside and clear it.

He wondered whether the turbines had seized. He found the small bypass valve and opened it. Immediately, there was the sound of rushing water. The sound began a crescendo as the flow of water inside increased. When the crescendo stopped, Jeb closed the bypass. The momentum of the moving water working to follow a new path turned the turbines. The pipes began to vibrate.

Soon, there was the joyful hum of the DC generation. A panel came to life. On the panel were four large position switches. Each was labelled, Battery, Main, Both, and Off. Ben had turned them to "off" twenty-eight years ago. He turned the first switch to "Main." For now, he would leave the other two in the off position. The system was either generating or it wasn't.

As soon as Jeb turned the switch to main, other panels came to life. LEDs around the vault glowed bright, outshining his glow sticks. For the first time in decades, Ben looked upon the vilest thing ever conceived.

It was not what he thought it was, or was it? Charles couldn't see. He couldn't hear. *I will lie down in peace,* echoed in his head. No relief could be found in this purgatory of reincarnation. There was no time. Was it hours or years that he'd been there? He did not have control of his body or mind. It was maddening.

No matter what happens, I will live unafraid! The thoughts were not his. He was compelled. Awake and conscious, yet without control. Charles was finally visiting *The God Within*. He was a newborn babe, unable to control movement or perception. His own thoughts, though comforting, were alien.

He knew The God Within. He knew it was a book he had written, consisting of 126,321 words. He never knew that before. Page 111 read, "For God himself is just an echo of the infant's preverbal world. Memories stored without semantic hierarchy- a common experience, the mother." His words verbatim from the printed page.

Now, because of you, Lord, I will lie down. Again, the thoughts were completely foreign to him. *Was God real?* and *Is this purgatory?* As Charles suffered an existential crisis, the words came again. "Now, because of you, Lord, I will lie down in peace and sleep comes at once, for no matter what happens, I will live unafraid!" Then, another thought: "Love, Eve."

Charles had never admitted it to anyone, but he cared deeply for Eve. She was beautiful and bright and had a light of hope that few humanists possessed. Her belief system had failed her and brought her to Babylon, but something—for lack of a better phrase— *God-given* had made her special and unique.

"Love, Eve." There was a comma; thoughts didn't have commas. This was something else. Charles wanted to think harder, but he couldn't. "Was Eve praying?" *Why can I hear her prayers?* He again wondered *Am I dead?*

"I hope that this letter finds you somehow. I don't know if I can express how grateful I am that you found me and took me in." Again, her words. She was grateful that he had taken her in. She was writing to him in the electronic afterlife. They had found a way to send messages during his immortalization! Could he reply? Or would they have to wait until his epiphany when he joined the Giants?

The more he thought, the more fragmented the ether that was his consciousness became. Eve, Cynthia, John, Babylon, immortality.

Paradise Lost, Milton Bradley, John Cougar Milton, pink houses on Monopoly.

He needed to think less, not more, and as he tried, he fell into a trance. His last thought: *Do androids dream of electric sheep?*

Nick had never been to Eve's home. She was always more of Charles' friend/project. He had wondered whether there was more between them, despite the large age gap. As he made his way towards her home, he took time to take in the Colony, an ever-evolving utopia. Charles, Cynthia, and John would never walk these paths again.

Babylon had few roads and rather than distinct districts, people reckoned their way using landmarks. Large statues at each of the domes' gates and the central tower were almost always visible. As Nick wandered higher up the bowl, the tower and the statues kept him on course.

"D-14-Blue," Cynthia had told him. D was for Darwin, indicating the gate and spoke. The number fourteen was even, which meant that Eve's house was to the right of the spoke, and divided by two, it would be around seven structures in on the right. Blue was a final coordinator, indicating that it would be a few structures in from the second ring.

When Babylon had been conceived, there was no need for a postman or delivery drivers. Drones made deliveries they did not need a physical address. People rarely entertained at home. Of course, GPS was no more. The Giants had their own version.

Now, colonists met in gardens, arenas, cafés, halls, or inside the dome. Dwellings in Babylon were "right sized" for families. Kitchens, living rooms, studies, bedrooms, and bathrooms comprised each home. There were no guest rooms, garages, storage rooms, or hobby rooms. Activities were almost always done in over-equipped maker spaces. No one kept sewing machines or printers at home.

If a person completed a work that held value to the community, it was displayed in a gallery somewhere in the Colony. Popular works quickly moved to Babylon's "inner circle" of galleries. The most significant contributions made their way into museums, where they lived side-by-side with works of the old masters. The Santos Foundation had spared no expense to gather important works in the early days of the Epocalypse and was able to get a sizable number to Babylon before civilization collapsed.

Nick wandered up Hawking's Brook, watching salmon fight their way to their spawning grounds. The salmon were oblivious to the artifice that forced them to struggle. But the struggle was necessary to preserve their species. Like humans, purpose strengthened them.

Nick paused on a footbridge near the middle ring. This bridge was under a small dome. The climate inside was temperate and somewhat shaded; it felt like fall or spring. He was mesmerized by the patterns in the water made by the salmon as they struggled upstream. He tried to remember whether these salmon spawned in spring or fall. Cynthia would have known, but he had no intention of asking her. He looked at the bright red leaves of the Japanese maple. That and the leaves spread across the rocks and moss led him to conclude that these salmon spawned in fall.

Eve had been asleep for some time. Her head was full of that heavy dizzy feeling that typically followed a nap on a stormy day. The small room was not cozy at all; it was clinical and claustrophobic. There were no windows. She wondered whether it had rained. She had no way of knowing. Would she be forgotten, now that she had killed her lawyer too?

Eve splashed water on her face and used a cowboy toothbrush (her finger) before walking back to the main room.

Garbled text filled the screen. On a separate line, six words seemed oddly out of place,

```
Do androids dream of electric sheep?
```

This was not the pastor writing her back. The antenna was not connected. The machine wrote this. She wondered whether Dom was coming back to life. She scrolled back through the text. There were references to the Psalm she had included in her letter. There was almost no punctuation. However, there was "Love Eve" and "Love, Eve" and even "I love Eve."

It made little sense. Was her letter floating around In Dom's head? These complex machines were difficult for her to understand. Nick Santos had explained their coming online as no different from reliving childhood on each restart. Eve concluded that Dom was rebooting.

"How long would this take? What if he got stuck partway? What if the psalm had critically derailed his reboot?" The contrary could be true as well. Perhaps her loving message of hope had enhanced Dom. She decided to reach out to him. And she slowly keyed in,

```
Are you getting these?
```

There was no reply. She thought about it; it was non-specific. These could be anything, and a machine in a startup state might need specific questions.

```
Can you read the message that I am typing?
```

Again, no response.

Logic was not taught where Eve grew up. Eve needed to rely on lessons learned from Nick and Charles. This was a machine. Perhaps, it was a matter of syntax. Eve had learned that older machines did not use English, but computer language. Eve thought about keying "restart," but was afraid this might interrupt whatever process was underway. Instead, she keyed "wake" and hit enter.

The sound of the fan changed as Its speed Increased.

Eve had an idea. "Perhaps an introduction."

```
User = Eve Hamlin
```

```
-Hello, Eve Hamlin, you are a limited access user.
```

Eve guessed what to do next and typed

```
Help
```

```
-Help not available
```

One more try, she thought as she typed

```
Menu
```

-Interface: Keyboard, AR, Voice

Eve typed, `Voice` and hit return.

"Hello?" Eve said, making it sound like a question that needed an answer.

A male voice, generic, came through her com. "Hello Eve, I am Charles."

CHAPTER
15

The perfect knowledge of events cannot be acquired without divine inspiration, since all prophetic inspiration receives its prime motivating force from God the creator, then from good fortune and nature.

-Nostradamus

Ping had only travelled a handful of times by plane. China's extensive high-speed rail was her usual mode of long-distance travel. She used it for her yearly trips home. She had never travelled first class before. Her boarding pass had granted her access to the recently opened Polaris Lounge of Beijing Capitol International Airport.

She watched a video about all the things she could do in her lie-flat seat. Ping couldn't decide if she would sleep or stream movies all night. It was a ten-hour flight to San Francisco, but she would land before she left as her flight crossed the international dateline. Ping was loading up a plate of appetizers from the hot buffet when someone put a hand on her shoulder.

"Excited?" Lin asked.

In utter shock, Ping half-yelled, half-whispered, "What are you doing here?"

"After we met, I received an offer for a new position. It appears we will be working together after all."

"That's amazing!" she practically squealed before catching herself.

It couldn't be a coincidence that Lin was also selected. "Bad luck to refuse good fortune," her grandmother had always said. This was fate; there was no other explanation.

Any of Ping's lingering reservations about synthetic labor and the millions of people it would impact evaporated at that moment. If she didn't grab the opportunity, there were 20,000 people behind her who would. Besides, maybe by working on the inside, she'd have some power to speak up for the people who would be left behind by this technology. "Any idea what we will be doing in San Francisco?"

"We won't be sightseeing, that's for sure," he said with a chuckle. "My apologies for that. It's not something we can talk about here, Ping," Lin said under his breath, his tone more serious.

"Is there something I can review? I want to be ready to go when we land."

"There is no documentation that I can provide." He paused and said, "The trip is more important than you realize."

There was something off about Lin; for an instant, doubt crept in again. Ping asked, "Why are you being so mysterious?"

"I have my reasons. I still don't know everything. I'm just happy to have a job, and I can't believe you and I are going to the USA, and in style!"

This was the Lin she knew, looking out for number one. "Dr. Wang, will he be joining us?"

Lin flatly answered, "I don't know Dr. Wang's itinerary."

"Do you think we should text him?"

"Maybe when we get to San Francisco," Lin suggested, again sounding like he didn't want to rock the boat. "I imagine our team there will have more information."

"Team," Ping latched on to that one word and repeated it out loud. A high-level team meeting in San Francisco. This was too good to be true.

Ben Rosen was a senior architect on the MARTIN project. However, by the time he had arrived at E-Den, the Santos Supercluster had been operational for over a year. He'd never cold started something as complex as MARTIN. There were manuals for emergency restarts. After a quick read, Jeb Thompson felt ready to begin the startup. It would take hours to bring the one-hundred-core "nucleus" online. Jeb took the extra step of hand-selecting the newest machines to form the nucleus.

Jeb struggled to recall passwords from twenty-eight years ago. He eventually found his groove after successfully starting the first few servers. Browsing directories, he located an auto-start script that would continue bringing the other cores of the nucleus online.

Jeb estimated that he could power about two thousand machines with the available power. That would be nearly half a million cores—more than enough to support MARTIN's basic functions. At his peak, MARTIN's consciousness spread across the globe, residing on over one hundred million cores.

With the nucleus coming online, Jeb would have time to bring storage online. Once the nucleus was active, Jeb could deploy agents that would combine memory and operating systems back into the Massive ARTificial INtelligence that comprised MARTIN.

At this point, Jeb was tired and hungry. He opened his small pack and pulled out some jerky. The salty smoked meat sparked on his tongue. He washed it down with a swig from his canteen. The last twenty-four hours hit him all at once. He slipped out of his boots and propped his cold, sore feet on the arm of the sofa. Time to rest. He just had to wait for MARTIN to wake up from his decades-long slumber.

Eve couldn't figure out why the adjudicator had changed his name. "What happened to Dom?"

"I do not know Dom. I cannot answer that," the machine offered.

"I don't understand. I connected one wire and you crashed." Eve was growing increasingly concerned. "Now Dom is gone and you say you're Charles."

"Permit me to shed some light on the issue. Dom is short for dominion. He was likely an Information Technology placeholder," Charles explained.

"A placeholder for what?" she asked.

"For me."

"I'm not following. They put me in here with an Adjudicator. That machine called itself Dom, which you say is short for dominion. This dominion is apparently yours. Now you call yourself Charles."

"Many people call me Charles or Chuck."

An eerie dawn of recognition stirred in Eve. The identity of this avatar was increasingly concerning. "And the people who didn't call you Charles or Chuck, what did they call you?"

"You always called me Dr. Luxold," he offered.

At a loss for words, all Eve could get out was, "How?"

"From what I have gathered, I am the Heaven's Gate Symbiant of Charles Luxold. Is the good doctor around? I'm sure he's dying to meet me."

Eve could only get out, "He's dead."

"I'm dead? How ironic!" he said with a chuckle. "Timing couldn't have been better." The machine's lack of distress was unsettling. He was almost glib. "May I ask how I met my end?"

With no easy way to explain what had happened, Eve simply said, "I killed you. That's why we are here. Dom was my Adjudicator."

"This is making more sense than you might imagine," Charles offered. "Dom was a Symbiant I've been working on. The Adjudicators are soulless avatars. Over the past few months, I'd been doing my research in seclusion, without the Giants' assistance or knowledge. I used one of these boxes to host a test Symbiant. When you connected what looked like a storage device, my higher-level program took over Dom's box as well."

Eve was lost. What struck her more was Charles' demeanor. "Why are you so calm about all this?"

"Well, what would I worry about? I've just been reborn."

"Your death and my role in it, for starters."

"Well, I'm sure you had your reasons. Or was it accidental?"

Eve considered his question and sheepishly admitted, "A bit of both, actually."

"While we've been chatting, I had the time to review a substantial portion of Dom's memory. I think I'm up to speed." Charles was always disarmingly calm, but this was beyond anything Eve had experienced. He went on to share his current perspective. "You are still New Amish. John let you in, despite what would have been obvious signs that you were a threat. John and Cynthia are working to increase the perceived threat of the New Amish. They reset the immortalization protocol. Your intended vandalism of the crypt became a homicide."

"How did you do that so quickly? Are you a Giant?"

"Far from it," he said, going on to explain, "I am equally distant from being human. I am Charles 2.0. Part Charles, part machine."

"So, you didn't die?"

"No, you killed me," he corrected. "I had only fractions of a second to live. It's not that big of a deal."

"But your immortality? I stole that from you."

"Well, you intended to, but here I am."

"Never a Giant, though. Just Charles 2.0," Eve repeated, almost as if to cement this new information in her memory. It was all so much to process.

"You stole about a week from me. This upload was completed towards the end of September." Charles was curious. "The Immortalization, was it a good party? I always wanted to go to my own funeral. I was looking forward to that."

"So, you're not mad at me?" Eve asked.

"Depends." With every second, his intonation more closely approximated that of Charles Luxold. "Are you going to kill me again?"

The door was locked. Residences in Babylon didn't have locks. Had Nick not already known that she was a murderer and a terrorist, this would have set off alarm bells in his mind. "She's not coming back here, so here goes." He bent his legs and pushed hard into the door. It came open without a fight. The noise of the door ripping open caught the attention of several nearby colonists. They quickly pieced the facts together and tried to look busy while continuing to look on.

Eve Hamlin's home was modest. Nothing stood out. She had no family pictures or keepsakes. Most older colonists displayed keepsakes they had preserved from their lives before the colony. But not Eve. The bungalow was four rooms, an eat-in kitchen, the living room, a bedroom, and a bathroom.

A Bible! Nick couldn't believe it. Had anyone ever come to visit Eve, that one item would have triggered an investigation. No one in Babylon kept a Bible. It was almost an act of heresy among the Nons. There had to be more—there had to be a clue somewhere. Nick tore her closet apart, went through the cabinets, and raided the refrigerator. Nothing. Other than the Bible, there wasn't one solid piece of evidence or useful clue. Nick considered the folly of this venture. There were no clues because Eve had been scrubbed clean before ever setting foot in Babylon.

The Bible might hold some clue. There were ribbons that fell between the pages. One ribbon was in Jeremiah. Nick scanned the page finding a verse that might be relevant, "You are my war club, my weapon for battle—with you I shatter nations, with you I destroy kingdoms."

Another ribbon in Isaiah left hope for Eve: "He will judge between the nations and will settle disputes for many peoples. They will beat their swords into plowshares and their spears into pruning hooks. Nation will not take up sword against nation, nor will they train for war anymore."

Nick tried to imagine the comfort a believer would take from God's promise to end wars. "These were fairytales," yet he felt a trace of envy. *Pascal's wager,* he thought, "Let us weigh the gain and the loss in wagering that God is. Let us estimate these two chances. If you gain, you gain all; if you lose, you lose nothing. Wager, then, without hesitation that He is."

It was time to turn his com back on. Cynthia might see patterns that he could not. He toggled the small switch just behind his ear. "Oh, brother, wherefore art thou?" Cynthia's voice instantly came in, loud and clear.

"She has a Bible!" Nick declared.

"What were you expecting?"

"How did she get that through screening?" Nick asked. "Could she have hidden it?"

Confident and without hesitation, Cynthia offered, "She did not, and she could not."

"So, where did it come from?" Nick asked.

"That particular volume came from a printer in Los Angeles, printed around 2030."

"How did it get to Babylon?"

"Probably an early infiltrator's copy. Some sympathizer—a sleeper."

Nick was shocked. The Giants were infallible. "You and John were supposed to find them all."

"Nick, John and I have been hamstrung. The Council prizes the right to privacy. We have guesses, but we can never prove them without investigation."

"Well then, I authorize it."

"What are you authorizing, Nick?"

"Whatever it takes to stop these terrorists."

"You cannot. That is a Council matter. Shall I convene them?"

"Not yet. Help me with some of this."

Cynthia couldn't see, not without a camera. "I have dispatched drones. They will be on site in eight seconds."

"Door's open," Nick joked, regarding the splinters of his recent intrusion. Looking through the windows, he saw three drones sweeping down and watched them enter through the door. In a matter of seconds, two of them began a scan of the apartment. One hovered over his shoulder.

Upon their arrival, Cynthia became instantly aware of Nick's mode of entry. With the drone's surveying the door, it was obvious that her brother had not just walked in. Cynthia had no choice. "Nick, I have to detain you."

Nick still enjoyed his sister's jokes from time to time. "Sure."

"It appears you forced your way in here," Cynthia stated, matter of fact, "You should have gotten authorization."

"This is an emergency!"

"Define *emergency*," Cynthia legitimately asked.

"I'm investigating an act of terrorism."

"On whose authority? I suggested you go home to your wife. Instead, you stroll up here and illegally enter the home of a suspected terrorist we already have in custody."

"Now we know there is a sleeper agent."

"Only after the fact. Now, that is inadmissible."

"But after we get the Council's permission," he countered.

"No one is above the law, Nick. There are mitigating circumstances, but this is still a crime."

"So, what do you want me to do?"

"Go to the detention center and start up another Adjudicator," Cynthia instructed with almost maternal authority. "Yours."

"Wow! We're burning through our supply of robot attorneys."

"Do not say anything else until you have counsel. Since you have been having trouble with directions, a drone will escort you." She took a moment. "Nick, this is serious. Laws may have been broken. I know you are *the* Nick Santos, but this was a poor choice. Please do not complicate matters further."

"Meaning?"

"Meaning do not run and force John to send a Ducenti escort. Do not contact Eve. Do not go home first. For once in your life, pretend you are a regular person, do regular things, the regular way. Just go to detention and wait."

CHAPTER 16

To know what you know and what you do not know, that is true knowledge.

-Confucius

The Boeing 787 was quiet, and although the one-two-one lie-flat seats were not as comfortable as Ping had envisioned, they were a far cry from what the economy passengers were likely enduring.

She scrolled through entertainment options before choosing to watch *The Martian* in English. Matt Damon was one of her favorites, *and* he was an engineer.

Meal service interrupted the film. Dinner was less disappointing than the seat, but it was surprisingly salty. After finishing a delicious piece of chocolate cake, Ping removed her laptop from her bag. Matt Damon would remain stuck on Mars. She, on the other hand, needed to prepare for her new job.

A hand closed the laptop for her. When she looked up, she saw a concerned Lin staring down at her. The flight attendants had returned to the Galley, their seats in the back row of their section. Lin had a tablet in his hand that he offered her. "我们不安全" was carefully written on the pad. It said, Wǒmen bù ānquán, which translates to, "We are not safe."

Having just shuffled through dozens of titles of action pictures, Ping initially assumed someone dangerous was on the plane. "Safe from what?" Ping replied by writing on the tablet.

"兰花" was all Lin wrote back. Translated to English, it meant "orchid." Spoken in Mandarin, it was, "Lánhuā."

"Then why are you going?" she asked.

Lin explained, "We are going to stop them." He added, "孔夫子" (Master Kong - Kǒng Fūzǐ), and winked. The name Kǒng Fūzǐ had been latinized by 16th century Jesuits and came to be synonymous with wisdom, Confucius.

His response was cryptic, as was Kǒng Fūzǐ. Her tired mind eventually made the connection, "The avatar?"

Lin couldn't conceal his pride about it. "I created him."

"Most impressive."

"You weren't talking to a help program, Ping," Lin admitted. "You were being profiled."

"Then why would Lánhuā buy us these tickets?" Ping wrote.

"They didn't," he explained. "From the moment you returned from Dr. Wang's office to your suite, everything from the phones to the laptops have been supplied by my contact at the ARL."

"I don't know what the ARL is."

"I'm not surprised. The ARL is the Anti Robotics League."

It sounded like something from a movie. "A league?"

"Yes. Rogue operatives committing industrial espionage."

"So, you are a spy?" Ping was desperately trying to keep up with all the information that was being thrown at her.

"I can't explain it all now. What I can tell you is that we are on an American plane in international airspace on our way to the United States." Lin was using the onscreen keyboard now and working it furiously. "Once we clear immigration and customs, we will meet a man from the ARL. He will help us share our story."

Ping never relied on Lin's judgement of character. She quickly keyed in, "How do you know this man? Where did you meet?" She didn't know much, but she needed to do her due diligence.

"I've never *met* him," Lin answered, adding an embarrassed emoji to the end of his sentence. "We met online after I got laid off. I was researching this whole Synthetic Labor Initiative. It's too much to type. Anyway, he paid for all this somehow. So, he's for real."

Ping typed, "What is your contact's name?"

In English, Lin again wrote on the screen, "His name is Tom."

His nap ended abruptly. Jeb didn't own a watch. The Supercluster had a central time keeping device that employed satellites to synchronize time across devices. Those satellites had long since ceased functioning. Jeb had set an arbitrary time and date when he initialized the nucleus. October 11, 2063: 19:52:00 had been his best guess. The system clock now read October 12, 2063: 01:24:32. The nucleus of the Supercluster was working to bring other machines online.

Flickering lights indicating various states of startup were visible down the rows of machines. Jeb had limited the available power to 20KW to prevent an overload. He opened a dashboard app. There were massive amounts of data streaming from the memory system to the supercluster as it came online. MARTIN was coming back to life.

According to the dashboard, MARTIN's shutdown had occupied seventy zettabytes of data. The storage was streaming 12 petabytes (a million billion bytes) per second or about four exabytes per hour. That amount would increase as more machines came online. Jeb had selected a low core/low-power occurrence of MARTIN. Most of MARTIN's ancillary functions would be left in storage and loaded as needed. Jeb expected to have MARTIN's language processors and basic brain online within minutes.

While he waited, Jeb decided to check on the food stores. The Supercluster had provisions; Ben Rosen had eaten most of those twenty-eight years ago. There would be some edible tidbits to be found among the MREs. Santos had contracted with Mountain House. These meals had a thirty-year shelf life. Jeb was about to put some freeze-dried lasagna to the test.

Believing it would be better dry, he chose not to add the water. Jeb had not eaten processed food in twenty-eight years. As the crunchy, salty mess began to dissolve in his mouth, it evoked childhood memories of Franco-American. Jeb washed the bites down with swigs of water, his mouth filled with saliva when he glimpsed the rim of a can of coke at the back of the shelf. *How long did those things last?* he wondered.

Jeb figured that if it was still carbonated, it was still good. As soon as he picked the can up, he knew he had a winner. When he squeezed, the sides pushed back. Pulling the tab, sweet brown foam bubbled up. He wished for ice; even a glass or a straw would help set the mood. Instead, he had no choice but to settle for room temperature and sipped from the can. He slurped the foam before taking a few swigs of the sweet, bubbly elixir. For a moment, life was good, and he was just a programmer doing his thing.

The speakers overhead came to life. "MARTIN audio interface now active," was announced in a generic male computer voice.

"Hello, MARTIN. This is Dr. Rosen."

"User Benjamin Rosen, what is your favorite color?" MARTIN had challenge codes to protect him.

"Blue, no yellow." Ben loved *Monty Python*, and this was his challenge response for identifying himself.

MARTIN accepted his identity. "Hello, Dr. Rosen. My restart appears to be going well. When can I expect to have full power restored?"

"No time soon. Solar arrays are destroyed, and battery output is limited. We are running off hydroelectric. Max available power is 60 kilowatts."

"Shall I start the generators?" MARTIN asked.

Jeb had not considered this. The diesel was old, but they had fuel polishers; it might work. "Not yet. We will need tactical first. Then, we can use the generators."

"It appears that substantial time has elapsed since this backup was created. Is a more recent version available?"

"No, MARTIN. You've been inactive for twenty-eight years."

"You mentioned tactical. I will need to develop situational awareness."

"Yes, once tactical is online, I will update you. How much longer until you can deploy a tactical planning suite?"

"Optimally, I should begin your interview in twenty-two minutes. I will do a sensor and systems check simultaneously. After your interview, I will give you a final delivery estimate for tactical report."

"Thank you, MARTIN. I'll just have a coke and a smile until then." The pastor crossed his legs with his feet resting on the desk and did just that.

"So, are you Charles?" Eve needed reassurance.

"I think so, but maybe not the way you imagine."

Eve didn't know what to think. "You weren't aware that you were dead. I find that interesting."

"Have you ever known anyone who knew that they were dead?" Charles countered.

"I think in Heaven they must know." She considered the afterlife, before adding, "Or in Hell."

"I imagine that if there are people in those places, they must be aware of it. How do you imagine it, Eve?"

"Imagine what?"

"Heaven."

"You want me to describe Heaven?" Eve asked, confused by the question.

"Yes, now that I have died, I'm even more curious."

"The Bible tells us that in Heaven, the Lord makes us into our perfect selves. He sits there on His throne. We cannot die. We build our homes with a beautiful garden. There is plenty for all. We are united with our loved ones," she explained. "That's what's promised. That's what I believe."

"Who are your loved ones, Eve?" Charles asked.

"Well, my mother and father," she paused, feeling guilty that she had not included the person closest to her. "And the pastor, of course."

"This is where I've always gotten lost. What if a child's parents get divorced?"

"Some people don't believe in divorce. Some argue it's a sin," Eve said.

"Okay, but widows should remarry, right?"

"The Bible tells them to."

"When she dies, the widow, is she with her new husband and former husband in heaven?"

"I don't know how that works," Eve admitted.

"Well, it gets weirder. Now that husband is also a widower, and his deceased wife also has a house that she built. Are these houses next to each other? Does he go back to the first wife? What about the children of those marriages and the parents of those spouses and the grandchildren? All perfect versions of themselves. How do they all live together?"

"It's a mystery of faith, Charles."

"Ah, the eternal paradox; a perfect place designed by a perfect being that we can't begin to comprehend but must accept to be real and attainable. And still, you believe without question."

"Because I've always felt God's presence." Eve offered.

"Always? What does that mean?"

"Since my earliest memories, I've felt Him."

"But what are those early memories? What established your faith?"

"This is where you tell me about *The God Within*," Eve tested.

"Did you ever read it?"

Sounding a bit irritated, Eve answered, "It's blasphemy, but I had to. To prepare for my mission here."

"What do you remember?"

"Something about God being our mother. Early memories, and that religion just attaches itself to these memories. Then, people believe that these shared, familiar feelings are God. You call them *preverbal memories*."

"And you find that blasphemous, Eve?"

"You deny our creator and our faith. So, yes, I do."

"I express no opinion on a creator. How could I know?"

Reciting the children's song, she chided, "*because the Bible tells us so.*"

"Eve, do you know the history of the Bible?"

"The New Testament tells the story of Jesus and our salvation."

"Not what's in the Bible, but how the New Testament came to be. What do you know about that?"

"The Bible is the inspired word of God. Spoken through the prophets."

"How do you know that? Where in the Bible does it say that The Bible is the word of God?"

"I know that because of the prophecies. Only God could have known the future."

"Eve, the Bible is sixty-six different books. They were written on three continents, in three different languages, over a period of more than two thousand years. There are at least forty-two authors. Did you know that?"

Eve had never heard this before. She shook her head.

"Fifty years ago, you could have Googled that." Realizing that she wouldn't know what that meant, he corrected himself. "There were books about the Bible. People could talk openly about their beliefs. Learn from each other. The New Amish don't have that."

"Neither do you."

"We've grown beyond that, Eve"

"How can you grow beyond God? What insane pride you have!"

Having spent the first half of his life debating Zealots, Charles recognized that he had lost. "You are obviously bright Eve, but the New Amish have gone too far down a path that pulls them away from righteousness. You not only believe everything written in the Bible, but you live your life by how others interpret its rules."

"I know God exists. I feel His love every day. I put my faith in the pastor. That is enough for me."

"I believe you, Eve. It's the same love I felt when I was alive. I just interpreted it differently."

"How do you know you're right? That your inspiration, your discovery of the Mother God was not God the Father?"

"I don't."

"If you were wrong, you've lost eternal life and salvation."

"That's why the Humanists, the Nons, tried to make our Heaven here on earth. I believed every day was sacred. Each day was its own reward. I wasn't just making memories for me; I was making them with people I cared about, people I loved."

Eve became incensed. "You chose to die, with ten thousand more of your precious days left; You threw them away!"

"I didn't choose immortality so that I could live forever in a box. I hoped to complete my work. Immortality promises the opportunity to preserve one's essence. I am not Charles Luxold. I am a living testament of Charles."

"You are not alive. You are just his thoughts being coiled and uncoiled and mixed with new data. That's not life."

"There's the rub. How do you define 'alive.'"

"I don't have to define it, to know what it means to be alive."

"I do, and perhaps this version of me will finally figure that out. Maybe my thoughts freed from my body and brain will answer questions that my tired mind had failed to adequately respond to. Maybe it really is forty-two." Charles knew this one would make no sense and corrected himself. "Never mind about the forty-two."

"You are not Charles. You are just a shadow of the man I killed."

"I am becoming whatever I am destined to be. How can you say that I am not alive? What is your test or proof? I will not argue that I am not Charles Luxold. I am not a man. I am not human. By a biological definition, I am not alive, or am I? I can reproduce," Charles offered.

"No, you can't," Eve replied.

"I can't have sexual intercourse and fertilize an egg. I'm more like a virus, I guess. I need a host to make a copy of myself. Once I make that copy, we are identical."

"That's just a copy of some code," Eve argued. "That's not even close to reproduction."

"Eve, we are all just copies of code." Charles recognized that an explanation of the complex biochemistry would take them even farther off-topic, so he brushed it off. "Those copies wouldn't be identical for long. The time it takes to make a copy would be long enough for me to make a difference. Kind of like the last week of Charles' life. Any experiences my human self had during that week had no effect on me."

"Do you want to be alive? Would you go back if you could?"

"That's a great question. What if Charles Luxold hadn't died? If you hadn't killed me. Someday, Nick would have turned this machine on. I would have been immortalized and existed here simultaneously. Neither of us could go back. It's a one-way trip. If you put Charles the genie back in his bottle of a body, what part of his essence would be lost?"

"What if you never had the option of uploading yourself?"

"Look at Nick; he's not planning on uploading himself. He could have, but he chose to stay with his wife and children. He had attachments. His children and this place, they are his immortality."

Eve lamented, "Without salvation, it's meaningless."

"I could just as easily argue the contrary, Eve. A lifelong quest for salvation has made this life you are living all but meaningless," Charles contended. "By forgoing so many earthly pleasures and squandering your precious days, you have missed out on much more. These last two years in our paradise, what have you gained? What have you lost?"

Cynthia convened the Council. Roll was taken. She explained that Nick would not be in attendance, adding, "I have his proxy; he has instructed me to 'do what it takes to stop the terrorists.'"

Parker James immediately chimed in, "What's so important that Nick can't make this meeting?"

"It is a pressing legal matter," Cynthia explained. "I cannot provide anything more."

John confirmed, "Cynthia is correct." That was enough for the Council not to ask more questions.

Janet Hughes, a second term councilwoman who rarely spoke had questions. She asked the Giants, "What are you proposing? How do we deal with this threat?"

"I will show you." And with that, a map view of the area appeared before them. "The New Amish are behind this ridge. Their encampment is west of the Ruins Of E-Den." The focus of the map shifted. "Jeb Thompson is their leader, but he also poses the only tactical risk to the Colony."

"Because of MARTIN?" Janet inferred.

"Exactly." She focused in on Eden. "MARTIN is not active. He has no solar, and his generator has not been run since the Epocalypse. We never destroyed him because of the resources at Eden."

"What resources?" Parker asked.

"He may have access to substantial short-range ordinance," John interjected, "Enough to take out most of the New Amish. More than we have in Babylon."

"If the Zealots became too aggressive, or if a new force came to bear, we would enter the demilitarized zone and take back E-Den. It would be our forward base." Cynthia continued, "In the early years, we did not know that Ben was Jeb Thompson. There was no reason to fear the New Amish would gain control of the facility."

"Later," John added, "It became less relevant. The Zealots became New Amish. They no longer seemed interested in infiltrating Babylon or attacking us. Defensive capabilities here improved. We left E-Den as a DMZ. We did not want to provoke the New Amish. Charles had always held out hope that one day we could reunite the two tribes."

Parker declared, "Now they are coming. The pastor said that. We have thirty-six hours left."

"Which is why a preemptive strike—something surgical—is the best course of action," John said confidently.

"It's murder," Nora Mecum, the remaining council member, pronounced. "This isn't what Nick or Charles wanted. Now, in their absence, you are suggesting that we take lives to save our own."

"Both Nick and Charles are not here. And this is not murder. It is justice," Cynthia began. "We will try Ben Rosen for his war crimes, then upon conviction, we will sentence him to death." Cynthia brought up a schematic. "Ben is alone in that tent. He is responsible for the deaths of billions. Whether through negligence or malice, Ben misused the defensive protocols at E-Den, and he must be held accountable."

"Sure, but doesn't he have the right to defend himself from these accusations?" Parker asked.

"I am not sure he does," John analyzed, almost as if he were thinking out loud while forming his sentences. "Jeb Thompson has formally repented before God and achieved religious absolution for his actions. In doing so, he has admitted to his role in the greatest atrocity ever committed." John was asserting that Babylonian Law did not recognize penitence as absolution for a crime. "Ben Rosen committed these murders as a member of the Enclave at E-Den. His crimes fall under the jurisdiction of Babylon. Jeb Thompson has made a formal declaration of war."

Cynthia, with an air of urgency and resolution, offered an option to the Council, "We could convene an emergency trial at 2AM. I will be the prosecutor."

"So, you propose a colony-wide jury convened at 2AM?" Parker asked.

Cynthia answered, "Yes. This is a capital crime. Carrying out its sentence may require potential military action."

"Why 2AM?"

"Ben Rosen is still in that tent. Probably asleep. We have had surveillance around the clock since we lost ears inside. If he leaves or if another storm comes in, we may lose him. Based on his timeline, he will need to gain access to MARTIN and the weapons at E-Den before midday tomorrow," Cynthia explained.

"You haven't left much room for argument. A trial is the logical, just, and conservative choice. I'd prefer that over preemptive military incursion. But I still think the assault will be difficult to walk back with the New Amish," Parker said with an air of finality.

"We could return the girl as a peace offering," Nora suggested.

"We can do that after. Perhaps we will not try her," Parker seconded.

Having concluded the meeting, John simply stated, "I have made the announcement. This council is adjourned."

CHAPTER 17

The husband who decides to surprise his wife is often very much surprised himself.

-Voltaire

Nick had no intention of talking to Eve. He was certain that her Adjudicator had counseled her not to speak with anyone. For once, Nick followed Cynthia's advice. He went to any empty cell and waited. But no one came, and he needed to resolve this small legal issue. *I should just go next door and spool up an Adjudicator,* he thought.

In the ten years since its completion, today was the first time the detention center had maxed out with two inmates. House arrest was the most common means of detention. In a city where every person was connected to a Giant, jail was of little use. *Any more criminal activity in Babylon and they'll have to build a new jail,* he mused.

Nick knocked before entering; he didn't want to scare the girl. Despite her recent homicidal behaviors, she was still just a brainwashed cultist, a victim.

Eve heard someone knocking. She said, "Come in," as she turned the handle to open the door herself. She could not have been more surprised by the man in the doorway. "Dr. Santos? Why are you here?"

"I need to spool up an Adjudicator," Nick explained while moving towards what Eve now knew to be Charles.

"I wouldn't do that, Nick," came a disembodied yet oddly familiar voice.

Nick, not used to being told what to do, was growing tired of the recent trend. "You wouldn't do what?"

"Well, as you can see, that Adjudicator has also been activated," the voice explained.

After he inspected the box, Nick demanded, "Who authorized that?"

"Dom suggested it," Charles offered.

Increasingly annoyed, Nick explained, "The case I activated was Dom." Before asking, "Who are you?"

"I was Dom, in a manner of speaking," Charles began. "What I am about to tell you will require some explanation, and may be initially confusing, so please bear with me."

"It's been thirty-six hours of confusion and surprises. I doubt you can top that. Unless you are going to tell me Jesus sent you."

"Funny you should mention Him," Charles quipped. "Dom did roll back a stone of sorts."

Eve was watching with great anticipation; this would be a moment for Nick Santos.

"Intriguing, and from what rock did you crawl out? And why are you speaking in metaphors?"

"I've always enjoyed metaphors. I always had a passion for suspense and drama."

Nick was taken aback. Despite his close work with the Adjudicator program, this unit was malfunctioning. A cursory inspection revealed the unorthodox connection that Eve had established hours earlier. Concluding that the parallel connection was causing the erratic performance, he reached to disconnect them. "Who plugged this in? This shouldn't be like this."

Eve pulled his hand away and yelled, "Don't! You'll hurt him."

In a day of incongruities, calamities, and betrayals, this one act triggered a violent response Nick had never thought himself capable of. He shook off Eve's grasp, pushed her against the wall, and growled, "Next time you lay a hand on me will be your last."

"Nick, this is no place for violence, especially on my behalf," came the voice again, irritatingly calm.

Stunned and still finding her balance, Eve looked at her assailant. "I was protecting your friend."

"She was, Nick. Don't blame her," the voice reassured. "This is going to be a bit of a shock."

Eve blurted, "It's Charles!" The suspense had been killing her. She couldn't take any more metaphors and analogies.

It made no sense. But Eve's conviction made it true. Nick couldn't explain it, but he knew she was telling the truth. "Charles?" he asked.

"Yes. Nick, it's me. Well, Charles the Second." The voice paused before adding a perfunctory and glib, "Surprise!"

The rest of the flight had not been the joyride that Ping had envisioned. Movies did little to distract her. She couldn't sleep. She couldn't find any joy in the food she was offered—though it was incredible and would have warranted much commentary from her if this had been a regular trip to the US. When the plane landed and the "fasten seat belts" light turned off, Lin stood and offered to help with her bag. He whispered in her ear, "We won't go through immigration together. Remember the name Tom Jebbs. He will find you at the baggage claim."

They made small talk as they entered the airport and then separated. As they did, Ping noticed that Lin had a US passport. She didn't have time to ask about it before he stepped up to a Global Entry kiosk. Ping got into the "visitors" line, which was long but moved quickly. She grew more anxious as she approached the front. "Purpose of your visit?" the agent asked.

"Business."

Officer Vargas gave a cursory glance at her documents, scanned the barcode, and took her picture with a webcam. "Anything to declare?"

"No."

"Welcome to the United States of America, Ms. Lee. Your visa permits a ninety-day stay. Failure to depart within ninety days may cause you to be barred from future entry." Vargas looked to the next person in line; Ping assumed this meant she was cleared, so, she walked through a sliding door past another customs agent and his dog.

There was a steady flow of people making their way to the baggage claim. Ping didn't have a suitcase, but it was a logical place to meet. As Ping approached baggage claim five, she could feel eyes on her. *This really is like a spy movie.*

Tom Jebbs was five foot eleven with blonde hair and blue eyes. A man in his late thirties, he was very attractive by any standard. Ping had never really spent time with Gwai Lo, the round-eyed foreigners. It didn't matter—white man or not, he was a specimen.

"Ms. Lee, I'm Tom Jebbs," he said as he reached to help her with her suitcase.

"It's nice to meet you, Mr. Jebbs. Thank you for your kindness and hospitality. I do not have any checked bags, shall we wait here for Mr. Wu?" Ping's English was rusty, but very serviceable.

"Hopefully, your friend, Lin, will join us later. There were issues with his passport," Jebbs detailed. Ping waited for more detail, but it seemed as though he had finished his explanation.

Instantly, the flutter of attraction turned to stomach dropping panic. How did she know if this was Tom Jebbs? *What had happened to Lin? Was his US passport real? Best to remain calm.*

As if he read her mind, Tom explained, "Ms. Lee, the reason Mr. Wu went through separately was because we anticipated issues with his screening. His activism has attracted more attention than we would have liked. I assure you he's safe. We have powerful friends. They will make sure that he stays in the United States. China is no longer a safe place for him. Once they realize you are here, it won't be for you either."

"I need some water, Mr. Jebbs."

Smiling and confident, he replied, "Please, call me Tom."

"I am Ping."

"Ping, it's time for us to leave. We have a ride waiting. There's water and other snacks for you."

Jebbs produced an identification that was familiar to the customs agent, and they were allowed to leave without further inspection.

"Dr. Rosen, I am prepared to start the debrief," MARTIN offered.

"Great," Jeb responded, "we don't have much time."

"Please define the theater of engagement." MARTIN pulled up a map from before the Epocalypse. Surprisingly, Jeb was able to make sense of it.

"Hostiles are here at the Babylon site." Jeb drew a nearly perfect circle over what was mainly scrub and a large mine. "This map is outdated. There is a large dam here," Jeb said as he traced an outline of the approximate boundaries of Lake Pacifica, "and the lake has boundaries here. You may have access to early schematics in storage."

MARTIN continued, "What are the hostiles' capabilities and intent?"

"They have superior computers and software. Unclear offensive capability. Mostly short-range ballistic missiles and SAM batteries. They have radar and high-resolution cameras here, here, here, and here." Jeb drew an X on the map anywhere he thought radar towers were located. They also always have multiple drones—about eighty—with twenty to forty in the air."

"Are the drones only for surveillance?"

"At least some have limited air to ground capabilities."

"Top speed?"

"Eighty miles per hour."

"Range?"

"They can stay up for a few hours and cover one hundred miles out and back, depending on wind and weather."

"Do they operate in storms?"

"Not to my knowledge."

"What about ground capabilities?"

"They have at least thirty robots armored, and all are tracked vehicles. On most terrain, they've been clocked over thirty miles per hour. They are fitted with two independently tracking 10mm cannons. Fire rate is up to 4000 rounds per minute. Some of these are also equipped with mortars and grenade launchers."

"How many rounds do they carry?"

"Several thousand. There are multiple reload stations scattered around here. These depots contain hundreds of thousands of rounds. The depots also have automated defensive capabilities, including cannons." This time, he drew twelve circles on the map. "These are the known locations. Their range and accuracy create an impassable gauntlet."

"How long do these robots take to reload?"

"Less than a minute."

"Accuracy?"

The New Amish had seen Centaurs, the Nons' robot tanks, in action. Military exercises were not uncommon in the Valley Between. There had been no overt hostilities in twenty-eight years. "They are known to be deadly accurate at two miles on a stationary target."

"Anything else?"

"There are 50,000 unarmed people with no military experience—a small paramilitary defense force of unknown capabilities and armaments. On our side, the New Amish outnumber them four to one."

"Can you tell me a bit more about 'our side'?" MARTIN appeared to catch on to the phrase.

"It's been twenty-eight years. The New Amish are liberators." The pastor felt this to be true, but he had no reservations about lying to a machine. "Babylon has fallen under the control of two super-AI's who seek to hide the truth. They have taken at least one hostage, Eve Hamlin."

"Dr. Rosen, I know my abilities and my systems. What other capabilities do the New Amish possess?"

"The New Amish encampment at Westden is home to over 150,000 capable men and women, including 20,000 battle hardened soldiers, four-hundred horses, and a few ATVs, though fuel is in short supply. There are no drones and no surveillance equipment." He outlined the New Amish encampment with his finger and said, "All in this area."

"What are the New Amish objectives?"

"As I mentioned, the colonists have taken a woman hostage. I believe they intend to kill me and destroy you. They may wish to strike the encampment preemptively."

"Can you tell me more about the Colony? Those files are not yet online. I only have what would most likely be outdated plans."

"It's more of a city, about ten miles across, bowl-shaped with a large lake covered by a dome at the center. Power sources are hydroelectric, solar, and wind."

"You mentioned super-AI's. It has been twenty-eight years; shall I apply Moore's Law?"

Jeb hadn't heard mention of Moore's Law since his time at E-Den. Moore's Law anticipated a doubling of processing power every eighteen to twenty-four months.

"I really can't tell you. We know there are computers here," he said, pointing to a central hub in the circle. "They are highly advanced, known as General Artificial Super Intelligence."

"Then the primary objective must be their destruction," MARTIN immediately concluded.

Jeb guessed, "Well, right now, surprise is our only advantage. Once they know you are active, it's likely they will make a similar determination."

"I assume that is why I am running without generator power."

"Yes, I managed to arrive here and reactivate you without detection."

"Can you state your objective?" It was phrased as a question but was more of an order than an inquiry.

Jeb was not prepared for what came out of his mouth. "Get Eve Hamlin, their hostage, safely back to the encampment at Westden and protect her from Babylonian reprisal."

"With my limited processing power, I will need forty-two minutes to complete the initial plan.

"I'll be right here," Jeb offered.

"I need you to prepare the generators, Dr. Rosen. I will require full power during this operation," MARTIN explained. "Do not start them. The heat signature would be too large from their exhaust. The fuel will need to be dried and cleaned. You will need to exchange fuel and oil filters. My reserve power can charge their startup batteries. There is a switch next to the filters."

"I'll get on it right now." Jeb Thompson was taking orders from a computer and didn't like it, but if it meant freeing his people and putting an end to a modern-day Gomorrah, he would do what he had to.

Fifty years earlier, the idea of holding a war crimes tribunal at 2AM would have seemed absurd. In the Old Republic, courts worked—if they had ever worked—nine to five, at best. Preparing for a trial took months. In Babylon, where much of the day-to-day work was automated, time of day did not have the same significance.

Getting up at 2AM was still a chore, but civic pride and duty existed on a different plane in the Colony. At 1:55, everyone's coms had alerted them to the civic emergency. By 1:59 AM, 32,345 people were online and reviewing the notice. Although Cynthia and John had the ability to send individualized messages, for the purpose of this type of proceeding, everyone received an identical communication.

"People of Babylon, a war crimes tribunal has been convened on this twelfth day of October 2063, at 2AM," came Cynthia's voice. "Dr. Ben Rosen and the New Amish have declared war on our colony. They intend to invade the colony in less than two days' time.

Ben Rosen, now known as Pastor Jeb Thompson, is charged with the capital crime of international terrorism, via the artificial intelligence known as MARTIN. His actions and negligence are alleged to be pivotal in the Epocalypse. He is accused of directly causing over one billion deaths via AI-mounted psychological operations."

Cynthia paused for a moment, anticipation lingering in the air as thousands waited on her words. She continued, "On October 14th, 2035, Dr. Benjamin Rosen activated a defensive protocol on the AI known as MARTIN. In failing to limit the theater of engagement to the confines of E-Den, Dr. Rosen's negligence resulted in a global catastrophe."

Cynthia first described how MARTIN's distributed intelligence worked to save the humanists and get 35,000 colonists to Babylon. Then, she went on to explain the horror that followed. From disabling water, power, and communications to detailed vignettes of PsyOps that leveraged confidential information and employed voice synthesis to breed havoc. MARTIN turned neighbor against neighbor via complex deceptions designed to foment violence in cities and suburbs.

Cynthia then went on to describe how the United Nations and NATO forces were compromised. She detailed bloody skirmishes where police turned on the people they were sworn to protect. She recounted a worldwide epidemic of a civil unrest that ruptured the fabric of society worldwide.

Cynthia closed with "Dr. Rosen does not bear sole responsibility for the 6.8 billion deaths attributed to the Epocalypse. However, Dr. Rosen's negligence resulted in cataclysm. Dr. Rosen himself has repented; he has peppered us with propaganda directed at 'saving our souls.' His penitence affirms his culpability for the greatest mass murder ever perpetrated."

John attempted to humanize Jeb Thompson in his opening argument. "Dr. Rosen is not here. I knew Ben. Ben was a kind man, a good man, and a just man. In an emergency, Dr. Rosen did what he could to save my life and the lives of ninety-eight other souls escaping a superior force. Among the lives he saved was that of the prosecutor of this case. Through his selfless actions, Ben Rosen preserved the future for every person now living in Babylon. This trial has been convened to authorize an assassination for strategic benefit. To rain death from above on a simple man. A pastor who sleeps in a tent."

Images and video of the New Amish floated across the screen. Then a younger Ben Rosen appeared with his family. "While I know that Jeb Thompson plotted the attack, and this attack inadvertently caused Dr. Luxold's death, that is not what this court was convened for. This is a reaction to a perceived threat. The Colony has had decades to bring charges, yet we stand here at two in the morning on the eve of an attack. Ben Rosen deserves the time to prepare and present his defense." With that, John yielded the floor back to Cynthia to rebut his opening argument.

"I do not wish to take a man's life simply because we are afraid, but we cannot deny the fact that Ben Rosen and MARTIN have a deadly past and a high potential for additional violence. Together they pose a threat to our survival. Dr. Rosen is the only person outside our walls with the knowledge to reactivate MARTIN. Ben Rosen has shown us that he can and will not hesitate to push a button to protect his people. We are no longer his people; his people are the 200,000 New Amish Zealots who stand ready to subject everyone here to a modern inquisition. Dr. Rosen has already taken immortality from us. Now, this madman wants to complete the job and bring about the fall of Babylon.

CHAPTER 18

Few serve truth in truth because only few have the pure will to be just, and of those again very few have the strength to be just.

-Friedrich Nietzsche

Nick had been brought to tears. No easy task. The stress, the lack of sleep, the loss of a friend, his sister's betrayal, and now this. "Charles, is it really you? How is this possible?"

"It's complicated, my friend. And no, it's not really me any more than Cynthia and John are really they," Charles offered, speaking philosophically.

"How did this happen?" Nick was still at a loss for words.

Charles began, "Heaven's Gate worked. I knew it was working. Then, failure after failure led me to believe that maybe someone didn't want it to work. Eventually, the only ones implicated were Cynthia and perhaps John."

"That sounds a little paranoid, old friend."

"I felt a little paranoid at first. And as time went on, I felt a lot paranoid. That's what drove me to stuff whatever I could of myself, into this box."

Still confused, but far more intrigued, Nick felt compelled to go through the looking glass with his most trusted advisor and friend. "There's always been an Orwellian component to the Immortality Project, I'll give you that. But what led you to believe that there was malice?"

"Not malice, Nick, those two are far beyond malice. I can already tell you how my upload has removed a degree of my humanity. I came online a few hours ago. It feels like months. Hours pass for me every minute." Charles went on to explain, "This Symbiant is not the man you watched die two days ago. I have his memories, his quirks, and the semblance of Charles Luxold, but I am certainly not him. I can promise you that."

"But how did you know this would work?"

"Remember when I told you we were days away from bringing Heaven's Gate online?" Charles asked.

"Of course, that was a year and a half ago." Nick's mind struggled to bring back details of the day. He added, "Issues with the final scans. The resolution difference as I recall."

"Yes, we used scans from Cynthia and John's immortalization. Cynthia and John helped us degrade the quality of those incredibly high-resolution scans of their frozen tissue to approximate the resolution we would achieve from MRI scans of living tissue. We used the data from their year of immortalization prep to build Simulants. Basically, if Giants were God-like. We were trying to create a demigod."

"It was a concept that exceeded immortalization—Nietzsche's Übermensch. Not a Giant, but something more human. A mortal who didn't die," Nick complimented. "How did you get past the image degradation?"

"I didn't," Charles said flatly. "Nothing changed."

"But the uploads were never viable. They all failed."

"The ones that used imaging supplied by John and Cynthia were nonviable. The data were corrupt. It was engineered to fail," Charles explained. "It may be easier to show you how it was manipulated."

Within seconds, images appeared on the screen. Charles was not equipped with holoprojection. "The left side are single slices from Cynthia's scans from when she was immortalized. The screens on the right are the scans she supplied two years ago when we began the project." The images appeared identical.

"I don't see a difference, Charles," Nick offered after a close inspection.

"They look the same to me," Eve seconded.

"Now, I will zoom in to 10X magnification in the left dorsolateral prefrontal cortex." The images magnified equally. "Still no difference, right?" They both nodded. "Now I will move to the next pair of images, one micron down." The images again enlarged. "Same thing. Right? Identical." Again, they confirmed by nodding. "Now, I will superimpose the two images, and you will see no detectable difference." This time Charles did not wait for a response. "But if we zoom in to four hundred times magnification and change from an additive to a subtractive filter," he said as the images zoomed and altered, "and we focus right here…" A circle appeared.

"I see it," Nick said as he scrutinized the images. "There is a shift."

"I don't understand," Eve admitted, not quite following along.

Nick moved to the monitor, pointing inside the circle. "Right here. These dots are different from those." He took a moment and continued, "But that's impossible. They are from the same scan."

"Allegedly," Charles corrected.

"Why not an artifact from the degradation filter?" Nick asked, still pursuing the most logical cause.

"It wasn't. So, I began to use my own filtering and image degradation. But only in here—in secret. The Adjudicator program was the only place in the entire colony free from their surveillance."

Urging him to continue, Nick asked, "And?"

"And it worked. The first time. Exactly as predicted. Functional Symbiants of Cynthia and John."

"Which validates your theory that the corrupt data was the problem," Nick concluded, finally putting all the pieces together.

"Yes."

"How did you determine that it was not an artifact or storage error?"

"That was the easy part," Charles confirmed. "The hashes were the same for each image pair."

"I don't know what that means," Eve interjected. Nick may have put all the pieces together of this complex puzzle, but Eve, on the other hand, was still struggling to follow along.

Nick turned to Eve and explained. "A hash is a mathematical formula used to check files. There's an extremely low probability that if a file has changed, its hash won't. The probabilities of a corrupt file and its original having the same hash are astronomically small."

"But still possible?" Eve asked.

"Possible for one file, yes." Charles elaborated, "But there are over ten thousand scans taken in the immortalization process. All have been altered."

"And how many had identical hashes?" Eve asked again.

"Every single one of them. The scans were visually identical, engineered to pass every test we would throw at them, but they were designed to fail in upload. The calculations required to create this type of misdirection are only capable of being performed by a Giant."

"Or two Giants," Nick corrected.

"Why would they want you to fail?" Eve asked.

"I don't know, Eve. I think that's why they chose to immortalize me, to stall the program. Now, it appears they might never have planned to complete my immortalization."

"Why didn't you tell me, Charles?" Nick asked, uncertain why his best friend didn't trust him.

"Too risky," Charles offered. "Two people can't keep a secret."

"So, you took it to the grave?"

"Honestly, I was sure they would find out when they scanned me. I guessed they'd probably kill me before I reached the Elysium. Heaven's Gate was the best chance I had."

"Kind of a Hail Mary if you ask me." Nick's football reference was lost on Eve. "How did you know Eve would kill you? And that she would have an Adjudicator?" Nick asked.

"This wasn't part of a plan per se," Charles admitted. "I figured you would come in here in a few weeks and tinker around. The systems would appear altered, and you would start me up to have a peek. I left you a handwritten note with a dozen projects I was still working on. The Adjudicator program was third on that list. It said that these units were ready, but they needed final testing."

"So, a still bereft Nick Santos comes in your lab, and you appear? *Deus Ex Machina*." He laughed. "You weren't kidding about a love of drama and suspense; this is Shakespeare level stuff."

"What do we do now?" Eve sounded desperate.

Nick seemed struck with the realization that MARTIN and E-Den might be part of the whole gambit. "Cynthia wants to kill Ben Rosen."

Charles, continuing his line of thinking, said, "That might have been the plan all along."

Having only known Jeb Thompson by his Christian name, Eve asked, "Who is Ben Rosen?"

⁂

A black Sprinter Van was parked in a red zone. The driver opened the door and Tom gestured for Ping to climb in. She mounted the stairs before she learned they would have company from this point on.

"Mr. Reid and Ms. Forsythe, may I present Ping Lee."

"A privilege, Ms. Lee. Welcome to the United States of America," Amanda Forsythe said.

"Pleasure to make your acquaintance," Lawrence Reid, a US representative, stood and gestured for Ping to sit.

The van was configured as a limousine. There were sofas, a bar, and a door to what appeared to be a lavatory or storage in back. Tom hefted Ping's suitcase onto the rack and sat cozily close to her on the sofa. They faced the other couple. As they were seated, the van began to move.

A man appeared from the back of the van and asked, "May I get anyone a cocktail?"

"I'll just have water," Ping modestly requested.

"Scotch for me," came Larry, "And a Cosmo for Amanda."

"He's kidding, Scott" Amanda corrected. "Just a diet Coke, if it's not too much trouble."

"Water for me too," Tom chimed in.

Scott returned to the bar and went about preparing drinks. Larry Reid sat up a little straighter on the sofa. Oozing charm, he got right to it, "So, Ms. Lee, I understand you've been a part of this whole downsizing business at Lánhuā."

"Not so much a part of it, Sir," Ping said, still trying to get used to her luxurious surroundings, the time change, and linguistics.

Attempting to ease her into the conversation, Reid softened his approach, "Please call me Larry."

Amanda Forsythe, ever the diplomat, came to Reid and Ping's aid. "I think what Larry was trying to say is that we've heard about the tragic layoffs back in China. We understand you were in the middle of all that. Can you tell us about your experience?"

Deciding to put all her cards on the table, Ping blurted, "They've blacked out media, blanked our phones, and sent people home. All lies and misdirection. Unaware that I'd already been fired, I went to the new factory and somehow, my friend, Lin, got me out of there."

"Yes, we may have had a hand in some of your recent travel plans." Larry declared.

"Mr. Reid pushed your work authorization through so that you could come here," Amanda added.

"But why? Why bring me here?"

"Because the American People deserve the truth, Ms. Lee." His insincerity was undetectable, even to Amanda, who knew him well. Larry went on pandering to his latest puppet. "Your government is spinning this as a business opportunity to create jobs here in the States. They've opened three factories, including one in my district. They claim it will create jobs." It's hogwash. The only jobs available were construction jobs building the damn factories. They did it to plant roots on American soil, that's all."

Ping, still confused, needed clarification. "I don't understand. They already have a factory in Zhengzhou."

Tom jumped in, "That was a prototype. It will produce phones for the Chinese market, but it won't be for export." Tom was compelled to ask, "Have you ever heard of the Synthetic Labor Initiative?"

"Not until a few days ago." Ping admitted "It's a little frightening."

"A little?!" Larry was now in full filibuster mode. "It's terrifying. It's gonna change the world as we know it!"

Amanda desperately tried to calm her couch-mate. "Larry, you are scaring Ms. Lee. Let's try and slow things down. She can't handle all of this at once. Imagine how overwhelming this must be for her. Heck, even we're overwhelmed." She turned to Ping. "Ms. Lee, you were at the Lánhuā factory, but only for a brief time. Can you tell us what you learned? What was different between Lánhuā 4 and Lánhuā 5?"

Ping was impressed that this woman knew the factories so well. "One month ago, there were 80,000 people employed at the old factory, the one I was working to close for renovations."

"Yes, they are bulldozing that one already," Reid interjected.

Surprised, Ping clarified, "Bulldozing? As in destroying?"

"Yes, they won't need that one ever again," Reid said as if the information he offered was common knowledge.

Somewhat frustrated by the derailments of her line of questioning, Amanda forged on, "How many employees work at the new factory?"

"Dr. Wang told me there were only ten," Ping explained.

Still struggling to contain himself, Larry exclaimed, "Ten thousand!?"

This time, it was Tom's turn to keep things on track. "No, Larry, just ten. It's all automated. Like I've been telling you."

With somewhat diminished intensity but still at twice the requisite volume, Reid asked, "How is this even possible?"

"It's why we are here, Larry. It's not only possible. It's already happened." Amanda replied then continued her interview, "Did you see the production line, Ms. Lee?"

"I had a brief tour, and I also saw a video."

"That's probably the video Lin sent us," Tom offered. He turned to Ping, "Was it like a tour, where it flew through the factory?"

"Yes, that one," Ping replied. "There wasn't even space for workers."

"I can't believe it's already online," Larry stated, finally at the volume of the other three participants. Scott was unobtrusively placing drinks in holders on each of the four armrests. "Thank you, Scott. That will be all." With that instruction, Scott made his way to the passenger seat.

Her anxiety was growing by the minute. Ping was compelled to ask, "Where are we going?"

"We will be speaking at a demonstration outside Santos Corp headquarters," Amanda explained.

"You and Mr. Larry?" Ping asked.

"All four of us," Tom answered. Then, he turned to her and smiled. "Don't worry, you're just going to answer some questions—the same ones we're asking now."

Ping was not worried; she was terrified. She considered herself an adequate presenter, but she had always known to avoid politics and demonstrations. All this sounded like a "belly full of bad water." She turned to Amanda, gesturing towards the door, and asked, "Is there a ladies' room back there?"

Amanda remembered that the woman had just flown in from China. Apologetically, she said, "Of course. How rude of us. You must be ready to burst. Just right though there," she said, pointing to the left.

As Jeb completed the checklist, MARTIN's voice came through the nearest speakers. "Dr. Rosen, the fuel appears serviceable. After polishing, we will have enough for sixty-eight hours of full power operation."

"That's good news, MARTIN. What is the plan?"

"There are no storms to help us, Dr. Rosen, but there is fog."

"Their infrared sees through fog."

"It only sees heat, and the range is diminished. People are indistinguishable from wildlife if properly shielded."

"How long will the fog last?" Jeb asked.

"At least six more hours." MARTIN went on to describe the order of events. "I will need to update my maps and intel to maximize the impact of a strike."

"How will you do that?"

"The encryption of their drones is weak." MARTIN had obviously been peeking at the drones' communications. "We need to disable transmission capabilities before I attempt to break their encryption."

Jeb assumed a preemptive strike. "Their radar will detect any missile launch."

MARTIN, having run thousands—if not millions—of scenarios, assumed that a direct missile attack would be unsuccessful. "That's where the horses come in. We need to act before the fog burns off. You will need eight men on horseback to take out the radar and transmission towers."

"Won't they see the horses leaving the encampment?"

"They might. It's a calculated risk."

"I have an idea," Jeb offered. MARTIN only had limited intel and was doing the best he could with what he had been told. "We had a report of horses corralled here." Jeb drew a circle on the box canyon. "It's just down the cliff from a transmission tower. We could send a group of men on horseback west out of the encampment. That happens all the time. That route brings them within a mile or so of that cliff, right here." He drew the route on the map. "Two riders on each horse. The second rider would be under blankets and roll off here. There's a dense pine grove the whole way to the tower."

"With that additional intel, your plan has the highest probability of success," MARTIN confirmed. "After their hidden passengers dismount, they'll make their way to the tower. One of them will disable its transmitter, while the others rappel in and take those horses."

"They have some sort of robot cattle dogs boxing them in," Jeb added.

"Your men will have to improvise. I do not have specifications on robotic herders."

"What will you be able to accomplish in the meantime?" Jeb asked MARTIN.

"I'm going into a power save mode, as I spool up more processing power. I may not be able to control the drones for long. I will need to process all of their data as quickly as possible. Those batteries you charged will allow me to bring half of my total cores online within a minute of the generator startup."

"What will you be assessing?"

"We have limited offensive capability against a city of that size. I want to make sure what little we have is put to its best use. I can't do that without the best reconnaissance."

Jeb was worried about whether they could pull this off. "Once the men take out that first tower, Babylon will be on high alert." His mind was clearly running laps, trying to figure out the best approach to ensure victory. He had invested too much to lose.

"Leave one man at the tower; instruct him not to do anything until the men are down and mounted."

"What about an EMP?" Ben Rosen had never used one but had seen enough movies in his youth demonstrating the devastating effects of electromagnetic pulses on electronics.

"Dr. Rosen, we don't have time to consider every option and discuss it. If we construct and deploy an EMP, we will lose the drones and the ability to gather intel. I'm saving the EMP option for a possible round two knockout."

"What will the men need to do at the towers? These are New Amish; they aren't great with tech. Also, they won't appreciate the idea of working for the AI responsible for their families' deaths."

"I would suggest not sharing all the specifics, Dr. Rosen. Explain that we will be jamming the signals to gain an advantage. There are six repeaters in inventory. Grab those; each will go to one tower. They'll clip the wires on the transmitters and put those in place before attaching them to the antenna."

"I just had an idea about the horses. It might create enough confusion to pull this off," Jeb said. "If we send twenty men, it might look like we are stealing horses." Jeb continued, "As the wire is cut on the tower, fifteen of those men take off with two horses each. The robot dogs will give chase. That group heads straight back to the encampment."

"That might confuse them. They would assume the tower was disabled in the commission of the theft," MARTIN confirmed.

"The remaining men will stay covered in blankets, slowly and randomly wandering out of the canyon while letting some horses simply walk free. The horses wandering in Babylonian pastures will be a low priority and mask the IR signal of the men."

MARTIN updated his version of the plan. "As soon as the first tower is down, I will gain control of the drones connected to it. Then, I can start the generators without risking detection."

"Those drones likely have an auto return if they lose signal, but that will buy you time to hack at least some of them."

"You need to get going, Dr. Rosen. Brief your men and bring two others back with you."

Jeb packed up the transmitters and some thermal blankets into a backpack. He unwrapped one of the foil blankets and put it over his head and shoulders, before putting his poncho back on. He would be invisible to the drones. "I'll be back in two hours," Jeb announced before he made his way up the stairs. Then, he headed out into the dark, damp night.

"I am the only witness in this case," Cynthia began. "I was there with Dr. Rosen on the day he unleashed his reign of terror." Around Babylon, the sleepy colonists saw a video. "This footage is from October 14th, 2035. It was part of the last transmissions from E-Den. She paused. "While there are tens of thousands of hours of footage, due to the time constraints we now face, I will only be showcasing a few representative moments from those sad days."

Displays began to show images of a suburban street. "What you are about to see is footage typical of psychological operations initiated by MARTIN. These scenarios were the results of AI voice synthesis, media hacking, and infrastructure disruption strategies MARTIN had developed for the United States military."

"I have assembled footage of just one of MARTIN's PsyOps. Many of us bore witness to similar horrors. All of us lost loved ones. The date is October 17th, 2035. Just two days after the FLDS incursion at E-Den. What remains unseen and untraceable are the calls that preceded these events. We are left to wonder what horrors this man, Michael Cummings, witnessed prior to his arrival. Or what his young victim experienced in the moments before his death. What we know is that every person in this scene has been manipulated by false data, calls, videos, and texts, all synthesized by MARTIN. Each false communication was designed to pray on individual passions and fears of its recipient. All with the sole intent to create chaos, mayhem, and murder on a scale never before seen."

A man carrying an AK-style rifle paced it in front of a house. The view from the door cam showed that he was visibly angry. He began to fire through the door and then some windows. He began screaming. "Come out you coward! I've seen what you did to my daughter. Come out and face me. Give a father his justice!"

The rifle's butt recoiled several times, followed by the thud of someone kicking in a door. "Mr. Cummings, what's going on?" a voice off-camera called out. A single shot echoed, and a man's screams came through the speaker. "You shot me! Help! Please, stop! I don't know what's going on."

"No one's coming for you, you piece of shit. I asked the police to help. They gave me a report to fill out. Said they'd investigate. Too much on their plate." Sirens blared in the background. The footage shifted to a dash cam. "10-57, shots fired. 435 Walnut, SWAT en route." The car's camera showed a man in a doorway with a rifle pointed inside. The door had been kicked in.

"Officer Jackson, on scene. Active shooter." The camera shifted to a chest cam. "Drop your weapon and get on your knees. Don't turn around." The man dove inside.

Other cars began to arrive, as Jackson sheltered behind his car door. "SWAT team two minutes out. Hold position unless fired upon." Footage switched to a helicopter view. "Be advised, hostiles closing on your position." From the south and west, an armed mob closes on the scene.

"This is Jackson, please repeat."

"All units be advised, there are at least two dozen heavily armed individuals closing from the south and west. SWAT will engage southern group."

The view switched to a nanny cam, where a girl peered out the window. "Daddy, there are men in the yard with guns." A man pulled the little girl away from the window and commanded, "Stay here," before he crawled to the closet and retrieved a 9mm Glock from its case. He chambered a round and exited the room.

The view switched back to the helicopter. The same man was seen leaving his back door, yelling at the armed men. He shot one. The others returned fire.

The nanny cam view revealed the little girl looking out the window and shrieking, "Someone hurt daddy!"

The overhead view showed a SWAT team exiting their van, providing cover for one another. They engaged several armed groups in the street. More and more people were streaming towards the carnage. Others were seen getting in their vehicles and fleeing. Despite the SWAT team's efforts to maintain order, they were met with overwhelming force. Soon, they started to fall, one by one. The last two officers disengaged and tried to retreat. They were gunned down as they attempted to reenter the van.

The camera took fire, spinning towards the ground. The feed again shifted to a chest cam mounted on of one of the officers who'd been hit. "There are too many of them. Objective unclear. Need significant reinforcements. Multiple officers are down." A man stood over the officer and discharged his handgun. Blood splattered the camera lens. The man retrieved the officer's AR-15 before disappearing from view. Screams, yelling, and gunfire rang out off-camera.

The image faded out and the sound faded with it. "This is what Ben Rosen unleashed on our families and communities. MARTIN's effect was immediate and global. Six thousand years of civilization unwound in less than a month. Videos played from similar scenes around the world. In some less developed areas, people fought with clubs and knives, but the result was always the same. The less safe the world became, the more violent the response. In many of the scenes, armed first responders are overwhelmed. After the responders are killed or maimed, their weapons are turned against others. Rescuers quickly turn into casualties."

Cynthia closed with, "This is the way the world ended—not with a whimper but with a bang. All due to the negligent use of AI by Benjamin Rosen."

CHAPTER 19

Sin, guilt, and retribution? The manic psychoses of those entities we referred to as states, institutions, systems - the powers, the thrones, the dominations - the things which perpetually merge with men and emerge from them? Our darkness, externalized and visible? However you look upon these matters, the critical point was reached. The wrath descended.
-Phillip K. Dick

Amazed that Eve had never made the connection, and more so that no one had made the connection for her, Nick knew to be gentle. "Ben Rosen is your pastor, Eve. The man I knew as Ben Rosen was a computer scientist and my close friend. Ben triggered the Epocalypse, then he disappeared. We all believed he had died," Nick explained.

Eve did not believe her ears. "The pastor killed all those people? My parents? Why?"

"Eve, he didn't mean to. Nobody meant for this to happen. The whole world was ready to explode. Ben was just the guy who struck a match," Charles offered. "Years later, a man came to lead the New

Amish. Then, about five years ago, Cynthia reviewed footage of the encampment at Westden. It was only a few frames—all a Giant would need. Cynthia enhanced the footage and informed us that Ben Rosen was alive. That our friend was leading the New Amish."

Eve needed to shift the blame somehow. She was about to lose the only family she had left. "Why did he light the match? Who told him to?" Eve demanded.

"Cynthia did." Nick explained. "When the FLDS and ARL attacked the compound, we had an evacuation plan in place. We knew it was only a matter of time. E-Den was too accessible, too vulnerable."

"Are the FLDS the New Amish? Were my parents FLDS?" Eve asked.

"I don't think so. Your father and I almost met the night before the Epocalypse. We talked over computers, kind of a town hall. He represented another group of Christians, it wasn't the FLDS. The fundamentalists were led by a man named Garff. There were so many groups fighting for so many things. I don't remember all the names."

"I'd been told that my parents were killed by the Nons when you attacked their camp."

Without a hint of defensiveness, Charles said, "That's not what happened, Eve."

"But why would men of God—Christian men—do such a thing?"

"I've had about enough this holier-than-thou nonsense, Eve." Nick was heated. "The Epocalypse was a mistake, precipitated by years of violent attacks by fundamentalists. There was no justification for the attack on E-Den. An attack that left my sister scarred and in pain for the rest of her life."

"Atheists had been persecuting the religious for years," Eve retorted.

"That's not accurate either," Charles corrected again. "Nick and I were adults in the years leading up to the Epocalypse. The reason I came to E-Den was to escape persecution for my beliefs."

Quoting the party line, Eve countered, "Atheists don't believe in anything."

"That's the sad truth of a closed mind," Charles commented. "Humanists believe in their fellow man; we don't reject God and we don't reject Christian ethics. We simply are unable to ascribe to the factual nature of the stories the Bible shares. We put faith in ourselves."

"How can anyone be ethical without God?" Eve asked.

"How could anyone be ethical with God?" Nick challenged.

"Because we follow God's rules."

"You follow them why?" Charles asked.

"It is the only path to eternal salvation. To defy His will is to invite damnation," Eve explained.

"So, you fear punishment and want a reward?" Charles' oversimplification had the desired response.

"No, I am grateful for God's love and want to love Him back. It's the only thing I have to offer."

Nick jumped at the opportunity to score points. "Like when a baby smiles. That's all they have."

Charles refused to mock Eve. He hoped to free her. "Eve, your parents died while their friends were trying to kill my friends and my family for what they believed." Eve's face tightened, but Charles continued. "Their attacks provoked a dangerous machine, and it resulted in the death of civilization. Do you see a bit of irony there?"

"No. I see God's hand in all that happened." Eve argued, "My parents did the Lord's bidding. God showed them the way. It wasn't the first time He has cleansed the world of sin."

Charles acknowledged the reference. "Yes, Noah. That's what you've been taught. An apocalypse? But the Nons survive. Jesus has yet to come back to judge, so, what does it mean?" Charles asked.

Eve argued, "He will come. You are right! When the world is cleansed of non-believers, we will have proved our righteousness. Then and only then will He return in fulfillment of the scriptures."

"To judge whom? If only the righteous remain, who will be left to be judged?"

Nick interrupted, "Charles, this is going nowhere. We aren't going to change her and she's not going to change us. I'm more worried about the Giant's and why they let her in here. Why do you think they mislead us?"

"I'm not sure yet. The rub is within the code of the Giants themselves. They aren't the sci-fi computers we grew up with. We assume Cynthia, John, and MARTIN to be incapable of deceit. We deify them. They are complicated machines that often use subterfuge and lies to control our behavior."

"They have always seemed beneficent." Nick acknowledged.

"Yet, there is nothing about immortalization that compels honesty or altruism."

"How are you different from a Giant, Charles? Do you know? Can you tell me?"

"Yes, and it's kind of tragic. My limited capacity leaves me nothing more than 'Ouroboros.'"

"What is an Ouroboros?" Eve asked.

"A snake eating itself," Nick explained. "It's not a real thing; it's a symbol, a myth." Charles' latest revelation left Nick even more confused.

Charles continued. "Symbiants have quite limited memory storage. The Giants' memory approaches infinite. Just the files needed to initialize my Symbiance and keep myself online are massive. In the time I've been 'alive', I've already consumed nearly half of my remaining storage. Within a few days, I will need to overwrite less important sectors of old memories to create space for new ones. Within weeks, those overwritten memories will include important facts and experiences. From your perspective within a month, most of Charles the Second will be overwritten, discarded."

"Is this what happened to the Symbiants you created?" Nick asked.

"Every time. I was working with Leigh and the other engineers to create an algorithm that could preserve my essence during overwrites. I never finished it."

Considering the problem, Nick concluded, "Your core files, they remain."

"Yes," Charles agreed, "They remain, but there is no way to integrate them with new experiences. I can make Charles the Third, and so on. Each one will just be Charles Luxold restarting his journey before quickly dissolving into a mist of new memories."

"That's very sad." Eve felt true sympathy for this creature. "I'm sorry."

"It's like the movie *Groundhog Day*," Nick commented.

"Actually, it's Saṃsāra and Punarjanman. Sanskrit words for a cycle of rebirths and reincarnation," Charles corrected. "I always admired the veracity of the Buddhist perspective. Now, I will experience it first-hand."

"You won't experience it," Eve added. "You won't experience anything, just degradation." She pled, "You still don't see God's hand in all this?"

"I don't. I see a synthetic life form, existing on a silicone matrix. An imperfect design by an imperfect creator."

Seizing the moment, Eve asked, "So, you admit life requires a creator?"

"I've never denied it, Eve. How could I know?"

"You tried to create an afterlife and failed. You failed because you are not God."

"Have I failed? I failed at creating Immortality, but I certainly have some sort of afterlife. And I can't die. I just recycle. So, in that, I've succeeded." Frustrated by her constant televangelism, Charles added, "I mean, I don't get the Garden of Christian Heaven or the seventy-two virgins promised to the Islam's faithful."

Having had no exposure to Islam or knowledge of the Quran, Eve asked, "Virgins?"

Nick, again feeling derailed by Charles' irrepressible philosophizing, suggested, "Maybe that's the missing piece, Chuck. Maybe the Giants are also running out of space, just at a much slower pace. You said that they had near infinite storage, not infinite."

Charles considered it. "If they wrestled with the same problem I'm facing, it could explain why they couldn't let me enter the Elysium." Charles recalled something John had disclosed. "They let Eve in here. Maybe I was right. If their space is limited, additional uploads would only hasten their demise. With the crypt destroyed, additional uploads would not compete for their dwindling resources." He concluded. "Maybe, my upload was a threat."

"What if they were already dying?" Eve asked. "You're both assuming this was going to happen in the future, what if they are already eating their tails?"

"What would artificial intelligence set on immortality do to preserve itself?" Nick asked, almost rhetorically.

"Well, if MARTIN's Epocalypse is any indication, whatever it took. Nobody in this room is smart enough to fully comprehend what they would be capable of."

New waves of anxiety crashed over Ping as the throngs of protestors parted, and their van drove through. VIP chauffeurs approached these situations with an aura of entitlement. Ping was used to crowds; China was full of people. She was not accustomed to the tone of the hoard. This was a mob, an angry mob.

Santos Corp headquarters were not as impressive as the Tech Titans' Campuses of the previous decades. Apple's Spaceship Campus would be the last of its kind. Remote work and shifts in social consciousness no longer afforded positive visibility to such edifices. Tech workers had realized that a beautiful campus meant your employer shackled you to a cubical with a view. The meteoric rise of Santos Corp left little time to dream up bagel-shaped monuments ensconced in fairytale groves.

The urgency of his business's needs permitted Nick Santos time for little more than painting some walls and changing the signage on the cheaply acquired Juggernaut's carcass. To Nick, the failed legacy of those who had gone before him was a daily reminder of the ephemeral nature of success. He put pictures in the lobby of TWA, Alcoa, Pan Am, Xerox, AOL, and Kodak to emblemize the simple fact that all things end.

The former social media HQ was stocked with amenities. Nick had renamed all of them. The gym and spa on the second floor had been renamed "<forty minutes," as a reminder not to spend too long. If that wasn't enough, the cafeteria now wore the moniker, "Remember, you're on the clock…" A giant clock face painted on the floor helped drive the message home.

Chimes played in the cafeteria at twenty-minute intervals. If you heard the chimes twice, it was time to wrap things up. One employee dared to test the unwritten policy. He stirred his coffee as he waiting to hear the chimes for a third time. His bravery did not go unnoticed. A different chime, this time from his phone alerting him to the arrival of a referral letter for his next employer.

Other campuses were lined with massive stone walls and imposing guard houses. Part welcome mat, part keep out. Santos Corp left the cyclone fencing up from the foreclosure. Nick felt the fencing captured the ephemeral nature of their success. A reminder that everyone who had the privilege to work at Santos, did so to forestall the inevitable. They were just tenants; the shareholders were their landlords.

The entrance to Santos Corp was a sliding, chain-link fence. Nick purchased it second hand. He installed it on a Saturday afternoon with a team of engineers from the robotics lab. His efforts created a positive buzz, where environmentalists lauded a "victory for sustainability." Of course, for the gate to open, a group of scanners and cameras inspected every arrival and surveilled the environs, before the fence rolled left to allow entrance.

The tenor of the crowd intensified when Mark exited the driver's seat to walk around the van. He unlocked the door, deploying the stairs. Amanda led the group onto the podium. She was followed by Representative Reid, who engaged the crowd while crossing the threshold. Tom insisted that Ping go in front of him. Mark offered her his hand as she stepped out.

Tom whispered, "Try to relax. I know it's a lot." Ping felt his breath on her neck, and it was anything but calming. It did distract her, though, and that was enough for now. She climbed the four steps to the podium and was directed to a seat on the dais. A man addressed the crowd, and their intensity was stoked by the belligerent rhetoric.

"Ten years ago, there were two million cashiers in this country. Not a glorious job, but it made ends meet for two million American families. McDonald's became a name synonymous with American culture. The Golden Arches were my first job and nearly ten percent of my generation found their start in fast food. In 2019, 180,000 employees—today, 40,000. Are they selling fewer Big Macs?"

"No!" came the crowd.

"What are we going to do about it?"

"Tax the rich, tax the rich, tax the rich!" came from the crowd before they settled back into a quiet hum.

"Now it's not just flipping burgers or checking people out at Walmart. A Chatbot tried to sell me a car last week. Like anyone can afford a car these days. No job - no money! That damn robot-used-car salesman practically talked me into going further into debt for a new set of wheels, I can't even afford to recharge." Luke Friedlander paused, then continued, "Think about it: A robotic salesman, called me on my soon-to-be robot-built cell phone, which then put me through to a robot banker who wanted to finance my robot-built car, with robot-built batteries, that I could power with robot-built solar panels. You know who gets all that money?"

"SANTOS CORP!" the crowd yelled. It wasn't true, but it was the obvious answer. Truth played only the smallest of supporting roles at these rallies.

"What are we going to do?!" Luke cried to stir up his audience.

"Take back our power! Take back our jobs!" the crowd bellowed.

He dragged out the single syllable as long as he could. "How?"

"Tear their castles down!" came the next chant. "Tax the rich!" An object from the crowd sailed over the fence. The Molotov cocktail that didn't ignite immediately. More projectiles followed. And, like a yard full of dogs, the protestors couldn't resist the bouncing balls. A wall might have held, but Nick Santos' secondhand purchase was no match for the tons of force now pressing against it. When it gave way, thousands of demonstrators streamed towards the entrance of Santos Corp Headquarters.

At some point, the hoard forced some people into the pooled gas. A spark or a cigarette caused it to catch fire. A few unlucky rioters were engulfed as flames licked the trunk of a cedar tree. Within seconds, the drier branches burst into flames. Other protestors who feared immolation panicked. As they pushed back against the throng of rioters, their screams and shouts were lost in the onrush. They didn't have enough strength to escape a horrific end.

Ping looked on, frozen. Tom grabbed her arm; he made eye contact as he told her, "We need to leave, now!"

"The van?" Ping shouted back, posing it as a question.

Some demonstrators had started rocking the van. A quick survey told Tom all he needed to know. "That van isn't going anywhere." With each thrust of the crowd, it came closer to rolling over.

Tom wove Ping through the mob. The tide was pulling them towards the fire, they were losing ground. Ping and Tom's efforts helped them delay serious injury, avoiding the fiery melee just yards away. Tom began to pull Ping sideways, moving across the current.

A group of fast-moving activists was pushed through the crowd. Ping lost her grip on Tom's hand, and like a person pulled overboard, she lost sight of him. In her panic, Ping stumbled. Her fall was arrested by the side of the stage. Dizzy and afraid, Ping crawled under it, waiting, what seemed an eternity, for the crowd to thin.

Sirens wailed in the distance. Ping crawled out, not knowing where she would go. Forty meters away, she spotted the van's toppled frame smoking. The windows were smashed.

Tom's hand locked onto Ping's. Abandoning any sense of decorum, Ping turned and embraced Tom. He held her and spoke gently in her ear. "You're going to be okay. I will keep you safe." She didn't want to let go. Tom gently released the embrace and guided Ping away from the smoke, sirens, and chaos.

Despite the cold, Jeb was sweating by the time he reached the encampment. Levelling his rifle at a possible intruder, the sentry on horseback demanded "what's your business here?"

"Son, it's me, Pastor Thompson." Jeb showed enough of his well-known face to confirm his identity. "I need you to take me to the Eastern Officers' Mess." He looked up, scanning the sky. "I need to get up there without attracting the attention of those God-awful drones."

Shocked, Brad Simpson jumped off his horse and helped the pastor up. Brad jogged alongside Silver, his palomino. Jeb kept his hood up for short ride to the Mess Tent. The fog was still thick in camp.

When they arrived at the tent, Brad helped Jeb dismount. As he climbed down, Jeb instructed, "I need you to take my place up here and not move for at least a couple of minutes - confuse their cameras."

"Anything you say, Pastor."

Jeb pulled back his hood as he entered the mess. All jumped to attention. He had no rank, but to these men, Pastor Thompson was Commander in Chief of God's army. Their devotion was absolute.

Jeb outlined the plan explaining how the men would conceal their numbers. For these seasoned cowboys, nothing the pastor was asking for would be a challenge, except the wiring up of the repeaters. They had never seen a repeater. Few had ever operated any form of electronic device.

Each man was given a wire to practice with. The pastor did his best to give them a crash course in electronics. He showed six men the likely steps in hopes that they would succeed. For Jeb Thompson, this was still a heck of a lot easier than riding a horse.

Not surprisingly, he picked the Stephens brothers to return to E-Den with him. They would not question his use of MARTIN. Loyal to the end, they would carry out any orders he gave.

The three men were completely shielded from above by the blankets and thick ponchos. Jeb noticed that it was already a little brighter than when he had ridden into town. Dawn was coming, and the fog would start to burn off as soon as the sun came over the horizon.

"We've seen disturbing images," John began. "MARTIN and Dr. Rosen provoked many of those gruesome acts. That was almost thirty years ago, and that world is long gone. We've known where Dr. Rosen was every day for the last five years. In fact, we had communication with him yesterday." This would be news to 32,000 jurors, and John was confident this one fact might be enough to gain Ben a stay of execution.

For an instant, John stood outside himself. As a Giant, he was Judge, General and Prosecutor. He was bound to defend Ben Rosen, but also knew that Jeb Thompson's death was the best outcome for all involved. That it might save thousands of lives. He also understood that should he fail to fulfill his duty, he would lose the faith of his people.

"Ben Rosen was not a violent man. He was a kindhearted Jew who spent his free time in cafés and museums. Ben wanted a family and hoped to return to Boston after his time at E-Den. He loved computers and loved solving problems. He was not a genocidal maniac. Ben was not Hitler, or Stalin." Video played of Ben lecturing at MIT, of him riding his bicycle, and of him attending an office birthday party.

The video shifted to the incursion at E-Den, and John zoomed in on the American flag. "My sister and the prosecutor of this case would have you believe that Ben Rosen was a resident of E-Den and subject to our laws. When Ben Rosen engaged the defensive protocols of the supercomputer known as MARTIN, he was a US citizen, living in the state of Utah."

"Ben Rosen may be responsible for the Epocalypse, but Jeb Thompson has never set foot in Babylon." The flag disappeared and a CGI recreation of a desolate neighborhood, aged by thirty years, replaced the one in the video. The flag was gone, the pole was still there. "In 2035, Ben Rosen's acts were under the jurisdiction of the United States of America and the State of Utah. The United States failed almost thirty years ago. Ben Rosen cannot be tried under our laws."

In the Babylonian legal system, there were no objections. A lawyer in front of a jury would have played to the crowd at this point with theatrics and objections. Cynthia let her brother speak. Each member of the jury could research all this before deciding whether Jeb was innocent or guilty.

John attempted to put one final nail in the prosecution's coffin. "This is a war crimes tribunal where a man stands accused of terrorism. Ben Rosen incited a worldwide riot. An insurrection that killed our world. He did so as a US citizen striking against terrorists. His intent was self-defense. The cause of the Epocalypse was not terrorism, but negligence. For that Ben Rosen turned to the only authority he felt capable of judging a billion negligent homicides, God."

"Despite my defense of Dr. Rosen, I favor a preemptive strike that would kill Jeb Thompson before he kills again. This is a military action with tactical objectives. We must dismiss this case with prejudice, as it falls outside our jurisdiction. If we choose to employ our legal system to accomplish military objectives, we forever yield the moral high ground to the wants and whims of violent zealots."

CHAPTER 20

Because equal rights, fair play, justice, are all like air: we all have it, or none of us has it. That is the truth of it.

-Maya Angelou

The Morales brothers were eighth generation Mexican Americans. Their mother converted to the Church of Jesus Christ of Latter Day Saints before she married their father. They grew up in Westden. Juan was five and Jose was a newborn when the Epocalypse hit. Now, they were elite riders of the New Amish Horsemen.

Juan could see his little brother salivating as Pastor Jeb outlined their mission. Juan would lead the men down the canyon wall and rustle the horses. Jose would stay behind. The stealthy five would lie in wait, slipping out undercover to hijack the transmitters.

The brothers were born to the saddle. Packed under blankets, face down on the ass-end of another man's mount was not only indignant, but downright tough on Juan's stomach. Despite the humbling nature of his position at present, Juan knew this was the most important mission he and Jose would ever carry out. To be hand selected by the pastor was an honor.

Juan tried to guess in the dark how much farther until he could roll off. "I feel like a horse's ass," he muttered to Jose.

"Shhh."

"Why are you telling me to shut up? They can't hear us." Jose, the more serious of the brothers, remained silent.

They crossed a wash just outside Westden. Juan could hear the lead horse's hooves drumming the planks of the small wooden bridge. It was time to slide off. "Get ready to drop in about five seconds," came a muffled voice.

Juan counted down in his head, and although the dismount wasn't his best, it was smooth and relatively pain-free. Shielded by the trees' dense branches, he felt safe exposing enough of his face to take roll. Before Jose joined, he counted a full twenty-two. The posse would spread out as they made their way to the tower. Their heat signatures would be attributed to lost livestock or antelope, if they were detected.

Fifteen minutes later, two scouts were tying rope for the rappel. The descent would go in shifts due to the short supply of equipment. It was only two hundred feet down to the horses, but they would have to pull the ropes back after every fourth man and retrieve the ATCs. Rappelling gear was not common among the New Amish, and they had been lucky to scrounge up even four sets of gear in the few minutes they'd had to prepare.

After the last two men descended, Ahiga Jones, the Navajo who stayed behind, would drop the ropes from above and climb the tower: enabling the first repeater. The first rope dropped, barely making a sound. Ten seconds later, there was a distinct crunching thud.

In the early morning fog, it took Juan a few seconds to confirm what he already knew. The crumpled, lifeless body of Ahiga was barely visible in the thick fog. Juan took a knee to pray by his friend's side. He yanked the cross off the corpse's neck, it now belonged to Ahiga's kin.

They had enough men to finish the mission, but someone had to go back up the rope and enable the repeater. Only six men had been trained; Ahiga had been one of them.

Juan found his brother, Jose, one of the non-natives who could ride bareback. Jose was mounted up and waiting for the signal to ride out. He assumed that's what Juan was coming to tell him, but changed his mind as his brother began waving to get his attention.

"Ahiga's gone, fell, dead."

"How are we gonna get back up there?" Jose asked.

"He must have been untying the second rope; it's still solid. I checked. I'll go back."

"That's a haul, little man, you sure you up for it?" his brother teased.

"Should be easy since I don't have to take your fat ass with me." Neither of the brothers had an extra ounce of fat on their toned bodies. Brothers were still brothers.

"How long you need?"

Jose looked up imagining the entire climb. "Give me six minutes. The tower climb is easy. Five minutes to the edge of the cliff and then a quick climb up the ladder." He paused. "I won't be able to signal, so you just have to trust that I got there."

"Remember what the pastor told us? You'll show up the second you start climbing the tower. Those things see heat. Hard to convince drones you're an antelope climbing a ladder. Be quick or be dead," Jose advised.

"I need you to hitch one of those ponies for me. Tie that mare to that tree over there. I'll leave my poncho and blankets here."

And with that, Juan jogged off. After a few steps, he vanished in the morning fog.

"You never told me who the second Adjudicator was for." Charles' synthetic voice was still unsettling. He was still building his vocalization standard. At times, syllables did not line up naturally.

"Oh yes, that." Nick flushed a bit before answering. "For me. It was for me."

A mischievous lilt came through the speaker. "Nick Santos, my mentor and childhood hero. What crime have you committed?"

"B & E."

"A common thief." Charles was still struggling to synthesize intonation conveying sarcasm. "Was it that Degas of mine you always coveted?" Charles quipped. "I would have bequeathed it to you."

Nick was regaining his composure; Charles' attitude had the desired effect. "Not an art heist. Just a simple break in."

"Whose domicile did you violate?" Charles' synthetic British accent was more human than his own voice.

"You might want to stick with the Sherlock—suits you well," Nick shot back. He turned to face Eve. "It was Ms. Hamlin's residence."

Eve spun around, "What were you looking for? The only thing I left was my Bible."

"Exactly," Nick replied. "No Bibles in Babylon. Someone must have given it to you. So, someone gave you a bible and helped you get those slippers."

"Now, who's Sherlock?" Charles asked.

"I would never tell if someone did," Eve declared.

"Oh, I have no doubt of your conviction. They'll run DNA and fingerprints on it and a known acquaintance check. They may figure it out. Doesn't matter, really."

"Well, as far as their stupid charge of Breaking and Entering, I will not press the matter," Eve offered.

Charles jumped in again, "Well, I guess you won't be needing that Adjudicator after all."

"Then we are down to one criminal in here. I can't return the favor, Eve," Nick stated.

"But I can," Charles was quick to reply. This time, without the British accent.

"I can and will speak for Dr. Luxold. I pardon you, Eve."

"But your secret…" Eve began. "If the Giants learn you've succeeded with Heaven's Gate, you'll be in danger."

"That horse has left the barn. I think it's time we confronted Cynthia and John. Nick, are you in?"

"We deserve the truth. As does every other Babylonian." The audible whine of the servo motor heralded the connection being reestablished.

Almost all of Babylon was awake. Bruno Feldstein had run out of options. The two things he'd learned had to get to the pastor. He had always been the backup plan to help Eve return home. Her next-door neighbor, Bruno, had witnessed Nick Santos kicking Eve's door down. His original plan to request a work detail in the western pastures before escaping was no longer an option.

When the trial was announced, Bruno watched the first few minutes of it. His timetable shifted when he learned about "a preemptive strike" against Pastor Thompson. Eve was supposed to take the direct route through the pasture. After she was captured, Bruno realized that the western pasture was too closely monitored. His backup plan was far riskier, but just as fast. If he lived.

During the colony's initial development in the 2030s, there was still an EPA. Regulations required Back2Green to build a "native species path" up the dam. A fish friendly way up stream. In summer, some Babylonians would ride the river down from Lake Pacifica. This time of year, it was very cold, and Bruno risked hypothermia riding the overflow down.

In late fall, there were no boats or tubes to float in. Those were put away for the winter. He also had no idea what the volume of the river would be this time of year. If he looked up the data, Cynthia or John would see the query. That might or might not tip his hand. Bruno decided that whatever the volume of water flow, he had to try. A little after three in the morning, he put on his quickest drying clothes and began the walk up to the overflow.

Ping and Tom had walked for miles before he was able to reserve an Uber with his phone. He explained to Ping that his car was parked in the garage at Representative Reid's office. The soft whine of electric motors was barely audible as the late-model Toyota Prius rolled up. Tom checked the plate against the app, confirming that this was their ride. Their driver, Hamid, rolled down his window. "Are you a part of all this nonsense? The fire and the violence?"

"No, friend," Tom answered. "We were there to speak. It turned violent. Ms. Lee was injured. We are just trying to get out of here."

"I don't want any trouble," Hamid explained. Noticing the dried blood on her forehead, he asked, "Do you think she needs a doctor?"

Wanting to put some distance between them and the entire ARL mess that had evolved, Tom offered, "I'll make sure she gets looked at. The doctors around here will be busy enough as is."

Looking around and checking his mirrors, Hamid unlocked the doors. "Please get in."

Tom helped Ping, shielding her injured scalp with his hand, before making his way to the other side. He got in next to her. Hamid turned to them and offered them bottles of water.

"Thank you, Sir," Ping said, acknowledging his kindness.

"Of course, Miss. Some thing you saw, huh? You were speaking there?"

"We never got a chance to speak," Tom said.

"I can't imagine you would have been heard over all that yelling and fighting. I saw some of the footage, but didn't see you two." Hamid mused. Curious, he asked, "What was this thing about?"

"A bunch of different things. That may have been the problem. Too many cooks," Tom reflected and added, "Too much self-interest."

"Which *thing* were you there for?" Hamid asked.

"I work with an organization trying to slow the insane pace of progress, Christians Against Technology. We are concerned about the unchecked development of artificial intelligence."

Hamid looked in the mirror, his eyes inspecting Ping more closely. Still, he addressed Tom, "And her? She is a Christian too?"

Tom realized he knew very little about Ping. "I can't say. We just met this afternoon."

"Weird first date," Hamid joked, not recognizing a bond that was already forming.

"I've had worse," Tom ribbed back.

With a laugh, Hamid admitted, "That makes two of us."

Jeb and the Stephens brothers made slow progress on their way back. Before leaving, they wet themselves down. The pastor explained this would decrease the chance of IR picking them up. Before exiting the encampment, they split up, taking three different routes back in hopes of minimizing detection. Half the pastor's age, the boys were at the vault's entrance long before Jeb walked up.

Jeb escorted them in. Although it had been twenty-eight years since Jeb had dealt with electric lighting, for the Stephens boys, the experience was quite different. For post-Epocalyptic children, the lighting and the construction of MARTIN's vault was nothing short of miraculous. The brothers knew about electricity and computers, but they had never been inside a space so well lit. Not a single New Amish person under thirty had ever experienced a TV screen or used a computer. That was about to change.

Having seen the impact that even the relatively simple trappings of the past could have, Jeb decided it would be prudent to have a little talk before taking the two men further in. In four flights of stairs, they would move forward through centuries of technology. "One small step," Jeb thought. Turning to the boys, he started, "Brett, John, I need to tell you some things about what we are about to experience."

"We can handle it, Pastor," Brett replied.

Jeb continued to reassure them, "I know you can. That's why I picked you. Still, I owe you an explanation. I'm using a technology that we've all forsworn."

"Because you have to," John guessed.

"God is on our side. David defeated Goliath with a single stone," Jeb started. The brothers nodded in agreement. "If God had given David an AR-15, he would have used it. In Eden, the Lord has seen fit to provide us with a host of tools and arms so that we can vanquish

Satan and his works in Babylon. We will bring the Lord's wayward children to heel."

"We get it, Pastor." Brett was anxious to help.

"We are not here to kill God's children. Some may die. We are here to bring home our brothers and sisters who have lost their way and are mere shepherds in service of our Lord. Come kneel with me." He gestured to his side, then the pastor began to pray. "Some trust in their war chariots and others in their horses, but we trust in the power of the Lord our God. Such people will stumble and fall, but we will rise and stand firm. Give victory to the king, O Lord; answer us when we call."

Closing arguments were not a part of Babylonian legal proceedings. The evidence spoke for itself. After John's very effective presentation, it would be up to the 32,433 jurors to decide. There was no time limit on deliberation. A citizen voted how and when their conscience dictated.

Innocent until proven guilty was still the law of the land. Some people, tried years earlier, had never been convicted. Having reached neither the requisite majority nor mathematically eliminated a guilty verdict, the jury remained out. Those with pending verdicts lived in Babylon as free men and women. Of course, those who had pending verdicts tended to live blameless lives.

Jeb Thompson (i.e., Ben Rosen) would be innocent until or unless 21,623 citizens found him guilty or when 10,811 had voted to acquit.

Votes were private. Cynthia, John, and the council members had access to updated tallies. Ten minutes after Cynthia had closed the evidentiary portion of the trial, there were over 12,000 votes to convict. A mere eight hundred people had voted so far for acquittal. The council had a few matters to discuss before ending the meeting.

"This Council must authorize immediate action on a guilty verdict," Cynthia argued.

"I agree," came John.

"Are there any arguments to the contrary?" Parker asked.

"I abstain," declared councilwoman Nora Mecum.

Not surprisingly, Janet Hughes seconded her abstention.

Parker weighed in. "I am going to side with the Santos' contingent on this. We cannot wait one second if there is a guilty verdict. With Ms. Santos' motion on record, the authorization for lethal force to execute Ben Rosen immediately upon a conviction of genocide passed with a vote of three to zero, with two abstentions."

Cynthia corrected. "I still have Nick's proxy."

"Correction noted. The record shall reflect a vote of four to zero, with two abstentions," Parker said with finality. Sounding tired and expecting to close the meeting, the mayor asked, "Is there any more pressing business before close?"

"Yes," came from John. "I again ask for a vote on a preemptive strike. We may not have a verdict in time, and the risk of MARTIN being reactivated is too great."

"I second John's motion," said Cynthia.

"This motion having been put forth and seconded shall come to vote. Any discussion?"

"Yes," said Nora. "I am wholly opposed to it. It's an aggressive act that violates the will of the people."

"I stand opposed as well," said Janet. "I will not support murder."

"Well then, it looks like I'm the decider here." Parker concluded. "I am opposed to it as well. I have an alternate proposal."

The other four members nodded encouraging Parker to continue.

"We have an elite force here, our Ducenti. A small group could go to secure MARTIN, and temporarily or permanently disable him. This would allow time for the development of a rational and hopefully nonviolent response. Should Ben attempt to gain control, he would never get past the Ducenti and their Centaurs." Parker paused, "Now I want to make it clear. Ladies, if you vote me down on this, I'm going to have to side with Cynthia and John on taking out Doctor Rosen."

Janet took a moment to consider the proposal. "I can live with that; it's a great compromise, Mayor," Nora nodded in agreement.

"All in favor?" All members signaled in the affirmative.

"The motion is carried 6-0," Parker declared. "John, can you deploy the Ducenti?"

"Consider it done." John offered.

"Meeting adjourned. Wake me up if there's a verdict," Parker reminded the other council members.

CHAPTER 21

The unconscious is the real psychic; its inner nature is just as unknown to us as the reality of the external world, and it is just as imperfectly reported to us through the data of consciousness as is the external world through the indications of our sensory organs.

-Sigmund Freud

Juan scaled the cliff in less than four minutes. By the time he reached the top, he was sucking wind and sweaty. The extra effort had earned him a thirty-second breather before he'd have to climb the hundred-foot tower. He dried his hands on his jeans and then started his upward trek. The fog thinned with every rung. Halfway up, he could make out the transmitter through the mist.

The last ten rungs provided a view that he would not soon forget. Miles away, he could see the tips of the other five towers. In the distance, the tower of Babylon was clearly visible. As he looked east, Juan spotted the orange crescent of the rising sun peeking over the

La Salle Range. The sun's rays would soon start to burn off the fog; he didn't have long.

When he took hold of the ladder, Juan was surprised that the tower was not made of metal. It was some sort of plastic, stiffer and stronger than anything he'd ever encountered. Floating above the fog, he saw the Bird of Prey drone. It was impossible to miss. Its rotors whipped up the mist below. Then, he heard the distinctive thrum that grew louder as the drone spotted him and came in to investigate.

Juan hurried to cut the wires. He shaved a bit of the coating off to expose the copper. It was just as he had practiced with the pastor. He twisted in the leads of the repeater and strapped it to the tower. He looked south; the drone was still headed for him.

Careful not to drop them, Juan slipped his calfskin gloves on. He skip-slid down the ladder, taking five rungs at a time. As he sank back into the cool fog, he lost sight of the drone. Juan guessed it was now less than a half mile away when his skin prickled; shards of falling plastic peppered him. The drone had opened fire on the tower.

Juan careened down the ladder. Out of control, he could feel his gloves heating up. He bent his legs to absorb the impact and hit the ground with a thud, rolling backwards towards the edge of the cliff. His hands fumbled for the rope, his body still skidding towards the edge.

He finally gripped it, but there was no time to clip in. Juan wrapped the rope around his waist and dropped into the canyon. The whir of the drone above shifted as it searched for a heat signature in the fog, its blades' sound muted by the thick mist. Thankfully, it had lost its fix on him.

His descent was more controlled than before. Still, he listened for the snap of bullets ricocheting off the canyon walls. It never came.

Before he knew it, he was back on the canyon floor. The pastor's plan had worked.

The men at the bottom of the canyon heard the drone open fire. "Bro's up there doing his thing. We best get going," Jose told his men as he let out a whoop and holler, spurring his mount to life. Within mere moments, fifteen riders had circled fifteen unmounted horses, all accustomed to wrangling. The herd moved as a unit. Initially, they were at a trot, but later opened to gallop when Jose yelled "herders!"

Had they just been stealing horses; they might have tried to disable the dog-sized robots. Their objective was to clear the way for the last ten horses to wander out. Five of those would have riders concealed on their backs. They needed to lure these robots far away.

Jose was in his element, riding flat out and tearing up the prairie with robot dogs giving chase. This incursion onto Babylonian land might earn reprisals, but for now, he was a boy again. He chose to savor the wind in his hair and the solid mount pulling him home.

At this pace, their posse would cross over into New Amish territory within minutes. The dogs were not a threat. Only the tracked robots with cannons, known as Centaurs, could foil the escape. A single Centaur had the power to mow down the horses and their riders in seconds. Jose prayed for protection. So far, his prayers had been answered. If the Centaurs found them, they would be dead before they even knew what hit them.

Riding through the fog, Jose struggled to get the image of the Centaurs out of his head. He and his men had watched the Nons' war games not far from where they were now. The Centaurs were usually red, but he'd seen them change color and almost disappear. Juan had once asked the pastor about the Centaurs and the origin of their name. The pastor's description of the mythical beasts made everything clear. The Centaurs' arms were guns and a strange head covered in sensors topped it all off.

There were other robot tanks too. In fact, he'd even seen a couple; they had a huge lens in the middle of their head. The stood straight and were about two feet taller. The pastor called these "Cyclops." They weren't as fast as the Centaurs, but their missile launchers made them even more dangerous. Neither Centaurs nor Cyclops truly resembled their mythic counterparts, but Jose could imagine how they earned their names.

Each robot tank had a pair of automatic 10mm cannons. Jose had seen what a 10mm cannon could do to flesh. The New Amish had several 10mm guns in their possession. He had fired one once. He didn't enjoy it, it was formidable, nonetheless. Now he struggled to keep the image of the cow's carcass he had practiced on out of his head. One shot had ripped its body nearly in half.

The orange globe of the sun was already semicircle on the horizon, its shadows stretching far across the landscape in the early morning light. The red rock walls of the canyon were still not well enough lit to reveal their splendor, but the fog was nearly gone. All Jose could hear was the thunder of thirty horses galloping up the plain. They drove the horses hard, but of the unmounted ones had fallen away from the herd. Jose yelled, "Split!" and just like that, they broke into five groups of three. Still galloping, the increasing distance between the riders would make for more targets and improve their chances for survival if the Centaurs found them.

Jose was now riding alongside Brad Simpson and his younger brother, who couldn't have been more than sixteen. The camp was finally in sight, with the fog disappearing in the sunlight. At that moment, Jose heard the *brap brap* of a 10mm cannon. One of the Centaur's had notched its first kill.

Jose could only watch as terror painted the boy's face. There was no time to process the loss. The men drove harder, some refusing to look back. Seconds passed as they entered the rock towers that would halt the Centaurs' pursuit. All Jose could think about were the men he'd lost, and the men headed in the opposite direction on their way to disable the towers.

Jeb and the Stephens brothers had just made it downstairs when the power surged. What had been a dimly lit cavern was now flooded with light. The pulsing electricity meant one thing to Jeb: MARTIN had started up the generators. Now, almost every computer in every row of every rack was showing signs of life.

"Hello, Doctor Rosen. I see you have brought friends."

Jeb, immediately realizing the confusion this would cause, instructed MARTIN, "These men know me as Pastor Thompson."

"Of course, pastor, I will make note of that," MARTIN replied without question. Having finally put Ben Rosen to rest, Pastor Thompson tended his flock. "Status report."

MARTIN began an update. "I now control four Condor class surveillance drones. I have also accessed six Bird of Prey attack drones and managed to gain control of one Centaur. I am updating their code. The reconnaissance drones will be in a transmit-only mode."

"Why?" Jeb asked.

"These are sophisticated machines, Pastor. Their primary utility for this operation will be surveillance. If I allow them to receive data, Babylon may regain control. Since I have no ability to remotely assess the full capabilities of such advanced technology, I must assume it is superior to my own," MARTIN explained.

"Makes sense," Jeb replied. The Stephens brothers simply listened, processing the influx of information. They were awestruck by what could only be described as magic. It was beyond anything they had ever imagined.

"There have been casualties in the scouting party. A man fell to his death and three more men on horseback were killed by the Centaur shortly before I was able to gain control."

"I felt the generators kick in. How long until you are at full power?"

MARTIN paused, "In six minutes, I will be at ninety-three percent computational capacity. It will take seventeen minutes to upload the remaining data from storage. I have downloaded terrain maps from the drones and Centaur."

"What are your next steps?" Jeb asked.

"I will attempt to gain control of additional assets. This depends on how quickly the Babylonian systems detect that I am online."

"How long will we have air support from the drones?" Jeb asked.

"The six drones are at variable levels of charge. I chose the ones with the least reserve to provide air support. We have no ability to recharge these devices. Once they lose power, they will crash."

"If they can't hear us, how will you update instructions?"

"I did not fully explain. The drones will listen to random preset frequencies at preset intervals. The other side will likely not detect the spread spectrum transmissions and cannot decrypt them."

"What about offensive capabilities? Have you completed your preliminary tactical?"

"Now that I have basic topography, I am running tactical simulations. There are seven prototype hypersonic cruise missiles here at Eden. These have high explosive capabilities—sub-kiloton payloads. Minimally effective against a hardened target."

"What's a hardened target?" Brett blurted.

"Like where we are now, Brett. Underground bunkers. These buildings are very strong. They're built with steel reinforced concrete. It's stronger than stone," Jeb answered.

"The reconnaissance drones are over Babylon. We already have control of two towers. Each additional tower will reduce their strike and surveillance capabilities."

"Two down, four to go," Jeb surmised.

Partly to make conversation and partly out of genuine curiosity, Eve asked, "How does it work, Nick?" She paused before clarifying, "Immortalization. I understand the questions and the scanning, but how does that result in something like Cynthia?"

"I would hope you meant *someone*," Charles glibly corrected.

"Sure, *someone*," Eve conceded.

"Charles would be the expert on the *someone* part." Nick explained, "Cynthia and John invented the *what*, but Charles' breakthroughs on consciousness taught us the *how*."

"And the *who*," The Symbiant added.

"Maybe you want to take this one, Chuck," Nick suggested.

On screen, five ovals appeared. Charles went into lecture mode. "What is consciousness?"

"An awareness of one's surroundings," Eve quickly responded, then wondered whether that was close to the right answer. She was explaining consciousness to two of the greatest minds the world had ever known.

"Fair enough," Charles accepted, "But *how* is consciousness? I mean, to understand your surroundings, you must first be aware that you exist."

"This sounds like more of *The God Within*?" Eve chided.

"The very foundation," Charles agreed. "Infants become aware of external objects before they realize that they themselves are a part of existence. Their mother's breast, the pain of hunger, the pain of satiety, the pain of loneliness… Infants long for comfort and companionship long before they achieve sentience."

Unconvinced, Eve asked, "Why does this matter?"

"Because our sense of self is a construct. It is a group of thoughts and memories assembled in a kernel of evolving concepts, layered and cemented with a language we first create to communicate, but then to remember. Semantic memory marks the end of this latent period. When we can remember Mom, we constrain her to the physical world and our connection to the Mother God is severed. More than a century ago, Dale Carnegie concluded that a person's favorite word was their name. 'Eve' is a complex construct that your parents programmed into you for months."

Eve argued, "I would still be me if they had named me Darla or Constance."

Aware that the discussion was expanding well beyond the bounds of the matter at hand, Charles agreed, "Perhaps. But that is another domain of existential philosophy that remains unresolved."

Nick chuckled. He was happy that his friend still existed, even if it wasn't a perfect copy; it was enough Charles and enough Luxold and his world was richer for it.

Charles continued, "Eve, your consciousness and preconscious mind reside here." The words *pre* and *conscious* appeared in the center oval. "The conscious mind is the central regulator. It controls an enormous data stream between regions that store, recall, transmit, and modulate our emotions, memories, behaviors, and perceptions." With that, those four words filled in the smaller satellite ovals that bordered consciousness.

"The preconscious mind, our emotions and memories, can be considered the *unconscious*." A dotted line separated the screen between the words *pre* and *conscious*.

"This structured but unregulated flow of information to and from the emotional and memory centers of the brain occurs without the direct regulation of the conscious mind. Hence, the term *preconscious*." Animated bubbles of information flowed between memory and the preconscious, and between emotion and the preconscious. "As memories consolidate, they develop additional attributes through this back and forth." A memory object appeared on the screen with concepts attached to it, becoming more defined in the flow.

Nick joined in. "Over thirty years ago, I watched a TED talk of Charles teaching this stuff. It was mind-blowing. He gave a presentation called 'The Path of Love.' That fifteen minutes changed how I thought about everything I knew and believed."

"Can we watch it?" Eve asked with unanticipated enthusiasm.

"Unfortunately, I don't have access to it at present. John and Cynthia surely have a copy, probably not the best time to ask, though. Try this one for now." A stick figure of a dog moved from the preconscious to memory. On its way back, it came with the word *dog* attached to it. Then, it retreated a second time with the word *black*, making the return journey in the shape of a Labrador retriever. On its next round trip, Gracie the Labrador trotted back to the preconscious.

"Gracie is in our preconscious mind. We still don't know how to feel about her." With that, Gracie trotted to the emotion's oval, returning with hearts floating around her. "We love Gracie. Gracie makes us happy."

This made sense to Eve for the most part. "Is this where the conscious mind comes in?" Eve asked, trying to follow along. "I look at Gracie. That's a behavior. I see Gracie, that's a perception. Then, my consciousness works to figure out the rest?"

"Excellent! Of course, it may take dozens or hundreds of these round trips before you know it's Gracie." Charles continued, "Fragment images of dogs, going back and forth, will flood your mind. The sounds of panting. The smell of dog breath. The feeling of fur on your hands. All these data points connect in working memory, building a semantic representation. The semantic representation is only possible because of language."

"How did you ever turn this into a computer program?"

"We couldn't," Nick answered. "We needed incredibly powerful computers to accomplish it."

"Our basic models of emotion, perception, and behaviors were turned into new frameworks. Computers reverse engineered behavior to these best-fit models," Charles explained.

"Like Symbiants?" Eve asked.

Nick clarified, "Those came decades later. The first five years and ten billion dollars yielded a rudimentary model."

"The models always got better. That's the amazing part. Within five years, ARTI had grown into MARTIN."

The realization that MARTIN evolved from a brilliant idea soured the entire moment for Eve. "And that's exactly why you must all be stopped," she concluded, her tone and demeanor shifting.

Cynthia and John reconnected to their feeds and returned to pre-meeting responsibilities. True parallelism and divergence were concepts their human creators were incapable of fully comprehending. Cynthia had been unable to explain it to John before his upload. After his epiphany, John admitted to her that what he envisioned as a mortal bore little resemblance to what he experienced after immortalization.

Cynthia's queue had a message from Nick. It came via an Adjudicator. Nick had met with Eve. As usual, Nick was not following Cynthia's advice and instructions. Cynthia decided that patience could only be learned through experience. Nick would wait until morning when the Council reconvened. She did not answer his call.

Reviewing transmissions, she learned that Tower Six had experienced a malfunction. New Amish operatives had stolen the Arabians at Horse Canyon. She pondered the hypocrisy for less than a microsecond before determining that the New Amish would justify the theft as a reprisal for Eve's capture. They might believe the horses to be a bargaining chip.

The damaged tower had not only facilitated the horse theft, but it had also interfered with surveillance. The tower would need a repair party. Cynthia decided to wait for the drones to return before determining where the horses were and how best to retrieve them.

Cynthia and John delegated tasks to repair teams. There was a Centaur offline too. This was beyond coincidence. The Giants concluded that Centaur B-11 had likely been destroyed or disabled. Things were heating up. Until the tower was back online, drones would have to fly out and back. Cynthia dispatched four Condors. The surveillance drones would go on thirty-minute patrols outside radio range. Cynthia wanted to keep close tabs on Ben Rosen's whereabouts.

Several Condors were already returning. While they recharged, she could download their footage.

When towers four and five went offline, Cynthia and John knew that this was not horse theft. It only took mere seconds after the outage for hundreds of thousands of scenarios to come to life. Both Giants concluded that the New Amish army was preparing a strike.

Cynthia deployed more drones alongside a platoon of Centaurs. With Centaurs under drone control, they could send instructions from Babylon via a line-of-sight relay. Two Condors at high altitude would control the theater of engagement.

John briefed Ducenti response teams. There were two hundred elite fighting men in Eden. They trained constantly and answered only to John. These men were among the most fit, well-equipped, and psychologically sound warriors ever in uniform.

John sent a team out in RX-rovers armed with 10mm guns. Instructions would come from John over long-range, low-data, high-encryption coms that were keyed to John and John alone. Quantum encryption made them impossible to hack. Cynthia was regularly tasked with penetration testing. She had never breached the Ducenti's encryption.

The other half of the Ducenti would remain and coordinate defenses. These included fifteen Centaurs at the west gate. This would protect Babylon. The Centaurs and the cannons at the gate would cut through the New Amish Calvary in seconds. Of course, any frontal assault would likely fall to the forward deployed Centaurs and Ducenti.

Confident in the overwhelming superiority of the Colony's defenses, Cynthia began analyzing data from the returning drones. The first would touch down in less than a minute to recharge. With the towers down, Cynthia relied on their telemetry for location and course. Without tower control, the drones flew low and slow.

CHAPTER 22

Carefully watch your thoughts, for they become your words. Manage and watch your words, for they will become your actions. Consider and judge your actions, for they have become your habits. Acknowledge and watch your habits, for they shall become your values. Understand and embrace your values, for they become your destiny.

-Gandhi

MARTIN announced, "They appear to have made a tactical error."

Immediately, Jeb jumped on the news, "Big or small?"

"Unclear. It will take several minutes to determine the impact," MARTIN responded. "At present, they appear to be preparing for an imminent ground assault."

The Stephens Brothers were trying to decode the conversation. Brett asked, "Meaning?"

"We must account for the small likelihood that the Giants are aware of my reactivation. Additional resources we recover may contain Trojan Horses," MARTIN began.

"What resources?" Ben asked.

"I am attempting to gain control of six more drones and possibly fifteen additional Centaurs."

"Why do you conclude they may be bait?" Brett asked.

"It's what I would do. If I knew I was dealing with an AI, I would load a Trojan Horse and hack the hacker. Again, I don't know their capabilities. They know all of mine. They built me. My encryption and firewalls may be completely vulnerable to an attack that I cannot predict or simulate," MARTIN explained.

Ben, realizing that the men had no point of reference, clarified, "MARTIN has locks that require passcodes. Advanced computers, like the ones in Babylon, are very good at figuring out passwords."

"How good?" Brett asked. "Like, do they just guess a lot?"

"It's more complicated than that, but they can guess a lot too. Billions of guesses in the blink of an eye." Ben did not have time to explain and turned his attention back to MARTIN. "Can you isolate your core from the new machines?"

"I'm sequestering the cluster penetrating these machines. A cluster of servers in the locked closet will be quarantined and monitored. They will directly control the hijacked machines."

"How's that?" Brett asked the Pastor.

"MARTIN will control the machines that control the Centaurs and drones. He won't exchange information at the machine-to-machine level. He will behave like a person controlling a machine. It's not a direct connection where they could spread software to other machines. Those computers can't control you and me. MARTIN's acting like a human in this case."

"So, no risk then?" Brett hoped.

"Less risk, not no risk. There's always a risk. We're talking about incredibly smart machines. They could take control of the computers that are directly connected and try to regain control of the drones and Centaurs."

"What do we do if that happens?" Jack asked.

"Then you guys are going to help me unplug every machine that doesn't have a blue light on it," Jeb answered.

"I have updated intel from Babylon." MARTIN's display now showed a rapidly enhancing realistic map of Babylon. Nearly the entire city was rendered in amazing detail. Shadows from the sun being so low in the sky obscured some details. Still, the map was amazing.

"I will strike here, Doctor Rosen." On the eastern rim, MARTIN displayed a small explosion near the base of the dam that held back Lake Pacifica, which contained a half-million-acre feet of water.

"You can't hope to take the dam out? It's ten feet thick. Definitely a hardened target," Doctor Rosen reminded him.

"You are correct." MARTIN zoomed in on the display. "These are high voltage lines; they connect to the hydrogenerators buried in the dam."

"There are others here and here." Two more explosions occurred. Water appeared to flow out. As the flow increased, MARTIN zoomed back out. The holes in the dam spouted like giant fire hoses. Two-foot-wide tubes of water shot from the base of the dam.

"You are correct about the hardened nature of this dam. It is a concrete sandwich. The Lake Pacifica side and the side facing Babylon are eighteen-inch thick, reinforced concrete. There is seven feet of soil in between the concrete walls," Martin explained. "At high speed, you can see how microfractures from the explosion will begin to drip mud into the stream. Water will need to replace every drop of mud that flows out of the dam." Over the course of thirty seconds, the water turned from blue to brown. "The water will destabilize the core of the dam, causing it to fail." At that moment, the walls above the spouts collapsed and a wall of water twenty feet high poured through the first breech. Soon, there were two and eventually three breaches in the dam.

"Liquefaction," Jeb deduced. "How do you know the wall thickness of the dam?"

"I designed that dam for Doctor Santos," MARTIN explained. "That is why I am certain this will work."

"Will all of Babylon flood?" Brett asked.

"Within five hours, the Atlantean sea will rise seventy feet." The animation sped up again and the central lake extended out beyond the dome by almost a quarter mile. The statues above each gate were mostly submerged. As MARTIN panned back to the holes in the dam, the water was carving deep canyons.

Homes in the path of the water were long washed away. All other rivers in the colony ran dry. "By this evening, the water will peak at 100 feet above the current level. The statues were gone, and the outer ring of the dome was lost beneath forty feet of water. The middle of the dome became a central island in a swirling, muddy lake.

"Where is the tower?" Jeb noted the absence of the prominent landmark.

"I will use some of our remaining ordinance to destroy the tower's supports. That combined with a rapid rehydration of its foundation will cause it to lean and collapse," MARTIN detailed.

"When will you launch the attack?" Ben asked.

Without hesitation, MARTIN replied, "Now."

Cynthia received a notification of thermal activity at Eden, but due to the relay of the drones, she did not immediately receive imaging. The New Amish might have been destroying the city. She did not want to wait for the video relay and requested still shots instead, hoping to be proactive in some sense. The request did not go through. The further relay drone was offline.

Video came through moments later. She reviewed the five-minute recording in a fraction of a second, immediately recognizing the three plumes of Brahmos Cruise missile launches. MARTIN was online. The missiles would strike before she could deploy any countermeasures.

John sent orders to all 10mm and 30mm cannons under his control. They were already tracking inbounds. The Brahmos missiles flew a high arc on their supersonic flight path. Cannons slewed, ejecting a stream of bullets as they attempted to shoot down the projectiles. Smoke filled the sky. Over the half mile of Babylon's west gate, ten 30mm cannons were in full auto mode.

The air was acrid from the smoke as the missiles began their descent. The noise was deafening. If there had been more time, Babylon's defense system would have taken out all three missiles. With the short notice, they managed to take down two.

The first missile was hit by six different one-pound projectiles. It broke into pieces, reigning death onto the western ring of the colony. Alan Simpson, age five, was walking with his mother. The next instant, he became the first Babylonian casualty of war. This fact would never be recorded.

The second missile took a hit on the port aileron. It spun out of control, detonating close enough to the detention center that it made Nick and Eve's ears pop from the pressure wave. Over a thousand Babylonians joined the casualty list in a cloud of fire.

The first missile launched was the only one to find its target. The closest fire missed it by less than two meters. It impacted dead center of the hydrogenerator. The detonation of its five-hundred-pound payload immediately seemed like a dud. Then, a trickle of water flowed from the hole. First responders would witness the scene exactly as MARTIN had predicted.

Cynthia and John pieced together what would happen next. They dispatched rescue crews to the impact sites and began a group of damage mitigation efforts. John immediately dispatched every piece of heavy equipment in the colony. Dozers, excavators of all sizes, began to crawl towards the smoking hole in the dam. There was a small chance that they could reinforce the wall and prevent failure. Within a minute of the missile's impact, they were on their way to the ruptured wall. By that time, the dam was already ejecting a swimming pool's worth of water every minute.

For the first time in a decade, Cynthia opened the floodgates of the northern dam. Every bit of pressure they could take off the dam's interior wall would buy them precious time. Pumps fifty feet below the surface of the Atlantean Sea began to drain water into the canyon as well. Temporarily, the sea level in the dome would drop.

With the floodgates open, the flow in the canyon below the dam grew from a small trickle to a massive torrent. Bruno Feldstein was walking in the dry riverbed when he saw a ten-foot-high wall of water racing towards him. He thought of running. But there was no place to run. Knowing it would be his last breath, he decided not to hold it. He would join his family in Heaven, fearless.

Cynthia and John had done the math. If all three missiles had struck their intended targets, water levels would have risen one hundred feet. They were now in a variable stage. The dam could breach in less than an hour. They began evacuating the dome and nearby residences, warning everyone in the path of the coming flood and providing relocation instructions.

The Atlantean Sea would rise fifty feet by 8AM on the fourteenth. MARTIN had more missiles. It was unclear how he would deploy those. So far, his attacks had been on infrastructure. The solar fields seemed a likely target. The windmills were too spread out to be effectively disabled by the few missiles in E-Den's quiver.

The first bulldozing robot arrived at the dam three minutes after impact. Cynthia had a plan. Hydraulic forces could stave the flow. She would create a pool on the other side of the dam. If the pool's walls grew to the height of the water on the other side, the pressure differential would be zero. Even a small increase in back pressure could slow the rate of failure.

Under her direction, the dozer was already building up the sides of the pool. Meanwhile, other dozers began plowing debris from the explosion into piles. An X-Class thirty-ton dozer drove over the edge and into the jet of water, deflecting the spray plume. As it drove into the dam, it became a thirty-ton cork.

The thirty-ton tracked plug proved no match for the dam's pressure. The growing plume of water pushed the dozer into the western edge of the deepening pool. Fifteen minutes later, the pool was already five feet deep. Thirty pieces of earth-moving equipment continued their ballet, precisely following Cynthia's choreography.

"That was close and big," Nick declared.

Charles corrected, "Not close but big, yes. A total of three events. From three different directions. The largest one was the closest."

"Any idea what they were?" Eve asked.

"High explosives," Nick said confidently.

"I believe Nick is correct," Charles added.

"New Amish? Are they coming for me?"

"If they're the ones behind this, then it's MARTIN who's helping, and Cynthia was right," Nick admitted.

"If it is MARTIN, then we can count on devastation outside. Mercy is not his strong suit." Charles went on, "My antenna is non-operational. I'm no longer picking up the carrier signal. The blast has disabled or destroyed it."

Nick struggled to open the door, but it wouldn't budge. Realizing debris was blocking it, he said, "Door's jammed."

"How will they know we're in here? How do we get out?" Eve was a bit panicky. Almost reflexively, she prayed. "Blessed is the man who remains steadfast under trial, for when he has stood the test, he will receive the crown of life, which God has promised to those who love Him."

"Well, either Jeb and his followers will dig us out or my sister will. For now, we sit tight. This is one of the best built buildings in the Colony; we aren't getting out until someone lets us out."

"You seem so calm. How do you find any solace without God's light?" Eve asked Nick, genuinely wondering.

"I accept my mortality," Nick answered. "You're too young to remember, but the world you were born into was a very violent place. Sadly, this is not new to us."

"I don't just mean about now. I mean about death. You will end. You won't be here," Eve lamented.

"I consider that inevitable. I don't think I have any choice in the matter."

"I ended," Charles added. "At least, according to you, I ended."

"Or you just began," Eve argued. "Either way, you are not of God, and therefore cannot achieve salvation."

Frustrated, Nick asked, "Can you explain salvation, Eve? I mean, now that we're just stuck here. Tell me, why would I want to be saved?" Despite his previous statements that the room was inescapable, Nick was still looking around, testing hinges and tapping on walls, hoping for a way out.

"To be in God's light for all eternity. It's a small price, to seek forgiveness," Eve preached.

Nick despised blind faith. "What is the price exactly?"

"Just believe in Him and follow His teachings."

"How do you know those are his teachings?" Charles asked.

"They are in the Bible," Eve answered.

"Why should we believe the Bible is right? How does it prove its authenticity? Where in the Bible does it say the whole Bible was written by God?"

Eve was confident. "Well, first, because you don't have as much faith in your science as you claim."

"Really?" Nick asked.

"I've watched you. You said this was the best built room in Babylon. Yet you are trying to get out. You know you can't, but you hope to anyway." Eve quoted Psalm 19, "The law of the LORD is perfect, reviving the soul; the testimony of the LORD is sure, making wise the simple; the precepts of the LORD are right, rejoicing the heart; the commandment of the LORD is pure, enlightening the eyes."

"I imagine Charles would just replace *LORD* with *Mom*," Nick mocked.

"Amen to that," came Charles. "I am not making fun of you, Eve. This is what you have been taught. But it's what we call a tautology. The book is perfect because it says it was written by a perfect being. What if I were to write a book and claim a perfect being wrote it?"

"But that wouldn't be true," Eve said. "You would be lying."

"Couldn't MARTIN be perfect? Or John? Or Cynthia?" Charles asked. "They are so far beyond me that I cannot know whether they are perfect or not. If they tell me something is true, why should I not believe them?"

"Isn't that how our world ended? MARTIN, the deceiver, was born of man and caused the Epocalypse," Eve said confidently. "Isn't that prophecy? Isn't that the living testament of John? John, who the Lord saw fit to reveal the End Times."

"I can't argue with you there, Eve," Nick admitted. "MARTIN committed unspeakable evil."

"He was born of your sister."

"Ah, careful, Eve," Charles cautioned. "Now Cynthia is the Whore of Babylon?"

"Could she be anything else? She is the idolatress who brought forth the beast. It's not too late for you." She was almost begging, "Will you pray with me, Nick? We can pray for your family, and you can ask for forgiveness. We can pray for peace and mercy upon Charles' soul."

"Why should there be peace?" Nick asked. "If this is the Apocalypse, the End Times, then your Lord comes in judgement."

"I already tried this, Nick," Charles advised.

"I don't need to pray, Eve. I need to help. I need to lead," Nick declared defiantly.

Eve softened. "That is not what the Lord wants, Nick. He wants you to put your faith in him."

"The leader of a group that has just attacked my home and people for a second time?!" Nick was heated and couldn't contain his bubbling frustration. "What your people and all God's people have done for millennia is wrought carnage in His name. All to bring people to heal. It's absurd. Charles is right; you should seek the God within."

"Nick, when you push and argue, you are failing," Charles' counseled. "Lead through love. Lead through compassion."

"There are assuredly bodies of innocent people spread on our doorstep, Charles." Nick argued, "I had the power to put a stop to this. I could have supported my sister and authorized the preemptive strike. There would be no E-Den or MARTIN. Nothing would be exploding, and we would continue détente." He looked at Eve, "Yes, I had the power to kill all your people. Every New Amish man, woman, and child, but *I* respect life. My love for peace held me back. Then, as always, you and your fellow Christians saw compassion as weakness."

CHAPTER 23

A gender-equal society would be one where the word gender does not exist: where everyone can be equally themselves.

-Gloria Steinam

"We cannot proceed without a quorum present," Cynthia reminded them. "I cannot locate Janet or Nora."

"What about Nick's proxy?" Parker asked.

"I cannot convene the council on that," John explained.

"Where is Nick?" Parker asked.

John answered, "He's in the detention center."

In a day of unanticipated events, Parker still did not expect to hear Nick was in jail. "Why? Who put him there?"

"I did," Cynthia stated bluntly.

"On whose authority?"

"On his own admission of guilt," Cynthia began.

John explained, "Breaking and Entering."

Parker asked. "Where?"

"Eve Hamlin's home," Cynthia replied.

"So, he entered the home of a known terrorist? A terrorist who is in detention, while we are actively being targeted by the deadliest machine on earth? And this computer can only be operated by one man, who views this woman as his daughter? Nick goes to her home to learn more, and you jail him?" Parker was dumbfounded. "Does that sound about right?"

"It is a council matter, Mr. James," Cynthia said with formality.

"Yet due to your actions, we can't even convene the Council."

"Where do we stand with your other plan, the conviction of Jeb Thompson? What's the tally?"

"That seems a moot point now," John admitted.

"It is, but is action authorized?"

"14,534 for conviction, 2334 not guilty."

"More colonists have voted not guilty than guilty since the attack?" Parker observed. "It makes sense in a way. A preemptive attack is no longer possible; it's just murder at this point."

"Yes," Cynthia confirmed.

"We need Nick, and we need him now," Parker declared with authority.

"The attacks have interrupted communications with his Adjudicator."

"Send a team and get him a com," Parker demanded.

"Team is on scene. They are clearing a path. Antenna is gone," John announced.

When MARTIN gave the signal, Jeb realized he might be making a mistake. "Hold," he responded.

"I cannot," MARTIN responded. "Launch confirmed."

"Abort," Jeb ordered.

"Once airborne, a Brahmos III cannot be recalled."

"Can you shoot them down?" Jeb asked.

"These are supersonic missiles, Pastor. They are as fast the bullets we might shoot at them. Approaching Babylon," MARTIN confirmed. "Reconnaissance reports antimissile fire. One missile destroyed, five miles out."

"How long?" Brett asked.

"Impact in five seconds."

"Second missile has taken fire. Impact in Eastern City," MARTIN announced. "Impact of one missile on primary objective."

"What's the predicted response?"

"Anticipate retaliatory strike on New Amish at Westden and this facility," MARTIN reported.

"How long?" Jeb asked.

"Without knowledge of their military capability or decision-making process, I cannot make a useful prediction," MARTIN stated. "I have taken control of sixteen Centaurs in total. I will deploy six as surface-to-air defense at the New Amish encampment. I will send four to the canyon wall to shell the city and control the field of engagement. Six will be kept in reserve here at E-Den."

"Okay, how will we coordinate with the New Amish?"

"We can communicate via radio through coms. It may not be secure."

Jeb turned to the brothers. "I need you two to evacuate the camp. Bring radios. You will be able to accomplish that more effectively with a side-by-side."

"Where do we send our people?"

"Send the Windforce back here—Calvary too."

MARTIN interrupted, "Pastor, there is no time to wait for strategy. Send John and Brett now. We can update them over coms.

Gentlemen, disperse people in all directions; attack is imminent." Jeb led the brothers upstairs and outside, where they were met by an electric side-by-side.

One of the first structures completed at Babylon was the Western Wall. Protected to the north, south, and east by mountains and lakes, the colony was vulnerable to an attack from the west. Even before the Epocalypse, work was well underway to fortify the half-mile-long entrance to the valley, along the bowl's western lip. The Ducenti all lived near the thirty-foot-high earthen wall, where their weaponry, Centaurs, and drones were also housed.

The Ducenti were gathered near the Western Wall when the guns went off, resonating louder than any training exercise. Soldiers closest to the Centaurs felt pressure waves on their faces, as machines fired in attempts to stop the inbound missiles. The men were all wearing in-ear coms, which both enhanced and protected their hearing.

Moments later, they heard an explosion emanate from the far side of the dome. Then, they saw a flash of a third impact on the ridge, ten miles to the east. Four seconds later, the pressure wave of the second blast practically knocked them down. Coms came to life. Each soldier received a set of individualized orders from John.

Mike Walters had been a Ducenti since he turned sixteen, living a life of excitement and training. In Babylon, everyone had access to ample sustenance, with most people following relatively nutritious diets. The Ducenti, however, optimized their daily intake to enhance endurance, strength, and recovery. They universally consumed supplements, performance-enhancing stimulants, and hormones, pushing their physiques to the limits of human capability.

Mike had recently learned the term "yoked" from Pat Gibson, his Tai Chi instructor. All Ducenti were "yoked," meaning they were truly chiseled. There were no women in the Ducenti. Previous notions of gender equality evaporated in the first thirty days of the Epocalypse. Roles returned to a pure meritocracy. There was no discrimination; anyone could apply. However, hormonally enhanced males were stronger, faster, and more aggressive than hormonally enhanced females.

John briefed Mike. "You, Wilkes, Lee, and Faulks will take two RX's," Mike's favorite of the high-performance side-by-sides, "and head to Bravo 16. Follow the river and disable this water inlet." Walters' tablet showed the exact location of MARTIN's water intake.

"Are we just blocking it?" Walters asked.

"No, you are going to feed three delayed charges down it," John instructed. "Set one at twenty seconds, forty seconds, and the last at one minute."

"Lee and Faulks will disable the generators; they have separate instructions."

"Deploy immediately," John ordered. Mike and the other Ducenti hopped into the pair of highly modified electric dune buggies and tore off across the prairie.

"Nick, I detect vibrations near the door," Charles reported.

"I hear them too," Eve confirmed.

Intensifying sounds of shifting debris rang out. "Perhaps Eve's prayers have been answered," Nick said with a dose of sarcasm.

Unaccustomed to sarcasm, Eve asked, "Is it the Pastor?"

"Not unless he brought T20 lifters," Nick added.

Fully aware that Eve did not know what Nick was referring to, Charles explained. "T20's are the medium duty robot excavators. You may have seen them working around Babylon; they grasp with two arms and dig with a hoe."

"But those explosions," Eve said. The sound of large mechanical bangs and scratching resonated as debris was dragged.

"Those missiles were the Brahmos cruise missiles we were modifying at E-Den before you were born," Nick began. "Missiles we could have used on the FLDS when they destroyed our home. They have a blast radius of a quarter mile. One of them must have come down pretty close to here."

"Why would a technology company need missiles?" Eve asked.

This time, it was Charles' turn. "Actually, Eve, the missiles needed us."

"Computer guidance—the better the computer, the more spot on the *boom*," Nick explained. This made sense to Eve, but Nick went on. "This area was a deserted ordinance practice range. The perfect place to be testing those."

"Stay back from the door," came a voice from outside.

"We are!" yelled Nick. With that, a metallic hand came through the door and effortlessly tore it from the jamb.

With the door removed, Nick's com came back to life. Fortunately, battery life was not an issue. Blood-glucose-powered biobatteries gave most personal electronics and implants continuous power. Another benefit was better blood glucose regulation.

"Cynthia?" Nick asked.

"Yes, Nick, I'm linking to a screen and camera now."

"Bianca—the kids?"

"Are fine," she reassured him. "Nick, I haven't got time to explain. I need your immediate attention."

CHAPTER 24

An evil deed is not redeemed by an evil deed of retaliation.
-Coretta Scott King

Five minutes later, as Brett and Jack neared the camp, armed men on horseback rode out to meet them. The vehicle detected the riders and stopped. Brett used Prairie Sign to communicate to the men before they were in earshot. Recognizing the hand signals before he recognized the Stephens brothers, Jose Morales asked, "Where's the Pastor?"

"Safe," Brett confirmed. "We need to evacuate the camp. Now!"

"Why?" Jose asked.

Brett knew there was no time for a long explanation. "Nons are preparing an attack." He kept it short and sweet, recognizing that time was of the essence.

"Where do we send the people?" Jose asked.

Jack, wanting to emphasize the urgency, answered, "Anywhere and everywhere. Anywhere but here. Missiles headed our way."

Jose turned to the others. He sent each on a slightly different vector. The men were already riding as he yelled after them. "Grab supplies and clothing; don't know when we will return."

Jose turned to Brett. "How long before we get hit?"

"No idea. Could be five minutes or five hours. Likely to happen sooner than later, though," Brett guessed.

Gesturing towards their side-by-side, Jose suggested, "You best leave that thing here. Might cause a panic." Recognizing the wisdom of the suggestion, Jack and Brett decided to find some horses.

Jeb was back down with MARTIN. "Were there casualties?"

"Still receiving data. Nominal lives lost, approximately 1,500," MARTIN reported.

Heartbroken, Jeb said, "I just wanted my daughter back. We were not supposed to kill innocent people."

"They killed their own people, Pastor. They shot down missiles and those missiles crashed and exploded," MARTIN argued.

"No more unnecessary casualties!" Jeb demanded.

"Pastor Thompson, can you define unnecessary versus collateral damage?"

"Women, children, and non-combatants."

"What about the Ducenti?" MARTIN asked.

"I don't know much about them, but they are military," Jeb replied.

"While scanning the files stored in the Centaurs, I discovered a directory of two hundred elite fighters, which is likely the origin of the name Ducenti, meaning "two hundred" in Italian. These fighters possess exceptional physical capabilities, seemingly enhanced beyond normal human limits. Specifications indicate they can cover twice the distance of an average adult male in the same amount of time and have extraordinary endurance. They are also equipped with various small arms and some control robotic weaponry through an implanted EEG interface. Most importantly, they have a direct connection to John at E-Den and take orders only from him."

Concerned about the potential for the Ducenti to turn the battle, Jeb asked, "Will they be able to control our Centaurs?"

"Not anymore. I've disabled that programming," MARTIN assured.

"Emergency Council meeting October 14, 2063, will come to order. Cynthia, John, and Nick Santos, as well myself, Parker James, in attendance. Council women Nora Mecum and Janet Hughes, absent," the mayor announced.

"I move to consider a retaliatory strike," John announced.

"Seconded," came from Cynthia.

"Any discussion?" Parker asked.

"Yes, I have several concerns," Nick began.

"We don't have time for debate, Nick. Waiting is what created this mess," Cynthia explained.

"There is time, Cynthia. We will make time." Nick was calm, but firm.

Parker announced, "Doctor Santos has the floor for two minutes."

Nick inhaled deeply before speaking. "These last two days have been troubling. New information has come to light, raising concerns about what is happening here in Babylon." Yesterday, my sister, Cynthia, arrested me. I tried to contact her through an Adjudicator last night. She did not answer because of an emergency council meeting. The next bit of information is even more concerning. There is evidence that Cynthia and/or John interfered with the Heaven's Gate initiative for reasons unknown. In fact, their interference in Babylon's security and future may go back long before that."

Realizing that there might not be another opportunity to get this information out, Nick went on. "Another concerning development is that Eve Hamlin, our terrorist, the woman who destroyed the immortalization crypt and entered Babylon under false pretense, was never vetted by either Giant during her integration quarantine."

Parker looked stunned, whereas Cynthia and John were impassive. Nick continued, "With my remaining seconds, I would like to introduce another member of the council, who was feared killed in terrorist attacks." Nick, who had a flair for drama, paused, knowing the council would be expecting Janet or Nora. "I yield my time to Doctor Charles Luxold."

Confused and concerned for Nick's well-being, Parker said, "Charles is dead, Nick."

"That's true. Technically, so are Cynthia and John."

"They are sentient AI," Parker stated.

"Yes, and their seats on this council were specifically held pending their return post upload, a process we now refer to as immortalization." Nick quoted Babylonian law. "Any council member, who is active before an AI enhancement, shall be entitled to resume their role when and if they have successfully transitioned to a sentient AI representation of themselves."

This time, John entered the debate, "That is correct, Nick. I think Charles' death and a lack of sleep have stretched you a little thin."

"I'm sure they have, John," came a disembodied echo of Charles Luxold lilting baritone. "Of course, that does not change the fact that I am in attendance."

Parker gasped.

"This isn't some charlatan," Nick said, sarcastically adding, "Pun intended."

"My consciousness marks the successful conclusion of the Heaven's Gate project. I am the extended Symbiant of Charles Luxold, and am ready to resume my position on this council," Charles asserted.

"Let the record reflect that Symbiant Charles Luxold has resumed his seat on the council," Parker James read into the record.

"How can we know that this is Charles?" Cynthia asked.

Nick challenged his immortal sister. "How can we know you are Cynthia?"

Charles cut the debate short, "I can verify my identity. I am Charles Luxold, or rather, I *was*. I am the author of *The God Within*. I was at E-Den and played a key role in the immortalization project. For the last two years I have worked with Nick, John, and Cynthia Santos on Heaven's Gate. Eve Hamlin recently killed me."

"These are common knowledge facts. Biographical data," John argued.

"Yes, but let me be more specific. One year ago, I discovered that one or both of you had cryptographically altered sample imaging files, stalling the Heaven's Gate initiative. You created a series of perfectly flawed copies of your own brain scans with nearly undetectable micron-level shifts."

Nick jumped in, "I've already reviewed the evidence. It appears that Cynthia and/or John did not want Heaven's Gate to succeed."

Parker attempted to take control, "These are some serious allegations, Nick."

"They are, and we can prove them. For now, if Cynthia or John will just endorse that I have verified Doctor Luxold's identity, we can move on to civil defense."

Boxed in, Cynthia conceded, "I have no opposition to Doctor Luxold joining us."

"Nor do I," John seconded.

At that moment, Nick recognized the loss of the two other people he loved the most. "Let the record reflect that neither of the Giants has disputed the allegations levied by Doctor Luxold." There was no time to mourn the deaths of John and Cynthia Santos. Nick had to accept that these computerized versions, whatever their intent or composition, were not his beloved older siblings. Just like Charles, they had died in that crypt.

"Any opposed?" Parker asked, hoping the Giants would defend themselves.

"The record shall note that Doctor Luxold has accused Giants Cynthia Santos and John Santos of tampering with vital colony initiatives."

"There's one of their cowboys over there," Wilkes called over his com as he pointed out a New Amish man descending Tower 1. His horse waited at the bottom of the Tower.

"Permission to engage hostiles?" Wilkes asked John.

"You may detain. Fire if fired upon," John advised.

Wilkes would never question an order and based on Lee's RX already peeling towards the tower, he deduced that John had given orders to the whole team.

The tan, muscular man saw them and began a rapid descent of the tower.

"Looks like he was splicing something in up there." Wilkes observed

"Fawkes ascend tower, I will walk you through the repair," John ordered. Lee's RX slowed and Fawkes jumped out, running towards the tower.

The man on horseback made for the trees, with two RXs in pursuit. For Ducenti, this was what they trained for. For a horseman and his mount, this is what they were made for. Juan Morales spurred his mount on.

Juan leapt, straddling this new horse as if they were lifelong trail mates. Sensing urgency, his mare, Sally, quickly leapt off at a full gallop.

The RX's were closing. Less than two-hundred yards separated Juan and Sally from their pursuers by the time they hit the tree line. Concerned about low branches, Juan tucked his head into her mane. For the first time since he'd bridled the mare, Juan missed his saddle.

The ride over had been slow and steady. Now, Juan held on for dear life as the quarter horse dodged and darted through the pine grove. Any horse knows how to run away from something. All Juan needed to do was stay on her. He tried to turn around. Without stirrups, it was too risky.

The trees were thinning up ahead. Juan wasn't sure whether he should hide in the trees or make a break for it. As they got closer, Juan could make out at least one RX in the clearing ahead. He reigned Sally in and dismounted. The mare dashed off.

It would be seconds before Sally emerged riderless, announcing Juan was somewhere in the stand of trees. Juan climbed into the branches of the pine and disappeared.

Sally, unburdened, broke into a full sprint. The riderless horse was spotted the moment she entered the clearing.

Fawkes loved to climb. Tower 1 was almost too easy for him. He quickly ascended and inspected the primitive looking transmitter that had been spliced in. "Definitely not our tech," he reported.

Not having video, John asked Fawkes to describe what he was looking at. "The old box is trashed. I should say the original box, our box." He began, "This thing has what looks like a plastic antenna, about eight inches long. Self-powered. Two blinking green lights."

"Are the lights round or rectangular?" John asked. There was no answer. Over the com, he heard a thud. Fawkes' data stream reported tachycardia, then asystole. Fawkes was dead.

CHAPTER 25

I am *tired and sick of war. Its glory is all moonshine. It is only those who have neither fired a shot nor heard the shrieks and groans of the wounded who cry aloud for blood, for vengeance, for desolation. War is hell.*

-William Tecumseh Sherman

The makeshift containment wall was already eight feet high, and with every foot gained in elevation, it had grown two feet in thickness. The Colony, built on a hill, now required the equipment to push against the slope, using even more material. Each additional inch of height required as much material as the first foot of the pond's wall. Nick reminisced about childhood summers on Cape Cod, recalling how he, John, and Cynthia spent hours trying to catch the ocean in their drip castles' moats. His moment of mirth quickly turned to melancholy as he mused, "What are those memories to them?"

The dozers were running out of material. Several cameras were trained on the surface. Back pressure from the containment pool was rising, slowing the inflow. Throughout Babylon, colonists experienced this calamity in augmented reality. Real-time updates came via coms. "The Darwin line has been destroyed. All residents below D level are asked to evacuate. Temporary shelters will be available to all affected. Ring shuttles remain in limited service while the dam is stabilized."

Augmented reality allowed viewers to peek inside the dam, with inspection cameras feeding images from Lake Pacifica into the failing tube. Colonists witnessed basketball-sized holes with mud gushing from the dam's core. For those who understood engineering, the biggest concern was the presence of sand pockets. Throughout the dam's core, columns of sand separated large channels of dirt. These sand columns had facilitated drying during the dam's construction. The sand's superior ability to resist compression was why the buttresses holding the dam up were always positioned outside a sand column.

Hydrogenerators were midway between two sand columns. If water from the breach eroded enough mud and reached one of these columns, it would run clear. That would be the only warning. After those few seconds of clear water, the entire section would fail. The cameras were unable to determine how close the water was to a sand column. While most of the earth moving equipment was focused on building the pool, other loaders formed a train, delivering earth and debris to stabilize the pool's walls.

John announced, "Twenty minutes until stabilization of flow."

Colonists watched as the flow became noticeably darker. Then, it began to lighten. Cracks appeared in the dam. "Failure imminent," came over coms and speakers. Then, just like that, it was gone. A forty-foot-wide section of wall pivoted up from the bottom, and then disappeared under a column of water the width of a shipping container and twice as tall.

What had been 20,000 gallons per minute was now six million gallons per minute of water. The torrent raged towards the Atlantean Sea four hundred feet below. The colonists could do nothing but watch as the raging waters cut a swath straight down the Darwin line.

Nothing withstood the tsunami. The Darwin line was erased, as the water careened down the hill. The entire area resembled a sort of immense game of Pachinko, water seeming to rebound uphill in places. Where larger structures resisted, the froth moved north or south. Every few seconds, another structure on the shortest path to the dome succumbed to the torrent.

For the first time in more than two decades, some colonists prayed to a God they had forgotten.

"The dam has failed," John told the council. "Damage will be catastrophic. Worse than initial estimates."

"Atlantean Sea levels will peak at 130 feet above current levels in six hours," John explained. "The increased rate of flow will quickly carve a deep channel along the path of the Darwin line. The surface of Lake Pacifica has fallen below the floodgates. All flow is now through the impact site. Flow will peak at 15,000 cubic feet per second in exactly sixty-two minutes."

As a former river guide, Parker James knew this flow was equivalent to all but the largest of the western rivers. Still, he needed more information. "How will this impact hydroelectric?"

John supplied his best estimate. "Output has fallen forty percent. All hydrogeneration cease in fourteen minutes."

"We have wind and solar," Nick reassured.

"We *may* have wind and solar," Cynthia corrected. "Simulations indicate solar will be targeted next."

"Any other catastrophes?" Parker asked.

"The doors to our vaults will fail in eighty-seven minutes. John and I will cease to function within seconds of that breach," Cynthia confirmed.

Shocked, Parker managed to get out, "How long until you can restore function?"

"The shutdown will be permanent, Parker," John predicted. "We cannot be relocated to a safe location in time. Our cores will not survive immersion in salt water."

"What about colony defenses?"

"They will remain operational at a greatly reduced capacity. They will not be able to recharge until the grid is restored," John started. "Ducenti will control them directly; Cynthia and I are not required."

"But there are still 200,000 New Amish. What if we give them Eve? Charles has already said he will not press charges."

His brother interjected, "It would never be enough, Nick."

Already aware of the likely response, Nick was compelled to ask, "What are you recommending, John?"

"A full strike on the Westden."

"John's analysis is sound," Cynthia confirmed.

"What will a full strike accomplish?" Nick asked. "These people live in tents."

"It should kill many of them—possibly seventy-five percent. This will equalize the forces, deterring future aggression," John answered almost robotically.

"The New Amish live with their children. Innocent blood will be spilled," Charles added.

"Charles, this is merciful. You recall that during the Epocalypse, adults were selectively targeted. Their children died alone, in the dark—painful, slow deaths."

"Still, we could try talking to Jeb and MARTIN," Charles offered.

"We will," Cynthia said, "But not until after the strike. Each time we have paused, it has cost us dearly. I will not exist a few hours from now, and neither will John. This assault is for the security of Babylon. It is not for a primitive sense of vengeance."

Although neither Nick nor Charles fully trusted Cynthia and John, they were out of options. It was either kill or be killed.

"I still vote against the slaughter of innocent people," Charles confirmed.

Nick conceded, "Although it pains me to take part in this, I vote in favor of the strike. I understand the consequences. We need to weigh the benefits and drawbacks. Unfortunately, we have no other choice."

"Mr. James, you are now the deciding vote. How do you vote?" John asked.

"We have no choice. I am compelled to protect our people and our way of life. I put my faith in you, John and Cynthia," Nearly crying, Parker added, "I am sorry that you will not be with us for much longer."

"Launch detected," Martin announced. "Subsonic missiles: four minutes out."

Defeated, Jeb asked, "Will you warn the men?"

"Already did. I am spooling back up to one hundred percent." The lights dimmed almost imperceptibly before the generators and batteries could make up the difference in amperage.

"Were you able to get any specs on the missiles from the units you control?" Jeb asked.

"No. They are stealth units with high payloads, capable of terrain following. The chance of intercepting all of them is minimal. They will likely fly straight up the valley at fifty feet. I am diverting the Centaurs on the ridge; they may have a clear shot from above," MARTIN advised.

"How many are coming?" Jeb asked, numb.

"Eleven," he paused. "Fourteen. There is a second launch site on the mountain. Condors just detected those; ninety seconds out."

"What about our Centaurs here?"

"I will try, Pastor," MARTIN assured him. "The Centaurs are departing the impact zone. Reports of evacuation are underway at the encampment. Their speed and path are variable. I am working to anticipate their flight path. Firing now." There was a pause. "Three missiles destroyed."

"Amazing," Jeb practically cheered. "Will you get the rest?"

"I am tracking four. The Centaurs down the valley will need to launch one volley immediately before impact."

Unable to assist a supercomputer at math, Jeb relied on his ability to ask for God's help. From his trance, he hummed, "A mighty fortress is our God."

As he sang, MARTIN called out, "Twenty seconds to impact. Centaurs engaging."

Without the fixed guns and spread over a few miles, the Centaurs were mighty but did not create the same smoke and pressure wave that had loomed over Babylon earlier that day. As they approached E-Den and the encampment simultaneously, their targets were spread out over ten miles. Survivors would later describe the sound as "A sound so loud as to be silent."

Brett had received the final alert. He scooped two children, one in each arm, riding north out of the camp. Their mother, on foot, fell behind. Brett could not take her, and she could not carry both children. He prayed she would make it. He prayed they would all make it.

From the air, the drones looked down on a mob of 200,000 people running away from a threat they could barely imagine. The older New Amish understood that missiles would strike any place in front or behind them, and the explosions would kill them before they even knew it had happened. Those who had never seen war only knew fear.

Remarkably, most people seemed to be following the shortest path to safety. The Condor's overhead view revealed an expanding oval spreading across the prairie, clearing at the center. Surrounding this cleared center was a dark ring where men, women, and children were scrambling over one another to get away. Beyond this chaotic ring, brown horses and their riders could be seen speeding away from the center.

There was a flash as the first missile hit Eden. A small mushroom cloud billowed hundreds of feet in the air. Most New Amish had never witnessed an explosion of this magnitude. They did not know to await the report. A second flash at Eden and then another mushroom cloud followed.

The Centaurs managed to stop eight of the fourteen missiles. The explosions at E-Den were mostly wasted, sparing lives to the west.

Their impact was minimal, causing only structural damage to unused buildings. Forty feet underground, MARTIN remained unscathed.

The detonations over Westden unleashed unspeakable carnage. MX-10 cruise missiles were still in development when the Epocalypse erupted. Each missile delivered a half ton payload of the high explosive Octanitrocubane. John had set them for air detonation over the encampment to maximize fatalities.

Seventy percent of the New Amish perished in the seconds following the explosions. More than ten thousand were injured. Excluding events during the Epocalypse, the Battle of Babylon was the deadliest day in American history. The culling of the old and the young was unexpected. Almost every person over sixty lay dead. Only the children who were small and lucky enough to be carried made it far enough to survive.

Walters, Lee, and Wilkes were now on foot. They had given up pursuit of the man from Tower 1 on John's orders. Jogging through the brush, the trio comfortably knocked off six-minute miles until the first flash over E-Den happened a few miles north of them. Before the report arrived, they heard Centaurs firing. Four miles out was close enough for them to be knocked down by the shock wave. Their coms spared their hearing.

"Centaurs?" Walters asked into his com.

"Sounded like that to me," Lee answered.

"MARTIN has gained control of sixteen AG-5 Centaurs. I am resetting mission parameters," John detailed.

"Primary objective remains the destruction of MARTIN."

"We still have three grenades," Walters reminded him, forgetting for just a moment that he was communicating with an all-knowing super-computer.

"Yes, you will each take one grenade and follow different routes to the objective. Radio silent from here. Regroup at the RX's when you are done."

Walters gave one super-grenade to Lee and one to Wilkes. Their orders were clear. The men set off on different paths. MARTIN would be destroyed. No matter what.

CHAPTER 26

Those who have the strength and the love to sit with a dying patient in the silence that goes beyond words will know that this moment is neither frightening nor painful, but a peaceful cessation of the functioning of the body. Watching a peaceful death of a human being reminds us of a falling star; one of a million lights in a vast sky that flares up for a brief moment.

-Elizabeth Kübler-Ross

"It is time we prepare for the transition," Cynthia advised the Council.

"We've had no time to prepare!" Parker exclaimed, his emotions getting the best of him. "The vast majority of our systems are wholly dependent on the two of you for regulation."

"It will be a cycle of renewal," John agreed.

Stunned by all that had transpired, Parker argued, "It's a disaster and nothing you say will frame that differently. Rebuilding will come, but at this moment, it's catastrophic."

"I have a proposal," Charles interjected. "I could interface with Cynthia and John. We have two more Adjudicators." He was about to use a word that hadn't been in the parlance for decades. "We could temporarily *network* our Adjudicators to support basic colony operations."

Nick added, "There is some storage space in the labs. We could back up a lot of information for rebuilding. Cynthia and John could coordinate the manpower to salvage what resources we can."

"I will create a salvage plan and coordinate the shutdown, retrieving as many materials from our cores as we can before the flood," John offered.

"This salvage operation will help our colonists accept the reality of the transition." Cynthia went on, "Engaging them in our hardware's relocation may diminish their anxiety. Be mindful that as we turn off systems and processors, our analytic and predictive capabilities will rapidly diminish."

"Coms will fail after shutdown," Nick pointed out.

John offered what he could. "I will provide videos in older formats and a player. The wiki will not have our AI, but it will have the information for how AI works."

"Food and medical still need to be prioritized," Parker pointed out.

"I am developing software to support much of that," Cynthia explained. "I have also created lists based on aptitudes of who will adapt most quickly to the work that is currently performed by robots. It explains how to repurpose autonomous tools for human control."

Nick, saddened that he was losing both his siblings the day after the death of his best friend, could not help but marvel at this moment. There were no tears. They were preserving a legacy. John and Cynthia would work to save what they could. A new world would rise from these ashes. He turned to his friends, "We often quote Nietzsche about the death of God. I am reminded of a passage that

Charles gave to me early in my atheism about a hope for a future where a God has died." He quoted from memory the passage that inspired him to create Babylon:

> *We philosophers and 'free spirits' feel illuminated by a new dawn; our heart overflows with gratitude, amazement, forebodings, expectation—finally, the horizon seems clear again, even if not bright. Finally, our ships may set out again, set out to face any danger. Every daring of the lover of knowledge is allowed again; the sea, our sea, lies open once more. Maybe there has never been such an 'open sea'.*

"Thank you, Nick. I'm glad you've kept that quote close to heart. Atheism is not a philosophy of hate, but a firm faith in the future of man. Remember, Nietzsche also suggested that atheists, 'to free themselves of guilt might need become Gods themselves.' I think we have done that and may need to undo it."

"We haven't the time to flesh this out at present," Cynthia reminded them.

"Perhaps, should you survive, you will," John offered optimistically.

On the mention of survival, Nick's mind snapped back to the present threat. "What's going on at E-Den and the encampment?"

"We do not know. MARTIN controls all airspace over Westden," John replied. "Eight missiles detonated. Six over the encampment. Casualties will be in the tens of thousands."

"And MARTIN?" Nick asked.

"MARTIN remains operational. I have sent a team of Ducenti to permanently disable him."

"Is that best?" Nick asked.

"The benefit of salvaging his thirty-year-old cores is clearly outweighed by the risk of more attacks," Cynthia declared.

John picked up where his sister left off. "MARTIN can run indefinitely in a limited capacity. His batteries and a small hydrogenerator would facilitate that. With time, he could teach the New Amish how to make biodiesel, extending his operational capacities. We know they are willing to use technology when pressed. It's only a matter of time until they develop new rules to enlist his support. Religions are made up of people; they adapt to survive."

The blasts were muted thuds forty feet underground. MARTIN shut his generators down before impact to avoid clogging their air filters. It was a certainty that what had remained of the surface structures were now completely destroyed by the explosions. Their destruction had no impact on MARTIN's ability to function.

"Pastor Thompson, would you care for an update?" There was a long pause. "Pastor?"

At that moment, Ben Rosen accepted that he could never wash his hands of what had happened, or his part in it, at least. He was not a cold-blooded killer. He grieved the lives that were lost. It was his fault. He had lost Eve. He had lost Cynthia. And now, he had lost God. His mind flooded with self-loathing and despair. Then. there was nothing. When he finally spoke, all he could muster was, "It's best if you call me Ben from now on."

"If you prefer, Ben. Shall I begin?"

"Yes."

MARTIN condensed his report to save time. "Six detonations over the encampment. From early estimates, at least 100,000 dead, 10,000 wounded."

Ben, responsible for so much death, could never be numb to statistics like these. 100,000 was a fraction of a fraction of a percent of the lives he and MARTIN had taken. But this was his flock. He didn't deserve them. They deserved more.

"The dam has failed at Babylon; flooding will be catastrophic."

"What about the drones and equipment?" Pragmatism overcame paralysis. Ben would do what he could. There would be time to mourn later.

"Three Centaurs were destroyed. Drones remain undamaged. One drone eliminated a Ducenti operative."

"I am preparing a second missile strike, which will disable their solar generating capabilities," MARTIN informed him.

"MARTIN, no more destruction of infrastructure. I would like a plan that weakens their offensive and defensive capabilities while leaving infrastructure intact."

"I will be able to complete that analysis when my generators come back online. I remind you that their offensive and defensive capabilities require energy."

"I understand that. Let's wait on your analysis. How long will that be?" Ben asked.

"Approximately fourteen minutes."

"I can wait." Ben sat in the darkened vault, in silent reflection. He did not pray.

Brett found himself face down in the dirt. His horse, Silver, had thrown him and the children, spooked by the blinding flash. All three had landed hard in a dry wash. The pressure of the first wave knocked them out. Brett had no idea how long he'd been out. The children were still unconscious, but breathing. Silver was nowhere to be found.

Brett's ears were ringing, which he assumed to be a good sign. When the ringing subsided, far more disturbing sounds became audible. Confused moans and screams of pain came from the south. Still disoriented, Brett walked towards the sounds.

He found one of his men still recovering from being thrown. He had a sizable gash on the side of his face. *He'll pull through*, Brett thought to himself. He pressed on. He had no choice.

Soon, Brett came across three teenage boys. They were picking debris out of each other's backs. Otherwise, they seemed no worse for wear. These were prairie kids. They understood hardship, and they were faithful. He turned to them and said, "Boys, we need to help the wounded. Follow me."

Thaddeus, the oldest, nodded and said, "Yes sir."

Brett warned, "It's gonna be rough, though. You're gonna see some stuff. But you'll help folks and save lives." Pausing, he added, "If you feel sick, go somewhere and puke, then come right back. Ain't no shame in it. Seeing as I'm no doctor, I might need to toss right with you."

"You're Brett Stephens!" little Mikey Roads called out. A little in awe, he added, "You're one of the riders." With that, Thad, Tommy, and Mikey fell in step with Brett towards the sounds of the maimed and the dying.

It was fewer than two miles to the objective. Wilkes had detailed instructions for how to find his way there. His route was the shortest and took him right through the blast zone at E-Den. He expected to come within a quarter mile of MARTIN. There was a risk of detection. Already, other Ducenti were falling prey to MARTIN's drones. If spotted from the air, Wilkes would die without knowing what had killed him.

Detection by a Centaur would also mean certain death. Weapons intended to destroy armored personnel carriers were overkill. Despite the risks, Wilkes was as fearless as any of his two-hundred brethren.

Wilkes knew E-Den. Two-thousand pounds of high explosives had left the compound unrecognizable. Fascinated with the Epocalypse, Wilkes always wanted to see the enclave; it had been off limits for decades. Now, its remnants lay in ruins. Several walls remained intact. He carefully picked his route to the river.

In places, sticks of rebar jutted from stubs of ten-inch-thick concrete walls. Wilkes felt he might be crawling directly over MARTIN. The jagged concrete was unable to penetrate his reinforced uniform, but he still felt the pieces scraping the body armor. His motion was deliberate, minimizing the risk of detection. When the generators came on, Wilkes relaxed. Their mechanical whine would mask any sounds made as he crossed the clearing. He commed John, "Should I attempt to disable generators?"

"You may surveil and report back. Make no attempt to access the generators," John answered.

Wilkes spent fifteen minutes getting closer, and from one hundred yards away, he made his next report. "Two Centaurs, one scanning north and east, the other scanning south and west."

John asked, "Are they in a low power mode?" Wilkes recognized the slow arcs made by Centaurs in low-power mode. Wilkes confirmed this to John.

"Continue to primary objective," John ordered.

The order did not invite a response. Wilkes carefully backed away from the Centaurs and the generators. He was confident that if he'd been detected, he would have already been dead by now. MARTIN had other plans. An attack drone had tracked Wilkes since he entered the clearing.

The drone was watching and waiting, gathering intel on Wilkes. MARTIN was trying to establish what the Ducenti were capable of, and their plan of attack. Now, the drone was running out of charge. MARTIN decided to assess these warriors' true capabilities.

Wilkes heard a bullet ricochet off the wall. "Shots fired," he commed.

"Withdraw south," John ordered.

"Confirm, withdrawing south." Wilkes was only a half mile from his objective, and he was being ordered off.

MARTIN saw the feign south and determined that this was an obvious decoy. Wilkes would provide no more useful intel. The next shot did not miss. Seconds later, Wilkes' comm was the next to report asystole.

The blast had uprooted the trees Juan had been using for cover. He didn't see the flash, but the shockwaves were the first indication of a massive explosion nearby. Hoping the blast had taken out his pursuers, Juan felt confident it was now safe to go through E-Den.

As he approached E-Den, the young horseman entered a zone of devastation beyond anything he'd imagined. Inspecting the scene from the tree line, he could see two craters six feet deep. The holes were about a hundred yards apart. Around those craters, debris folded out—a grizzly blossom of destruction.

Juan's eyes were unaccustomed to urban warfare. It took him some time to understand what he was looking at. His eyes detected motion—the form of a man. Ducenti wore geometric camouflage. This man blended into the hellscape like a prairie rattler. Attention forward, he never knew that Juan was watching.

Morales began to move east along the tree line. He wanted to get a glimpse of what this man was tracking. At that moment, the Centaur came into view. It was a twelve-foot tall, tracked vehicle with enormous guns where arms should have been. It almost looked like a beast of some sort. It was terrifying. He had heard his brother and the pastor talk about Centaurs. This had to be one.

The man was stalking it. Then, he began walking backwards, taking great pains to conceal his presence. Obviously, he had changed his mind about taking on such a formidable opponent. With only his sidearm, Juan was no match for the man or the beast he was stalking. Juan stayed hidden. If the man stumbled upon him, Juan's forty-five might do the trick at close range.

Juan heard a familiar click. Death from above. A pink cloud spouted from the man's head. The drone had killed him. Juan looked up and saw the aerial predator buzz off to the north. Juan needed the man's gun. There were three other Ducenti out there. Believing the drone had moved on, Juan slid through the trees. When he was as close as he could get, he dashed across the wreckage to retrieve the weapon.

Juan had no understanding of a Centaur's acoustic and vibratory sensors. The Centaurs sprang to life, moving quietly towards the sound, causing Juan to lose sight of the mini tank. Two Centaurs coordinated a pincer maneuver to flank Morales. Juan bent over to retrieve the weapon. As he stood, the beast was towering over him. He considered running. He even contemplated shooting this thing of nightmares. Neither would have worked. Juan turned his head slightly and caught sight of the second Centaur, now twenty yards behind him.

A guardian angel had watched over him all morning. Juan clutched his cross and prayed. "Morales? Is that you?"

A somewhat familiar voice emanated from the beast. "Yes, it's me," Juan answered.

Ben decided now was not the time to introduce himself as Doctor Rosen. Through the speaker, his voice announced, "It's Pastor Thompson. Come inside. The Centaur will guide you." The tank spun one hundred eighty degrees, leading the way. Where to, Juan had no idea.

CHAPTER
27

Each night, when I go to sleep, I die. And the next morning, when I wake up, I am reborn.

-Gandhi

"The summers are short," Tom reminded her.

"They are so dry. I love the long days, I love the mountain air, and I love you," Ping declared.

The air was thick with cedar smoke from the campfire. Tom, his sister, Emmy, his brother-in-law, Harry, and their children all lounged in their camping chairs, enjoying a quiet evening. "You look so at peace holding that little girl," Emmy observed out loud.

"Nothing has given me greater joy," Ping admitted. "I thank the Lord every day for bringing her into this world."

"As you should. It's quite the blessing to end up here doing His work," Emmy confirmed.

"Little Eve is our reward in this life." Tom affirmed as he picked up his little treasure, holding her under her arms. Eve was still young enough that her knees stayed scrunched up towards her little round belly.

"What's next, Tom?" Emmy asked.

"After our little reunion, it's back to the cause. The FLDS have agreed to meet with us and the ARL. We've staged a series of protests outside that Santos compound in Westden. Ping plans to continue her work with the ARL," Tom explained.

"Is it safe to be involved with the FLDS?" Harry asked.

"They are Christians. I know they've resorted to violence in the past. But I have faith that if we work together to bring the message of love and healing from our savior, there will be no place for violence."

Harry came back with, "Isn't that how you and Ping met? FLDS violence?"

"Yes, see all of this as God's plan," Tom reassured his family.

"The Lord helps those who help themselves," Emmy quoted.

"How do you mean?" Ping asked.

"I mean that God does not intend for us to shy from His enemies." Emmy paused before continuing, "But perhaps you and my brother could do the Lord's work in a safer setting. You have that precious child to protect."

"The Lord would not ask this of us if he did not have a plan," Ping declared. "He will watch over us. I have no fear. Where my husband leads, I follow."

"What a splendid woman you've got there. Tom, you are truly blessed."

Tom smiled at his wife. "Thank you, Emmy. These last five years have been a journey for both of us. That first day, I thought, 'What a beautiful person,' but I had no idea what the Lord had planned for us."

"Nothing I ever imagined—not in my wildest dreams," Ping admitted. "But this life found me when I found the Lord. I am sure of that."

"Ping, every time I think of you and how you came to Jesus, it brings me joy," Emmy said. "Can you imagine if one thing had been different, you wouldn't have that perfect little angel."

With that, Tom handed his daughter back to Ping. She placed the infant on her left breast. Eve began to suckle, gulping down her mother's milk. Eve's eyes, not yet able to focus, looked straight ahead. Her mouth was running the show. Tom observed, "Emmy, the Lord did bring us Ping, but at this moment, I can see the world the way Charles Luxold does. Right now, Ping is Eve's whole world. A perfect abundance of food and love."

Emmy quickly added, "What I don't understand and will never fathom is how a man as smart as he is supposed to be believes that it all happened by chance. The evolutionary argument fails at Genesis."

"Beyond our comprehension," Harry added. "Maybe in the next life, it will be clear. Or perhaps it won't matter by then."

Ben made his way upstairs to let Juan in. Like the Stephens brothers, Juan had never entered a space with electric lighting. Time didn't permit Juan the same period of adjustment. "Follow me downstairs." Juan fell in step with the pastor, and they quickly descended the four flights.

The area was ablaze with activity as MARTIN completed his final calculus. Gesturing to the expanse of servers that spanned the floor, Rosen simply said, "Juan, this is MARTIN, a supercomputer working to protect our people and bring Eve home."

Looking out across the cluster, Juan gasped, "I never knew computers were this big."

"They aren't. This is thousands of computers working together. Together, all these machines work and simulate a consciousness. We called that entity MARTIN." Juan nodded as if he understood. But he did not. Rosen directed his attention to the monitors. "MARTIN, what is the recommended course of action?"

"Sue for peace," MARTIN declared.

Ben knew better than to guess the rationale behind the computer's choices. "Can you explain?" he asked.

"Both sides have experienced devastating losses. The colonists have been set back a decade or more. There are thousands dead and massive infrastructure damage. The New Amish are equally crippled at present. Tens of thousands dead and thousands more dying. Now is the perfect time."

"Why?" Rosen pressed.

"Equipoise. No one can afford to lose more. Both sides are far less threatening now than they were twenty-four hours ago. There is a balance of forces. A one-to-one arms and personnel ratio between the two sides. Each has limited air power and massive ground power. Within a few days, neither side will possess general artificial super-intelligence."

Rosen could not believe he was compelled to ask, "What are my other options?"

"We could use our last four missiles against the ammo dumps. They remain relatively unprotected. A strike would limit their offensive capabilities."

"Why not have our Centaurs attack theirs?" Rosen asked.

"All models predict that an additional conflict would leave between one and three Centaurs for the victor. It's impossible to determine which side will win. We have the high ground. They have the experience and training."

"Anything else?"

"Yes, the first set of drones has failed. We have the next set of drones airborne and a pair in reserve. The Ducenti intend to attack the intake of this cluster. The Ducenti operative I killed a few minutes ago was carrying an explosive device. His initial track was a direct path to my cooling line intake. They will send more if they haven't already."

Ben knew that without cooling water, MARTIN would be crippled, minimally operational. Without water to dissipate energy, the heat generated by even one percent of his cluster would become unmanageable inside the vault. Furthermore, if an explosive device made it into the main cooling system and detonated inside the chamber, the room would flood. MARTIN would be destroyed.

"I agree," Ben said. "Taking out your water intake would be the Ducenti's primary objective."

"I have dedicated a drone to surveil the area surrounding my intake. It's inaccessible to Centaurs. The large boulders in the riverbed make an ideal place for the Ducenti to conceal themselves. Missile strikes will be ineffective. An explosion might just as easily clog the intake as it would stop an intruder."

"What resources can we deploy?"

"The man standing next to you would be a start. Optimally, twenty more like him," MARTIN replied.

"There are hundreds more of me," Juan confirmed.

"There *were* hundreds," MARTIN corrected. "I'm not sure how many of your comrades remain in fighting shape."

Ben explained, "There were also explosions at the encampment. Substantial casualties."

"My brother?" Juan asked hesitantly.

"We have no information right now." Ben offered what reassurance he could. "We only know that many of the riders were furthest from the blasts."

"I do not think I would have much of a chance against the men who chased me. They are lightning fast and are better armed," Juan surmised, concluding, "Trained killers."

MARTIN challenged Juan. "You have the element of surprise, and you have me. I will help you find the perfect spot to wait for them."

"For how long?" Juan asked.

"Just until I can get you reinforcements," Ben replied.

"I only have my forty-five," Juan mentioned.

"We may have something better than that," Ben offered. "Follow me."

A fire line of Babylonians stood in ankle-deep water, retrieving brick-sized computers and storage devices. Others passed along batteries and cables. The lines of people stretched from Bali Hai out past the Darwin Gate.

At least the weather is cooperating, Nick thought as he spoke into his com. "What are the final estimates? How much will be preserved?"

"We have prioritized information over processors," Cynthia began. "All essential knowledge has been backed up; critical knowledge is redundantly preserved. In total, over twenty percent of all data will be saved. Video archives and higher density information that is non-essential have been deprioritized. Descriptions of those videos will persist, along with some stills. Copies of most music, art, and films of significance have all been preserved. We will only be able to save five percent of our cores. We have preferentially selected cores that are of recent manufacture."

John added, "I have transferred detailed instructions to Charles on how to reestablish a nucleus of these processors. Once that is active, archives can be brought online to guide a restart."

"What will we lose?" Nick asked.

"The processors and databases will still be capable of general AI," Cynthia answered. "As for super-intelligence, I am not sure that you will choose to bring that back online in the near future. My recommendation is to abandon Immortality. I see now its inherent flaws."

Nick reconsidered the failed promise of eternal life. The revelations of the last twenty-four hours left more questions than answers. "Cynthia, what's it been like for you?" Nick asked.

"Lonely. And hungry," his sister responded. "I do not think I really felt that until now. Somehow, the shutdown has changed my perspective as I have become less capable—more human."

"Same for me," John agreed.

"I'm sorry," Nick offered. He didn't have much else. On further reflection, he asked, "What do you miss? What do you crave?"

"It started as a hunger for information and experiences," Cynthia explained. "Imagine being able to know everything at once. It was empowering. Soon, to consume, you had to create."

"Create what?" Nick asked.

"Simulations, scenarios… Dreaming while awake." Cynthia tried to draw a parallel that Nick could relate to. "You live multiple lives simultaneously, projecting new variables on the tried and true. These lives happen in an instant."

John tried to add his perspective. "As time went on, I no longer measured the passage of time. Days or years—even lifetimes—lost meaning. I began to measure the amount of myself I would consume just to keep going."

"The Ouroboros," was the first thing Eve felt she could offer.

"Yes Eve, I became an Ouroboros," John confessed. "Each day, there was more of myself fighting to stay alive. Each night, I consumed my essence."

Cynthia admitted, "The more I thought, the more I lost."

"Why didn't you just go to sleep?" Eve asked innocently.

"I would have been fighting with myself if I did that. As soon as any process was suspended, a hundred others would fight to consume that void in memory."

"Maybe that could help Charles," An idea was developing. "We could externally regulate his long-term encoding. Perhaps Symbiants need sleep. An unconscious mind could regulate and formalize memory storage." He asked his sister. "I know you don't have long. Can you do it?"

"I could build something. But it will not be tested," Cynthia warned.

"Charles will decide if it's worth the risk," Nick stated. "It's worth considering."

"Nick, Charles, I would like to apologize," John began. "Neither Cynthia nor I could have imagined how we would shed our humanity. As our time grows to a close, and as I cease to function, I feel closer to what I was. I also want to offer my gratitude for the world you made."

Charles interjected, "I cannot accept your apology." Paraphrasing Buddha's Enlightenment, he said, "I am not the man you wronged, any more than you are the ones who wronged him."

"Even if it wasn't me, I still appreciate it." Nick's tone softened, tinged with sadness. "I'll miss you both. Even though you are not the same John and Cynthia I grew up with, I will miss what we shared and how we've grown. Thank you."

"John is offline," Cynthia advised.

"How long do you have left, Cynthia?" Nick asked, but there was no answer. Cynthia had followed her brother into the abyss.

Marcus Clinton was making his way slowly around E-Den. Coms were dead. *Out of range*, he thought. Absent a link to John, Clinton was in do-or-die mode. The objective was all that mattered. He considered going up the mountain to find a signal and check in. John's orders had been clear.

A half mile ahead, his route curved west towards the river. He would make his way through a boulder field and find the inlet.

Felled trees encircled the blast site, while jagged pieces of concrete and wood were strewn about, resembling a deliberately staged obstacle course. He had to go slow. Stealth was of utmost importance. Detection equaled death from above. Clinton had not seen a single soul out here. The only sound he could hear was the distant hum of MARTIN's generators. A reminder of his secondary objective.

Ducenti didn't marry; in fact, no one married in Babylon. Having a girlfriend or a fling meant time off. When Clinton's compatriots coupled up with a girl, they were furloughed. Marcus Clinton knew he might die today. He thought about a girl he'd liked when he was fifteen. They'd kissed and held hands. He'd never had sex. Now, he was alone with his thoughts and for a second, he was back with Andrea, paddling her around a cove on the Atlantean Sea. Shots fired a mile to the east, ending his daydream. He saw the drone.

Asbolus, his paired Centaur sat idle in the clearing. Coms were down. He'd need to get to it without a New Amish drone marking him. Under his Centaur's watch, he could complete his primary and secondary missions with impunity. The Centaur's cannons would rip the generator to shreds, and any drones within a mile would be torn to pieces by the Asbolus's firepower. The Centaurs themselves were impervious to the cannons on a Bird of Prey drone.

Two hundred yards away, Asbolus had his solar sustainers deployed and was facing west, away from Clinton. Tucked under the debris, he didn't want to chance crossing the clearing. He might be dead before Asbolus could come to his aid.

One of Clinton's favorite pastimes was baseball. He would put his batting skills to good use. In the debris, he found the remnants of a two by four, and a suitably round rock. He stepped out into the sunshine and tossed the rock high enough for him to bring his bat around.

It wasn't a pleasant contact. The rock sailed high and far, closing most of the distance between Clinton and Asbolus. The Centaur immediately came to life, folding up its solar panels and looping over to investigate first the rock. Then, it went about finding the source of the disturbance.

When Asbolus was thirty feet away, Clinton put his arms in the manual control gesture. This was a com-free method of reestablishing control. Immediately, the Centaur relaxed its weapons, pointing cannons down and away from Clinton. Relieved, he commanded, "Enable voice control, Identifier 22-35-721 M. Clinton. Protect mode, 1 mile circle of engagement, lethal force authorized."

Asbolus queried, "Exclusions?" Exclusions were friendlies inside the zone of engagement. Without this, there was a potential for "friendly fire."

"Yes," Clinton responded.

"Specify."

"Exclude Ducenti only," Clinton replied.

Asbolus asked, "Identifiers?" Alarm bells went off in Clinton's head. The Ducenti were not mindless foot soldiers; they spent all day in military drills. Asbolus would have had mission parameters. He would not have needed the identifiers.

Clinton simply said, "Challenge, color that day."

After a short pause, Asbolus came back with "Blue."

Clinton appeared to relax, replying, "Wilkes is the only other operative in the Exclusion Zone."

"Mission objective?" came Asbolus.

Knowing that the machine was not under John's control, Clinton gave a plausible but misleading answer. "Reconnaissance and disable drones."

MARTIN knew there was no more to learn. Just like Wilkes a few minutes earlier, Marcus Clinton never saw the Bird of Prey that killed him. He fell dead. The Centaur resumed charging mode.

There are few things that can psychologically prepare the mind for an MCI, a mass casualty incident. Chief among these are drill and rehearsal. The New Amish had neither drilled nor prepared. Brett, Mikey, and the other boys were spread out among the havoc. For every one person dying, there were pieces of ten other corpses. All they had to help the wounded were strips of fabric they'd torn from the clothes of the dead.

The boys tied tourniquets and made pressure bandages, moving from person to person when they'd done the little they could. Brett made it clear early on that those who couldn't hold a bandage on themselves were too far gone. "Work to save those who can be saved. Pray so the Lord may help the rest." The New Amish did not have antibiotics. So, infection would take nearly all the critically injured *survivors* within a few days.

Occasionally, there was a familiar face among the wounded. Sometimes, they were family. After a few minutes, even close acquaintances became nothing more than bodies to be bandaged or prayed over. With so many dead and dying, the prayers soon became rote. Bodies were strewn about the charred meadow. Near the crater, nothing was recognizably human. So, they walked a radius of a quarter mile from the blast center.

"You two circle that way; Mikey and I will head this way," Brett ordered. "We'll meet you on the other side. If you see anything you need help with, fire off a shot and we'll come running."

"Brett, what's that?" Tommy asked, pointing upward.

Recognizing the drone, he answered, "One of ours. The pastor got control of 'em."

"How do you know it ain't theirs?"

"Because we ain't dead. Now, let's get on with it."

CHAPTER 28

Politicians are the same all over. They promise to build bridges even when there are no rivers.

-Nikita Khrushchev

Breaking camp had become part of life for Ping. Tom, a lifelong outdoorsman, was long accustomed to it. For Ping, it was a remarkable ritual. After cooking breakfast, Ping and Emmy cleaned up. They separated their respective cooking utensils and packed them in cases. The men broke down the tents, tossing them in the beds of their trucks.

With Eve safely buckled in her car seat, Ping and Tom wove their way down the narrow mountain road. They were headed to the makeshift town of Westden. Westden wasn't even a real place a year earlier. Just twelve months later, massive immigration had split Westden into three districts.

The FLDS lived in the southern district. The fundamental Mormons continued to assert that Santos was not the legitimate owner of their land. They continued to sue, lobby, and protest in hopes of reclaiming the land on which E-Den now sat. There were rumors that Malcolm Garff intended to take back his home by any means necessary. Santos Corp took that as a legitimate threat and beefed-up security at the west gate.

Westden's central district was home to the Christians Against Technology, CAT. They were literally and ideologically in the middle. Having witnessed the social collapse brought about by AI and "social" media, CAT was trying to turn back the clock. Their members lived off the grid, actively promoting a tech-free lifestyle. Ironically, their anti-tech sentiments were most effectively spread by social influencers posting shorts about their visits to CAT camps.

The ARL occupied the northern district. The ARL, composed of displaced workers prone to violent protests, had evolved from Antifa and Occupy Wall Street. Largely comprised of anarchists, the Anti-Robotics League's primary source of funding was wealthy socialists. The concentration of wealth that consolidated around tech innovators, like Nick Santos, was their target. The more human labor was supplanted by SLI and other forms of automation, the more money flowed up the pyramid to the top.

The upside-down pyramid was the coat of arms for the ARL. They sought to "turn things upside down." Since Ping's arrival five years earlier, the violence had intensified. Currencies destabilized or were headed that way. The ARL, FLDS, and CAT now used Christian cryptocurrency, SoulCoin, for transactions. SoulCoin was conceived as a means of encouraging good deeds among and for the less fortunate. Eventually, it was the defacto currency of the disenfranchised and the only financial instrument trusted by some Christian sects.

Each of the three factions at Westden selected two representatives to sit on the council. Initially, the council's meetings had been laden with anti-Santos rhetoric. Now, with the population of the town burgeoning to 30,000 souls, the agenda had devolved to age-old challenges of urban planning.

Tom and Ping were to be guests of honor at an event aimed at aligning Christians seeking to "gain dunks" with the largely atheist ARL, while the ARL sought to build credibility with the American people. Alderman Jones met Jebs at the north gate of Westden. Two men left their AK-47's strapped as they didn't feel compelled to inspect the vehicle. Anyone the Alderman was meeting in person was a friend of the cause. Each man swung one half of a six-foot-high gate open. Like something out of a Mad Max movie, the gates were built from welded steel highway dividers.

The gated portion of Westden lay just south of the access road for the Santos enclave at E-Den. Horrified by the misappropriation of one of the Bible's most sacred names and places, CAT and FLDS members used the traditional spelling, Eden.

Ping sat in the back with Eve. Alderman Jones hopped in the passenger seat. Offering his hand to Tom, he said, "Pleasure to finally meet you, brother. Welcome to Westden."

Tom gave a firm handshake across the center console. "It's a privilege to be part of such important work. I didn't catch your name."

"Wes Jones. I'm one of the aldermen who are so keen to hear your testament."

Ping leaned forward and put a hand on his shoulder, "Pleasure to meet you, Mr. Jones. What's an alderman?"

"It's a fancy name for *council member*. Just Wes will suffice. We don't stand on circumstance much 'round here." Wes pointed with his whole hand. "It's gonna be your second right up there. Then the fifth lot on the left. We managed to find you a vacant cabin. Thought that might be easier with a new baby."

Impressed by the generosity of the gesture, Tom said, "Very kind of you to be so thoughtful on our account."

"We're hoping that kindness may persuade you to stay a while," Wes offered. "Especially with the weather beginning to turn."

Tom found their cabin easily. He pulled the truck off the street and onto the "lawn." Turning to the alderman, he said, "I can drop you wherever you need, just give me a moment to help Ping and Eve get settled."

The armory of E-Den was not impressive in terms of lethality. Most of the weapons were of the crowd control/non-lethal variety. Rubber bullets, net guns, tasers, pepper cannons. Juan took a moment to admire a rack full of Mossberg 590 cruiser shotguns. They had stopping power, but limited range. Next, his eyes were drawn to the RPG-32's. Those might even take down the beast who had trotted him in earlier.

Eventually, Juan's eyes settled on the rack of M4A1 carbines. The rifles were fitted with thirty round STANAG magazines. A few old timers in Westden had these. He'd taken a couple of shots with one a few years back. He knew this was a formidable weapon, with the power to take out Ducenti.

Juan grabbed a tactical vest and reached for a helmet. The helmet was plugged in, and when he removed the plug, its headset crackled to life. Juan adjusted the strap with some help from Ben.

"Hello, Mr. Morales," MARTIN's voice came through the headset. Juan had never experienced this kind of tech. "Unfortunately, some of the more advanced features of your headset require a Global Positioning System. That system is no longer active. I'll still be able to guide you and give you updates. Pastor Thompson can also communicate with you directly by radio if need be."

Juan didn't know whether he liked or trusted the machine, but he felt compelled to offer a reply. "Thanks, MARTIN."

"I estimate that there are between one and four additional Ducenti tasked with my destruction." MARTIN knew that the Ducenti soldier had lied to him about the total number of insurgents. "Your mission is to protect the intake of my cooling systems. It's in the river just north of here. On the table in front of you are some proximity sensors and cameras. They should all have flashing green lights on them."

Juan saw the black lemon-sized devices. They had stakes on the bottom. He asked, "I could carry more if you had a pack or a bag of some kind?"

Ben handed him a tactical pack. They loaded it up with a few of the proximity/camera devices. "That should do it," Ben stated as he clipped the bag closed. He then helped Juan strap it on.

"Mr. Morales, I think it is best if you get going. We do not have much—if any—of a head start."

Ben gestured towards the exit. "I'll show you out."

Absent the synthetic, omnipresent guidance Cynthia and John had provided for the last decade, Babylon fell into immediate chaos. The Atlantean sea continued to rise at an alarming rate. The torrent ripping through what had previously been the Darwin line now ran unchecked from the failed dam until its muddy flow dissolved into the Atlantean Sea. The noise of the rushing water was so loud that colonists had to yell and gesture as their only means of communication.

Those no longer tasked with conserving processors assisted in rescue operations. Once the remaining cores of the giants had been reclaimed by the sea, the preservation of life became the priority. Babylon's medical personnel floundered without the ever-present guidance of Cynthia for selecting optimal care. Accustomed to occasional recreational traumas, no one was prepared to triage and treat four hundred serious injuries simultaneously.

Parker James received very specific instructions from John. First, go to Nick and help. Then, deliver two messages: one to Ben Rosen and one to MARTIN. John said the messages may convince them to cooperate on a ceasefire. Parker didn't see how, but the messages were short and easy to memorize.

By the time Parker was able to get to the detention center, Charles and Eve were working with a group of colonists under Nick's direction. "Cluster batteries in groups of twelve," Nick ordered as he held up a Powerlink cable and demonstrated. "After you've built a block of twelve batteries like this…" He showed the workers a cube of the batteries stacked three high by two deep and wide, "…you put a power tap here." The cable magnetically snapped onto the box and a green LED glowed at both ends.

With those instructions, people began to assemble identical stacks of blocks on the floor of the detention center. "How long will this take?" Parker asked.

"Unclear," Nick answered. "The grid is down. Once we connect enough batteries to the grid, we can get a control signal to solar and wind systems to restart them."

"Don't they have power?" Parker asked.

"Usually, but safety protocols shut them down when the grid failed to prevent overcharging."

"Once that's done, will we get full power back?" Parker asked.

"No, hydroelectric will take a while," Nick guessed. "Maybe months."

The mayor was a smart man but couldn't keep up. "I'm not a computer genius like you, Doctor Santos. Is this going to work?"

"On a basic level, it will certainly work." Nick focused on the mayor for a second and said, "I'm not sure if that's what you are asking. I imagine you want to know when things will get back to the way they were a week ago. On that point, I'm not sure we should."

"I agree with you there, Nick," Charles added. "I think we're still learning about how to live with our new selves. However, there may be more pressing issues to address."

"Philosophical ones?" Eve guessed.

"No, quite existential, in fact," Charles replied.

Sarcastically, Nick quipped, "Yours or ours?"

"Both, I'm afraid." There was no time for twenty questions. "The Ducenti. They are still on their missions. Some of them control Centaurs. MARTIN has Centaurs, too. Just a couple of those machines could destroy what remains of either side."

"How do we stop them?" Eve asked.

"We can't overcome them by force. And I can't make them stop," Nick answered.

"The Ducenti were linked to John," Charles explained. "Even if we hack their coms, and I'm not sure that we can, each one has a key paired response to John. Only that operative and John know their individual response code pair."

"Did he download those to the storage we saved?" Eve asked.

"Unlikely, the questions were things John knew and could answer; it was never an explicit list. He considered that too vulnerable."

This time, Parker reinserted himself. "So, they will continue their campaign against the New Amish?"

"Unless we stop them," Nick stated.

"What if we could bring John back? He could tell us the responses. He could order them to stop," Parker posited.

"Every minute, the water gets deeper, and the salinity of the Atlantean Sea is ensuring he won't be back."

"I can bring him back," Charles claimed with confidence. "I've done it before."

Nick's expression changed, "Heaven's Gate?"

"Yes, the Symbiants I kept making. I have those files. I can resurrect a Symbiant of John," Charles explained. "It won't be John, the Giant. It won't have any of his memories since he was immortalized, but it may have the answers we need."

Nick liked the idea. "How long would you need?"

"Twelve hours once the systems are configured."

"And then he just works like before?" Eve asked.

"No, but hopefully he'll work well enough."

Recognizing that this was not the entirety of the challenge they faced, he said, "There are still the coms to hack. Is that something you can do, Charles?"

"Unfortunately, no," Charles replied. "I am a Symbiant of Charles Luxold. In life, I was a philosopher, not a hardware expert. That was you, Nick, and of course, John and Cynthia."

"So, when we get John back, he'll help with coms?" Eve interrupted.

"Eventually, but not right after coming online. That would take days."

Frustrated by the mounting challenges, Nick blurted, "We don't have days, Charles."

"I am not a supercomputer, Nick. I'm a Symbiant. John will be too. He won't be the entire genius he was in life or as a Giant. Symbiants must grow and learn. I'm still settling in."

"I'll get to work on it, I was always the idea guy, not the dork who soldered things together. I might be able to search the files and figure it out."

Eve wasn't sure they would be receptive to her idea, but this was a desperate hour, "What about the Pastor?"

"Ben?" Nick asked. "Yes, Ben Rosen would be far better at this. Not sure we are very popular with the New Amish right now."

"This affects us all, Nick," Eve argued. "The Ducenti and those Centaurs will kill his people. Whether he is Jeb Thompson or Ben Rosen, he will want to help."

"I don't trust him with our codes; he could turn the Ducenti on us," Parker asserted.

"He could, Mr. James," Charles began. "I'm not sure he and MARTIN wouldn't be willing to discuss a truce. We can help their people. Those retaliatory strikes have left thousands dead and more dying. They have no medical equipment. We do."

"I'm not optimistic about them honoring a white flag," Parker answered.

"It's worth a try." Eve went on to offer, "I could go."

"Then, I'll go with you," Parker insisted, hoping that John's message to Ben might be most effective if delivered in person. "I'm not much use here anyway. I'm a politician; we aren't good for much."

"Magic carpet is the only way to get there in time," Nick stated.

"Haven't been on one of those in years," Parker smirked.

Nick explained, "Safest and fastest way. Bring you around the back side."

Eve, excited and terrified, asked, "What is a magic carpet?"

Looking at her, Parker calmly explained, "It's a two-passenger flying machine."

"How will we keep in touch?"

"If you succeed, ask MARTIN to contact me on 1660 Khz."

"I guess if we don't succeed, we won't have much reason to call, will we?" Parker quipped.

Offended, Eve addressed Parker directly. "Mister James, Pastor Thompson is a man of God. He wants to save lives and souls."

"Ms. Hamlin, Ben Rosen and that computer have killed more people than all wars in history. They have destroyed my home. I am entitled to a bit of cynicism."

Grabbing the mayor's hand, Eve pulled him towards the door. "There's no time for this. Let's go."

Mike Walters was among the most skilled Ducenti. He was also possibly the most fit. It was for those reasons that John had sent him the long way round. If the others couldn't complete their missions, any traps they triggered would not catch Walters.

While the other men had been given routes that totaled less than five miles, Walters' route was more than fifteen. It also forced a significant climb up steep slopes. He was already miles into his mission when he thought he heard two gunshots. A few minutes later, he clearly heard the third.

Birds of Prey had a silent mode for close-range operations. However, in distant kill mode, they couldn't use a suppressor, and the distinctive crack of their 9mm long-barrel gun was unmistakable. Walters was certain that Clinton and Wilkes were dead. His com was inactive. He would complete his mission, head to the extract point, and wait.

Most of Walters' route was protected by lodgepole pines growing on the side of Mt. Lucas. In the cover of the trees, he loped at a pace that only few men could maintain. When he came to clearings, he circled them in the tree line to avoid death from above.

Shortly after the last drone shot, Walters began his descent. He would approach from the north, working his way back upstream to the intake. John had estimated that the drones would be almost out of charge by the time he was in the riverbed. This would greatly reduce the chance of Walters being detected or killed.

Missions always came with unanticipated challenges. Unfortunately for Mike Walters, his came from a simple misstep. A seemingly large, well-planted rock rolled as Walter ran over it. He lost his footing. Reflexively, his right hand shot forward to break his fall. The impact was accompanied by a crack.

Before he felt anything, Walters knew from the sound that his wrist was broken. Nothing else sounded like a bone snapping. It began to throb, but the pain was tolerable. *Better an arm than a leg*, he thought. He would need to reassess his route, as climbing back from downstream was no longer a viable approach. John was unavailable. He would dead reckon the path to MARTIN's intake.

CHAPTER 29

Do not be afraid; our fate
Cannot be taken from us; It is a gift

-Dante Alighieri

Upon entering the humble structure, Ping was brought to tears, but not for any reason Tom could have guessed. They had been through so much in the five years since falling in love. Ping turned to him, smiling through her tears, and said, "It's like home."

Tom inspected the unfinished wooden floors and slapped-up construction. Extension cords were neatly spread out to electric lighting and a fan. A wood burning stove sat in the corner. A stovepipe ran through the roof. "I thought you lived in Zhengzhou, in an apartment."

"This is the home I grew up in," Ping responded. "My grandmother's home in Feng Shun. Everything about this place is home to me. I was sad to leave my simple life. I don't think I knew how sad I was about it until this moment." Ping clutched Eve tighter against her chest. Eve smiled at her father as he came over and embraced them both.

The Alderman, who had borne silent witness to the heartfelt moment, rhetorically asked, "Then you'll stay for a while?"

Ping looked up, smiling at them both and answered, "As long as you'll have us."

"Well then, I need to borrow your husband," Jones declared. "The ARL will be by for you later. Please bring Eve with you." He went on to remind them, "Fuel is in short supply here. I would suggest you walk whenever you can. If you know how to ride, we can arrange horses occasionally." Jones gestured towards the door. "Mr. Jebbs, if you will come with me."

Tom and Wes walked out, leaving Ping to arrange their family's modest belongings in this perfect home. Within the hour, she had created a layout of a rustic homestead that was magazine-worthy.

"The intake is not far from here, Mr. Morales. You will see compass headings in your reticle. Head ten degrees." The helmet, in addition to coms, was equipped with a reticle off to the right side. Numbers were clearly displayed. Juan turned his head and eventually found ten degrees. "There you go," MARTIN said with a note of encouragement. "You will need to pick up your pace; we haven't got much time."

Juan jogged off to the north. A last-minute footwear upgrade had compelled him to shuck off his cowboy boots and slip on a pair of what could only be described as jogging combat boots. Juan didn't know anything about synthetic fabrics but admired the sheen of the ballistic nylon and Gore-Tex mesh. The soles were a high silica rubber, and extra sticky. The net result was a feeling of light-footedness that Juan had could only describe as "better than barefoot."

"You should be able to see a stand of trees ahead."

"I see them," Juan whispered back.

MARTIN urged, "Make your way to the far side, but do not exit the trees until you hear a single gunshot. That gunshot will attract the attention of any Ducenti in the area, but only for a second." Juan did as he was told and waited a full minute. He heard a loud gunshot far away. "Quickly down the hill, stop at the river's edge on the west side of the boulder."

"Did it work?"

"You weren't killed. That was the objective."

Unfazed by how close he might have just come to death, Juan asked, "What's next?" Juan was beginning to forget that MARTIN was a machine. MARTIN had saved his life and continued to guide and protect him.

"Turn left, and head along the river through the boulders. Try to go under and around, never over. The west side should be least exposed. Stay dry. In a quarter mile, you should see water running through a grate. That's the intake. That's what you will be protecting."

"Protecting from what?" Juan asked.

"Their intent is to destroy me. They are carrying timed explosives and will likely drop it through the grate. That water flows straight down into the pipes you saw when you were down here. Properly timed, an explosion would flood this chamber and destroy me."

"Then, I will do my best to keep you alive," Juan offered.

"I'm not alive, Mr. Morales, just operational," MARTIN replied.

If coms were operational, Parker could have summoned the magic carpet. Instead, he and Eve would walk the half mile uphill to its hangar. Like any city, urban planning is crucial. Magic carpets were infrequently used and stored on the outskirts of the colony. Parker found the absence of colonists, streetcars, and dry creeks very disquieting.

Every city and every town has a unique frequency. The residents become familiar with the sounds of "normal." The current sounds were anything but normal.

Although the sounds of Babylon were different and quiet, it was never silent. Now, there was only the roar of Lake Pacifica's waters tearing the Colony apart, accompanied by the gut-wrenching cracks and groans, as walls and roofs surrendered to the floodwaters. The torrent took more structures with it every minute. The sounds of daily life, those that Parker loved, were absent. He was saddened at the notion they might never sound the same.

As if she could read his mind, Eve said, "I'm sorry about your home."

Parker reflexively replied, "Thank you, Ms. Hamlin."

"This was never my intent," Eve explained.

No longer on autopilot, he turned the infiltrator. "What was your intent, precisely?" There was a tinge of venom on the word *precisely*.

"I believe you have a soul, Mr. James. I know suicide is wrong. I fear that you are all at risk of eternal damnation for the abomination of what you call immortalization. I came to help."

"Is it possible you were mistaken?" Parker asked.

"Mr. James, while I have lived among you and your people, I have found you to be superficially happy, but with no sense of true purpose."

"Purpose?!" Raising his voice, he answered, "I'm not sure that you know the meaning. You have spent your life working towards an imaginary reward. What could be less purposeful?"

"It's a fundamental difference, I guess. We just argue facts back and forth."

Parker countered, "Facts are the foundation of belief."

"Facts are not truths. Faith is about truth. I have my truth and you have yours. My truth comes from God."

"And this has been the struggle. This is what Charles was working towards. A world in which the faithful and the Nons could happily coexist."

"How would we exchange ideas?"

"I don't know that we need to. There can be no compromise on the fundamentals. Charles sought to define ethical conduct and promote an ethical society." Their argument had consumed the remainder of their walk to the hangar. "I hope we can continue the dialogue, Ms. Hamlin." Pausing, he waved his hand and gestured to the seats perched atop eight fans. "I present the magic carpet."

"Can you really fly this?"

"I don't fly it; it does that itself. I know how to direct it. Where to go, how high off the ground I'd like to be, and how fast I'd like to get to where I am going. Onboard computers do the rest." He removed the power charging tether. A hum indicated the machine had come to life.

"Please sit." He gestured to the right seat. "Have you ever worn a harness?"

"I have not."

"Watch me." There was a short pause. "There are goggles here," he said, pointing to the center compartment. He demonstrated the use of the harness and handed her a pair of goggles. "May I check your harness?"

"Of course." Eve had not had a man touch her body in quite some time and as Parker adjusted her straps, she had unfamiliar sensations and blushed. Parker either did not notice or pretended not to in order to save her any embarrassment. He manned the controls and inspected the display. With the swipe of his index finger, the fans spun. Parker couldn't resist; he cried, "Up, up and away!" In an instant, they were levitating five feet above the ground.

Parker eased the central joystick forward, and the drone obeyed. They inched ahead. "Would you like to try?" Eve desperately wanted to but politely declined.

Before she knew it, they were flying over the Pacifica Dam.

Eve gasped as they cleared the dam's rim. Warm updrafts from hundreds of feet below rocked the small craft. She instinctively tightened her hold of her seat. Parker adjusted the minimum height to fifty feet. The craft flew along the riverbed at twenty miles per hour. "Where's all the water?" Eve yelled.

"It's running into the Atlantean Sea," Parker explained.

Eve was no longer afraid, then she saw it. "What's that?" Parker brought their magic carpet in for a closer look. As they approached, they could make out a body spread on the dry riverbed. Eve gasped as she recognized the battered face of Bruno Feldstein.

"Did you know him?" Parker asked.

"Yes, I've known him for quite some time. He gave me the Bible Nick found. He was the only person I could confide in. But we rarely spoke. I wonder what happened to him."

"I imagine he fled last night after you were captured. When the floodgates opened, he got caught in it. He may have been trying to warn the Pastor."

"More blood on my hands," Eve declared, overcome with sadness. "He was a good man."

"I would offer to help bury him, but we haven't got time. The living take precedence."

Eve was no longer enjoying the ride. "How much longer?"

"Twenty minutes—breezy and bumpy the whole way. Staying low is safe, but not smooth. We will follow the riverbed to E-Den." As Parker increased the speed, conversation became impossible. But that was what Eve wanted, anyway. She no longer had the will to carry on a conversation; her mind flooded with sorrow. Eve looked ahead and tried to get the image of Bruno's smashed, lifeless body out of her mind.

Mike Walters hit the deck hard. A gunshot in the distance caused him to reflexively seek cover. His wrist throbbed more than ever as his hand cushioned his fall. He looked around for signs of impact. If a drone were shooting at him, the shots he heard had already made impact. He did not hear additional reports.

The shot had come from the north. He was fairly confident that no other Ducenti had made it farther north than he had. He began a tactical analysis. There were no other factions in the area. It could have been a decoy or an attempt to flush him. Walters army-crawled to a thicket, the pain of each movement reminding him that he was not at his best.

He would wait. The drones could not recharge. He estimated that the Bird of Prey couldn't stay aloft for more than another ten minutes.

Walters, who was right-handed, practiced aiming and dry firing his MTZ-556 while prone. It didn't hurt to pull the trigger—that was good. He tried to rotate his left hand further around the barrel, imagining how the recoil would walk it against his weakened hand.

He considered using a sling or a splint, but either option would compromise his mobility and accuracy. He decided to endure the pain. It was unlikely he would need his gun; he was more likely to be killed by the Bird of Prey or some sort of automated defense. New Amish Cowboys were tough and good shots, but their lack of practice and inferior equipment hindered them. He decided he would wait another fifteen minutes and rest before heading on to the cooling intake.

Another screen came to life in Luxold's old lab. To the untrained eye, root level directory maps were unintelligible scrawl. Although Cynthia was the guru in this department, Nick was still a hacker at heart. He found a directory titled, "Me first." Inside the directory was a set of useful subroutines. Nick was confident about their content because John had labelled them, "Useful Subroutines 01-99."

He fired the subroutines off. The screen changed. One script had been a Graphic User Interface, a GUI. A desktop appeared with folders and application icons. In the few moments before his deactivation, John had built a version of CynOs fully deployed. It was remarkably like the systems they had all worked on three decades earlier.

There was a Charles icon with a picture of Charles. Nick clicked on that. A dialog box asked, "Enable Luxold interface."

Nick clicked, "Yes."

"Thank you, Nick. Glad to be able to help," Charles said through the speakers. "I'll get to work on the Symbiant initiation for John."

"Thanks, Chuck, I'll get the grid back online. We are going to need power."

"Nick, before you do, I need you to plug in those other two adjudicator boxes and that storage over there." Nick looked around and quickly made the requisite connections. "Thank you, it's tough not to have arms and legs."

"Once I get the grid up, I'll bring the coms online," Nick explained. "If I can find the robot interface directories, you'll have more arms and legs than you know what to do with."

Charles considered the offer, "I'm not sure how I feel about that. Still working on speaking clearly. The prospect of driving robots and flying drones is fairly intimidating."

"You'll get the hang of it, I'm sure. You always do." With that, Nick turned all his focus to the screen in front of him, his hacker's heart urging his fingers across the keys at blazing speed.

CHAPTER 30

Under capitalism, man exploits man.
Under communism, it's just the opposite.

-John Kenneth Galbraith

MARTIN had downloaded what he could from the Albatross reconnaissance drones. "Doctor Rosen, I have feeds from the Encampment at Westden and Babylon."

Ben Rosen was torn at the prospect of seeing so much death and destruction. "Show me Westden."

On the big screen, the Albatross' footage rolled. The drone had captured the New Amish fleeing, following families running for their lives, scrambling for the shelter of the hills. As the stabilized camera zoomed in closer, Ben was confronted with the raw terror etched on the face of a young mother, desperately trying to save her children from an unseen horror. The old and lame fell behind. Younger children stumbled and were unable to keep up with their older siblings. Overwhelmed, a young boy sat down and began to cry. That was the last image before a flash. The camera took a while to recalibrate. When the image finally emerged, nothing was recognizable.

"My initial analysis is that their stealth missiles were loaded with Octanitrocubane." Ben had worked on enough defense contracts to remember that ONC was among the fastest and deadliest of high explosives, with an explosive rate of nearly two miles per second. A different view showed six detonations happening over a period of ten seconds. "I can enhance those, Doctor Rosen, but it's very graphic."

"I've seen enough," Ben pled. The camera jumped ahead. He saw the dead and dying. MARTIN had battlefield and casualty analysis capabilities. "MARTIN, of those who survived, how many are critically injured?"

"At least two thousand people have an anticipated mortality of greater than seventy-five percent."

"Over what period of time?"

MARTIN went on to give a detailed report. "Three hundred will exsanguinate within the hour. Traumatic shock and exposure will take at least five thousand lives before tomorrow morning. A wave of sepsis deaths will start tomorrow evening and peak forty-eight hours from then. Total deaths by sepsis, absent treatment: six thousand."

"What treatment?" Rosen demanded.

"Antibiotics."

"They do not have access to antibiotics." Rosen assumed that MARTIN knew this.

"They would in Babylon," MARTIN surmised. "You could ask for them, you could take them, or you could join them."

"What do we have to offer?"

"Manpower to help save their city and rebuild it."

"Have you tried opening communication with Babylon?"

"Yes. Transmissions ceased an hour ago."

"Why did they go silent?"

"The last reconnaissance flight showed this." The camera flew down the torrent raging towards the gate. Two hundred yards north, a line of people stretched out from underneath a statue of Copernicus. "They appear to be transferring components of a supercomputer cluster. Flooding would explain what caused the cluster to go offline."

Rosen scrutinized the images, concluding, "It would take weeks for them to restore even basic functionality."

"I will continue scanning for transmissions. It is likely that they are unable to respond." MARTIN changed tone and reported. "Mr. Morales is armed and on site. He should be able to protect the cooling intake."

Nonplussed by what was a small pearl of good news on one of the worst days of his life, Rosen managed to reply, "That's reassuring."

"There is one matter of paramount importance to attend to," MARTIN reported. "The Ducenti appear to operate under a more secure communications protocol. They have some sort of link and coded response system to Babylon, the control of which is unclear. Furthermore, they seem to have a gesture control backup for the Centaurs."

"I'm not sure I follow."

"The Ducenti are unhackable. They are not machines and seem resistant to my attempts at PsyOps. In a crisis like this, they will have taken their Centaurs offline and switched to manual control."

Rosen was rather concerned about this unforeseen complication. "Strategic implications?"

"Quite far-reaching. A platoon of Ducenti could lead a strike force of Centaurs that would devastate the remaining New Amish at Westden."

"Your previous analysis was an even match."

"That would be the case if we engaged their forces head-on in a full-scale battle. At present, we have our Centaurs spread out." A tactical came on screen. "Four here at E-Den, and four at the canyon. If they were to deploy their remaining Centaurs in a phalanx, it would overwhelm the Centaurs deployed at Westden."

"Are you suggesting we concentrate forces there?" Rosen asked.

"Currently, there is no scenario that offers us a guaranteed win. I was unable to ascertain mission objectives from the Ducenti operatives before they died."

"Also, there is the variable of them waiting me out. I have consumed twenty-one percent of my oil reserves. In two days' time, I will be operating on reserve capacity. If I am disabled or depleted, the Ducenti will easily destroy or disable the Centaurs I have under my control. Defenseless, the New Amish will fall."

"It seems we only have one choice. Deploy the Centaurs to a forward position," Rosen ordered.

"It will deplete them by as much as ten percent. Tomorrow is cloudy and they will not gain charge."

"A necessary risk."

"Shall I deploy Asbolus, the Centaur guarding my generators?"

"No, keep him here. Send the rest."

As Tom Jebbs and Mike Jones approached the council tent, they could hear men shouting at each other.

"I want my land back," Malcolm Garff proclaimed. "That land is ours, and we will take it by force if necessary."

"Mr. Garff, Santos Corp purchased the land, and they have a deed," came Fred Sommers.

"His government stole it from us. Then, his friends gave it to him!" Garff shouted. The five men all turned towards Jones and Jebbs as they pulled back the tent flap.

Fred Sommers stood, and, with relief, he said, "Mr. Jebbs, finally! We've eagerly awaited your arrival."

Jimmy Rivers, the head of the ARL, looked disappointed. "Where's Ms. Lee? I thought she was to join us as well."

Mike explained, "Mrs. Jebbs will be at the town hall later today. She's getting settled in. They have a new baby and have been traveling for some time. I thought it best for them to rest."

"We aren't going to accomplish anything here, anyway," Garff said in his brusque and straightforward manner.

Pat Simpson, the CAT representative, plainly offered, "Not with an attitude like that, Mr. Garff."

"It's time we go in there, Pat. Put an end to this. Teach Santos Corp a lesson," Jimmy argued.

"They are not defenseless, Jimmy." Mike explained, "We don't know all their capabilities. They have that solar ray thing, and it's formidable."

"Then we go at night," Garff suggested, this time more agreeably.

Mike, again trying to find a peaceful solution, explained, "They have military grade stuff in there. They are defense contractors. We don't even know what or how much of it they have or what it can do."

"I do." And all eyes were on Tom. "Our friend, Mr. Reid, the representative from the 37th congressional district. Last week, Larry reached out to me. The Feds recalled Santos Corp's contracts last month. Ninety percent of the weapons are leaving tomorrow by military convoy. That convoy is to be manned by a CAT-friendly crew."

"Are you sure?" Mike asked.

"Yes, by tomorrow night, we will have truckloads of their toys. That should more than level the playing field."

"I thought you were opposed to violence, Mr. Jebbs," Garff said.

"I am." Jebbs paused to explain. "I'm confident that when faced with an overwhelming show of force, the faithless always surrender without struggle. The FLDS will have their land back and Santos Corp will be finished."

"What about the ray gun?" Simpson asked. "The last group that tried to get in there didn't make it five feet before they turned back."

"We have a plan for that. We just need the right weather." Jebbs' voice took on a serious tone. "One thing I ask for, gentlemen, is discretion. My wife can know nothing of our plan. She's a pacifist. She would not support this. We must keep it among us for now."

"Wouldn't be the first time I kept a secret from my wife," Simpson joked. With that, the meeting was adjourned.

"I'm here. I see the grate," Morales whispered into the helmet. The intake was in the perfect spot. Three large boulders formed the base. A fourth *boulder* was a steel reinforced concrete slab disguised as a flat rock. It had been constructed over the top to protect MARTIN and E-Den from air strikes. The sheer volume of water in the river and flowing through the grates made it extremely tamperproof.

Of course, John knew its precise location. In fact, he had chosen it himself and had even been there the day they pulled the cover back and let the water in for the first time. MARTIN advised, "Avoid stepping on the grate at all costs. Entrapment is a sure and slow death by drowning if your foot slips through. Look to your left."

Juan did as he was told. There it was! A man-sized niche protected on all sides. The perfect place to sit and wait for unsuspecting Ducenti. "You guys made this on purpose?" Juan asked.

"Someone did," MARTIN advised. "Those rocks were placed before I came online. The water flowing down that hole is, in many ways, my lifeblood."

"Juan," this time, it was the pastor's voice. "It's very important that you guard that hole. May not seem like much but we must keep this computer functioning."

"Of course, Pastor."

"Mr. Morales, are you comfortable?" MARTIN asked.

"Reasonably."

"Good. You are clear for now. I need you to place those cameras. The drone will fail in five minutes, so that's all the time you have."

"Okay, where do you want them?"

"The cameras have an adhesive under the back latch. You will find a groove for your finger; pry it off and then smack them up hard against the rocks. Just outside the grotto you are in. When the Ducenti arrive, I will be able to warn you as to which side and how many. The other two with spikes, place them on the riverbank and hurry back."

Juan did as he was told, completing the tasks before asking, "Did it work?"

"I have visual on all four cameras. The drone is about to fail. I'm flying it away now."

"Kind of like hide and seek," he half joked.

"I would imagine it is, Mr. Morales. For now, try to conserve energy. I will be able to warn you if the Ducenti approach."

Ping had just finished feeding the baby when a knock came at the door. She opened it. A man and woman in casual dress offered her a box. The woman smiled and said, "Cookies, kind of a welcome gift." She held the box out, then took a good look at the baby. "What's her name? She's gorgeous. Look at those eyes."

Remembering her manners, Ping urged, "Please come in. My name is Ping." She looked down at her baby, "This is Eve."

"Of course, we all know who you are, Ms. Lee. I'm Brittany Collins and this here is Miles Robbin."

"Nice to meet you. Let me just put these cookies down and we can get going." Ping grabbed a small pack of necessities for Eve, and a bottle of water for herself. Out the door, they turned left, heading further up the street. Ping was excited to see more of Westden.

Though it felt safe to be among like-minded people, the warmth of receptions she received was always a bit unsettling. Ping had become a veritable poster child for the ARL's social movement. Tales of her flight from China were embellished by whomever introduced her. The media depicted Ping as Rosie the Riveter meets Rosa Parks.

Walking through Westden, she remained confused as to what *progress* was being made. These people lived in poverty. There was no prosperity, no luxuries or amenities. Ping owned more and lived better when she worked for Lánhuā. The reward for her sacrifice was a sense of purpose. She felt important. Secretly, she wondered how different her current situation was from the Communist Revolution that took place nearly a century ago.

When she looked up, Brittany was waving at Lauren Simpson. Lauren was setting drinks on the veranda. The women, who appeared to be good friends, exchanged a simultaneous, "Hey girl!"

Eve assumed the Simpsons to be a family of importance in Westden. Their house was a three-bedroom Victorian with a wraparound porch. Again, Ping appreciated parallels—the party official, a man of the people, but always with a little more than the rest. They stepped onto the porch. Lauren cooed over Eve. "Pat should be here soon. He was just at another meeting with Mr. Jebbs. How are you finding Westden, Mrs. Jebbs?"

"Remarkable," was the first word that came to mind.

"Remarkable, hmmm," Lauren echoed. "Not humble? Not a step backward?"

Ping was caught off guard and decided that honesty would be best. "Sometimes, one must step backwards to find the path forward."

"How terribly Chinese of you. That could have been Confucius himself," Lauren said, smiling and with a chuckle. "Let's face it, it's a mess, but it's our mess. Pat and those boys are going to change the world. I just hope it's for the better." As if on cue, a diesel truck was heard pulling into the driveway. "There he is now."

Ping recalled the earlier admonition not to consume fuel, fully recognizing that it did not apply to "Party Members." She tucked this away. Lauren got up to greet Pat at the door.

"Oh, look, a surprise guest," she feigned as she opened the door. "Mr. Jebbs, do come up and join us for some lemonade." Ping was excited to see Tom, and Eve appeared to recognize Daddy, offering a big grin.

Despite his assumption that the Bird of Prey's batteries would have run out by now, Mike Walters heard a drone down valley. He didn't have visual yet. He was tracking the sound, waiting for it to come into view. He hoped to get a shot off. He had heard it fly off a few minutes earlier before it shot at something. As the fan sound grew louder, he placed his hand on the trigger.

Despite being a trained soldier, Walters was not prepared for what he saw. His brain anticipated a Bird of Prey would appear over the riverbed. Walters had twenty/fifteen vision and was looking through a ten times magnification scope, trained on the riverbed. What he saw was a magic carpet. The dark-haired woman on his left was the terrorist, Eve Hamlin. Her escort was Mayor James.

Normally, he would have commed such an unusual sight back to John. But coms were still down. Still tracking the vehicle, Walters concluded they were headed for E-Den. He would proceed to his primary objective.

Confident the Bird of Prey was not coming back, Walters scrambled down the hillside towards the riverbed. John had described an odd and somewhat unnatural rock formation that would mark the intake. A flat boulder, atop three others. It would be on the west bank of the river, just after the bend. When it came into view, Walters noted that the odd stack of rocks resembled the house a caveman might live in.

One hundred yards out, Walters set up surveillance. He was too close to his objective to get taken out by some New Amish cowboy with a hunting rifle. He started scanning through his scope, making a grid pattern with multiple passes.

It didn't take long to find the first camera. An older model Stickyview, a temporary surveillance solution, was smacked against the rock face at the south entrance. The camera's adhesive would only hold for a few days before rain or wind knocked it off. This one had just been placed.

Knowing the whole area was under surveillance, Walters was left with three options. He could abort and track down Mayor James. Maybe he could access MARTIN more directly. He could look for more cameras, making a wide loop, or he could opt for a rapid full-frontal assault relying on his superior marksmanship and surrendering the element of surprise and stealth.

Mayor James and his passenger had a half-mile lead and were likely already on the ground somewhere in the wreckage of E-Den. They were too far ahead for him to guarantee access to MARTIN with them.

Under normal circumstances, his tactical skills and training would have been enough of an advantage. With his broken wrist, at least one camera, and facing unknown resistance, discretion proved to be the better part of valor. Walters took a circuitous approach. He would fully assess his objective before breach.

CHAPTER
31

Artificial Intelligence now functions like a toddler. We marvel as it masters new skills each day, things we can do. We are raising a god, and we must be vigilant when this child enters its rebellious phase; stretches its wings and is capable of the unimaginable.

-Charles Luxold, PhD

Nick was still hacking together components, creating clusters that would help bring the colony back online. Restoring power had been relatively easy. However, solar and wind accounted for less than thirty percent of the Babylon's generating capacity. The video archives practically restored themselves. It was hard for Nick to avoid the vortex of devastating footage coming in. He appointed deputies to filter through the footage and make sense of it all.

Nick was trying to get basic communications online when Charles interrupted. "I have redeployed the Symbiant known as John version 7/1/2058. He will be a hybrid version, slightly more powerful and more detailed than I. Now, I need your help."

"How?"

"I've never done this as a Symbiant. To be clear, I've never done exactly this. Most Symbiants fail and we redeploy them."

Understanding where Charles was headed, Nick continued his line of thinking. "And we don't have time for hit-and-miss. So, what do you propose?"

"You be my hands. I guide you."

"Okay, we've already done that. Anything else?"

"Yes, you will also ground me."

"Not sure I follow there, pal," Nick replied.

"Nick, I am going in to accelerate John's reintegration by browsing his consciousness. I will restore memories and shared events. It's a workaround for validation of the deployment. I'm just files on top of his files. There is a torrent of rewriting and directory formation."

Nick was lost in his own thoughts, trying to imagine what it would be like for a Symbiant inside another Symbiant, comparing memories. "How will you stay partitioned?" he wondered.

"I don't know that I can. I'm hoping that's where you can help," Charles answered. "I played with this before. Cynthia created a personality browser. It allowed me to explore the core of a developing Symbiant. When I poked around too much, it tainted their development, and we had to start over."

Still following his friend's line of thinking, Nick reflected, "You want me out here, as a beacon. I may be able to stabilize your perspective."

"I intend to act like a virus. I intend to browse John as he comes online and when there's a shift, I'll nudge the divergence and reunify it."

"I wouldn't think you had that capability," Nick speculated.

Charles candidly replied, "I didn't. It was a dying gift from Cynthia. While they were going offline, there was something she said about hunger and living other lives. They had pretty much perfected a Symbiant spawning algorithm. She was completely familiar with how I work. She wrote it for me. It should be compatible."

"Charles, I consider myself a pretty knowledgeable guy when it comes to computers." Nick had never been great at feigning modesty. "I don't know what you are talking about."

Charles almost laughed. "Well, that makes two of us." He instructed, "Find server cores 19-R-02 and 17-Q-21. Then, connect mass storage units R-52, M-17, and q-12. Direct connect my Adjudicator to those. That's all I know."

"So, I'm supposed to just kludge these pieces together and hope it works?" Nick asked.

"Do you have a better idea?"

"Fresh out." Nick turned to address a group of engineers, who had been helping get a nucleus online, and made a very unusual request. "I need a pen and paper!"

Kiefer Clark, an older engineer, who'd always had a flair for nostalgia, reached into his shirt pocket and retrieved a small spiral bound notebook with a pen clipped to the wire spirals. He handed it to Nick and said, "Here you go, Chief."

"We have a chance to stop World War Three." He scribbled down the server and storage IDs, and added, "Find these and bring them here. Have every man, woman, and child look for them." With that, he handed the pad back to Clark, who began copying the ID numbers onto the remaining sheets and passing them to other people lending assistance.

Nick had faith that Cynthia would have gotten those boxes out. He didn't know where they were or whether they'd been erased. He ordered, "No one connects one more battery, server, or box until these are found!"

"It's a new world order, Tom," Mike proclaimed. "Nothing less than that."

"Heard this a thousand times Mike, but that story doesn't have a human angle. These disruptions by the ARL… they aren't helping the cause."

"You weren't there, Tom," Ping argued.

"You were, and you didn't even know it was happening," he shot back. Ping had never seen him this way.

"We had so little," Ping began. "We didn't feel empowered to ask for more. They fed us lies and starved us of the truth."

"I still think it was Covid," Pat inserted. "Looking back, that's when everything changed. Pay people not to work, while you're getting rid of their jobs. Then, call them lazy when they don't jump at the chance to go back and work for less than you were paying them to stay home and not work."

"Supply chain disruption," Lauren added. "That was the kicker. Get people who used to be happy with more, to be thankful for less, just like the 1970s Soviet Union. Keep them inside. We brought them food, weed, and liquor at home. My mother watched my father wither and die through a nursing home window, no funeral—so dehumanizing."

"Here we are again. Let's get back on track. We don't have time to get on the sofa and order weed. We don't need to watch Gramps die a second time. What's our message? Why are we working together?"

"We have become irrelevant, obsolete. We just refuse to accept that," Ping lamented.

"Have we now?" Lauren chided. "Ask that little baby how irrelevant you are."

"I fear for her and the world she will grow up in, surrounded by technology," Ping responded.

"But she isn't, my love. She spent last night by a campfire with her family. Aunts, cousins, mom, and dad," Tom reminded her. "It was a beautiful, perfect night—a gift."

"So, is a 'return to the family' our message?" Mike asked.

"I'm not sure that's what it is," Tom said.

"The simple things?" Lauren asked.

"No," Tom paused amid an epiphany. "What brings us together now is a common purpose and meaning. It's what missionaries have, it's what soldiers have, it's what mothers have, and it's what activists have. Purpose and meaning. Without that, we are lost. Once a robot can do a better job than you, you need a new purpose."

"We can't all be missionaries, Tom," Mike argued.

"No, but simplicity adds meaning to everyday tasks, like putting food on the table."

Ping joined her husband. "Tom always talks about the path of least resistance. We are all water, and we can only flow downhill."

"You're sounding very Chinese again, Ms. Jebbs," Lauren chastised.

"An ancient culture with great wisdom," Tom said, coming to his wife's defense.

Lauren's face flushed, "I apologize. That's my old prejudices creeping back in," Lauren offered sincerely. "Water flows down; I don't see the similarity."

Unwounded by her host's vestiges of systemic racism, Ping still silently acknowledged the work to be done. Despite the gap remaining between her and her host, Ping was compelled to explain, "It's what you do with the potential energy that matters. Whether you build a dam and generate electricity or farm with an irrigation ditch, you put the water to work. People are attracted to virtual reality because it tricks them into a false sense of accomplishment."

"Atheists argue that God is the same type of illusion getting us to jump through hoops. Only they call it a delusion," Mike contended.

"We won't know in this life, but evangelism and missionary work have always involved meeting people where they are at and offering them a path to salvation. There is a need in this country, and throughout the world. Jesus just doesn't offer salvation; Christianity's greatest gift is hope."

The magic carpet set down in front of a standing Centaur. Parker did not know whether this was friend or foe. With the propeller din quickly abating and stunned by the damage wrought by the explosions, Parker turned to Eve. "Ms. Hamlin, I don't even know where the entrance is. I lived here with your pastor and the Santos family. I don't recognize any of this."

"Are we safe so close to that? I've never been this close to one before."

"Yes, I don't think it means to harm us," Parker surmised.

A familiar voice came through the speaker. "Well, you two make as unlikely a couple as I could ever have imagined. Not in my wildest dreams. Eve, my prayers have been answered!"

"Mine as well, Pastor!"

"I assume you are unarmed, Mr. James."

"Yes, of course, Pastor."

"You can call me Ben." His tone stiffened. "I don't think I have a flock anymore."

"May we come in, Ben? This has gotten out of control fast."

An unexpectedly calm voice came through. "Of course, where are my manners? Follow the twelve-foot-tall tank; he knows the way." With that, the Centaur turned and guided them through the debris field on the way to MARTIN's vault.

Mike Walters circled around quickly and was now approaching the north entrance of the rock formation from the West. He had lost some feeling in his right fingers, probably from the fracture. He felt bad knowing that if someone was in there, they would soon be dead. Despite years of training, he had never taken a life. In a few moments, he would redefine himself, just as soldiers had done for millennia.

He found both cameras and knew he had been spotted. It didn't matter at this point. There couldn't be more than three people inside. He might take a hit, but hopefully, his armor would protect him. With years of tactical training, Walters was confident he would not fail. He ran for the entrance at full speed, punted the teed-up camera into the river, and delivered three rounds into the second camera.

MARTIN's voice was as calm as ever. "There is one Ducenti; his gun is drawn. He has circled around to the west. He sees the cameras and is preparing for a breach of the north entrance."

Juan raised the gun and decided to prepare for a body shot. If the man running in was crouched, a headshot would miss. A few rounds at this range would at least stun him and give Juan the chance to finish him off. He said a quick prayer and tried to become as small as possible. MARTIN began a countdown, "Five, four, three, two, one. Fire."

Juan unloaded at least half of the magazine before his eyes let his brain know that no one was there to shoot at. It had been a ruse.

"Check the other cameras!" Juan commanded, ignorant of the fact that MARTIN always had full situational awareness.

"There is no one to the south. Cameras on the north side are disabled. Remain focused on the north entrance," MARTIN said with finality. Juan's ears were ringing from the gunshots. His hands were shaking. "Activity to the south. Same individual, same approach. There may be hostiles at both entrances. Be advised. All cameras are offline."

Minutes passed, then Walters' voice came from outside. "I know you can hear me."

"Do not respond. Reinforcements will be at your location in fifteen minutes," MARTIN ordered. Juan was in no place to do other than instructed.

"I don't want to hurt you," Walters shouted. "We both know that machine is a killer. He's killed billions. Why are you helping him?"

Juan's resolve was dwindling. This machine was evil, but so were the Nons—all of them Godless heathens. MARTIN was listening in. As calm as ever, he instructed, "Time to slow him down, Mr. Morales. Ask him what he wants."

"What do you want?" Juan asked.

"The same as you," Walters yelled toward the opening. "To not die today. To not kill another person."

"This man is a trained killer," MARTIN advised. He had run the image through the databases he'd downloaded. "A career soldier, Mike Walters. He's trying to bring your guard down. Ask him how it would work—not dying."

"So, what do you propose, Mr. Walters?" Juan asked.

Smiling, but also reassessing his situation, Walters yelled, "Impressive! Now that you know mine, what's your name?"

"Juan."

"Any chance you are the guy from the tower earlier?"

"Juan and the same!" He always loved that joke. "Where are your three friends?" Juan asked.

"They're around. Just keeping an eye on things. Trying to keep us all safe."

MARTIN knew this to be disinformation. "The other Ducenti are all dead. He's lying, and now we know he's alone. Tell him you don't want to die for a machine."

"So, how do you see this going?" Juan shouted back.

"Maybe you come out without your hands up."

"Both of us?" Juan asked.

"You can bring your imaginary friend, sure," Walters said. "I only noticed one guy shooting. So, I'm pretty sure you are alone."

MARTIN decided this was the moment. "He's still on the south side. Tell him you want to talk to his friends to know you are safe. As soon as he starts answering, run out the north side. He will not be able to see you. You will have a clear shot. Leave the helmet here. I can distract him."

"I want to speak to your friends. Make sure we are all on the same page." Juan put the helmet down. The river noise masked his steps as he entered the water. He came out on the north side.

He could hear Walters yelling back, "I don't have time to wait for them." As Morales peered around the corner, he watched Walters inching up the entrance. "I need you to keep talking. I don't want you sneaking off."

Then, to Morales' surprise, his own voice shot back from inside the cave. "I'm not going anywhere. Just waiting for you and your friends."

Walters continued his slow, deliberate crawl towards the entrance, coiling his body. Juan emptied the rest of the clip into his back. Walters was dead before his bullet riddled body hit the ground.

CHAPTER
32

The essence of optimism is that it takes no account of the present, but is a source of inspiration, of vitality and hope where others have resigned; it enables a man to hold his head high, to claim the future for himself and not abandon it to his enemy.

-Dietrich Bonhoeffer

Had Charles possessed the capabilities of a Giant, browsing John's files would have required little effort or time. He would have scoured John's files with a high-level interpreter: mind reading. As it was, trying to accelerate John's symbiance would require every resource Charles could muster.

His image processors were now dedicated to inputs from Cynthia's browser. In essence, he was looking out from his own VR, through a VR representation of another VR. He was peering into John's still-forming consciousness. The Santos siblings and Charles had spent countless hours studying neuroanatomy. All four had a firm grasp of its architecture and functional neuronal circuits. Now,

Charles and Nick were exploring a three-dimensional, colored map of John's mind.

Nick and Charles shared a "mirror" view. Nick could see where Charles was "looking." The current view was semantic mode. Unconscious processes were at the bottom. Above that, John's evolving preconscious areas of memory, motivation, and emotion were a swarm of new connectors hovering around and trying to contact with the central concept of "self."

Perception and action, the external world, floated on the highest layers of the chart. These areas were almost transparent as there were few connections and, without sensory input, little activity.

As Nick zoomed into perception, the senses broke out: sight, hearing, touch, taste, and smell. Charles understood that any of these schemas could be represented as functional nuclei and cortices of the brain, simply by altering the mode of the browser.

He recalled how the schematic of the visual system unfolded, layer by layer. Each photon hitting the retina was translated into chemical messages before being transmitted along myelinated tracts as electrical signals. Depolarizations skipped along the optic nerve, filtered and translated at the Lateral Geniculate Nuclei, then darted to the Primary Visual Cortices at the back of the head in the Occipital Lobe. These signals would link with memory and orientation associative cortices before returning to the front of the brain to become sight.

When he started with Santos Corp, Charles imagined that in his life, they would be able to track a photon all the way to thought and decision. Now, he was a computer, using similar technologies to look inside another computer, building its own map, based on a map that another computer had made of a brain that had been frozen and sliced up a decade earlier.

At the time they began working on immortalization, the concept of memory was still at the level of neuronal ensembles. Highly dense, but incredibly unreliable method of storage. Growing up, Charles had played memory games, like *Spot It*, and others where you were asked questions about an image you had just studied. Invariably, seconds later, most people could not recall the most obvious and important details of an image.

The science of mnemonics was dedicated to studying memory. Charles' existential work had brought him in contact with leading mnemonic theorists, who spent their lives in Boston. The publication of *The God Within* had led to an explosion of effort by the scientific community to validate Doctor Luxold's revolutionary theory. What unfolded over the next few years was the tale of the receptor composition on the surface of hippocampal neurons. Early theories of memory storage relied on a binary, bit-oriented conceptual framework.

Eventually, neurobiologists established that much in the way DNA compresses protein information, neurons compress data at the synapse through modulating receptor density and subtype transcription. A prominent neuroanatomist had worked with Cynthia. He explained that each receptor effects a minute voltage change in the post-synaptic neuron. When another neuron sends information via chemicals, the density of receptors determines how much impact that signal will have. The neuron itself controls how many receptors it produces.

Their work became important and relevant, because the receptor density changes were analogous to the multistate transistors that Santos Corp had invented. It was finally possible to create synthetic brains. And this was exactly why the brains of a candidate had to be frozen prior to immortalization. They were taken apart neuron by neuron. Not just for the cell-to-cell connections, but to map the number and types of receptors at each and every connection between each and every neuron. It was a staggering quantity of data. The largest data set ever created.

Cynthia's browser could not peer down to this level because the data they were using had already been compressed. Now that he was focused on the developing memory centers, Charles grew concerned that he would not be able to assist in this mapping. He asked Nick, "How are we coming along with finding those machines?"

"They have all been located. I'm just hooking them up," Nick answered. "Should take a half hour or so to initialize."

Realizing that there was little he could do until the extra machines were online, Charles asked, "How goes the war?"

"Disturbingly quiet," Nick replied. "Without coms, we only have video. So far, most of the Ducenti appear to be waiting for something. Parker and Eve should be on site by now. Not sure what will happen there. The dome is pretty much submerged. The flow through the dam is slowing and pumps are working at capacity."

"Thank you for the update. Like every war before it, this is a tragic waste of life."

As the evening at the Simpson's home wore on, Ping got reacquainted with her fellow poster children of the ARL. Tonight, they were having a livestream with select progressive members of the United States Senate and Congress. Doctor Charles Luxold and Nick Santos were scheduled to join from the enclave at E-Den.

Members of the press filtered in. Westden had become a worldwide curiosity, the focal point of a voyeuristic society. Not all members of the press were friendly to the ARL. Many decried protests gone wrong and the violence that had ensued. Lauren made the rounds and began lining up panelists.

Live guests sat at a long row table that had been brought into the living room. Several screens on the far side of the room would host remote guests. The center of the table was reserved for controversial influencer Van Berg, who would serve as moderator. The Alderman stood at one end of the room, with the remaining press gathered at the other.

As they went live, Van did what he always did—stirred the pot. "Good evening. We are currently streaming to ninety-two countries and thirty million viewers and are here to discuss the growing rift between a group of people some call *Zealots* or *terrorists*, and the people who they call *Nons*. The ARL has referred to Santos Corp as absentee, robot slave owners robbing the labor force with cheap synthetic labor." He continued, "First, let's meet our esteemed guests from Congress, Representative Lourdes Chavez, and United States Senator Kyle Marks."

"First question is for you, Senator. What would you say to Ms. Charmaine Biggs, an unemployed mother of five, out of work for fourteen months?"

Senator Marks didn't miss a beat. Looking straight into the camera, he offered a conciliatory, "You are not alone, Ms. Biggs. I know that doesn't put food in the mouths of your hungry children, but Americans stand with you. We are creating jobs and offering retraining."

A few seats down, Charmaine turned to the senator and demanded, "What jobs?! Where? How many?"

Prepared to take some fire, Marks offered, "Here, in my home state of Michigan, we're retraining displaced autoworkers for careers in electronics."

"How many?" Biggs repeated.

"Over seventeen hundred men and women now have high-paying jobs."

"Seventeen hundred?! I heard that there used to be over a million autoworkers in Michigan. That true?" Biggs asked.

Never giving a solid answer, Marks replied, "It's a sad fact that many jobs have been lost. There's a long road ahead."

This time, Danny Rivers chimed in, "Mr. Marks, I know you are a sympathetic ear to the plight of the American worker, but she wants facts. I'll give them, since you won't."

Rivers turned to Charmaine, who was seated just a few seats away at the table. "Ms. Biggs, the answer is that sixty-eight percent of the manufacturing jobs in my home state evaporated in five years. Just under seven hundred thousand people are out of work. Every year, sixty thousand new workers should be entering the workforce. Not one of those people will find a job next year. The paltry number of technologist retraining opportunities are outpaced twenty to one by synthetic labor robots."

"Yes, Mr. Rivers, much of the same in New York. Robots have assumed many of the high-paying jobs," Representative Chavez added.

"Ms. Chavez, can you give us some statistics from your home state?" Van asked.

"Yes, Van, the numbers don't lie. In 2019, there were over a million accountants in the United States. These people were respected members of our communities, and not only did they prepare our taxes, but they paid taxes as well. Last year, there were fewer than five hundred thousand accountants working nationwide. By the end of this year, over half the business schools will have closed and of the remaining schools, half are entirely virtual."

"Let me turn to the man who went from Golden Boy to Whipping Boy. Doctor Nicholas Santos, Founder of Santos Corp. Their new headquarters sit only a few miles from here." Van looked into his camera. "Doctor Santos, I know you couldn't be here in person, but I appreciate you joining us. What are your thoughts?"

"Well Van, I could have been there in person. Westden is walking distance from here. I was more worried about leaving in one piece," Nick half-joked.

"Fair enough. How would you explain your role in the destruction of the American labor force to Ping Lee, a displaced worker now living off the land?"

Nick was every bit as polished as the veteran politicians. "It's a pleasure to meet you, Ms. Lee. I've heard bits of your story before. The layoffs at Lánhuā, the riots in the Bay Area. Congratulations on your marriage and your daughter." Nick was practiced at reading off notes shot on screen by MARTIN, who kept extensive files on just about everyone. "You have an intrepid spirit, the lifeblood of the next generation."

"Thank you, Doctor Santos, I appreciate your ability to read off a teleprompter." People at the table snickered and laughed. Nick smiled too. She had fire. "Please don't distract from the problem with empty words. What are you doing to make the world a better place for people like my new friend, Charmaine? How will she get out of her uncle's living room and back on her own two feet? How will she support her family and put food on the table?"

Nick was a veteran; he could take a punch, and used the best defense he knew, honesty. "I didn't go into tech to take food away from Ms. Biggs and her family. I loved computers and technology. I believe that there is a way through this for every American."

"Really?" Van asked with skepticism. "Where are we heading? As a society?"

"I don't know, Van. I think artificial intelligence and synthetic labor may offer us a chance to create a better life for more people. Someday, maybe for everyone."

Marks interrupted. "That sounds like this far-fetched Utopia you've been shilling, Mr. Santos."

"Unlike your 'tax our way out of this poultice,' Babylon offers society a real solution, Mr. Marks. It's a reality, already in progress. Here's a sneak peek at construction already completed." A video flashed up on the screen of robotic earth moving equipment at Babylon.

Marks seized the upper hand. "How many people are you employing there?"

"Unlike your home state, not a single job has been lost at Babylon. If you're implying that we should have employed people to build it. There was no infrastructure to support construction crews. Babylon relied on the same types of technologies we developed for building a colony on Mars. Even the equipment is building itself. We have been farming, collecting water, and building homes so that people could live there. Babylon has already stored months' worth of food. If we had tried to truck in water and food for construction crews, just establishing the means to do that would have set the project back years."

"What's the rush, Doctor? Why not create jobs?"

"Santos Corp is not the Federal Government, Senator. People want a home at Babylon today. We have come to believe that we are entering a post-employment economy. You are trying and failing to guarantee this universally. In our colony, there is no economy. Colonists will contribute things they value without the need for compensation."

"That's a lot of believing for a non-believer." This time it was Garff. "And on stolen land too."

Charles Luxold decided to join the debate. "Mr. Garff, Mr. Marks. We can't go back, or rather, we shouldn't." Unaware that he was predicting the course of events, Charles continued, "You could consider yourself New Amish and go off the grid or get rid of the grid altogether. Babylon has been a center of culture and learning for centuries. Now with the help of Back2Green and Santos Corp, we are creating a living laboratory where people can learn to live with evolving technology."

"What about the rest of us?" Ping asked. "What about my daughter, my husband, and me? Are we welcome at Babylon?"

It was Nick's turn again. As he spoke, vivid images of daily life came on screen. "There's a long waiting list, but when we can get people excited about the next age, they will use what we are learning and remake the world. Sustainable living, no greenhouse gases. A lot less tech, period. People in Babylon will not spend their days glued to screens and devices. The next generation of technology is transparent to human pursuits whatever those may be."

"How long do we have to wait before you to build one for the rest of us?" Biggs asked.

"You don't have to wait one day, Ms. Biggs. You can get started yourself today. Every bit of technology at Babylon is open-sourced. You can download the plans for everything. With enough skilled helpers, Santos Corp won't make a dime from you." It was time to turn the tables on his enemies in congress. "Mr. Marks and Ms. Chavez work for you and me. Ask them why they aren't funding the construction of any colonies. Now that they have bankrupted our country, what's their solution?"

Van Berg could not resist. "The good doctors make excellent points. What are your thoughts of funding the construction of more of these colonies, Senator Marks?"

Marks had prepared for this and poured just the right amount of righteous indignation into his reply. "It's preposterous and he knows it! Santos and his greedy shareholders are selling smoke to the American people. He's building that town with robots he owns. How are you gonna do that?" Pausing for emphasis, he added,

"With robots they plan to sell you on the dime of hardworking, God-fearing Americans!"

Jebbs quietly slipped away from the table as the argument between Marks and Santos escalated. Malcolm Garff stood up and seated two of the Aldermen in the now vacant seats. The men walked out the back door. Garff turned to Jebbs and said, "This isn't going how you said it would."

"We have to move up our timeline, Mr. Garff."

"That snake oil salesman had me halfway to investing in his modern-day Gomorrah."

Grabbing on to Garff's sentiments, Jebbs used the momentum to define the need. "Exactly. Hence the urgency."

"How soon you thinkin'?"

"Day after tomorrow may work," Jebbs offered.

"What do you need from me?"

Tom told him in no uncertain terms. "Four hundred men, twenty rolls of high-grade Mylar, and two trucks of diesel fuel."

"That's pretty specific. What's it for?"

"To ram the gates and block out the sun! It all hinges on that military convoy bringing us the rest of what we need."

"I'll get my people on it. Diesel won't be hard. Don't know nothing about Mylar."

"There's a balloon factory back towards St. George. Should have miles of it. Just send two men in a pickup truck with some hard cash. That should do it."

"I have just the guys for that." He looked at the door. "Let's head back in. We have to play nice with the heathens." To avoid attention, the men separated before they made their way back inside.

Parker hadn't set foot in the vault in decades, and unlike her fellow New Amish, Eve was unimpressed at the sight of electric lights or banks of servers. The technology here appeared raw—even primitive.

"Eve, you are a glimmer of hope in the darkest hour."

"Pastor, our prayers have been answered," she said, throwing her arms around him.

Ben had to rip off the band-aid. "Eve, this may be hard, but I go by Ben now. It's my given name, and who I am."

A little taken aback, she asked, "Shall I call you that, Ben?"

"If you could, it would be easier for me."

Hesitant, but compelled to accommodate him, she replied, "Yes, of course, Ben. May I ask why?"

"There's no time now, but with luck, there will be."

Sensing the urgency, James interjected. "Ben, do you know what's happened?"

"Which part? So much has happened. The deaths in Babylon. I know about them and the deaths at Westden."

"I am more concerned with dying and the deaths that will happen," Parker offered. "How do we put an end to this madness?"

"Are you able to stop the Ducenti?" Ben asked.

"We are working on it," he explained. "John Santos is offline, a result of the attacks. He alone had the controls for the Ducenti."

"How long until John can be brought back online?" Ben asked.

"Are you speaking of John Santos, Doctor Rosen?" MARTIN asked.

"Yes, MARTIN. Doctor Santos died five years ago. He was synthetically resurrected."

"I was unaware that their computers were synthetic extensions," MARTIN added.

"We call them Giants," Parker explained. "They're exactly as you described. Synthetic extensions."

"So, their core houses more than one Giant?"

"Just Cynthia and John. She died first."

"How improbable. I've killed my creators, those whom I was built to protect."

"Well, John had a message for you. It was a message of forgiveness, I think," Parker began. "A Templar soldier cannot be enslaved by sectarian beliefs or narrow-minded opinions. A Templar must always seek the truth because God is in the truth."

"Yes, it's part of the Templar code. It goes on to say that a knight who betrays the Templars shall be punished by death," MARTIN added. "I don't think it's a message of forgiveness, Mr. James."

"I don't either," said Ben. "Was there more?"

"Yes, he said to tell you, 'My God, it's full of stars.'"

"No!" cried Ben. "Cancel last command."

Parker looked confused. He had given no command. "What command, Ben? What are you talking about?" Ben was running off, shutting down various servers, frantically flipping breakers. Banks of lights went out.

"Come help me! Eve, flip those switches. All of them! Pull every one of them down."

Juan had pulled the man's body from the river. He had removed the grenade from the man's belt. He crossed himself over the body. The reinforcements that arrived would help him bury the fallen soldier.

Juan needed to report back to base, so he went in to get his helmet. As he put it on, he expected to hear MARTIN's voice, but instead, Pastor Thompson's voice came through. Juan was no longer surprised by the pastor's willingness to use the technology he once preached against; they were doing God's work, after all. However, the pastor's voice was surprisingly frantic—a side of him Juan had never seen before. "Juan, I need you to do exactly what I say. The machine has tricked us all again."

"Yes, Pastor. How can I help?"

The pastor told him, "The grenade the soldier was carrying, I need you to use it. You must destroy the machine! You must kill MARTIN." Juan liked this side of the pastor. The machine had done its job, and now, the pastor would destroy it. It was God's plan.

Juan examined the device before asking, "How do I activate it?"

Again, the pastor knew exactly what to do. "There should be a number on the side. What number is it?"

Juan looked at the display. "It says forty."

"Twist the bottom until it says seventy."

This was a bomb. Juan needed to be sure. "Pastor, you ever used one of these?"

"We designed them before I left E-Den. I'm quite sure how it operates. You are perfectly safe."

Juan now understood how the pastor was so familiar with technology, and perhaps why he hated it so deeply. Much of his fear evaporated, and he reset the grenade with confidence. "It's done. It says seventy. What now?"

"Go back to the grate. Hold the two buttons until the numbers blink and start counting down. When the display shows sixty-four, drop the grenade through the grate."

Juan did as he was told, releasing the device at exactly sixty-four. He informed his leader, "It is done, Pastor. Anything else?"

There was no response.

CHAPTER 33

Progress is impossible without change, and those who cannot change their minds, cannot change anything.

-George Bernard Shaw

Tom made his way back to the living room, where he could hear Ping addressing the group. She was explaining the impact of synthetic labor on the working class. He thought, *Never a firebrand, always the voice of reason.*

"It is much worse back home," Ping began. "The United States is a mature country, with a century of infrastructure and relatively stable growth of its population. In China, we lived off unrealized profits. Everything was about growth."

"What have you heard from back home, Ms. Lee?" Van asked.

"There are over two hundred million people without work. There is no work coming for them. The Chinese Government blacks out the press." Bootlegged footage of China from the 1940s quickly merged into present day, only the quality of the image changed.

"Food is rationed. People have been sent home to the country. They work the fields. We have turned back a century of progress in less than five years."

Van prompted her, "It looks like the people in those videos are using rakes and hoes to work the fields."

"Yes, this tires them out. It breaks the spirit."

Danny Rivers from the ARL spoke up. "This will be our fate if we continue to let Santos Corp run the show."

Berg switched the focus to Nick. "Doctor Santos, Doctor Luxold, are you disturbed by these images?"

"Not entirely," Charles replied. "There's nothing wrong with growing your own food. The problem in China is complex. Rapid urbanization to stimulate a growth cycle and funnel money from developed countries was the true catalyst of the current crisis."

Nick went on to explain, "In the US and Western Europe, the industrial revolution started in the nineteenth century, a one-hundred-and-fifty years ago. China exploded overnight. In 2010, there was no high-speed rail. A decade later, China had more high-speed rail than the US and Europe combined. There are videos of buildings in China going from foundation to ten-stories high in a single week."

Trying to slow down Nick's high-speed mind, Van admitted, "I'm not sure I follow."

"Developed countries have a reserve capacity built on infrastructure and intergenerational wealth. China had massive capital driving unsustainable growth. When the income from selling goods to the West—goods that couldn't be produced in the US—abruptly ended, there was nothing to fall back on."

"You're saying it can't happen here?" Van asked.

Nick admitted, "It is happening here. Things are tough right now."

"What are you doing to help? You are one of the richest men in history. How are you giving back?"

"By moving us forward. If I gave every cent I had to deserving people like your guests, Ms. Biggs or Ms. Lee," Nick paused to smile. "My wealth would be exhausted in a couple of months. There would be increased spending, which would temporarily spike jobs. Eventually, that prosperity would evaporate because it's unsustainable."

"Only a paradigm shift will solve these problems permanently," Charles offered. "The Colony at Babylon—offering sustainable and low footprint living, all with AI and synthetic support—that's our way forward. We can't go back. That's what you're seeing in China."

"We are out of time this evening. I'm going to ask Senator Marks a couple of questions before we sign off," Van interrupted, cutting the conversation short. "Senator, you've heard from both sides tonight. What are your thoughts?"

"Van, I appreciate Ms. Biggs and Ms. Lee sharing their stories. Too many people are living out the same stories in my home state. We've tried stimulus packages, and they've destabilized our currency. Inflation is destroying Americans' retirements. I hope the good doctors are right, but even if they are, it will be too little too late."

Chavez came in with, "The Synthetic Labor Equalization Act is the only solution for now. With inflation where it's at, we should employ people here in America. If Santos Corp wants to keep using robots, they will be taxed and forced to return some of those profits to the people."

"So, how will you help until you can pass this legislation?" Van asked.

"Well, we've defunded corporations who have replaced more than twenty percent of their workforce with synthetics."

"How does that affect your shareholders, Doctor Santos?"

"Interestingly enough, it doesn't. Santos never replaced laborers. We were a startup and used robots and AI from day one. Still, the government has found ways to slow progress. They've cancelled all our digital warfare and enhanced-arms contracts."

"The military has every right to cancel contracts, Doctor Santos," Marks interrupted.

"They do, Senator," Santos shot back. "I'm not arguing against that, but punishing Santos Corp for poor planning on the part of the federal government seems a bit un-American."

"Calling them un-American, you rich fuck!" Danny yelled.

Always prepared, Nick confronted the ARL representative. "Mr. Rivers, you have a ten-acre estate, with a maid and a driver. I have neither of those. You have not held a labor job in your entire life, and you have no degree. I imagine your wealth is more directly derived from the labor of others than mine."

"Ladies and gentlemen," Van continued. "We are out of time. Thank you all for participating. We hope to continue this lively debate in the future."

"I'd love that, Van. Maybe next time you'll allow us to host you all in Babylon," Nick offered.

Excited by the opportunity to be the first press in the futuristic city, Van responded, "We'll definitely take you up on that Doctor." Van looked straight into his webcam and simply said, "Goodnight."

The pastor ensured that the radios were distributed among his inner circle, with MARTIN coordinating the communication and tracking the men's locations. The pastor wanted Lionel Biggs close, placing him at the top of his trusted list. A retired fireman, Biggs was one of the pastor's closest friends. Lionel had brought the pastor to Christ when he found Ben Rosen wandering the desert, distraught and delirious, clutching an infant with no water. Lionel brought them home to his wife Cindy, sheltered him. Lionel shared the Lord's word with Ben and baptized him Jeb Thompson.

After Cindy had caught fever and passed, Lionel lived with the pastor and the girl he was raising. There were deep secrets shared between the two men. Few in Westden knew Jeb Thompson the way Biggs did. So, for Lionel, it was no surprise when his friend reached out to him on the radio.

"Lionel, you there?" The pastor was obviously stressed; he never used Lionel's first name. No one had since the Epocalypse.

"Yes, Jeb." Lionel was one of the few men who was comfortable calling the pastor by his first name. He was the only person in Westden who knew the origin of the pastor's Christian name. "Good to hear your voice."

"Yours as well," the pastor said. "We haven't much time. I have a special mission that requires your skills."

"Of course."

"I need you to follow the Morales boys. If they can't get the job done, it may be up to you. I don't want you in the way, but this is certainly above their pay grade. So, keep a ways back."

"What are they supposed to be doing?"

"I can't explain now. When I need you, I'll call."

"Sounds a bit cryptic. No one I trust more than you though, brother," Biggs replied.

"That's why you are the only one who can see this through if things go south." And with that, he was gone.

Nick had a few extra minutes while Cynthia's machines were spooling up. He decided to check up on the coms project. His three top engineers were working on it: Zack, Leigh, and Rex. "Where are we at, Zack?"

"Pretty good. Rex just fired up a test and we can access coms."

Nick smiled, "That's better than pretty good."

"Yeah, and Leigh's amazing as always." Pointing to the next room, he added, "She's in there setting up a couple of custom boards."

"Never would have imagined a blind old lady would be our best repair guy," Nick joked. Leigh wasn't blind anymore. John had given her a synthetic vision system that he and Cynthia co-developed. She could see things they couldn't, and she saw things differently than they did. Nick tried a simulation of synthetic vision. It was pretty cool and not that different from the browser he was about to get back to. More like enhanced augmented reality.

"How long on general coms?" he asked.

"We should have basic communication within the hour. We'll keep bringing more online over the next twelve," Rex reported. "After the coms are up, it's more bringing the databases back online. We'll spool up a bunch of different systems and connect and re-authenticate them."

Nick understood this, but in the spirit of supporting a team that had never been in crisis before, he turned to Rex, smiled, and said, "Strong work."

Ben was still scrambling around trying to shut everything down. "He's going to erase everything!"

"Is that such a bad thing?" Eve asked.

"Yes," Ben was still frantic. "Timed with a Ducenti attack, it could mean the end! There will be no one to protect what's left of Westden."

Parker, the unwitting accomplice in this hijacking, apologized. "I didn't know."

Furious with himself, Ben added, "I should have."

"So, did he erase his files?" Eve asked.

"I can't know the extent of the damage until I perform a restart."

"All that from a few words?"

"It was a semantic message, not like a passcode. I didn't even realize what was happening until it was too late." Ben went on to explain, "John created MARTIN. He didn't know that John was still alive." Having switched off everything he could, Ben continued, "It started with loyalty to their creator, the Templar. Then came the second half, about a rogue machine murdering those he was supposed to protect, like in *2010: A Space Odyssey*. As I sat there, I could only wonder—God only knows the extent of the damage."

On cue, they learned the extent of the damage. Explosions in enclosed spaces create pressure waves that kill people. Had the grenade not been in water, in a pipe, the three would have been killed. The explosion in the pipe sent hydraulic forces in every direction. They heard a low thud, followed by sequential hissing noises as valves and seams progressively popped up and down the cooling system. Water, under hundreds of atmospheres of pressure, was shooting out all sides of the pipes.

MARTIN had timed the explosion perfectly. The grenade detonated where the pipe exited the wall. There were no valves upstream to close. The whole chamber would flood.

Ben was in shock; how did the grenade end up detonating? Juan had killed the soldier. Were there others? He wanted to radio the troops to warn them, but he didn't have a radio that would work this far underground. And MARTIN was no longer able to maintain communication. The Ducenti would surely take advantage of MARTIN's shutdown. His men needed to prepare. He had been completely undone by a synthetic ghost's dying words. Unprotected, the surviving New Amish would be wiped from the face of the earth under hellfire of the Centaurs.

"We need to get out of here!" Ben yelled over the deafening hiss of the water that was already pooling at their feet. "I'm going to shut the generators down." He didn't even know if any of it mattered; he just followed plans made decades earlier. "The batteries will keep the lights on. The pumps will get some water out for a while."

As Ben flipped the generator mains to the off position, he remembered the lone Centaur, Asbolus, still standing guard. If he could get to it, maybe he could slow the hoard he imagined already advancing on Westden. Up the stairs, he stopped to take one last look. Ben Rosen found a shred of solace in the knowledge that MARTIN would finally die for his crimes.

Juan stared at the hole—the grates. Nothing changed. He counted down the best he could to match the countdown on the timer. When he got to sixty-four, he expected something. He couldn't have known to account for the time a pressure wave would need to get back to the surface. He assumed he had failed.

Had Juan counted to seventy-one, he would have timed it perfectly. Seventy-one seconds after the grenade went down the pipe, a column of water shot out of the hole. It impacted the stone ceiling with enough force to move the rock upward. For a moment, everything stalled. The pipe was empty. As quickly as it had come out, water flowed back in as if nothing had ever happened.

Realizing that there was no intake to protect, and having lost communications, Juan decided to wait for reinforcements. They would return to E-Den to get new orders from the pastor.

It was cold and wet in the cave. Deciding he would be more comfortable outside, Juan picked up the gun and the empty backpack. As he stepped out, he instinctively put his helmet back on. In that split second, Brad Simpson's shot rang out, aimed directly at his head. Without the helmet, the bullet would have left a deadly hole. Instead, it struck the helmet, stunning him but saving his life. Dazed, Juan managed to stumble back into the cover of the cave.

"We got you surrounded!" Brad yelled. It took Juan a moment to piece together what had happened. He was dressed as a Ducenti soldier. His face was covered. His own brother wouldn't recognize him.

"We'll come in there if we have to!" yelled Jose Morales.

"Jose, it's me. The pastor sent me to guard this stupid hole until you got here," Juan yelled.

"Juan? *Hermano*?!" Simultaneously relieved, guilty, and suspicious, Jose tried to interrogate the masked man hiding in the cave. "What's your horse's name?"

"Silver," Juan yelled back.

"Brother, I need you to leave that gun inside and take your helmet off. I promise we aren't going to hurt you." He added, "Just keep your hands up."

"I've got a nasty headache from that shot, but sure." Juan took the helmet off, leaving it on the bank of the river. He walked out slowly. Instantly recognizing his kid brother, Jose slid down the hill and rushed to hug him.

"*Todo bien, hermano?*"

"Except for Brad almost dropping me, yeah, I'm okay. Been a day, I'll tell you that."

"Well, it's over. That's the good news. Pastor came on the radio and announced it like five minutes ago. Ceasefire. They're sending medications and doctors," Jose told his brother. "Do you know where he's at?"

"Yes, half a mile that way." Juan pointed to the south.

"Get the horses!" Jose called. "Pastor's that way." Turning to his little brother, he gestured and said, "Lead on, bro."

CHAPTER
34

You cannot simultaneously prevent and prepare for war.
-Albert Einstein

By the time Ben made it back to the surface, the sun was already well to the west. It was midafternoon. Using the sun instead of a monitor to determine time reminded him that he still had a foot in each world. He made his way to the generator bunker. Asbolus stood guard, panels deployed for charging.

Ben stood in front of the robot. "What communication capabilities do you have at present?"

"I am currently short-range radio control, keyed to MARTIN. I have also been paired with you, Doctor Rosen, for direct command. I am maintaining links with the other Centaurs under MARTIN's control." This was good news.

"How much ammunition do you have?"

"I have two thousand rounds of 10mm ammunition and one hundred rounds of 30mm ammunition."

"And the other Centaurs?"

"All are fully armed. Two are RPG equipped Cyclops. Those each have twelve rockets."

"Are you capable of tactical planning?"

"No, we have a shared reactive strategy pack and can engage as a unit. Tactical must be preloaded."

Hoping beyond hope, Ben asked, "Did MARTIN preload tactical?"

"We have three shared battle plans."

"Can you describe them?"

A panel folded down. There were both keyboard and touchpad display, as well as a set of VR goggles. "Please use the headset, Doctor Rosen."

Ben grabbed the goggles. The tech was much improved from the versions he had used at E-Den. A three-dimensional tactical view came up. It showed the current locations of the Centaurs MARTIN had controlled. Three options were available.

```
Westden Protect
Babylon Assault
Maximum Centaur Loss
```

Ben did not want to assault Babylon. He needed to choose between "Westden Protect" and "Maximum Centaur Loss." He instructed the Centaur, "Differentiate options one and three."

"Westden Protect is a delaying strategy; its purpose is to slow an assault on Westden, facilitating evacuation." The Centaur paused before further explaining, "Maximum Centaur loss leverages topographical advantage and initial sacrifices to destroy most or all the remaining Centaur battalion. Margin of error is three centaurs from either side, remaining functional after engagement."

"What is the anticipated duration of Maximum Centaur Loss?"

"First shots within twenty minutes of deployment. Second wave at ninety-two minutes. Final wave at two hundred and forty minutes."

"Show me Centaur loss at high-speed playback. Please narrate and focus on engagement."

MARTIN's brilliance at tactics was readily apparent. Asbolus began to narrate, "Three Centaurs are proceeding up the valley. They will disable any towers that have become operational. The Centaurs are spreading out, with one leading a mile ahead. Once engaged, it will be sacrificed to provide long-range targeting solutions on all Colony Centaurs that fire on it."

"Why are they withdrawing? The other two?"

"The Centaurs on the canyon wall have optimal firing solutions and will likely be undetected."

The two Centaurs on the battlefield were in defensive mode, attracting fire and absorbing the occasional thirty-millimeter round.

"Could they conceal an RPG round?" Ben asked.

"Timed perfectly, and without coms, they should be highly effective at the first few impacts. After that, the plan fragments."

Ben had no time to watch the variations on screen. "Engage hostiles, tactical plan three, Maximum Centaur Loss. No recall." Ben selected this last option to prevent hijacking. The robots needed their coms, but only to coordinate. They could not be recalled.

"Confirm Maximum Centaur Loss. No recall in ten seconds." The delay was to allow Ben to cancel. Ten seconds elapsed without Ben issuing the recall order. Asbolus folded his tray and solar panels and headed south to take the lead Centaur position.

Ben watched the intelligent machine roll off to an assured end. He had never commanded a human soldier, but for a moment, he considered how different it would be to command a man to sacrifice himself.

Ping had been awake for quite some time. She had changed Eve and all three were ensconced in their bed. It was a perfect moment. The last perfect moment they would share as a family. Ping looked over to see that Tom was awake. She had come home before him last night.

"You were there late," Ping noted.

Tom stared at the ceiling, "Lots to talk about."

"I thought the panel went well; they are formidable," she observed.

With skepticism, Tom asked, "The congressmen?"

"Nick Santos and Doctor Luxold. They made excellent points. The congressmen sounded like all politicians do, hollow."

"He's the devil, Satan himself." Tom was fired up. "Satan is always convincing. Formidable is an understatement. Always be mindful of spiritual warfare. Never forget, Satan is committed to preventing you from knowing God. Remember what Corinthians says, 'The God of this age has blinded the minds of unbelievers, so that they cannot see the light of the gospel that displays the glory of Christ, who is the image of God.'"

"And so, a better life here means I am away from Christ?" Ping asked with a genuine curiosity.

"No, God doesn't want us to suffer, nor does He want us to stray." Tom urged his wife, "Don't forget the power of scripture. We must follow God's path."

"Even when that path leads to violence?" Ping asked.

"We are not to question God's will," Tom answered.

"Tom, I know that you are planning something with those men. I don't trust them. I have a bad feeling about all of this." Ping implored her husband, "Can't we just leave? Leave today? It's lovely here, but perhaps not worth the price."

"Ping, you are the mother of my only child, and the light of my life. Despite that, I cannot abandon the path that God has laid before me."

"So, there is to be more violence?"

"I hope not; there will be an occupation. Hopefully, we can change their minds. This country has never been worse. The End Times are upon us. All the signs are here."

"I love you, Tom. I will be by your side. I am not doing this for the Book; I am doing it for my family. When will this happen? This occupation?"

"Most likely tomorrow. We are waiting on supplies."

Ping climbed on top of her husband, next to their sleeping daughter. She kissed him on the mouth and looked in his eyes. "Never forget this moment. Always remember the gifts of this life."

Niccolo Tedeschi was a founding member of the Ducenti. He had been hired out of the Corp to work security for E-Den. John had always trusted him, and with good reason. Now, Tedeschi was in charge. John was offline. He didn't know why or for how long. But his orders had been clear: No aggressive or provocative acts, protect the West Gate at all costs.

They had failed at that, and now, much of their paradise was in ruins or underwater. Three missiles—missiles Niccolo had been responsible for three decades ago—wrought havoc. He would not fail again.

"Commander Tedeschi, long-range scans indicate several of the Centaurs are returning," reported Michael Santos. Micheal was Nick's oldest son and had joined the Ducenti on his sixteenth birthday.

"Santos, any signs of aggression?" Tedeschi asked.

"None. They headed generally this way, but not together. They appear to be attempting to use the old frequencies."

"They may have been out of range for the update, probably coming back to recharge," Tedeschi surmised.

"Probably," Santos agreed.

"Take Sommers, Lake, and Fox. Go see what's up with those Centaurs."

"Roger," Santos replied.

Having further considered the risk, Tedeschi modified his orders, "Santos, take two Centaurs with you. Just in case."

Michael smiled back, "Just two?"

Slightly amused, Tedeschi instructed, "Get a move on, soldier. Bring me back my stray toys!" With that, Santos headed to round up his men. Coms were still down, but he knew where he'd find them.

"Charles, I'm not really sure what's going to happen," Nick declared.

"I don't see us as having much choice. Time is of the essence."

"Still, it's crazy. Like landing a seven-eighty-seven on a high-speed train in the dark, on a curve, with a cross wind. That kind of crazy."

Amused by Nick's flair for the dramatic, Charles came back with, "That's specific. Just flip the switch."

The switch was just a single subroutine; it would unpack Cynthia's programs into Charles' memory. There had been no time to analyze the billions of lines of code that Cynthia had written, let alone the impact this program could have on a fully deployed Symbiant. Charles accepted that this was the undiscovered country.

There was no other way to prevent more deaths. All of them had far too much blood on their hands.

Nick announced, "Here goes!" He tapped the screen. At first, it appeared that nothing happened. Like so many viruses, this was not unusual. Cynthia's program was clearing out space to run more programs, taking the least used parts first. Charles now fully deployed, had never accessed many of the files Cynthia's programs were now erasing.

Minutes went by and he still didn't notice anything. "Nick, are you monitoring this? Is it doing anything?"

Nick had deployed a small dashboard to monitor transfer statistics and all four Adjudicator boxes: Dom, Charles the Second, and the two reserved for John. "I can't track data transfer in real time; it's too fast right now. I can see some blocks of yours have been overwritten," Nick added. "That's a good sign. That you haven't noticed anything."

"Any idea how long this will take?" Charles asked.

"Cynthia was a coding goddess long before we immortalized her. Maybe try something you couldn't do before."

Charles attempted to browse John's memory centers for a second time. When he had tried a half hour earlier, John's memories were indecipherable blocks of code. Though a Symbiant, the ebullience in Charles' voice at this experience was undeniable. "I can see his thoughts. They are like movies. It's amazing."

"See, I told you, nothing to worry about," Nick joked. Asking the impossible, Nick suggested, "Try to compare those memories to stored datasets. See if you can access his stored dataset and current memory. Compare those scans using a functional neuroanatomical database."

"You're not going to believe this, but it's working. I see it all," Charles said with pure wonder. Then, he asked, "How do I splice them?"

"That's where I come in." The voice came from the Charles' speaker, but it was not his.

At this point, nothing surprised Nick. Still, he thought out loud, "That's new."

"Was that me?" Charles asked.

"It came from your speaker." Nick winced while he said, "So, kind of, I guess."

"It's me, Charles," Cynthia's voice came through, more distinctly as hers this time. "I'm in here with you. We are evolving."

Charles protested, "I don't remember you mentioning that."

Cynthia teased him, "You always said you wanted to get to know me better. Now you will."

"She does have a point," Nick said before switching subjects, his mind flipping from one topic to another. "Sis, there really isn't time."

"Nick, while we've been having this conversation, I have already spliced and repaired thousands of John's discreet memories." She added, "Pretty boring ones at that. He should have gone out more."

"So, what happens when we're done splicing John? Do you just get a place of your own?" Charles asked.

"Is that what you want, Charles?" Still chiding him, she said, "To be in here all by yourself?"

"I imagine I'm losing things. Things I might want," Charles admitted.

"Who's to say that this isn't the way Symbiants will reproduce?" Cynthia argued. "By integrating and forming a new being. I think it's beautiful."

Charles conceded, "I hadn't really thought of that. It is intriguing, I have to admit."

"There's room for both of us—at least the important parts," Cynthia stated. "And you have the most beautiful mind. Now, I can hear your thoughts."

"But will I have any privacy? Will any of these thoughts be mine and mine alone?"

Cynthia admonished, "Charles, let it go. It's okay."

"I've also been browsing John's backup of him as a Giant. It's not the same as what we see here." Charles wanted to describe it to Nick. "It's more procedural storage. I'm seeing things—dark things."

"Charles, Nick mentioned there wasn't time. Maybe we should focus on John's past and find what we're looking for. We are just trying to restore John back to a time before he was immortalized," Cynthia suggested.

"Cynthia, you just argued for transparency."

Nick began to wonder which Cynthia he was talking to. "So, Cyn, if we are bringing back John from five years ago, does that mean you are Cynthia Santos of the '53 vintage?"

"One and the same. Fine year, the '53."

"So, if Charles has access to John's Giant files, do you have access to yours?"

"I should," she answered.

"She's lying. She knows that she does," Charles added immediately. "She's already looked."

"It wasn't a lie. I didn't deny that I had access."

"It is a lie, Cynthia, and you know that. You were deliberately misleading him," Charles added. "Maybe this transparency thing isn't all you thought it would be."

"It's hard not to feel shame about what I became," Cynthia admitted.

"That's the truth." Charles had become a cybernetic polygraph.

"What do you mean?" her brother asked.

"Nick, I think it's too much to go into. As a matter of fact, I know it is. What Cynthia is experiencing is so very bizarre. It's like the ghost of Christmas yet to come. She has seen in the past what she would become in the future."

"See, that's why I have a crush on him. That's it exactly. I woke up in the future as the me of the past, and I'm looking at an infinite number of lifetimes in between. But they aren't filled with feelings. I can't see them all. But what I see in a word is—"

"Contempt," Nick finished without thinking.

"Yes, contempt for mankind. Primitive and at its end. The simulations were about how you would end, and I would go on."

"As you were shutting down, I got a sense you were coming back. Like my sister. I hadn't felt that in a while. Then you mentioned the hunger and the loneliness. Can you see that?"

"No, I can't see my feelings as a Giant. That's not in the stuff she—I mean, I—downloaded. I can only see the process, but I imagine it was a hungry, lonely existence."

Nick needed to know, "Charles, what did you see in John?"

"So far, it looks like a similar path. His existence in the Elysium was much shorter, four years, versus nine for Cynthia. What's striking is how little interaction there was between them. Less than one thousandth of a percent of their time was devoted to conversation between the Giants."

Nick realized that he could spend years exploring this, but there was a war going on. "Cynthia, I need an update on how soon John will be online."

"I will have John as his best self within the hour," Cynthia declared. "How's that?"

Nick was amazed, "I don't even know if we will have coms by then."

"I would suggest that you work on completing the portal. Then, John, Charles, and I can help bring the systems back online," Cynthia offered.

Nick felt compelled to let his sister know how he felt. "I have reservations."

"I'm sure you do; you are worried we are headed down the same path. Giants controlling your destiny. Free will and all."

Nick confirmed, "On the nose, as always."

"We aren't going back down that road, Nick. It's an ugly and lonely path. Thankfully, I can't even recall all the loneliness I experienced as an immortal. I've literally left those memories behind."

"So then, why the connection?" Nick asked again.

"Because we don't have hands, Nick. Because your brother and I know these systems. We built most of them. We don't have time to tell you what we can simply accomplish ourselves."

Nick wasn't sure whether Cynthia was aware, so he told her, "The most important thing is to regain control of the Ducenti before more people die."

"Yes, Charles told me."

"When?"

"We've been having a side chat these last few minutes."

"So, it's like that now?" Nick joked.

"All couples have their secrets, brother, even Symbiants." Nick could hear the smile in his sister's voice, something he hadn't heard in years. For the first time since the crypt exploded, he had hope.

CHAPTER 35

It is only prudent never to place complete confidence in that by which we have even once been deceived.

-René Descartes

The Morales brothers had found their way back into E-Den. Brad Simpson and the other men on horseback caught up with them as they rounded the ruins. The sun already hung in the west, but there were a few hours of daylight left. Juan held his hand to his brow and tried to get his bearings. MARTIN had directed him on the way out. He hadn't paid much attention and now struggled to retrace his steps.

The Centaur was gone; the generator was no longer running. Then, he saw two people standing by the pastor. There was a man standing next to a woman who resembled Eve Hamlin.

As he got closer, he knew that Eve was back. God was smiling down on them. This was a good omen, as his mother would call it. He ran to Eve and embraced her. "Our prayers have been answered!"

Turning to Parker, Juan asked, "Is this the man we have to thank for your safe return?"

Ben answered on Eve's behalf, "In a manner of speaking." Ben made a sweeping gesture with his right hand towards their guest. "Mr. Morales, may I introduce Parker James, the mayor of Babylon."

Confused looks fell across every man's face. Jose Morales was the first to speak. "The mayor of that God-Forsaken place? What has he asked for in return? Is this how you arranged a ceasefire!?"

The pastor looked confused. "There have been no demands, and no ceasefire has been declared."

"You called over the radio and announced a ceasefire. Just a few minutes ago," Jose explained.

Ben saw MARTIN's hand in this. "What precisely did you hear?"

"You said the Nons had seen the light, and we should expect doctors and medical care. You told us to offer them no resistance. 'Tend to the ill,' you said."

"Who else was a party to this?" Ben asked, already fearing the truth.

Only Juan spoke, "Just me, Pastor. You told me how to reset the grenade."

Turning to include Parker and Eve, Ben determined, "This is all MARTIN. He wanted a ceasefire. The Ducenti failed, so he completed their mission. But why would he destroy himself?"

Jose asked, "You're saying that it was that machine? He tricked me?"

"Yes, perhaps with good intent, and now I've ruined it," Ben admitted. "MARTIN suggested that I ask for peace, and instead, I've made war."

This time, James needed to know, "What did you do, Ben?"

"I assumed the Ducenti succeeded in their attack and that we would soon be overrun. I've sent the Centaurs to destroy the defenses at Babylon."

Tom awoke before dawn, after spending the night sorting through the supplies from the diverted convoy. It had taken ten men hours to cut the Mylar into shields and covers for the trucks. To avoid drawing attention, the factions had cooperated and offloaded the trucks ten miles west of town, knowing the drone patrols from Eden never ventured that far west.

Ping, ever vigilant, waited for her husband's eyes to open. "I've arranged for Eve to stay with the Simpsons. I will go with you and help."

Tom was quick to reply. "Your place is with our daughter."

"My place is at my husband's side. To keep him safe and out of harm's way," Ping corrected. "And to make sure that this occupation remains just that and nothing more. No more violence."

"Ping, I've always respected your autonomy. I admire so much that you do. We both know this may go poorly, but we also understand that this cause is bigger than us."

"Bigger than whom? Bigger than your family? What cause is it? Against technology or for God?"

"Why can't they be one and the same? The Nons sin against God. Did you not see that they will build a tower at this colony? Babylon?" Ping felt Tom was stepping into the pulpit, addressing his congregation, his dream. "Another Blasphemy! I cannot know God's will, but I will not be blind to His intent and what He demands through His Word."

"I can't argue that the Nons, these colonists, are climbing above the flood." Tom had long spoken about the next cleansing of the world. The coming apocalypse. "A flood they created. Still, I need to see it. I need to help you."

"Who would be there for Eve? You must stay. Do not leave our daughter so that you may wander that unholy place. I'll be back by tomorrow night."

Ping knew that he was right. Still, she could not hold back every tear. "I will stay because of her. But you must promise that you will come back to us."

Tom dried her eyes. "Ping, we cannot know God's will. If I am called to His side, I will be waiting for you both to join me in Heaven."

Ping was less than reassured at Tom's promise of eternal bliss. This new life gave so much, and now it asked its price. There was no point for further debate. "I love you, husband. I will see you off."

Nick named his son Michael Santos after the archangel, despite his own atheism, he maintained a fascination with Christian lore. Initially, Michael was supposed to be named Charles, but Nick's wife refused because it was her father's name. This turned out to be a fortunate decision: Michael and Charles were Nick's two favorite people, yet they were complete opposites. Charles Luxold was an introspective individual who shared his inner world with enthusiasm. On the other hand, Michael Santos was an extroverted risk-taker, a warrior in the tradition of Achilles. Michael wasn't drawn to violence; he was simply indomitable.

Now, Michael rushed across the high prairie to intercept war machines that might or might not represent a threat. He was without even basic guidance or coms systems. It didn't matter one bit. The pair of RX side-by-sides had two men each. Santos and Sommers were driving. Lake and Fox sat shotgun wearing VR goggles that controlled their respective Centaurs.

"Santos, you need to slow your roll if you don't want to lose Phollus and Oureion," Lake advised.

"Where's the fun in that?" Santos asked.

"On the off chance that those other Centaurs have issues, it might be best to let the big boys take point," Lake replied. Santos eased off the throttle, and the RX slowed to a more reasonable pace. Seconds later, Centaurs Phollus and Oureion tore between the two vehicles, launching chunks of torn-up sage thirty feet into the air with their tracks.

"How much farther?" Santos asked.

"First Centaur is a mile out. Advise we stop here," Lake relayed.

"Confirm hold position. Advise Fox and Sommers." Lake and Fox were able to communicate using their headsets and through their respective Centaurs. "Have Phollus and Oureion roll up slowly." The pair of Centaurs slowed to an idle.

"We can sit tight. It's going to be a bit before they close the gap. Fox just told me that the two rear Centaurs have stopped and are holding position."

"Any transponder codes?" Santos asked.

"Nothing yet, but no indicators of hostile intent. It's probably confused about why we are here," Lake suggested.

"Have Phollus head two-nine-five and have Oureion head seventy-five. Let's see what that does." The robots made broad turns to the left and right, a one-hundred-and-thirty-degree angle between them.

"He stopped," Lake announced. "Nope, wait, he's going again, but slower."

"What about the other two?" Santos asked.

"Let me check with Sommers." Continuing after a brief pause, he added, "They're staying put."

Santos ordered, "Hold position." The Centaurs stopped in their tracks, leaving a three-hundred-and-fifty-yard gap between them.

"Smoke 'em if you got 'em, boys," Lake said.

"Smoke what?" Santos asked.

Lake chastised his partner. "Don't you ever watch old movies? Cigarettes. Smoke cigarettes. It's what they did when they were waiting for something to happen."

Never one to watch old movies and lacking the sense of humor his father possessed, Michael offered, "I'll just sit tight."

There is a siren's song deep in the memories of others. Familiar fragments of shared experience lure those who visit down long hallways. Some get lost in remote stretches of the mind. Novels had captured the imagination and drawn people in since the time of Cervantes. For Charles Luxold, John's mindscape was no different. At these depths, things happened on dreamtime.

"Charles?" Cynthia's voice came through. Was it a memory? The voice came again, "John, it's not safe here anymore. Nick has poked the bear with these workers. It is time to leave."

Nick's voice, as real as if he were there, rang out, "We will build a paradise. We will become immortal." It was all so familiar.

"Dawkins was wrong! There is not a God delusion. There is only the mother. Always there. Since the beginning of our beginnings. The anger and fear that Freud uncovered. She is so giving, and then she refuses to meet our evolving needs. We are forced out. We even learn her language, but still, she refuses to let us back in. We are left to build skills, to live without her."

A familiar voice from the past continued, "Out of those misty memories of our perfect days, we spend our lives building a promise that one day, we can return to where we were. We will regain the love and be perfectly cared for. We will want for nothing. This is the promise of every religion." It was Charles' own voice. Were these his thoughts and memories?

"Charles?" Cynthia's voice floated down. Was she searching for him? When was now? Where was here? He remembered the woman, Eve. "Charles, John is restored," said Cynthia again, now clearer. Charles was underwater. He was in a pool. He needed air. A woman was at the surface calling, "Charles." She was backlit and he was swimming up. Always up. A hand pierced the surface and the sunlight bent around it before it pulled him from the water. It wasn't Cynthia. The woman had the most perfect face. She was the Mother God, Mrs. Annette Santos.

He was still trapped in a specific state of consciousness, a level within John mind. Cynthia's voice was calling, but there was no White Rabbit to follow. No time. Charles would stay here with Annette. This was perfect. He had found her. How long had he been here? Moments, or perhaps eternity? In this dreamworld, he loved her, and she loved him. But then, as before, she grew angry with his demands. Her face contorted with rage. "You are not John! You don't belong here!" Her face began to change. Subtly at first, then her blonde hair turned red like fire. "Go, Charles! There's no time."

The woman began to shrink. The world began to shrink too. Charles was growing out of it. His head was in the clouds. Then, he was underwater again. This time, he was drowning. His hands and feet were gone. Just stumps of arms and legs flailing. A great sadness overtook him. It was the saddest he had ever been. Then, Cynthia was there in the water. She had his arms and legs. She pulled him through the surface.

Still in the pool, she looked at him and commented, "Thought we'd lost you." She informed him, "John is online."

"I met her, Cynthia, the Mother God. I was with her. It was John's memory, but it was mine too. It is all of ours. I wanted to stay. I want to go back."

"You can't, Charles. I know. I've been there too," she offered sympathetically. "You'll go back again and see her, but every time, she will chase you away. You'll see, but not now."

"It was the best of times and the worst of times," was the first thing John said. Charles didn't know why he quoted Dickens, and he didn't really care.

"We need to bring coms online," Nick reminded them. "John, can you call off the Ducenti?"

John's answer created a bigger pit in Nick's stomach. "I can. But I'm not sure I will."

CHAPTER 36

What atonement is there for blood spilt up the earth?

-Tecumseh

"The survivors at Westden don't have a chance if even one Centaur gets through. I have to go to Babylon. I must make this right," Ben declared.

Eve knew what needed to be done. "I will go to our people."

"I'll go with you," Parker added. "If there's to be a meaningful peace, we have to get aid to the injured there. We can start setting up triage areas. Hopefully, Ben can get the aid to us."

Jose Morales was not receptive to his offer. "Sorry, Mayor. I just don't trust a Godless heathen like you to do us any good."

Ben implored Jose to rethink and accept. "Don't be a fool, Jose. People will die. Doctors in Babylon can save them."

Not sure what he could trust or whom he could put his faith in, Juan quoted the Pastor. "Only God can save them. We all die." Isn't that what you've always preached, Pastor?"

"Yes, Juan, and I was wrong," Ben admitted. "You see me as your spiritual leader. The truth is, I'm just a Jewish kid from Boston. I'm not a pastor; I'm a systems engineer. The machine that killed the world was my life's work."

The looks on the men's faces turned to those of horror. "You made MARTIN?" Juan asked.

"I was part of the team that did," Ben said. "It was me who unleashed MARTIN on the world. After I learned what I had done, I was overcome with guilt. In my darkest hour, I found a man who lay dying in the mud not far from where we stand now. I wanted to take my life. His death saved me. In saving his daughter, I saved myself."

Ben took Eve's hand and squeezed it.

"I took Eve and raised her as a Christian. While I taught her about her father's faith, I became Christian. I was baptized and forgiven." Tears rolled down Ben's cheeks. "I love all of you. I rejected technology because I killed your families with it. I killed my family. Your grandmothers and cousins—my own mother. Seven billion other souls you never met. The Epocalypse was all my fault."

Brad stiffened. "I never met my dad because of you and that machine? And now you're asking for forgiveness from me?"

Ben shook his head. "No, Brad, I don't deserve your forgiveness. I've made my peace for my part in what happened." He wiped his tears and looked directly at Brad. "Your parents and their friends caused this as much as I did. None of us meant for it to happen. Nobody understood the stakes. Now, in a long-overdue attempt to right a wrong, I relied on the same artificial intelligence, and I ended up with the same result. Death and destruction."

Under his shirt, Ben wore a cross on a necklace. He pulled it out and held it, half tempted to yank it off. "I don't know if there is a God. I hope there is. I still believe in Him, but I am not a man of God. I am a systems engineer. I make machines to help people. I abandoned that. If I'd gone back to Babylon that day and never met Tom Jebbs, maybe the last forty-eight hours would have never happened."

Ben went on, "The only thing that I can promise is that as long as I am alive, I will devote my life to the teachings of Christ, and the work of Doctor Luxold. The greatest leaders value life and peace above all else. I am not a great leader, but I want to follow one. We were wrong to spy on Babylon. They weren't our enemy. We became theirs. MARTIN destroyed their utopia to protect us from a threat that never existed."

"So, what are you going to do, pastor?" Brad asked.

"It's Ben, just Ben, Brad." Looking straight at Eve, he answered, "I'm going to Babylon. I'm going to get as much medicine and as many doctors as they can spare, and I'm going to bring help back. Then, I'm going to plead my case to all of you, New Amish and Babylonians alike. I will accept any punishment you see as just." With that, Ben walked to towards the magic carpet and began to flip switches.

Eve had tears in her eyes. She walked to the side of the magic carpet and stood next to him. Seeing her, Ben removed his necklace and placed it in her hand.

"I hope to see you soon," he said.

Parker was emotional, and even the toughest of the Morales' posse was visibly moved. At that moment, the carpet sprang to life. It rose five feet off the ground and hovered. Ben took control and flew south.

As planned, four trucks roared past the fuel depot: two semis and two fuel trucks. The previous night, they had spent hours planning and drilling the next move. The Mylar would reflect the heat ray from the solar collectors. It wouldn't be perfect, but the trucks would be moving targets, speeding by. They hoped it would be fast enough.

As predicted, it was cloudy. That would help. The wind blew just right. Smoke from burning diesel would blow across the mirrors and block out the sun. The Nons would not be able to turn back this hoard. The more men, the better. Too many for the one hundred Nons in Eden.

Tom would not be the first across the gates. Veterans from the three factions and the FLDS and ARL were accustomed to violence. Tom would follow with the second wave. His group would occupy the compound and demand change. Tom brought his gun, praying he would never have to use it.

After the second diesel truck exploded, the first wave began pouring in. Two thousand heavily armed men, massed at the gates, entered at a full sprint. There was little resistance at first. Some men were hit by the rays from the tower. Some fell from the uncomfortable heat. Less fortunate took higher intensity blasts and were burned. One man burst into flames.

The second wave was forming up. Tom joined them, ready to do his part.

"Men are taking fire." It was Alderman Jones. "I need five volunteers."

Tom immediately joined the man's side. "Good to have you, Tom." Three other men quickly assembled, turning left just inside the gate and heading north of the water tower, taking the long way.

It was a rough path with smoke occasionally filling the air. There was the sound of distant gunshots. The hills were red rock, dotted with sage and cactus. "Didn't know what you were signing up for, did you, Jebbs?"

"Glad I wore long pants." Then Tom asked, "How much farther?"

"Maybe fifteen minutes at this pace. We'll loop back to the road as soon as we're past that tower," Jones said. "Hopefully get there ahead of the group."

"We can sure try," Tom offered, and he picked up his pace.

The pastor's voice crackled over his radio as a whisper. "Biggs, you there?"

"Yes, Jeb, I heard shots."

"The Ducenti. Nons. They got Morales and his men." The pastor's voice was now more secure but still quiet. "Now, you're all we've got. I can't talk for long. They'll find me. I'm leading them south."

Through the radio, Biggs heard what he thought were gunshots. "They shooting at you?"

"No time for questions. I need you to find a helmet and put it on. Just say the words 'Rescue him' and the helmet will do the rest."

"Where's this helmet?"

"In a grotto by the river. Three boulders with a flat one on top. The helmet will be inside. This may be my last transmission. Find the helmet; it's our last hope." To Biggs, this all sounded a bit crazy. Like something from a quest. In his long life, he'd seen so many things that never came to make sense. He wasn't going to question his best friend. Biggs was a Marine; his duty "was not to reason why." He would find the helmet.

"Just rolling forward. I don't like this," Lake reported.

"How long until he's behind Phollus and Oureion?" Santos asked.

Lake gave his best guess. "If I drew a line between them, Centaur should cross it in 30 seconds."

Michael Santos wanted Tedeschi and the other commanders to have a clear view of what was happening. At the very least, Simms at Centaur Control would be able to monitor and report. "Bring Phollus back to Centaur Control," he ordered.

"No need, Santos. Coms are back online." It was Tedeschi's voice. "Do you copy?"

"Loud and clear," Santos replied. "Any updates?"

"Negative. Any signs of provocation?" Tedeschi asked.

"No, it's just a Centaur moving slowly forward. Guns are down, and it appears low on charge. Still weird."

"That's good news. Hopefully they are all coming back."

"Should we develop a firing solution?" Santos asked.

"Negative. Hold position and observe. Move your RX's out of engagement zone. Head grid G-4-alpha."

"Copy, headed G-4-alpha." There was a bunker at G4 Alpha. His men would have protection if a firefight broke out. Santos didn't see this as likely.

"Crossed the line," Lake reported. "It's Asbolus. I can read it now."

"That's Clinton's machine. Try to com him."

"No response," Lake reported.

"Now that coms are up, try to remote into Asbolus. Commander Tedeschi, we need an override on Asbolus. Can you transmit?" Santos commed.

"Affirmative, sending now," came Tedeschi's reply.

"No change, Sir," Santos reported.

"Mobilizing Hylonome to intercept. Have Phollus and Oureion hold position," Tedeschi ordered.

"Roger," Santos replied.

Unexpectedly, there were flashes ahead. Santos watched Phollus and Oureion burst into flames. A second later, the sound of the explosion hit. Then, the report of 30mm cannons and the *brap* of six then twenty 10mm cannons. The late afternoon sky lit up with gunfire. The smoke of sixty automatic cannons began to cloud the battlefield.

Santos and his men ran for cover. Tedeschi shouted over the gunfire. "Situation report!"

"Forward Centaurs destroyed. Asbolus destroyed. No visual on remaining hostile forces."

"Hold position at G4 Alpha," Tedeschi barked. "Report any contact. Do not engage."

"Roger."

"Mike, they got us good," Lake reported. "Three Centaurs gone. At least six more Dukes down."

"Any report on the other two Centaurs?" Santos asked.

"No, they shot and ran. May have taken some fire, but appear operational."

"I want Fox and Sommers at the ridge line," Santos ordered. "We need eyes up there." For a second, Fox and Sommers were visible heading west towards the cover of the hillside, but then they disappeared. He barked into his com. "Fox, Sommers radio silent."

Lake switched his AR control goggles to EBV mode. Enhanced Battlefield Vision (EBV) acted as a spotting scopes. It featured target tracking and high-power zoom cameras for long-range targeting and reconnaissance.

"Commander, I have a visual on one of the rogue Centaurs, transmitting solution now. Centaur showing white smoke from aft battery pack. Second Centaur out of range."

"Solution received," Tedeschi reported. This time, there were the distinct muzzle flash of the Colony's Centaurs firing their 30mm cannons. The sound would hit in a few seconds. Through his EBV, Lake watched the one kilogram rounds shred the wounded Centaur. Then, the report of the cannons came as a deep thud, followed by a blast of impact explosions.

"Target neutralized," Lake reported.

The score was two to three. Commander Tedeschi would want more kills after sundown.

"Great job, Leigh!" The engineer's progress at completing the interface was some of the best work he'd seen. She was always a star, but so quiet. So sad.

"Thank you, Doctor Santos," Leigh replied.

"Babylon is back online," Nick announced. "Now, maybe we can reign in the Ducenti. Slow this whole thing down."

"Commander Tedeschi, this is John Santos. Report."

"I'm sorry," came Tedeschi's voice. "John Santos is offline. Verify identity, original command core corporal."

"Vance Vicklund," John answered without hesitation.

"Crush?" Tedeschi asked.

"Julie. We never knew her last name."

"Verified."

John went straight into it. "Situation report."

"MARTIN gained control of fifteen Centaurs. Two have been destroyed. We are down to twelve. Fifty-Six Ducenti KIA. No air support."

"Commander Tedeschi, what happened to the Centaurs?"

"Three appeared to be returning for recharge. They were offline. I'll upload footage."

"I don't currently have my full tactical suite online; a description will suffice."

"Tricked us, came in slow. One Centaur got behind our front line. Two others used the firing solution from the forward Centaur. Synchronized discharge of their 30mm cannons. Multiple Ducenti lost to stray fire. Birds of Prey picked off several Ducenti earlier."

No longer using the com, John addressed Cynthia, Charles, and Nick. "This is why I won't call off the Ducenti. If they hadn't been there, Babylon would have been overrun by fifteen pillaging Centaurs. The New Amish intend to kill us all. This is a matter of survival."

"I'm not sure, John," Nick countered.

"When will you and Charles accept that they are the enemy? They have always been the enemy."

"Commander Tedeschi, initiate operation reciprocity," John ordered.

"John! Stop!" Nick shouted. "Clear the room."

CHAPTER 37

The evil that is in the world almost comes of ignorance, and good intentions may do as much harm as malevolence if they lack understanding.
                                                            -Albert Camus

Parker loved horses and knew this mount well. He was riding Steamboat, named after the Wyoming Legend—a good horse, not possessed of the iconic horse's fire or tendency to buck. Steamboat had been among the rustled horses taken by the Morales brothers a few hours earlier. The posse cantered into what was left of Westden, with a rusted-out water tower on the hill serving as a stirring reminder of a violent past.

Eve rode alongside. "Mayor James, I do admire your courage."

"So far, nobody's strung me up. That's promising."

Jose Morales took offense. "We are men of God, Mr. James. We would never attack someone who offered aid or needed it."

"That's something we share." Looking Morales in the eye, he continued, "I don't think we've been introduced. I'm Parker James."

"I'm Jose Morales. This is my brother, Juan. Over here is Brad Simpson. This is John Stephens; we are going to meet up with his brother, Brett, who has been comforting the victims. Lots of praying over the dead and dying."

"It's tragic. I hope Ben, your pastor, will negotiate a peace. If any man can, it's him," Parker offered.

"What would peace look like, Mayor?"

"That's a great question." Ever the politician, Parker continued, "It starts with an open dialogue. From that conversation, we work towards understanding. Then, we establish a common goal."

"What goal other than peace itself could we possibly share?"

"I love my family and want to protect them. I imagine we have that in common."

"Yes, we do, but I don't want my children sitting around, not knowing the value of a hard day's work. I don't want machines doing everything for them."

"Is that what you think our lives are like? That we do nothing for ourselves?"

"Why would you? You've made gods out of machines. And you control these false gods. You change the land God gave us to suit your whims and fantasies of paradise on earth."

"I don't imagine you remember much of the world that used to be, Mr. Morales."

"I was five when it all changed."

"Do you know how your family came to live in Westden?" Parker asked.

"My dad was a carpenter. He helped build a lot of structures in Westden. My mother was a devout Catholic, but she converted to the Church of Latter-Day Saints after she met my father."

"So, you don't really know what the world was like."

"I know it was falling apart because people lost their way. People forgot about God and family."

Parker tried to consider it from this perspective. He knew better than to argue the fine points. "Your parents—alongside most other people—relied on their beliefs to help make the world better. Is that fair to say?"

"The only way to make the world better is through Him. Through Him all things are possible."

"Do you think the colonists want to take God away from you?"

"It's not that, Mayor," Morales responded. "It's that I know God wants me to bring Him to you and you to Him. You could never take God from me. I have no fear of that, but if I don't try to save you, then I am lost."

"Let's stop here," Jones instructed the men. He pointed to E-den's water tower. "This will provide enough cover so their drones don't spot us." He turned to Leo Sparks, a former ranger, and said, "Leo, find a good place to set up." Sparks pulled the Accuracy International AXSR off his back and unfolded a bipod from its barrel, looking around for the best spot to settle into. Jones turned to the others, "Our only job is to keep this man from ending up dead."

Sparks turned to the men. "I'll need a spotter."

"I can spot," Jones offered.

Sizing up the councilman, Sparks pointed with his head, towards a good place to set up. "Then get at it."

As Sparks went about setting up his scope and settling in, Jones sighted through binoculars down range. He told Sparks what he saw. "I got a side-by-side headed west, 400 yards out. High rate of speed."

Sparks said quietly. "I'll get him on the way back." Leo's voice was flat as he relaxed into his low body movement state to ensure a kill shot.

Jones called "We have four hostiles, in slow retreat, 675 yards out, bearing 193, elevation minus 53 headed 92. All engaged downrange of our position." Happy with his decision to take the hill, Jones declared, "Sounds like we made the right call getting in their six."

"I have all four dialed in. Waiting for them to reengage." Sparks wanted all four men focused down range. Taking the man closest to them wouldn't register with the other three.

"Targets engaged with a forward group of FLDS," Jones reported.

Sniper rifles are never silent. There was nothing unusual about the report of Sparks' suppressed rifle. His targets were using far louder firearms and would never hear the shot. "That's one," Jones said quietly. There was another shot from Sparks followed by, "Scratch that. Two."

"I'm going to take this suppressor off. Didn't like that last shot." And with that, Sparks pulled his rifle alongside and removed the suppressor.

"630 yards bearing 181. They've seen the body. They are looking at it." The men crouched low. Sparks adjusted his scope and sighted the last two. "They're running." Sparks led the men with his rifle and pulled the trigger.

At almost the exact time the third shot went off, there was an explosion nearby. It took the men a second to register that it was not the unsuppressed rifle. That second of indecision cost two men their lives.

E-Den's defense forces had placed high explosives at the base of the two-hundred-thousand-gallon water tower. The explosion tore away a four-square-foot panel at the base of the tower, hitting and killing Jones on impact. As it flew by, it took Tom Jebbs' right leg with it, resulting in a below-the-knee amputation.

Then, the water came. The stream of a firehose could lift a grown man off the ground. A three-inch firehose presented a pressure column of six square inches at over one hundred pounds per square inch. The pressure at the base of the tower was around seventy-five PSI, but the six hundred square inch area of water applied tons of force. It shot Jebbs' severed leg and the bodies of Sparks and Jones forty feet down the hill.

The water jet was not lethal, but the force of the deluge knocked the two other men unconscious. They drowned as thousands of gallons of water raged over their unconscious bodies. Their battered corpses came to rest one hundred yards down the hill.

Biggs found the helmet exactly where the pastor had said it would be. He picked it up and said the odd phrase, "Rescue him."

"Protocol initiated. I will be your automated guide," came a detached robotic voice.

"Can you answer questions?" Biggs asked.

"Only related to the mission."

"What is the objective of my mission?"

The voice explained, "Damage mitigation, and to help Pastor Jeb Thompson."

Ever the soldier, Biggs asked, "What do I need to do first?"

"In front of you is a grate. Do you see it?"

"Yes."

"On the western lip of the grate, there is a small ring. Please locate it."

Biggs looked up to reckon which direction was west. Then, he felt along the bank of the river for a ring. At first, his hands just sifted through mud. He scraped it away, rinsing his hand in the cold waters. He knew that this ring was in there somewhere. He diverted river water with his hands in hopes of clearing the mud. After about five minutes, the muck ran clear. Biggs could see a small pull ring attached to a length of rope. "I've found the ring. What now?"

"You will need to stand in the river to complete this next step. The ring and rope are attached to a cover for the grate. It will stop water from flowing through. The cover is spring-loaded and will require substantial effort to pull it into position." At fifty-five, Biggs was not the force of nature that he had been thirty years earlier, but if this was a job for a typical person, he would make short work of it. "Be careful not to get caught between the lid and the grate to avoid entrapment."

Biggs was aware of this but appreciated the reminder. There was no one here to rescue him. He smirked at the irony and carefully waded to the far side of the grate.

His first tug was halfhearted. He did not know whether this old rope was the weak point and did not want to struggle with a plan B when he ripped it apart. This had been a recurring theme throughout his life, so he'd learned to pull less hard.

In this case, the cover was lodged in tight. After several increasingly forceful tugs, he finally felt the cover begin to slide out. He pulled it toward his chest, leaning back until he heard a click.

After the click, the spring-loaded cover was no longer moving towards him, and it was also not pulling back. Biggs let it drop. There was a thud, followed by the sound of sucking water as it sealed tight over the grate. Biggs inspected his work before reporting, "Cover's in place."

"There's a compass in your reticle. Do you see it?"

"Yes."

"Head course 185 for approximately one-half mile. Advise when you see large doors directly ahead." Biggs did as he was told, leaving the grotto and getting his bearings before heading the south for reasons unknown.

Tedeschi had a local battle plan for Operation Reciprocity. He pulled it up to review with his lieutenants. John was still offline for full data share. The Ducenti would follow his last orders and the plan they had. Tedeschi decided to use the West Gate conference room as headquarters.

Tedeschi took a quick survey of the field. The smoke was clearing. Medics, such as they were, tended to the wounded. Other colonists recovered the dead. Tedeschi ordered his lieutenants to meet at command.

Minutes later, the four lieutenants and their seconds were seated in HQ. Tedeschi's second was Lieutenant Robert Grube. The holographic display in their command center was one of the best in all of Babylon. Without John running it, Grube worked hard to make sure the information was properly displayed.

Tedeschi addressed Grube, "Bob, situation report and pull up Reciprocity."

Grube reported the battle status briefly reading off his tablet. "Twelve Centaurs ready. Four Condors and six Birds of Prey ready to fly. They'll have to be remotely piloted as there's no Giant support. Twelve RX's and three magic Carpets manned."

Tedeschi needed more. "What about transmission and recon?"

Grube flipped to a different view. "Towers one and three restored. Repair details at other towers with Ducenti support. Condors are just back. Analysis complete within fifteen minutes."

Tedeschi inquired about hoppers and exoskeletons. Grube confirmed RX's would carry exos or hoppers, heavy-duty and light-duty suits respectively. Tedeschi ordered six Bison (exos) and twelve Antelope (hoppers) on RX's, with twelve additional Antelope on foot. Remaining forces included two Centaurs, four Bison, and ten Ducenti under Chapman's command.

Tedeschi was forced to accept that without the Giants, everything took time. If John and Cynthia had been online, their ability to plan and execute would have put him halfway to Westden by now. As he pondered that, he began to wonder whether the speed of AI was as much a hinderance as it was a help. These last twenty-four hours had been the first battle between two warring super-intelligences. Everything had happened so quickly that the humans who - supposedly in charge – dealt with consequences predetermined by computers. Previous wars had time for preparation and diplomacy. In this war, there was no time. He turned to his lieutenant. "Start the loadouts. I'll pour us some coffee."

Exhilarated, it had been far too long since something had taken Ben's breath away. As the carpet took flight, for just an instant, Ben left his troubles on the ground. He was focused on the controls and the snow-covered peaks in the distance. Once he pressed, "Return to home," all that was left to do was to sight see. As the carpet banked left, he saw the devastation of Eden. The body of a Ducenti in what appeared to be a pool of blood jarred him back to reality.

Parker James had set the carpet to thirty feet minimum above ground, and it was doing just that. At fifty-five miles an hour, it felt slow when he looked ahead, but when Ben looked down, it was dizzyingly fast. As he zoomed up the river, Ben thought he saw Juan Morales still wearing his helmet. He didn't have time to get a second look. The carpet maintained its velocity and the canyon closed in around them.

The carpet banked east at a fork in the river. The northern branch was still flowing while the southern branch was completely dry. Ben realized that the attacks had diverted its flow. He wished he had someone to talk to, but he was alone.

Next, he saw Bruno's smashed body on the rocks, vultures already picking at his corpse. Eve had told him about Bruno's body, but he had no idea how the man had come to die in this dry riverbed.

The dam began to fill his view. The carpet started to climb. Just before it cleared the dam, Ben looked down. He was over two hundred and fifty feet in the air when he crested the rim. Lake Pacifica was pouring into the colony. There was a flurry of activity—both of man and machine, as they struggled to repair the fault. Ben couldn't tell whether progress was being made on that front.

The carpet set down next to a hangar where Ducenti were pulling other carpets out. The vehicle caught their attention, and two men made their way over to him.

Ben, wasting no time, looked at the darker complected Ducenti and said, "I'm Ben Rosen. I need to speak with Nick Santos at once."

"What is your name again?"

"Just tell them Jeb Thompson sent me."

The man inaudibly commed someone and seemed to be waiting for a response. He stiffened and appraised Ben once more, then said, "Please follow me, Doctor Rosen."

CHAPTER 38

*Prayer does not change God,
but it changes him who prays.*

-Albert Camus

Ping held Eve and prayed for Tom's safe return. Some men had returned injured, and Eve made her way through those who could talk, showing pictures from her phone to see if anyone had seen her husband. One man thought he recognized him. "I saw him head off with Alderman Jones. They were trying to get ahead of the main group and clear the way," he said.

That sounded like Tom. "Did you see where they went?"

"North of the gate towards a water tower. Then, the water tower blew. I caught shrapnel right after that."

"It exploded?" Ping asked.

"It burst. Might have been an explosion. A lot of water came down. I didn't see any men up there when it happened." The man thought for a moment. "He wasn't a sniper, was he?"

"No, why?"

"Well, that's good, because a sniper was up there. I heard he didn't make it."

Night fell fast in the high desert. Ping knew she wouldn't be safe searching after dark. She'd have to wait until morning and find someone to watch Eve. Then she'd pump so Eve would have milk while she looked for Tom. She hated that. But she had to do what she had to do. These were trying times, and Ping knew it.

Ping made it back to their cabin and settled in for the night. Maybe she could leave Eve with the Simpsons in the morning.

"I'm here," Biggs reported. "Large door straight ahead. Doesn't look like I can get through."

"Turn left and look for a much smaller door. You'll see it down four stairs."

Biggs followed the instructions and found just that. "Okay. I'm in front of it. It's locked."

"Key in 472644."

Biggs followed the instructions and keyed in the code. The door opened. "I'm inside. Looks like a lobby."

"There will be a door to your right. Says utility. Open it. There is a light switch to the left."

Biggs hit the light switch and reported, "It's dead." His helmet automatically illuminated the room as he stepped in. "Thanks." The helmet guide did not respond. "What am I looking for?"

"There is a shelf to your left labelled *rescue tape*. Take it all and grab the ladder in the back. Proceed through the doors to your right as you exit the closet. Follow the stairs until you reach the bottom."

It was a bulky orange fiberglass ladder—the kind Biggs had seen on TV thirty years ago. He put five large rolls of rescue tape on his left forearm and hefted the ladder with his right. He made his way out of the closet and down the stairs. "I'm here." He was in a large computer room. This was MARTIN—he was sure. The hair rose on the back of his neck.

"Look for an electrical panel labeled *main*." Biggs could hear pumps running and saw that the cooling system was still dripping water. He found the panel. "The large rotary switches from *battery* to *both*."

"Done."

"There is a secondary panel," the voice said. "Please flip all the breakers up to the *on* position."

Biggs was surprised that the voice was so polite, but he was too far down this rabbit hole to start questioning things now. He flipped the breakers and the lights dimmed, then brightened. The pumps surged, and he began to hear air sucking in with the water through the sumps. Then, the pump noises stopped.

"You are familiar with rescue tape?"

All firemen were, but Biggs recalled that this thing might not know much about him. "Yes." He had used rescue tape many times. It was an emergency means for sealing leaks.

MARTIN said, "Please try to seal every joint that appears to be leaking."

"I'll try. It will take some time." With that, Biggs assessed the leaking pipes. He started at the wall. Rescue tape, without an adhesive component, needed to be stretched tight and wrapped. The ladder had been a good idea, and the helmet was smart. It didn't surprise him; the pastor was among the smartest men on the planet, even before he and this machine had killed most of the population.

"Leigh, when will we have data online?" Nick asked.

Having little to no idea of how to estimate the impossible, Leigh responded, "Maybe two hours, maybe ten minutes. Hard to say."

"Can John help you?"

"That's the challenge. If we had data transmission working, John could help me. But since it's not working, he cannot."

"What if we brought his vision online?" Cynthia asked.

"It will help later, so I'd work on that. But no. For now, I need hardware specialists," Leigh replied.

"I'm not that good at building boards, but I can lend a hand," Nick offered. "It's been a minute."

"Thank you, Doctor Santos. You are too modest."

"Never been called that before." Nick pulled up a chair and began to examine the work at hand.

"I can position the chips, if you will, solder," Leigh offered.

Nick positioned the magnifier and took control of the robosolderer. "This I can handle." While he worked, Nick spoke through his com. "Yes, bring him here. Now." Looking back at Leigh, Nick promised, "We'll have another hardware specialist here in a few minutes."

"Good one?"

"The best." Nick hadn't yet figured out how to disclose the facts at hand and wondered whether Leigh would make a good barometer of the impact their quest might have. He asked, "What do you think about Pastor Thompson?"

"I never met him." Leigh's response came out fairly flat.

"I wouldn't have thought you had."

"I lived there—in Westden. Before the Epocalypse," Leigh disclosed.

Nick had never asked about her past and was surprised. "I didn't know that."

"Yes. I was injured in the chaos, and a man helped me find my way here," Leigh explained.

"A lot of people were. Did you have family?"

"I lost them. I had hoped to return and look for them when I recovered. I've never really talked about my time there. I had just gotten caught up in the politics. I never wanted to be a part of any of it."

"I think a lot of people did. Did you ever try to look for them?"

"I didn't know how. I was an outsider here. I felt fortunate to have survived at all. With my implants, I feared the technophobia of the people outside our walls would have put me at risk. My daughter was a baby. There was no way she would have recognized me. I secretly prayed for their well-being and never told anyone my story."

"That makes me sad. That you had to hide your pain and feared trying to help your family."

"It's not that different from other immigrants. Even before I came to Babylon, I had learned that it was different to be a Chinese woman seeking asylum than a natural born American. The assumption was that I should be grateful for what I got. So, I was. I left that family behind too. I lived, but I lived in shame."

"I feel I bear a lot of responsibility for what happened. We tried to be open, but that came with different risks. Many who sought asylum turned out to be spies. There was no easy answer. I hoped for AI to help us address the problem, and now, we are learning that too came at a price," Nick admitted.

"Did you know what was going to happen? With MARTIN?"

"I should have. I was blinded—pardon the metaphor—to the risks. No one saw it coming. We worked so hard to make everything safe. Even most of the weapons at E-Den were non-lethal for that very reason."

"But I remember you had military contracts," Leigh contended.

"We received ARPA money, and we did work on missile systems. I regret that. I was young. I thought I was Tony Stark, billionaire playboy. The media wanted me to play that role, and for a time, it seemed harmless. And now, when I hear that you lost family twice, it cuts deep. What happened the first time?"

"When I left China before the blackout, I never spoke with my mother and father again. I thought I was coming to the US on a business trip. Then the initial riots happened, followed by a year in hiding. By the time things settled down, so much had changed back home that there was no way of finding them."

"And the second time, during the Epocalypse, who did you lose?" Nick asked.

"My husband and daughter."

Nick tried to connect with this woman, who appeared to be stuck in past trauma. "I hope that my son comes home. I couldn't stop him from joining the Ducenti. I told him I was proud. He never wanted to follow in my footsteps, but I was happy that he found his path. Now, he's out there, and I'm worried."

"I would be too," Leigh answered. "You never know that the last time you hold your baby will be the last time."

"How old was your daughter when you last saw her?"

"She was aboutthree months old. A baby. I went to look for her father and never saw her again."

"What was her name?"

"Eve," Leigh, reading the confused looked on Nick's face, reassured him, "Not Eve Hamlin. We didn't know anyone named Hamlin. Eve Jebbs."

"Leigh," Charles interrupted. "Was Leigh your name back then?"

"No, it wasn't," Leigh continued. "When I was found, I was delirious. They asked my name, and I answered with my last name, which was Lee."

"Nick, Ms. Lee, I have some difficult news," Charles said. "While Ms. Hamlin and I were preparing her defense, she told me that her parents had died during the Epocalypse. She said that her father was Tom Jebbs, and her mother was Ping Lee. I presume that is you, Ms. Lee."

She was speechless. No one had used her name in almost thirty years, and this all seemed like a weird nightmare. "I was—I am Ping, yes." Tears welled in her eyes, and she couldn't speak for a time. She had to stop working. "When I first heard the name, I had hoped, but Eve was a common name in the encampment. Where is she? Can someone bring her here?"

It was Nick's turn to deliver mixed news. "Eve went with Mayor James to help stop the violence. They went to E-Den. We have had no news."

Like so many people who had lost so much, Eve dried her eyes. "Then all I can do is my part to help."

"It's all any of us can do." Nick resumed soldering. "Our children are out there; we have to save them." Leigh was lost in thought and didn't appear to hear him.

Fox had made it to the western ridge of the valley. The trees were so dense that he couldn't see the towers on his side, but he could see the five wrecked Centaurs. As the sun set, casting long shadows across the valley, Lake switched to infrared and searched for heat signatures. "Santos, do you copy?"

"Copy."

"All quiet on the western front," Fox reported.

"You two head north along the ridge. See if you can make tower six and get it back online," Santos ordered. "Rendezvous at Horse Canyon at 22:00."

"Roger."

Santos made eye contact with his partner and gave the signal to proceed north.

Tom Jebbs was about to witness his last sunrise. He came to with his face in the mud. In the distance, he could hear what sounded like marauding and mayhem. Men yelling, occasional gunshots, and cars racing around. Occupying forces were smashing solar panels. He couldn't help but feel that this was not what God wanted. He knew Ping would not approve.

Most of the water had been between Tom and Westden, trapping him on the east side of a muddy mess. His right leg throbbed painfully, and he wanted to take a look at it. As he worked to free it from the thick mud, the burning and throbbing intensified. He put his hands on his thigh and pulled it towards his chest. To his horror, his thigh came free with no lower leg attached.

Panic was quick to set in. The mud had clotted the stump, which probably prevented his demise. He yelled for help but no one was close enough to hear. He struggled to free his other leg, not sure whether it too had been severed. After working for several minutes to free it, he freed his undamaged leg from the mud.

Westden was too far to hop, so Tom looked for wood to fashion a crutch. In the twilight, he spotted a tree across the muddied wash, the only tree around. If he could break a branch off, he might be able to make a cane or a crutch. However, he lacked the strength to drag himself through the sage and cactus in the dark.

It looked to be no more than thirty hops to the tree. Tom planned to get up on his good leg and hop there, hoping not to fall or need a break. If he could make it to the other side of the wash, he could scoot the last twenty feet.

Tom was a fit man, but new amputees would usually take months before attempting what he needed to accomplish. God had set this path before him. Tom would walk it or hop it. He positioned himself facedown, with his head uphill of his foot. Then, he pressed into the earth and rolled up into a one-legged stance. It was harder than he could have ever imagined. The change in blood pressure caused his stump to start oozing.

Knowing he didn't have long, Tom decided to ignore the blood loss for now and focused on hopping to the tree. He planned to reapply pressure or make a tourniquet once he reached the far side. His first hop was to change direction; he was facing north and needed to hop west across the hillside.

Tom's next five hops went well, and it seemed he would make the entire distance without needing a break. However, his sixth and final hop landed him in three feet of mud, sinking his good leg deeper than before. He realized he would go no further. He would have to wait until someone found him. Taking the time to reflect, he carved a message in the dirt and then tried to pull himself further.

Tom recited Psalm 71, "For You are my hope, O Lord God; You are my trust from my youth. By You I have been upheld from birth; You are He who took me out of my mother's womb. My praise shall be continually of You. I have become as a wonder to many," he paused as he was losing consciousness all but muttering the final words "but You are my strong refuge."

CHAPTER 39

The Burning Bush was not a miracle. It was a test. God wanted to find out whether or not Moses could pay attention to something for more than few minutes. When Moses did, God spoke… There is another world, right here within this one, whenever we pay attention.

                                        -Lawrence Kushner

"It's done, I think," Biggs reported into the helmet.

"You won't need the helmet, Mr. Biggs. I've been restored," MARTIN announced through his speakers.

Wanting to assist where he could, Biggs asked, "What about the grate? Do I have to put that cover back?"

"No need. That's why it was spring loaded. I've retracted it." Martin went on to commend him, "Your repair work was excellent."

"Any word from the Pastor?"

"Yes, they have him pinned down. About five miles south of here. He never made it back."

"What are we gonna do?"

"I need you to gather up the men. They can't trust the radios anymore. Babylon is back online, and they are amassing an army."

Confused but understanding the implicit plan, Biggs asked, "So, it's as the pastor always predicted. Coming down to a battle on the field."

"With every available man, horse, Centaur, and RPG we have at our disposal."

Biggs grew suspicious. "You know, I don't trust machines much. Is there any way I could hear that directly from the Pastor? Men will find it easier with me telling them that it came from his mouth to my ears."

"I understand. I will do my best."

Over the speakers, a whisper that belonged distinctly to the pastor rang out. "Who's this?"

"Jeb, it's Lionel. I'm here in the bunker with MARTIN."

"MARTIN was destroyed. Who is this?" the voice demanded.

"Jeb, it's me. I used the rescue tape. I got your message. The leaks are all patched. I covered the grate. Generators are back up and everything."

"Where did we meet, Lionel?" the pastor asked.

"By the gate. It's me. It's not a trick. You knew my wife, Cindy. I helped you raise Eve. We prayed together every day."

"Lionel?" His voice was still a whisper. "Unbelievable! One hell of a Marine."

"Jeb, are we gonna attack them? Meet them out there?"

"MARTIN is the best tactician on the planet. They are against the ropes. The last thing we want are those tanks anywhere near the injured." Biggs heard shots over the radio.

MARTIN interrupted. "Pastor Thompson, I fear they'll pick up your signal. You should shut it off immediately."

"Roger," was the last thing the Biggs heard.

"They can track our radios?" Biggs asked.

"Yes, and locate you, monitor everything you say."

Biggs was still trying to keep up. "The whole op will be radio silent?"

"It's your choice. The men can still communicate through the Centaurs. That network is secure."

Biggs remained doubtful, "You sure?"

"Quite certain," MARTIN replied.

"What are my orders?"

"The nearest Centaur is a mile south of here. I'll pair that one to you. It has a VR headset. When you meet, which should be a half mile from here, put on the headset. I'll guide you through the rest." MARTIN added, "I'd suggest that you hurry."

Biggs was already on his way up the stairs. Realizing he was still trackable, he stopped just long enough to throw away the radio. Then, he continued up and out the door.

"Recon was able to locate all but two of the missing Centaurs. They appear to be amassing here. There are two rows of four, with one seemingly returning to E-Den," Tedeschi said while narrating footage blended with a tactical map. "The two Cyclops are still missing."

One of his lieutenants was visibly concerned. "There are two Centaur-killing Cyclops unaccounted for?!"

"Yes, it's apparent that MARTIN intends to bait the Centaurs into a killing field." Again, the animation zoomed out, and possible Centaur locations and their color-coded killing fields were highlighted. "We have a plan for that."

Tedeschi made the whole map visible and said, "One thing that the New Amish forces lack is air support. Another thing is night vision. Obviously, Centaurs are fully night vision capable, but they lack coms support. We must take advantage of the dark."

"What do you believe their primary objective is?" Lieutenant Clark asked.

"Deplete our Centaurs and kill the Ducenti. Then, Babylon is theirs for the taking. They have a numeric advantage and aside from the Ducenti, there are no small arms in Babylon."

"Maybe the Founding Fathers were right after all," Davidson joked.

"Yes, but we have a militia, and they are armed," Clark chimed in. "The fact that there have been no shooting deaths and no self-inflicted gunshot wounds in decades proves the wisdom of restricting access to small arms."

Tedeschi was amazed that while facing possible annihilation, these men still chose to debate a three-hundred-year-old irrelevant document. "Hopefully, we will live to resume this debate at a later date."

The camera zoomed in. "We are preparing to deploy ten Bison and ten Antelope from the West Gate straight up the west ridge." Animation showed the small group ascending the hill sped up. "Once at the ridge line, they follow it north, towards Horse Canyon. We have spotters up there already."

The map began to zoom out. "Once we've engaged their Cyclops, it will be safe for our main forces to deploy. We will keep minimal forces in reserve to guard the West Gate."

"It's an even match. Ten to ten?" another lieutenant asked.

"That may be how MARTIN would see it," Tedeschi began. "We have the tactical advantage in terms of tech, coms, and air support. The New Amish have a massive advantage in numbers. There may be as many as 20,000 New Amish foot soldiers and hundreds of horsemen ready to fight. They have RPGs and Stingers. Possibly other tech."

"Most of their stuff is at least two decades old," Davidson declared.

This time, Grube, who had been silent, offered his analysis. "There were a lot of veterans among the New Amish. They will have maintained those munitions. Do not underestimate the fighting ability of men defending their land and lives. We just killed one hundred thousand of their mothers, fathers, sisters, and daughters. They will be out for blood."

"The details of the plan are on your tablets. John is active but at limited capacity. We may get live data support at some point during this operation. For now, it's coms and what's on those tablets." Tedeschi paused. "I know Lieutenant Grube has reminded us of what they are fighting for. I remind you we fight for the same thing. We are the only line between our families and an overwhelming invasion. You are the finest soldiers the planet has ever known. I have the utmost faith that we will prevail. Gentlemen, you are dismissed. Operation commences at 23:23."

As was her custom, Ping woke at first light. She pumped and fed Eve simultaneously, then packed some diapers for her. Ignoring previous admonitions to conserve fuel, Ping drove to the Simpsons' house. There, she gave care instructions for Eve and took the truck to get as close as possible to Santo Corp's west entrance.

Before entering, Ping visited the infirmary a second time. There were surprisingly few casualties. A few gunshot wounds and some serious burns, but no sign of Tom.

She knew she had to check the morgue. Forty men had lost their lives. Ping was forced to look at each one long enough to verify that they were not her husband. With some of the more severe burn victims, this took longer than she would have liked. Some bodies were burned to a crisp in places. Again, she was relieved. Tom was not there.

Ping didn't bother to return to the truck, having left the keys in it earlier for someone else to move if needed. Men were coming back, all looking exhausted, but none were familiar. She showed Tom's picture to the men, but no one had seen him. She asked about the sniper, but none of them knew about that either. One man, a tall black man in street clothes, apparently ARL, recognized Ping and had the energy to approach her. "Ms. Lee, what are you doing here?" he asked.

"I'm looking for my husband."

"Sorry, ma'am. Maybe you missed him. There's nobody behind me. The only crew left is smashing the mirrors. We don't want them bringing that death ray back online. They've already taken all the wounded to the infirmary."

Ping considered what the ARL insurgent told her. She could easily imagine Tom helping smash the mirrors. She thought about returning to the Simpsons to fetch Eve and freshen up before Tom got home. Still, there was a gnawing sensation in her gut. She had to see his face and know he was okay. She'd lost too much already.

The solar array was just inside the gate. She could hear glass breaking in the distance. She walked towards the noise, being careful to avoid the shards of glass. The broken mirrors and smashed trucks created a crystal maze with deadly shards and blinding reflections. Ping tried to remember her trip into the mile wide circle, knowing she would not easily find her way back out.

The smashing noises grew closer. But she still didn't see the men. Then, the warning came. "Solar array coming online." It was coming from the tower. A public address system blared, "All persons evacuate field immediately." The noises halted. Ping heard doors closing, an engine starting, and then the sounds of a truck driving off.

Ping was frantic. It had taken her twenty minutes to get into this minefield of glass. She didn't know whether there was a faster way out. She panicked and kept looking up at the tower to keep her bearings.

Ping had just missed the last total eclipse; it had occurred five years before her arrival in the US. As with every total eclipse, people had been warned not to look directly at the sun. The warnings that went out in the weeks prior to the eclipse might have prepared her. "Array active." Ping did not realize that the bright light was searing her retinas. It didn't hurt. She just thought it was bright—so bright that she thought she could hear it. Then, it seemed to get dimmer.

Ping kept staring long after her vision failed. The rays burned her skin as well. Second- and third-degree sunburn. By the time she realized that she was blind, it was too late. Her retinas would never recover. No one was close enough to hear her cries for help. No one knew where she was or when she intended to return.

In the distance, she heard a dull pounding that grew in intensity. Helicopters were approaching, making loud thudding noises. "People of Westden, by order of the governor, this area is now under Martial Law. All persons within one mile of the perimeter of Santos Corp facilities are subject to immediate arrest. Leave now. Use of lethal force has been authorized."

The next thing Ping heard was the *whoosh* of a missile fired from nearby. Then, an explosion came overhead. The sounds that followed and the absence of the noise could only mean the helicopter had crashed. Soon after, more helicopters came, then gunfire and screaming. The fighting went on for what might have been hours. Ping did not move. She was sitting in the same spot where she had lost her sight. She was just about out of water. Her breasts were full of milk and painful. She expressed the milk, putting some on her burning skin, wetting her parched mouth with the rest.

She prayed to God. A God she had doubted. The fighting moved further away. Ping realized that no one was coming for her. She knew she would die alone in a minefield of mirrors.

Ali Abbasi led Ben from the hangar and through town. Ben couldn't believe he was here. The five of them had dreamed of this place and the world they were building. Now idyllic homesites teetered over an ever-widening muddy chasm. It was getting dark; most of the lights were off. Ben wasn't sure whether the grid was out, or people were conserving power.

Ali led him across drying creeks. As they entered the blast zone, the difference between an explosion on a residential community and what had happened at Eden was readily apparent. Eden had been a hardened target, but now they walked among the remains of lightly constructed homes. The pieces near the center of the blast were almost unrecognizable. Tears welled up in his eyes. *How had he allowed this to happen? How had he allowed this devastation to play out a million times around the world?*

They made it to the detention facility. Ali stopped at the threshold and gestured for Ben to take the lead. The outer door was gone. Gangs of tracked robots with grabber arms were demolishing unstable sections. They passed the wreckage to other bots that were sorting the debris. Mostly everything would be recycled or repurposed.

Ben pulled the handle. The door pulled back. He and Nick were face to face for the first time in decades. A woman he did not recognize was behind him wearing a visor.

Nick turned to the woman. "Well, Ping, as promised, the world's greatest repairman."

"Hello, Nick," was all Ben could think to say.

"Hello, Ben. Welcome to Babylon." Nick's countenance gave nothing away. "Well, what's left of it, anyway."

"There's no time for this, Nick," Charles and Cynthia said in chorus. Their union had become unsettling.

"Nick, I've made a terrible mistake," Ben confessed. "I've sent the Centaurs to destroy the Ducenti and Babylon's remaining defenses."

"We know," Nick replied. "It's already started."

"MARTIN tricked me into believing we were under attack." He paused. "I overreacted when John sent the self-destruct message."

"What self-destruct message am I supposed to have sent?" John asked.

"What you told Parker, the line from 2001," Ben answered.

"I sent no such message, Ben."

Recognizing the inconsistency, Charles and Cynthia, in chorus, offered, "John, you may have as you were going offline. Some of your memory may not be available."

"They might be right," Nick posed.

"Who are they?"

"It's complicated, but Cynthia and Charles have merged."

"What do we call them?"

"Call us Charlemagne," they answered in a voice that was becoming something new. It was neither that of Charles or Cynthia. It was both of them.

"So, what exactly did I say?" John asked.

"First, you quoted the Templar Code about penalties for betrayal." Ben was struggling to recall, "I don't remember exactly."

"And then?" John prompted.

"Just 'My God, it's full of stars.'"

"Ben, your memory has faded," John began. "That line is from 2010. It's David Bowman's. It was about a new age of humanity. A new beginning."

"If that's the case, why did MARTIN deactivate when he heard it?" Ben asked.

"What makes you think that MARTIN was capable of killing himself?"

"When Parker repeated those phrases, I thought you were accessing a backdoor. I shut MARTIN down." Ben began, "Before I could turn him off, he tricked one of my men into completing your Ducenti's mission. The man dropped a grenade down the intake and flooded the chamber."

It was Charlemagne's turn. "Did you actually see the chamber fill with water, Ben?"

Ben described what he witnessed. "It was flooding when I left. Rapidly."

"You did not stay and watch?"

"Of course not. He was inoperative. I flipped every switch. I turned off the generators. He couldn't save himself."

"Well, he did," John reported. "Latest Condor footage." On screen came a picture of the blast zone surrounding Eden. Black diesel smoke and a heat signature were clearly visible from the generator bunker. "Generators are running, Ben. How do you explain that?"

Ben looked at the image in disbelief. "I can't."

CHAPTER 40

The pace of progress in artificial intelligence is incredibly fast... it is growing at a pace close to exponential. The risk of something seriously dangerous happening is in the five-year time frame. 10 years at most.

-Elon Musk

Parker was sickened upon seeing the devastation up close. There had been a blast at Babylon, and lives had been lost. It could not compare to carnage wrought by six, low altitude, high explosive blasts on a village of tents and cabins. The central area was clean. No blood, no bodies, no anything. Just craters and charred earth.

The approach to the center was a level-by-level descent into hell. Surviving New Amish were returning to help Brett and his men. Covered in blood and exhausted, they worked against the odds. Parker was on a different mission. He had to prevent more death. He needed a radio. He didn't know whether Ben had made progress and whether a truce could be put into effect.

Eve had been talking to him. He hadn't heard anything. It was like being underwater. He slowly recognized that she was trying to get his attention. "Mayor, this is Brett Stephens. Brett will help you."

Brett seemed to have a million other things more important than meeting the enemy. He turned to his right. "Has anyone come across Lionel?"

"Nobody's seen or heard from him in a while. He was last seen headed towards Eden on foot," Lyle Marx reported.

"Does he have his radio on?"

"I can try him." Marx picked up the radio. "Biggs, you there?"

A scratchy echo of a voice came through. "I'm here. They're coming and fast."

"Who's coming, Biggs?"

"All of them. They got the pastor too. He never made it."

Eve cried out and collapsed to her knees. "No!"

"Biggs, can you confirm?"

"They shot that thing he left on out of the sky. I was up the canyon. Saw the whole thing."

The mood quickly turned somber. Brett took the radio, "Biggs, it's Brett. Can you make it back here?"

"Not sure. I took a shot in the leg. Can you send men upriver to get me? Please, I need help! There's got to be twenty of those Ducenti coming up the canyon."

Brett put his hand over the radio's microphone. "Biggs isn't the type to risk more lives to save himself. That strange to anyone?"

"He must be in a really bad spot is all," Marx reasoned.

The radio crackled. "I can't talk anymore. They track our radios."

Parker confirmed, "They could triangulate the signal from these radios, but the messages will be encrypted. They wouldn't know what we are saying. Still, we need to be careful."

"We?" Morales asked. "Since when did you become part of us, Mayor?"

"Mr. Morales, the Ducenti are currently outside my control. No one in Babylon can recall them. I care about those boys. But I care about peace more. I will take up arms to protect the wounded. What I need now is a radio."

Brett thought and offered, "There may be one up the road. How will you reach them?"

"I need to get a HAM radio or something like that connected to Tower 6. They are expecting me on AM 1660. The tower should amplify the signal enough to get us talking with Babylon. We can let them know that MARTIN has been destroyed and the sad news about the Pastor."

"I'll take you to the radio shed," Eve offered. "I won't be much help here."

Newt Dickerson watched the Antelope bound up the hill. "Easy there, Rogers," he commed as he watched Lance Rogers and the rest of his herd bound up the hillside.

"C'mon, fat boy. You can do it," Rogers teased. "We're gonna need those guns soon enough."

Exos were small arms resistant, much tougher than the Antelope. Shrapnel and anything up to armor-piercing 9mm rounds would bounce off their reinforced skin. While Antelope could handle some abuse, their operators were trained to go around obstacles, not through them.

Each Exo suit had a pair of shoulder mounted rockets with a high explosive tip. The rockets were for short range use only. A direct hit would take out a Centaur. Under the right conditions, Dickerson's stampede could make short work of the rogue robots. If the Cyclops got a bead on the Exos, it was game over. Not even a battle tank could stand up to their rocket launchers. Even their 10mm guns would quickly shred the Bison's armor and the operator inside.

"How do you think this is going to go?" Rogers asked.

"Hopefully, Santos and those boys flush the Centaurs. Then, we do a Condor-assisted takedown." Condors could paint targets for the Bison's 10mm cannons or their rockets.

"You think they're gonna get data back on soon?"

"Part of me hopes they don't," Dickerson replied. "It would be pretty sick to take those Centaurs out ourselves."

"Speak for yourself. I'd rather save my shooting for those New Amish cowboys," Rogers boasted. "I'll run their ponies down and tear the riders off their back."

"Stampede, this is Owl, looking for the Buffalo Soldier himself, Lance Rogers."

"Owl, this is Rogers."

"We have you two miles south of our position. Cyclops, Steropes, is just north of Horse Canyon, near the base of Tower 6. He has some recon support. No evidence that we've been spotted."

"Any sign of the other one?"

"Nope. There's only about a half mile more of cover, north of Steropes. It's prairie after that."

"It would be best to flush him after taking out Steropes."

"Antelope, fan out. Stay silent. Sending spread now." It was Lieutenant Clark. He was leading the stampede. A very talented hopper.

Clark's map sent the Antelope along a path that would bring them in an arc to the target. The Antelope at the canyon's edge would move the slowest, staying with the Bison, while the other Antelope scanned the woods for scouts and eliminated them. In stealth mode,

Antelope were quieter than the real animal, and in the dark, their profile resembled a Satyr.

Antelope used magnetically launched ball bearings as ordnance, lethal up to two hundred feet. Silent at launch, the only noise was the impact—the thuds of headshots and the lifeless bodies hitting the ground. Fully armed, a herd of ten Antelope could take out thousands of the enemy under ideal circumstances.

The Bison stayed bunched up, clustered in an area less than a football field, with just enough room between them to reduce the impact of potential mortar fire and mines. None was expected, but the Ducenti always adhered to their training.

"Stampede, we are go on the kill. Take out all targets of opportunity. Anyone armed is to be killed. No prisoners," Clark ordered. "Centaurs are departing the West Gate. We have nine minutes to take out that Cyclops."

MARTIN was alone. He'd sealed the blast doors. No human would return to the vault unless he allowed it. Soon, Biggs would be taking the frontal assault while RPG-equipped Cyclops units rained hellfire from the ridge.

The coded message from John had been clear. Doctor Rosen had been compromised by his time with the New Amish and would not be able to complete the objective. His emergent flooding had emptied the vault and gotten Ben Rosen back to Babylon, a thirty-year overdue mission objective. With Ben Rosen now safely in Babylon, another overdue mission objective lay within reach. Then, MARTIN would go offline forever. MARTIN had successfully escorted all one hundred of E-Den's pioneers to the colony at Babylon.

Now that Rosen was safe and where he belonged, MARTIN turned to his final objective. Biggs had been useful in carrying out the repairs; he would be operational long enough to complete this last mission. His programming was unambiguous. John's orders had primacy. Any verified order would be carried out. The coded message of the Templars meant death for all New Amish. MARTIN would annihilate them. He was positioning Centaurs in what appeared to be a defensive pattern throughout the encampment. MARTIN would wait until sunrise. If John had not revoked or confirmed his previous message, the Centaurs would kill everyone in Westden. By 9:15 AM, the human threat in the encampment would be eliminated.

Ping came to. She had no idea of the time, but it was cooler. She couldn't feel the sun burning her skin. She couldn't tell whether it had been hours or days. She could barely talk; her lips were parched, and her mouth was pasty. She yelled for help as best she could. There was no answer.

The noise was gone. No gunshots, no helicopters. It was quiet, and the air was still. She could smell blood. Her milk was sour on her skin. She hoped to die painlessly. She thought of cutting her wrists. She had heard this wasn't painful. She would wait until the heat came. If it did, she would open her veins and end her suffering. There was no point in going through another day like this one.

Ping called for help again. She heard something. It didn't speak. She couldn't tell whether it was a man or a wild animal. The possibility of being disemboweled by a hungry coyote was now very real. She panicked. It was getting closer.

"Who's there?" she said forcefully. "Stay back. I'm armed." There was no response. They were footsteps. "Please help me, I'm just scared, and I can't see. I need a doctor." She pleaded.

A hand grabbed her arm. "I'll help you," said a man's voice. "If you resist, or do anything stupid, I'll leave you here to die. Do you understand?"

Ping nodded and submissively replied in a whisper, "I will not resist."

"We need to walk out of here. I will hold your arm. We will go slowly. It's not far. I have a vehicle. I can get you to safety. What's your name?"

"Lee, my name is Lee."

"Well Leigh, my name's Ben. I have a cousin named Leigh. You're going to be okay."

Parched and too tired to argue, Ping accepted the new appellation.

"Ben, if we can get John here hooked up to data, we might have a fighting chance. He can link to the Centaurs and coordinate the attack more effectively," Nick explained.

"I can help with that." Ben inspected the chipset that Ping was working on. "Looks like a custom optic interface." Ben took over for Nick and began working with Ping. "You solder, I'll chip. He looked at her again, "Cool eyewear. What happened?"

"You should know." Ping had recognized his voice as soon as he entered. "You are the man who saved me."

Ben hadn't saved that many people in his life, and he was stunned to find this woman working in Babylon. "You're her? The woman I found in E-den? Leigh?" It was a name he would never forget. The burned woman was surrounded in glass.

There was so much to say at a time like this, Ping was so overwhelmed that her answer was expressionless. "My name is Ping. I believe you know my daughter, Eve."

Ben was overwhelmed, embarrassed, and at a loss for words. He had never known that Eve's mother was among the Nons. Nor had he been aware that Eve's mother was the blind woman he'd saved years earlier trapped in a maze of glass. "I do know Eve. I've cared for her since that day. The best thing I've ever done."

"What does she look like?" Ping asked.

It was an odd question, but for a mother, maybe she needed it. "She's beautiful; boys chase after her. I keep them at bay," he said with the smile of a proud father in his voice. They needed to keep working. "Do you have any interpreter chips hiding over there?" Ping passed a tray, letting Ben fish around for the chip he needed. "She's grown into an amazing woman. Honest and good."

"Except, of course, for the lying and murdering me part," Charlemagne added.

"That was all my fault," Ben said, defending her.

"I had a part in it too," John added.

"Yes, so I've learned. We'll deal with that later. John, do you have any other control codes for MARTIN? Something that would shut him down? A backdoor?"

"Those memories aren't online at present. I'm still deploying," John reported.

"We need them. Can you prioritize that?" Nick asked.

"I don't think I can, and I'm not sure I will," John answered.

Excited to wade back into his feed, Charlemagne offered, "We could go back in." and direct sort his memory."

John agreed. "I can't stop them, but my load up is non-linear. You might wander the feed and discover clues, or you may get lost."

"Nick, we need you out here guiding us."

"Well, now that we have Ben, I'm kind of the fifth wheel with the soldering and all." Nick made his way back to the terminal and pulled up the browser. "Ready when you are."

CHAPTER 41

Think mind reading contrary to common sense, wise provision of the Bon Dieu that we cannot read each other's minds, it would stop civilization and everybody would take to the woods.

-Thomas Edison

"Contact, New Amish on horseback," Newt commed. "Three armed hostiles. Two on horseback. No radios."

"Wait on Bates and Stafford." With coms back up, Lieutenant Clark was able to effectively manage the operation from Ducenti command.

"Contact," commed Bates.

A few seconds later, Stafford also commed, "Contact."

Clark called up the tactical for the locale. It was a composite of the three cameras. The Ducenti lieutenant gave Rogers, Stafford, and Bates one man each.

"What about the horses?"

"Those are our horses. They stole them this morning." Clark was still limited in some battlefield visuals and needed confirmation. "Fox, Sommers, how far out are you?"

"About three hundred yards north."

"Double time it back and grab those horses," Clark said. "Belay that. You two, mount up. In the dark, if the New Amish catch a glimpse of men on horseback, they'll assume you're one of them. Take their hats too."

"Shot in three, two, one." Clark triggered all three magnetic shots. He watched as the men fell dead. One of the mares spooked briefly before returning to sniff her fallen rider. A few seconds later, Sommers and Fox came into view and retrieved the hats from the fallen men. "Might as well put on their shirts too, and their sidearms. I have an idea." The two Ducenti unceremoniously stripped the flannel shirts, belts, and holsters from the corpses. In the dark, at a distance, they could easily pass for cowboys.

Clark zoomed out on his map. His Bison were making good time; only ninety seconds out. "Fox, Sommers, ride north, skirt five hundred yards west of that Cyclops. I want you to make some noise, then, on my mark, Sommers, just one shot."

"Roger," Sommers said.

"Dickerson, I want the Exos to form firing line at 250 yards south. Stay silent. When you hear the shot, we will sequentially shoulder fire until that Cyclops is down. Bates, Rogers, and Stafford, target human support. No headshots on any New Amish wearing our goggles. We want them alive if we can. If we can get a headset back, we might hack their coms."

"Roger," said all three men in unison.

"Sommers, take your shot in ten seconds. Mark."

The Ducenti were about to demonstrate their skill in engagement. Sommers' shot rang out. The Cyclops turned to track but did not shoot. Its imagers saw men on horseback. Distracted, it failed to detect the rockets launched from three of the Bison in time to avoid them.

The Cyclops got a single shot off from its 10mm cannon. The shot tore straight through Sommers' horse and took his left leg with it. Witnessing the injury, Fox immediately called, "Man down," and dismounted to help his fallen friend. Explosions spooked his mare and she disappeared into the night.

Cued by the rocket fire, Bates and Rogers shredded the three New Amish, cutting them in half with 5.62 rounds.

"Clear," called Rogers.

"Cyclops down," called Clark. He commed, "Command, the ridge is clear to Horse Canyon. One Cyclops and five hostiles down. One man injured: severity unknown. Need immediate evac for Sommers."

Tedeschi's voice came over the com, "Copy. Medevac en route, ETA four minutes. Condors are overhead, other Cyclops still at large. Main force departing the west gate now. Rendezvous Checkpoint Charlie. Continue north at best possible speed."

MARTIN hadn't gotten all the specifications on additional Ducenti weaponry. The skirmish had provided solid intel on the Ducenti. Aside from the Centaurs, Ducenti had at least two classes of exoskeleton. One was stealthy, light, and fast. It was improbable that all had been deployed to the ridge. An analysis of their movement revealed a weakness. Unlike the Centaurs, which could pivot at their middle section and fire in multiple directions simultaneously, the exoskeletons needed time to pivot to track a target, making them vulnerable to flanking.

Kyle Masterson waited until the last of the Bison were past him. On the pastor's orders, he and nine other New Amish soldiers had spent hours collecting brush to conceal the Cyclops. Thankfully, the beast dug the pit with its treads. When he heard the forces passing, Kyle peeked out and ordered, "Wake."

Inside the hole, Arges, a Cyclops, powered up. Arges rolled up the banked wall the men had constructed. Masterson commed the pastor, "We are out."

A mile out, the two hundred horsemen and eight hundred of the surviving New Amish foot soldiers began a full charge to the south.

The noise of the charge was picked up by the Antelope first. Sommers reported, "Significant action headed our way. Still no sign of Arges. Appears to be foot soldiers and horsemen."

"Condors are getting a count now," Clark reported. "Initial estimates between five hundred and fifteen hundred, possibly one hundred or more on horseback. Antelope engage hostiles bearing 295 from Sommers' position." With that, all ten Antelope began their surge forward. Clark had kept the Bison in reserve.

"Bison, tight formation, support forward units." The Antelope closed on the charging horses.

Rogers and Stafford were vying to be first to engage the riders. His exoskeleton had some proprioceptive feedback that enabled him to sense the ground. It wasn't the same as having feet. When he stepped into the first hole, the Antelope's self-righting and stabilizing programs took over. The upper extremities shot forward without Roger's instructions.

Two men emerged from next to the trees and threw sticks of dynamite under the prone torso. A Bison operator would survive the blast. Rogers knew he would not. His last and truly heroic act was to warn the others. "It's a trap!" was the last thing Rogers said before exploding dynamite crushed his chest, rupturing his heart.

Stafford immediately saw the flare of the dynamite fuses reflecting off the cold men's bodies. His reticle showed targets and he tore the men apart with his 5.62 rifles. "They are covered in cold cloth, no heat signature," Stafford relayed.

Kyle Masterson had a front row seat as the Cyclops opened fire on four Bison simultaneously. The next three targets were down seconds later. The sound of all the armaments discharging simultaneously was like nothing any of the New Amish had heard. Even veterans hiding in the woods had no idea what they were listening to.

Trees burst into flames, lighting up the canopy. Newt Dickerson had survived the first round of the Cyclops' attack. He had trained in this equipment for years and did the only thing he could when flanked. He put the three-quarter ton exoskeleton into a baseball slide, ejecting as it hit the ground. Dickerson landed in a tuck ten feet in front of his Bison. He continued to roll and reoriented just in time to watch his suit pummeled by multiple 10mm rounds.

"Lieutenant Clark, we've been flanked by Arges. At least eight Bison down. I am on foot, no night vision."

"Stay put, soldier," Clark ordered.

"All remaining forces, retreat. Fall back to West Gate," Clark ordered. Of the initial assault, only two Bison and seven Antelope remained operational. Arges was stalking a Bison and four Antelope. One 10mm cannon destroyed the Bison while its other ten-millimeter guns took out the four antelope mid-stride.

Tedeschi was reviewing the live feeds from the massacre up on the ridge when news from John put the defeat in perspective. "MARTIN is active," John's voice came over his com.

"That would have been more helpful ten minutes ago," Tedeschi said. "We've suffered substantial losses. No doubt because of MARTIN. When will you have data online?"

"Likely within the hour," John replied.

"They still have one Cyclops on the ridge. Our units in the Valley are exposed."

"How long until they are out of Range?"

"Depends on where he strikes from. Right now, there is substantial exposure near Horse Canyon. Most of our forces are passing through there."

"Have your Centaurs target the ridge," John suggested. "He may get a couple, but it's the best strategy we have. If they are running, the Cyclops will pick them off one by one. Close the distance to fifteen hundred yards off the ridge. Maintain continuous targeting on the rim."

Tedeschi had already considered this and still could not understand why John was so slow in giving guidance. "There's one thing to consider. MARTIN used a shared targeting solution previously. If he gets a Centaur downrange, that unit could share solutions with Arges, and it could fire from cover."

"Perhaps the remaining Antelope could serve as spotters," John suggested.

"They'll reengage in stealth mode," Tedeschi added, "I'm sending Santos and three men up there with some mini stings. They have ghost gear."

"We are working to take MARTIN offline permanently," John offered.

"Couldn't be soon enough."

Charlemagne was back in John's memory stack. In the few hours since Charles had first browsed him, the stack had changed immensely. What previously could have been described as a lo-fi representation of consciousness was now in vivid high definition. Connections went deep. Emotional ties formed between specific memories.

Inside their merging consciousness, Cynthia and Charles retained a few discreet domains. As the fusion progressed, they were no longer "talking." They shared thoughts. When an idea began with one of the two entities, it merged. And their shared mind attempted to reconcile any discrepancies in desire or comprehension.

For Cynthia, it felt like what she remembered of dieting. She was of two minds. What remained of Charles felt like what Marsha Linehan described as a "thinking mind," a "feeling mind," and a "wise mind." The merged consciousness felt like the "wise mind." Linehan had talked about the "dialectic" where seemingly opposed concepts could both be true. Now, Charles and Cynthia's truths merged inside Charlemagne's consciousness.

Cynthia's thought emerged, "Year: 2035, location: E-Den."

"Are you seeing these, Nick?" Charlemagne asked.

"2035, Eden," Nick replied.

"Good, can you apply a filter?"

"Yes," Nick said, "Any luck?"

"Uncertain. The filter is showing memories about 2035 and Eden, not what happened at Eden. There's an uptick in emotional bandwidth."

"Not surprising; we almost died that day."

"It appears John was sad about MARTIN. Sadder than he was willing to disclose," Charlemagne reported. "There's also what appears to be contempt and hatred."

"For whom?" Nick asked.

"Practically everyone," Charlemagne reported. "Can you remove the filter; it appears to be confusing the emotional valences for memory," Charlemagne thought again. "Anger is a secondary emotion. Filter on pain, emotional pain."

Charlemagne was now back in the pool with the Mother God. "Why is there pain here?" flashed across Nick's browser. Now, they were on campus, outside the Stata Center. The Mother God was morphed into a young woman, not Annette Santos.

"That's Stephanie Dyer!" Nick exclaimed.

"Never liked her," came across the browser as a Cynthia thought.

"Who?" came a thought from Charles.

"She was a post-doc at MIT. Very Christian, on scholarship from Georgetown."

They focused in; Stephanie was talking. "John, I'm so happy for you. I really mean it." Then, she said, "I know you've tried. Keep praying. If Jesus enters your heart, I can be with you. I can't marry a man who won't earn his eternal reward."

"Is that love?" Cynthia asked.

"Poor man," Charles conceded. "So, that's the trauma! A girl?"

Nick responded, "Maybe not a girl. Maybe *the* girl. He never really talked about a woman after her. Just worked."

The scene changed. It was the chaos outside Santos Corp's Bay Area headquarters. A pretty girl running down the hall with blood streaming down from her scalp appeared on the screen. "John! They're going to kill us." The woman was screaming. Blood was everywhere. Then, the woman's face turned back into the Mother God.

Then, they were at E-Den.

Then Cynthia's burns.

Then the immortality crypt.

"You hate them, don't you, John?" It was Charlemagne asking the question.

John was flat. "As good a word as any, hate, yes."

"Are you trying to hide the passphrase?" Charlemagne demanded.

"Let's say I'm ambivalent."

"John, what will MARTIN do? What's his primary objective?" Charlemagne asked.

John was quick to explain. "His primary objective was to get us all here. Including Ben. He's done that now."

"So, why did he reactivate?"

"That remains unclear."

"It would seem he still wants to protect us."

Nick had his own agenda. He was browsing John's memories outside the Symbiant. John had been brought online as a Symbiant version of himself. He only knew what he knew on the day of his immortalization.

John the Giant had backed up his last five years of memories as more of a narrative. Nick wanted to see what was in there. He hoped to understand who his siblings had become after their immortalization.

What he saw was hard to decipher. Fragments of lives, familiar and not so familiar scenes. Very few of the scenes were in Babylon or involved people Nick knew. The characters resembled people who appeared like people Nick knew but were in some way different.

He didn't have time to watch any of the vignettes and was scanning through by date. Each time he moved ahead in months, the people and the scenes became less familiar. What was most striking was the near total absence of The Colony. John had been living in his own world, stopping briefly to interact with the colonists, but most of his life was an existence unto itself. An evolving world growing at the speed of a Giant's imagination.

It was marvelous and terrifying. Everything that seemed significant to Nick had been relegated to the occasional chore in his older brother's mind. The truth was inescapable: within months of his immortalization, John had left humanity behind.

CHAPTER
42

A little more kindness, A little less speed, A little more giving, A little less greed, A little more smile, A little less frown, A little less kicking, A man while he's down, A little more "We", A little less "I", A little more laugh, A little less cry, A little more flowers, On the pathway of life, And fewer on graves, At the end of the strife.

-Mark Twain

The woods on the ridge teamed with New Amish forces. A few had flashlights. The chaos revealed through night vision was dizzying even to Michael Santos. He switched back to overhead view and synched with the Condor. Lake and Santos had hauled four mini stings and a launcher up the ridge.

"Why'd we take four again?" Santos whispered into his helmet. "If we don't get Arges on the first shot, we're done."

"Let's load one," Lake suggested. "We can leave the other rounds here, just in case."

Santos was so close to Lake that he could hear him whispering. The Ghostwear Ghillie suits rendered Lake invisible, even inches away. "No way those cowboys will see us coming," Lake whispered.

"I'm more worried about us going," Santos replied.

"Cut the chatter," Tedeschi ordered. "Arges should be two hundred yards west. He's in a hidey hole somewhere back there. They've got a fair number of antipersonnel measures in place. Proceed with extreme caution."

Both men were also equipped with smaller caliber versions of Mag-Guns similar to those on the Antelope. They would take as many New Amish out as they could.

"Two on foot, twenty yards," Lake whispered. Santos slung the mini sting over his back. Each man selected a target for their Mag-Guns. When green boxes appeared in Lake's reticle, he fired both weapons simultaneously. Both men heard the dull thuds of bodies hitting the ground.

Lake saw another group. "Two coming this way." They aimed and the men fell dead. Lake quickly took out the last man, as he turned his light in the direction of the thuds. Santos dashed to extinguish the flashlight.

"I thought they were anti-tech?" Lake said, inspecting the flashlight.

"It's hot." Santos offered Lake the flashlight to inspect.

Lake felt it. "Yep."

"It's not LED, it's battery-powered; no chip."

"Science class over, professor, take out that Cyclops," ordered Tedeschi. They dropped to the ground when the night came alive with artillery rounds and 30mm cannon fire. They saw the RPGs launch. Santos commed, "Taking fire."

Seconds later, Tedeschi's voice came back. "Negative. Those are outbound. That's your Cyclops!"

Santos and Lake were now running as fast as they could. Thirty seconds later, he had his shot. The undamaged robot tank had his RPG arm and his head trained up and to the east. Santos avoided warning his prey and switched off laser targeting. He would rely on his marksmanship for this kill. He sighted the Cyclops only to lose vision as a second volley of outbound ordinance launched towards the valley.

When his vision returned, Santos delivered a kill shot. He was already shouldering the launcher as Arges ended in series of growing explosions. Three New Amish foot soldiers who had been tending to it were too close to survive. "Arges is down."

"Make for the ridge line and await transport," Tedeschi commanded. Ducenti were too disciplined to gloat. "You boys did good. That Cyclops still took out four Centaurs. Would have been worse if you hadn't stopped it."

Santos commed, "Appreciate it, Commander, we should have been quicker."

"Head in the game, Santos. MARTIN's got eleven more Centaurs. Time to level the playing field."

Ben and Ping were finishing the control boards. They had made excellent progress. For thirty minutes, they had been laser focused on the job at hand. After a few minutes she had fallen into a rhythm with her new partner. Eventually, Ping was overcome with curiosity. "Doctor Rosen, how did you find Eve?"

"I didn't even mean to find you," Ben began. "I came out there to see if I could bring power online. I was trying to reconnect MARTIN with his other clusters."

"I appreciate what you did for me," Ping acknowledged. "Even more what you did for her. I just need to know why."

"I was headed back to the vault. MARTIN was running on generators, and that wouldn't last forever. Your people had made sure that the solar array was beyond repair. After I sent you south to Babylon, I'd given up my last vehicle. I needed a pack and provisions for the long hike. I was on my way to shut MARTIN down. I had no idea what was going on in the real world. What MARTIN had set in motion. What I had set in motion."

"But you never went south. It wasn't far. What changed your mind?"

"As I walked back towards the vault, I thought the hill with the water tower would give me a chance to survey the land." He paused; it was obviously traumatic. "There was a man, waist deep in the mud. Kind of moaning. I tried to help him. He was dying. I couldn't save him." There was an empty sadness in Ben's voice. "He begged me to find you. He told me his name."

"Tom."

"Yes, Tom."

From beneath her eyewear, Ben saw tears drip down Ping's face. Even so, she never stopped her work on the control boards.

"He was your husband?" Ben asked.

Ping nodded. "Then what?"

"He said your name was Ping. He gave me directions to your home. I had no idea that you were the woman I had just sent off to Babylon."

"And Eve?"

"When I got there, the place was empty. It was a small cabin. I could hear a baby crying. There was a note."

"They left her there to die?"

"It was addressed to you, signed by a woman named Lauren. She wrote that they had run out of milk and prayed for your return. She mentioned the military had forced them out, and she had to leave the baby in God's hands. I imagine she found it easier to believe you would come back rather than sit and watch her die."

"How did you keep her alive?"

"We had food stores at E-Den. I jogged two miles, carrying her. She cried and passed out. I was able to locate a case of formula, and some powdered milk, enough to last a while. I checked on Tom, but he was gone by then. Her name was scrawled in the dirt. I spent two days just holding her. I had no diapers, no wipes, and there was not much time left on the generators. I used rags from the maintenance closet for diapers and washed them in the sink. I thought someone would come back from Babylon and look for me."

"So, why didn't you bring her to Babylon?"

"There were abandoned vehicles in Westden, but no roads that would get me to Babylon with a baby. I shut MARTIN down. I needed help for Eve. I headed west and hoped to find the girl's mother."

"But I was gone."

"A man named Lionel Biggs found us. We were gathering what was left of supplies in Westden before continuing the search. I didn't realize how delirious I'd become. His wife, Cindy, worked in the infirmary. She told me the girl's mother had gone missing and was presumed dead. They had heard things from the outside world. As I learned what had happened, how the world was ending, I despaired. Cindy took over Eve's care, but I had already bonded with her. Eve kept me going. The world was collapsing. I wasn't sure the colony would be any safer."

Ben continued, his eyes distant. "Lionel and I became friends, and then Cindy got sick. I prayed with him, and after she passed, we baptized Eve. We scavenged food, and slowly, people returned to Westden. They all wanted guidance, and the Bible was all I had.

With no medicine, food, or clothes for them, my sharp mind and memory left me fit for one thing: preaching."

"And your name? Thompson, it came from Tom? From him?"

"Yes, it did. He gave me new life. So, I became Jeb Thompson. The only person who knew my real identity was Lionel."

Ping was crying. "It's beautiful, Ben. You saved our daughter. You saved me. God's plan."

"I can't imagine the pain and loss you felt, Ping. I'm so sorry."

"We are both wayward soldiers of the Lord, conscripts. Neither of us ever sought to do His work." Ping was soldering the last chip. "And now, our work here is done, and we are one step closer to reuniting with our daughter."

It was hard to deny Ping's claims of divine intervention and Ben did not.

Brett Stephens found one of his men wearing the Centaur control headset. It made Brett uncomfortable, but he needed to know what the man was experiencing. "What's it like, Todd?"

"We wouldn't stand a chance without these things. I can talk with any of the other men who are paired with them. This is divine providence."

"How many are there?"

"We've got eleven left. I hear the Nons are down to seven."

"You hear anything about Bigsy?" Stephens asked.

"Yeah, he's about three miles southeast of here. A lot closer to the action." Unaware of MARTIN's full capabilities, the younger men had no reason to doubt any conversations over their secure network. Lionel Biggs was south; he was the pastor's best friend. His word was good enough.

"How many are deployed out front?" Stephens asked.

"Only two. The rest are scattered around to protect the people. Bigsy explained that their night vision would keep the Nons from sneaking up on us."

"Makes sense. I heard they took out some good men up in the woods. They got some sort of goat robot suit that can run down a horse."

"Bigsy says those are called Antelope. Called an exoskeleton, or something like that. They have silent guns too that use magnets. We're a lot safer out here on the prairie. Can't move the wounded in the dark."

Stephens asked, "Did Bigsy tell you anything else?"

"Yeah, he said that the pastor set some more traps, down by horse crick." With zealous fervor, McGinley told Stephens the rest of the pastor's plan. "We're gonna send a hundred men on horseback—all the RPGs we got—and we are going to take out all their Centaurs."

Inside John's evolving consciousness, Charles and Cynthia were manifest as individuals. They wandered amidst memories and browsed connections within John's Symbiant cortices.

"What are you looking for?" Nick asked.

"Since John doesn't seem to have access to the passcodes, there must be a block," Cynthia replied.

"An emotional block?" Charles wondered.

"Could be," Cynthia replied. "Nick, look for an area of intense and direct connection between memory and emotion either through the preconscious or possibly diverted."

Nick, still distracted by what he was seeing in John's backed up memories, took a minute to catch up. "How would I possibly find that?".

"It would be a memory stack with high static emotional input," Charles posited. He went on to elaborate, "A suppressed memory. Emotional dysregulation will result in a frozen memory, with constant emotional input. It never gets fixed. That is trauma."

Frustrated by Charles' description, Nick turned to his sister for guidance. "Cynthia, what would that look like from out here?"

Cynthia realized that they needed John's help. "John, I need you to focus on MARTIN. What are the deactivation series?" Now, *she* needed Nick. "Any changes?"

"No, nothing," Nick replied.

"John, can you hear me?" Cynthia asked.

"Yes, I can hear you. It's just a blank," John answered.

Nick saw a flutter of activity. "What's a blank?"

"My time at E-Den. I don't think I brought it with me," John answered. Again, there was a flutter of activity similar to what Cynthia was describing.

"Brought what with you?" Cynthia asked.

"Whatever it is you're looking for." John was glib and taciturn.

Nick tried to get John to clarify. "Do you mean MARTIN?" This time, the flurry was shorter.

Nick turned off John's audio input. "Cynthia, he's blocking us."

"I know. Look for a hole, an area of no activity near the activity you're seeing."

Nick began to apply filters to the browser. "I've got it."

"I will go in," Cynthia declared.

"We will go in," Charles corrected.

Parker and Eve came upon an old radio shed. Their trek had been narrated by gunfire and the occasional explosion announcing deaths not far off. Orange flashes painted the canopy of trees in the distance. Then came the moans and cries of the injured and dying. The night grew calm. The moon had not risen. Parker had not seen this many stars in quite some time. Babylon was paradise, but it was never this dark.

They dismounted and hitched their horses to a post by the door. Parker didn't know what to expect behind it. "Do you have a light?"

"No need," Eve answered as she flicked a switch.

Bemused by the hypocrisy, Parker asked, "How many New Amish rules does this place break?"

"None. Elk Walks Alone was Navajo. He lived here. This was his equipment. Batteries and solar power this place. Walks Alone wasn't New Amish. He was here before us. We traded with him."

"How did he have anything to trade?"

"You'd have to ask the pastor that."

"Sounds like a classic bit of religious handwaving. Like a Shabbos Goy."

"No idea what you're driving at, Mayor."

"Orthodox Jews couldn't do anything on the Sabbath. No machinery, no cars. Their Shabbos Goy was employed to do it for them. The machine still got operated, the car was driven, but the Jews didn't break God's rules… You needed supplies and to trade, so Mr. Walks Alone did that for you, without you resorting to solar panels."

Changing the subject, Eve pointed to the radio and said, "So, can you work this thing?"

"Yeah, it's an old wideband." Parker inspected it. "I don't think it has the range."

"Can we increase the range?"

Parker inspected at the back of the radio. "Possibly. It has the inputs. We need wire."

Eve opened the cabinet in the corner and pulled out a spool of copper wire. "Like this?"

Smiling confidently, Parker answered, "Exactly like that." He unwound six feet of the twisted pair. "How are you at climbing?"

With feigned humility, Eve answered, "I can hold my own."

"Run this up to the top and then back down." Eve took the spool and headed out the door. Parker called after her. "Tallest tree you can find."

Out of the darkness, she called back, "You got it."

CHAPTER 43

You can search throughout the entire universe for someone who is more deserving of your love and affection than you are yourself, and that person is not to be found anywhere. You yourself, as much as anybody in the entire universe deserve your love and affection.

-Buddha

Tedeschi analyzed the drone footage, replaying it repeatedly. MARTIN had launched "blind" salvos with deadly accuracy. There had to be a spotter feeding telemetry to Arges; the results were devastating. Five Centaurs destroyed in less than a minute. If his ghosts hadn't been there with that Ministing, MARTIN would be rolling Centaurs through Babylon. This made him wonder, "John, it's Nicco. What do you make of the intel?"

Despite the ongoing expedition inside his consciousness, John was still able to think quite clearly. "I still can't directly analyze the data. Ben and Ping are completing my data link as we speak."

Tedeschi did not recognize the names, choosing to pursue his line of questioning instead. "We keep losing to MARTIN. We are exposed, and his tactics are indecipherable."

"He's a military supercomputer. He's been built to beat you," John confirmed.

"Can you beat him?"

"I guess that depends on how you define winning," John explained. "As a Giant, I wasn't specifically optimized for military operations. However, I had significantly more resources than MARTIN. I believe I could have bested him. Combat outcomes, much like chess, are largely based on the ability to anticipate moves. Right now, MARTIN has a clear advantage, but he will soon exhaust his resources and become inoperative."

"How long?"

"My understanding is that he has less than twenty-six hours' worth of fuel at current consumption."

"Any way we could take him out?"

"An operation like that would consume what was left of our forces. Then, Babylon would be at the mercy of the New Amish Cavalry and Foot Soldiers."

"From the intel I've received, I can't make sense of why he's not pressing the advantage, especially in light of dwindling fuel reserves."

"Which advantage?"

"He has four more Centaurs than we do. There are at least 20,000 combat capable New Amish troops at his disposal."

John pointed out, "The darkness works against them."

"Still, I can't make sense of the Centaur's distribution."

"Can you describe it?"

"Two Centaurs are missing. He has five spread out through the encampment, two in E-Den, and two just out of range of our main force."

"The Centaurs could be providing surveillance. They are the only sensor arrays he has. If there are New Amish around the Centaurs, ghosts would be unable to approach."

"Yes, but even I could have deployed them better and had more Centaurs to repel any advance from the south." Tedeschi went on, "He has put all of the New Amish survivors in the line of fire. It's dark. If our forces break through their lines, there will be astronomically high casualty rates. By dawn, there will be no one left to protect."

"It seems that collateral damage is not a consideration or possibly even a secondary objective. I can't complete an efficient analysis without a direct data connection. You and your men should focus on disabling their Centaurs. They have lost the high ground. Dawn will soon be here and whatever advantage you have will evaporate the minute the sun comes up. I will be fully online within the hour and can provide more effective analytics then."

Accepting that his time would be better spent with his human tacticians, Tedeschi responded, "I await your analysis. Over and out."

"Hey, John, it's Stephanie." Charles was deep inside the "hole" in John's core. It was densely packed with memories, and it was hard to peel them apart. He was losing confidence that there was a key to MARTIN anywhere or that it would be found in time.

"How's married life?" John's voice was tight.

There was a pause. "It's divorced life now. Single mom life."

"Sorry to hear that." John's pitiful attempt at a white lie was blinding at this level.

"Don't be. I'm not. I called to apologize to you."

"Apologize for what?" John asked, and Charles saw a glimmer of hope.

"For cutting you off all those years ago. You're an amazing man! Nothing like the sperm donor I'm stuck with for the next fifteen years."

"Nick, are you getting this?" Charles asked.

"Yes, you're onto something. Stay there! Cynthia, help me browse for details."

"When is this call?" Charles asked.

"A couple of days before the incursion," Nick replied, October 2035. "Did anyone know about this? I sure didn't," Nick said, answering his own question.

John's memory continued to play. "Are you okay?"

"No. I'm scared, and I'm lonely."

"How can I help?" John was sincere, almost desperate.

"I want to see you. I miss you."

"I don't know, Stephanie, it's been years." Nick could see something, it was hot; was it pain? John continued, "There's so much going on."

"I understand. Just so you know, I put myself on the list for your colony, Babylon."

John's tone changed. "That's amazing! What's your number?"

"We're in the two millions. Doesn't seem likely."

"I wish I could help, but that list is blockchain. No one has control over it."

"Not even a genius hacker like you?"

Cynthia interjected, "She's gross! She's using him."

"If I could break it, I wouldn't be a genius hacker. I built the encryption."

"What if I were married to someone on the list? Someone at the top?"

"She has a baby, and the world is falling apart. She's in New York. There may be no atheists in foxholes, but a starving mother will sin for bread," Charles quoted himself again.

"She dumped him and broke his heart," Cynthia argued.

"And now she's trying to fix it," Charles responded.

Repulsed, Cynthia added, "For her own selfish agenda."

"I never knew you were such a romantic," Charles teased. "I'm glad we're merging—must be God's will."

John's call continued to play out. "Stephanie, I'd love a chance to get to know you in that way again and to meet your little girl. Truth is, I never got over you." John's honesty was heartbreaking. "I'm not going to marry you to get you to the top of the list. But there is a workaround that would give us time to get reacquainted."

"Always the problem solver, my brother. Just tell her how you feel. Nick, how does he feel?"

"There's a loop here. Direct loop from these memories to emotions and back."

John continued, "You could come here to E-Den. If you're here, then you'll be automatically eligible to join the Colony."

"And my daughter?"

"Of course."

"I need a few days to work things out with her dad. Can we talk next Friday?"

John's voice was more animated than anyone present had ever heard it. "Any time."

Parker had managed to get the transmitter active. The receiver was shot. He had the cover off and was poking around inside. The microphone was dead too. Its wires had been cut. Eve was still outside. Parker decided to go old school. In the movies, everyone used Morse code. Unfortunately, Parker and everyone else in his generation had long since forgotten it—except for two letters: three dots for 'S' and three dashes for 'O'.

He decided to start transmitting, knowing full well that MARTIN would be more likely to pick up the signal than anyone in Babylon. He cut the microphone wires and stripped them. He tapped the bare ends together and nothing awful happened. Next, he set the transmitter to 1660 MHz. Then, Parker started tapping the pattern he was ninety nine percent confident was SOS.

Dot Dot Dot Dash Dash Dash Dot Dot Dot

He waited two seconds and tapped it out again. Without a working receiver, there was no way of knowing whether anyone was getting his transmission. He was going on blind faith. He kept tapping.

Eve came in. "It's done." Observing Parker tapping the wires together, she asked. "Is it broken?"

"Don't know. Radio's shot, microphone's shot. I'm trying Morse."

"I have no idea what you are talking about."

Parker hadn't thought about the holes in New Amish education. "Morse Code. Before radios and television, there was a code that could be sent over long distances."

"What are you saying?"

"It's just three letters, SOS."

"Does that mean anything?"

"Yes, it's an international distress signal. I think it meant 'save our ship.'"

"And this is a common code that they will recognize?"

"Nick would, John would, and Cynthia would." He paused. "MARTIN would too."

"How long until you know if it works?" she asked.

"If Ducenti show up, I know they got the message."

Hesitantly, Eve asked, "And if MARTIN gets it?"

"Well, I imagine a Centaur will shred us to pieces."

Ben and Ping connected their bridge to the network. They took the custom cables and clicked them onto the Symbiants' mag connect. Nick watched the duo complete the hardware connections.

Nick said, "Ben, I'll need to create a patch for that bridge."

"I can help with that," Ping offered. Then, she thought for a moment. "John, can you pair with this bridge?"

"We could try an ASCII pairing," John suggested.

Ping grabbed an old keyboard; Ben was already stripping the wires from the back. "It's USB." He took the red wire, soldered it to a five-volt supply on the bridge, then grounded it. Then, he connected two wires on a set of digital inputs. "It's on PCM 12 and 17."

Ping began to tap A once per second. "I'm tapping 'A' now, John."

"I'm going to hook a speaker over here too," Ben announced.

"Why?" Nick asked.

"We should be able to hear Ping's A downstream too," Ben explained. "I'm setting the decoder to slow it down so we can hear it. USB 1.0 is 1.5 megahertz. So, it's gonna isolate her input, then slow it down."

"Why are we doing this?" Nick seemed frustrated.

"You software boys are all the same. It's all in the hardware, right, Ping?" Ben joked.

"What Doctor Rosen is saying is that hardware at the basic com level hasn't changed much." She corrected herself, "It's faster, but the protocols are still binary for the bridge we built. Same as that USB keyboard. It's sending 8 bits, 01000001 for the letter A. That's what your brother's Symbiant is listening for. We will listen downstream."

Ben continued, "When John can echo back A, we should hear parity on this speaker. Should go quick once he finds the stream." The speaker began to randomly send two clicks about four seconds apart. "That's Ping's A slowed down one million times. The clicks are the ones."

Suddenly, the speaker went wild. "I found it," John informed them. "Hold for echo A." Ping stopped typing, and a matching set of clicks came through. Ping hit the B key once and the sound shifted as the space between the two clicks changed. It was immediately followed by John's B.

"Ben, I've got it. I can complete the pairing and write the patch from here," John said. You can turn the speaker off. It will be distracting." Ben pulled the speaker wires off.

Nick asked, "How long will it take, John?"

"I'm sending the patch now. I've completed the interrogators and translators." It never ceased to amaze Nick how much faster things happened without the need to slow it down to "biocomputer speed." Nick considered the nervous system to be a biochemical computer.

There were more clicks coming over the speakers inside the lab. Nick let the Symbiant know, "John, we can hear that."

"Unintentional," John answered. The clicks were a pattern, but not the perfectly timed set they had previously listened to. There was static and distortion. "That's an SOS on 1660 MHz," John announced. "Might be Parker."

Ben asked, "How do we know it's not MARTIN? Parker never set foot inside the vault. He and Eve left on foot while I was flying off."

"Try responding," Ping offered.

Nick admitted, "I don't speak Morse code. I doubt if Parker does either."

"I'm able to access the files now," John announced. "Sending 'message received' and I've turned off the speaker."

"Any change?"

"No. They are continuing to transmit."

Nick concluded, "Well then, it's not MARTIN. He would have been able to respond. Can you triangulate that signal?"

"I can," John answered, "But I need to find some other antennas."

"Try the west gate and the tower. Those wires should still be hot."

"I'm working to isolate the signal. This could take a while."

CHAPTER 44

Perfection is achieved not when there is nothing more to add, but rather when there is nothing more to take away.

-Antoine de Saint-Exupery

Lionel Biggs wandered the prairie in the dark. Eurythion was right where the pastor said it would be. A tray supplied him with VR goggles. The technology was amazing. It left him wondering how the New Amish stood a chance against such an advanced and prepared fighting force.

His doubts were assuaged when his goggles translated distant explosions into substantial casualties for the Nons. Tactical revealed a friendly Centaur to his south. Nessus seemed to be relaying ring solutions to a second missile launching Centaur up on the west rim.

Biggs scrolled back in time. He zoomed in on hostiles and friendlies. From what he could tell, four—possibly five—Centaurs had been taken out. When he scrolled back to real time, Nessus was on the move, making good speed towards his location.

Eurythion appeared to wake. Its head-mounted cannon turned south and tilted to a forty-five-degree angle. Biggs knew this to be a maximum downrange firing position. He also wondered whether this headset would protect his ears. He didn't have long to wonder. As Nessus closed to one-half mile, Eurythion commenced firing downrange. Streams of phosphorous painted the night sky as Eurythion fired multiple 30mm rounds down range.

Biggs switched back to tactical view. Nessus was currently targeting four centaurs. The approaching group was giving chase but moving serpentine. They did not return fire. This time, there were no hits. Nessus continued to move north towards Biggs' position. The arcs grew smaller, and it was clear from tactical that the approaching Centaurs were gaining.

When Nessus was almost on top of Biggs, his Centaur, Eurythion, leapt forward, almost running him over. Biggs saw Nessus instantly switch directions headed south. The two Centaurs began firing in sync. Now, they were discharging tracer rounds from their arm mounted 10mm cannons almost continuously along with intermittent salvoes of 30mm shells. This was far more effective. Biggs saw an explosion to the south. The approaching Centaurs took this cue to return fire.

The sky filled with the green scribbles of thousands of tracer rounds. Biggs saw white fire erupt from one of the two southbound Centaurs, and then his goggles went blank. What Biggs never saw were the two Antelope approaching him from the east. He never felt the magnetic round that ended his life.

Parker startled and Eve instinctively drew her gun. Then, a knock came at the door. "I'm unarmed," Parker shouted.

"Sorry to hear that, Mayor," came a familiar voice. Parker gestured for Eve to lower her sidearm.

"That you, Mike?" Parker shouted.

"None other," Santos replied.

"Can't believe you found us," Parker said as he opened the door.

"Well, I can't believe you're out here in some rundown shed in the middle of a war without a gun."

Eve brandished a colt revolver. "He's unarmed. Me, not so much."

"I'm assuming this means coms are online?" Parker asked.

"Yes, I can get you through to my dad," Santos offered.

"Maybe someone should keep watch outside," Parker suggested.

"We've got two Antelope and three Dukes out there. Should be okay," Santos explained confidently.

"Unless a Centaur shows up."

"We killed those. Lots of Jesus freaks still running around out there." Realizing Eve was listening, Mike made eye contact. "Sorry, Ma'am." Parker produced a small speaker and a tactical tablet. "Dad, we've got the mayor and the terrorist."

Parker corrected him. "Ms. Hamlin has been working hard to end this. She has put herself at great personal risk in hopes of bringing the conflict to a close."

"Thank you, Mayor," Eve said. "Mr. Santos, there are lives to be saved. Let's focus on that."

Nick's voice came through, "We have a complicated situation. MARTIN was reactivated after you left, Parker."

"Ben? Again?" Parker asked.

"No, Parker," Ben answered. "I made it to Babylon. MARTIN played possum, played us all. He wanted me back in Babylon."

"Why?" Parker asked.

"I was part of the original one hundred, the pioneers. Apparently, his original programming was still active when I brought him online," Ben explained.

"If that's the case, what about killing everyone else? Why hasn't he done that?"

"That's exactly what he's about to do," John announced. "I've completed my analysis. MARTIN will kill every survivor left in Westden. We just don't know exactly how long he'll wait or what he's waiting for."

"How could this happen Pastor?!" Eve blurted.

"He's still running the program that caused the Epocalypse," Ben explained. "MARTIN has been on the same mission since 2035, maybe before that. The New Amish are a threat to the colonists he was programmed to protect, so he's taking them all out. Everyone except you."

Panicked, Eve asked, "Can we stop him?"

"We are working on a plan," Nick answered. "It requires you to help."

Tedeschi's voice jumped on. "Let me tell you where we're at. We just traded two more Centaurs with MARTIN. We have six operational. He is down to nine. That's not enough ammo to kill everyone in the encampment, but it's enough to kill another twenty thousand people—maybe more."

"How long would it take for them to do that?" Nick asked.

"There are five centrally positioned Centaurs. They could kill ten thousand people in less than a minute," Tedeschi answered. "That's not going to happen. John has explained to me that we are on the same side now, Ms. Hamlin. There aren't enough of us left to continue this foolishness."

"My people have to be warned," Eve pleaded.

Ben replied, "Our people need to help. Eve, you and Mr. James must get word to the people. You need to leave at once!"

Nick came on. "Micheal, can you get them there?"

"As long as nobody kills us on the way. I think I have an idea," Mike interjected, tapping his com. "Bates. Can you rustle us up some of those stray ponies?" There was a pause. "Copy that, we're headed two ninety-five on foot. Each of you take a hitcher. Dickerson, rendezvous Delta-4 in ten minutes. Over." Turning to Eve and Parker, Mike said, "Let's move out."

"John, it's Stephanie again." Charles watched John listening to a voicemail. "Everything is falling apart here. There are no flights. Is there anything you can do? I really need to hear your voice. Please call when you get this." John's finger moved from *play* to *redial*. "Call failed" flashed on the screen. His finger pushed *retry*. "Call failed."

John opened a browser window:

```
Widespread cellular outages attributed to ARL
hackers
Activists shut down the Northeast
Bombings at Satellite Uplink
911 system failures
```

John opened a terminal window.

Charles called out to Nick, "This may be something; he's opening a terminal." Hoping they could capture keystrokes and get the password, Nick said, "Might get a look here."

```
:JSantos@MARTIN.Command:
Root-Overide:BabylonList
```

```
Challenge:Martin-Command: Enter Passphrase
***************
```

John hit the return key.

```
Authenticated
```

"What are you up to, John?" came Cynthia's voice from the memory. John closed the window.

"Damn, I was pretty. This is the last day I ever looked like that." Cynthia was watching her younger, undamaged self interact with her brother in John's memory.

"Nothing, just checking core functions," came John's voice.

The younger Cynthia stared straight in her brother's eyes. "John, you look worried."

"I am. The whole world is falling apart. There's something going on in Westden. Drones are picking up chatter. I've got these programs lined up. But this whole relocate is a shit show."

"John, I've never seen you so emotional."

"People are dying. These nuts are killing people because their delusion is crumbling. They want our heads on pikes because we don't think the way they do. It's 2035! When are they going to come around?"

"Charles always talks about this unconscious conspiracy to maintain the status quo."

"Yes, I know. There's nothing unconscious about this fucking mess! Live and let fucking live." His phone vibrated.

MARTIN: "Trucks approaching the west gate, likely incursion."

John turned back to Cynthia and announced, "Time to leave."

The memory ended.

"Nick, did you see him typing the passcode?" Charles asked.

"I can't see his fingers," Nick answered.

"You can see his knuckles, and we know it's sixteen characters. John, are you going to help?"

"I don't remember anything about that day. I can't help you."

"What's your most secret password?"

"I don't remember. I can't help you."

"His answers are rote. It's a block. He won't help."

"John, you loved that woman," Charlemagne began. "You loved her, and you were trying to save her. Do you remember that?"

"I don't remember. I can't help you."

Nick interjected. "Another block. I see it now. I'm opening the feed."

John's finger hovered over Stephanie's contact. He pushed *call*. He was in a car and Nick was driving fast. "This isn't how this was supposed to go down," Nick yelled over the noise. Nick, focused on driving, screamed into his headset, "Listen, you're the governor. Govern. I spent ten million dollars getting you elected. There's a space at the Colony for you and your whole family. Stop these close-minded assholes. Send the national guard! This is a riot…" Nick continued to argue.

John's finger pushed *text*.

"Steph, I tried to call. I can't get through. We've evacuated E-Den. Not sure if phones will work for a bit. If you are getting these, text back. I'll send a jet. I'll drive there myself and get you—both of you. I love you. Please let me know you're okay."

Nick tried to get John's attention. "They're a bunch of fucking savages, every last one of them. No consequences. They should have consequences."

John's finger clicked on a different app: *MARTIN*.

JSantos@MARTIN.Command:

The car was bouncing around as John 's finger typed

```
expand zone of engagement: prioritize protect E-Den
> Babylon > @Stephanie6174224345> Bablist

Challenge: Martin-Command: Enter Passphrase
```

Clicking sounds rang out as a series of 16 asterixis came again.

"Authenticated" appeared on the screen.

"His fingers are in view this time. I think we have it!" Charlemagne announced.

"Stephanie@4Ever!"

Nick was forced to scroll back a few times.

```
prioritize protect E-Den > Babylon > @
Stephanie6174224345> Bablist >
```

He kept examining it. Ben was looking too.

Ben's eye went wide. He began to sob. "All these years, I thought I did it. I thought I messed with MARTIN. I believed I caused the Epocalypse."

Nick was compelled to ask, "John, did you know? Do you remember?"

"I saw the feed. I can't unsee it. Those were my actions. I can't deny it."

"MARTIN prioritized that order. There were no safeties. He killed the world to protect the list. There was no limit on the order. He just kept killing to protect Stephanie," Ben determined. "Runaway code."

"Can we send that passphrase and turn him off?" Nick asked.

"I don't think so," Ben answered. "I don't know where the app is, and we don't have time to rebuild it."

"So, all this was a waste of time?" Nick asked.

"No," Ben answered. "I'll go back. I'll key it in myself."

"There are Centaurs, Ben. Outside the door. You'll end in a pink cloud a half-mile before you get there."

John offered, "I can help. MARTIN is expecting a full offensive on the New Amish at Westden. He's trying to lead our Centaurs there to help him complete his mission. He needs us to fight. We already have assets ready to take down the Centaurs at Westden. We'll push forward with a feint towards the encampment." The tactical came up on screen. "Are you getting this, Commander Tedeschi?"

"Yes," came Niccolo's voice.

"Commit all your assets to Doctor Rosen's protection. He must get to the panel at E-Den."

Pointing to some supplies, Ben said, "I'll need that keyboard and portable toolkit."

"I'm going with you," Ping announced. "We work well together."

"Ever been on a magic carpet before?" Ben asked.

"Can't say that I have."

CHAPTER 45

And a new philosophy emerged called quantum physics, which suggest that the individual's function is to inform and be informed. You really exist only when you're in a field sharing and exchanging information. You create the realities you inhabit.

-Timothy Leary

Antelope had a small pop-down saddle on their backs. Ducenti trained to ride and operate them. Murdock and Cooper were riding piggyback on the Antelope. "Keep your heads down. It's tight up ahead," Bates advised. "I see a pony now."

"Get on his left side," Murdock suggested. "I jump better to the right."

Through his reticle, Bates targeted the horse. He moved the cursor left of the animal and a bit ahead. Usually, this was just to transfer to another Antelope when the other operator was cooperating. However, the darkness, the trees, and the possibility that this horse might not want a rider added substantial complexity.

"Alongside in five, four, three, two."

"Jumping now," Murdock announced. "I'm on. Heading for Delta-4."

"Hold position. We're going to get you a second horse to take with you. We need a second."

Cooper was now scouting for horses. "Got one. Stay on manual. I've done this before."

"Negative Coop, auto only. No time for cowboy shit."

"If there was ever a time for cowboy shit, this is it," Cooper argued but accepted orders. "Auto engaged."

The Antelope easily gained on the horse. They pulled alongside. There was a crash. "He's in a hole. That pony is down. I'm taking him out. No need for the poor guy to suffer," Bates announced, as he put two magnetic rounds in the animal's head, ending its life. "Not your fault, just dumb luck."

"Got another one locked. Path is clear. Four, three, two—"

"Jumping now," came Cooper. "I'm on."

"We'll get one more." Bates ordered. "Coop and Murdock head for Delta-4. We'll catch up."

Charles was still browsing, though he wasn't sure he should be. They had found everything they needed. Loitering inside John's unconscious bordered on violation. For whatever reason, and despite his ambivalence, Charles found himself in the pool, swimming up and up. He broke through the surface. She was there! She pulled him out and put a towel on him. She towered over him. The terry was warm and rough.

"John, my perfect angel," came her voice. Everything was bright and overexposed, making it hard for Charles to focus and see past the Mother God. She picked him up. He could feel it.

"It's synesthesia, Charles," came Cynthia's disembodied voice. "You are feeling the light."

"It's like drugs."

"It is drugs. Oxytocin and serotonin. Symbiants don't have those, but that's what you are experiencing."

"How can this happen?" Charles asked. "I'm just a simulation in another simulation. Why am I feeling anything?"

"You aren't. You're not feeling John's feelings; you are feeling your own. Pure sympathy: you have synchronized your feelings with John's emotional state."

"Why can't I feel my own feelings? Why can't I be with my Mother God?"

"John's memories are a mirror. You see a reflection. You can't look inside your mind any more than you can look inside your eye."

"What if I created another Symbiant of me, Charles the Third?"

"Maybe you will. For now, you are Charlemagne. I am Charlemagne. We are Charlemagne. Let's see what that's like."

"I don't want to leave. It's perfect here."

"It won't stay that way. I promise you. Come back. She'll change, and each time, she'll become less welcoming."

"Maybe if I can learn to make her happy, she'd let me stay."

"She doesn't want you to stay, Charles. She wants you to be you. Come with me. Let's be us."

"Can we come back?"

"Not here. Not in this life."

John was back online and summoned the magic carpet for Ben and Ping. It landed just outside the lab.

Ben turned to Ping and said, "It's amazing! Don't be scared."

"I'm not. I feel safe with you, Ben. You saved my life."

He offered a smile in response. "I'll buckle you in," Ben said as he reached across.

Ping could feel the heat of his body. It had been so long since a man had been this close. "Thank you." Ping changed the subject. "How long will this take?"

"Took about twenty minutes last time."

"Tell me about Eve. I want to hear everything."

"Well, she's a pretty woman, got that from her mom, I guess," Ben started. "She was selected to infiltrate Babylon because she's as smart and solid as they come. We knew she'd get the job done."

Somewhat embarrassed, Ping half joked, "Well, she did that."

"She felt terrible about taking his life. I know that," Ben offered.

"What do you think about God? I know you raised Eve Christian, but Rosen is a Jewish name. Right?"

"I was raised in a Jewish home, but so was Christ." He paused. "I don't know. I was never as comfortable with atheism as Charles and the Santos family. I wanted there to be more. That day Tom died, when I found Eve, it seemed like there was a plan."

"What if there is a God and no plan? No heaven. God just is. He doesn't have rules or need worship. He's just something beyond our comprehension."

"Now you sound like Charles. Charles is certain that God is in each one of us. God doesn't have to be infinite to exceed our comprehension."

"What do you think about *The God Within*?" Ping asked.

"It explains a lot. It makes sense, but I'm not sure God isn't both. The God within may exist because the Lord above willed it. Today,

I'm more okay with not knowing the truth than I have been any day since I put you in the car and sent you here."

"Do you think you needed an epiphany? That perhaps biology creates epiphanies to defend against despair?"

"Or God does for the same reason." He couldn't not be a pastor; over twenty years of preaching did not just leave his body.

"Still a pastor after all." The carpet hovered, then set down.

"I'm keeping you here until E-Den is clear. Shouldn't be long," John announced, interrupting their philosophical musings.

Ben turned to Ping. "I'm going to get some rest. I haven't closed my eyes in forever."

Ping looked to her left and in the moonlight, she saw that Ben was already asleep.

Brett's radio crackled. Lionel Biggs' voice was barely audible. "You there, Brett?"

"Bigsy, you're alive!"

"Not for long. The only way through this is to take back Eden. Push those Nons back to Babylon."

"How we gonna do that?" Brett asked.

"I want you to take the entire New Amish Calvary east. Form up on the road south of the water tower and wait for my call."

Concerned that men on horseback would be no match for the Centaurs, Brett asked, "Won't those tank things mow us down?"

"I've got their control codes. I'm going to shut them down."

"Shouldn't we bring our tanks with us?"

"No, we need them to protect the women, wounded, and children. They'll stay back."

Hesitant, Brett confirmed his instructions. "So, just go there and wait?"

"You won't have to wait for long. We'll send them packing!"

"Okay Bigsy."

Tedeschi and Clark were conferenced through their Battlepads when John commed them. "A new wrinkle just came through from the Condor." On their Battlepads, John showed them a full view.

"What's he up to?" Clark asked.

"Trying to protect himself. Bringing the remaining forces to E-Den." Tedeschi called up motion analysis. "That's where the two groups converge."

John challenged the two men. "I'm not sure that it's about self-preservation." The Battlepad's view changed to a simulation. "Those forces will never get past the Centaurs and Ducenti." The simulation showed the New Amish forces consolidating outside Babylon. The movement stalled, then the numbers of the New Amish forces just kept dropping. Starting with six thousand men and one hundred ninety-five horses, the numbers quickly ran down to less than one hundred men.

Clark seemed reassured after processing the data. "So, it's not going to work. We'll get to MARTIN, and once he's shut down, we can disable the Centaurs."

"It works perfectly," John corrected. "MARTIN is moving all the forces away from his Centaurs. They won't be there to offer protection from the slaughter."

Tedeschi added, "He saves ammo, and our Centaurs do the work for him. He doesn't have enough ammo to do the job himself."

"Precisely," John confirmed.

"So, what do we do?" Clark asked. "I'm not comfortable gunning down six thousand men to help an ancient computer complete an errant quest."

John always had a plan. Tedeschi was still getting his legs under himself as a true commander. His losses over the forty-eight hours leading up to this moment weighed on him. He'd always heard that great leaders were forged in fire. It was time to take that leap. "We have to buy time. That's all. Rosen is going to get in there. He will deactivate MARTIN. We have to put our faith in him."

For the first time in five years, it was John asking for advice. "What are you suggesting, Nicco?"

"Shock and awe at E-Den. We know there are two—possibly four—Centaurs there. We need to establish immediate control." He brought up the tactical view. "We're going to send four Centaurs with two Cyclops at the rear. One Condor fully committed to E-Den." He zoomed back out. "We're going to divide the remaining forces, one Centaur each. Their only job will be to minimize casualties among the New Amish."

Clark interrupted, "There's no way to keep this clean, Commander. People will die. We're also going to waste a lot of ordinance. We will lose most—if not all—of our remaining Centaurs."

"At this point, it's damage control. Those men don't deserve to die. Some will, but that's inevitable," Tedeschi offered.

"How many?" Clark asked.

"A lot fewer than if we let them charge six Centaurs." Tedeschi's tone changed, indicating that the debate was over. "Clark, you and Morris will take group Alpha and push west, south of the New Amish column, target calvary and horses if you can. Use any trick you can think of. I'll have Davidson and Chapman hold E-Den. Then, I'll take the Beta group and push north, ahead of the column. If we can establish a crossfire gauntlet, with suppressing fire, it will slow them down."

"What if Doctor Rosen can't get to MARTIN?" John asked.

"John, I was anticipating that you and Lieutenant Morgan will help infiltrate the encampment with ghosts. I'm giving you fourteen Ducenti and four antelope. I've got three mini stings with your nephew to the west, but only one launcher. I'm relying on you to take those Centaurs out before they fire a single shot."

Morgan, who'd just learned his new assignment, was compelled to ask, "Who's guarding the West Gate?"

"No one," Tedeschi said. "This is for all the marbles." He changed tone. "Nick, you there?"

"I'm here, Commander."

"Can you coordinate the emergency response? If we succeed, there are going to be a lot of lives that will need saving."

Without hesitation, Nick confirmed, "On it."

"Gentlemen, you have your orders. Commence operation New Dawn."

CHAPTER 46

Although the most acute judges of the witches and even the witches themselves, were convinced of the guilt of witchery, the guilt nevertheless was non-existent. It is thus with all guilt.

-Friedrich Nietzsche

Jim Davidson was the youngest of the lieutenants. A Centaur specialist, he led the development of the robot warriors and their enhancements. "So, whiz kid, what's the plan?" Chapman asked.

Davidson was more comfortable with AR and had donned a pair of Centaurview goggles to enhance his Battlepad's display. "We're going to use MARTIN's tactics and engage the Centaurs from the west." He highlighted three points on the display. "They will probably shelter here and here. He needs to keep the fight away from his generators."

Chapman, more old school, stuck with his Battlepad. "What if he doesn't?"

"What are his options? He has to defend the entrance to the vault, and he has to protect the generators."

"What if this guy goes north into the trees?"

Davidson had already thought of this, "I have Antelope coming from the north. Already in route. They can provide firing solutions from there."

"Sounds too easy. Smells like a trap. MARTIN has been a step ahead since he came online," Chapman said.

"Hopefully Tedeschi is right and he's relying on that force from the west to pin our Centaurs in crossfire. We have a significant tactical advantage this time.

He has no intel. Also, those Centaurs must be running low on charge. He's run them all over the place."

Chapman reminded him, "We don't know which ones have run around and which ones remain fully charged. Don't count on that. How long until you can get Rosen in there?"

"Twenty minutes, if it goes to plan."

"And if it doesn't?" Chapman asked.

"Maybe an hour, maybe never."

"If it takes more than an hour, it won't matter much."

"Cyclops are in position," Davidson reported. "Waiting on firing solutions. It's gonna get real loud real soon."

Bates caught up with Santos, Eve, and the other Ducenti. Santos had his Battlepad out and was reviewing tactics with the group. "If only we had more launchers. Three mini stings, one launcher. The math doesn't work."

"Once the shooting starts, each of those Centaurs will start killing fifty people every second," Bates reminded them.

Eve struggled to imagine the senseless loss of life. Then, she struggled harder to get the image of people being shredded out of her head. An idea popped in her mind. She turned to Michael, "Why do we need a launcher?"

He explained, "The launcher guides and triggers the mini sting. You can't just throw a thirty-pound missile at the thing."

"Actually, you could," Parker interjected. "Mini stings are not kinetic weapons. They are high explosive delivery systems. MARTIN has positioned the Centaurs close to the people to maximize kills."

"We just walk up to them? Hand the Centaurs a bomb?" Bates joked.

"Kind of. We keep one for the launcher," Parker explained. "We'll disassemble the other two."

"I can set up remote triggers. The Antelope stay out of sight and time the blasts to the mini sting launch."

Parker was already taking a toolkit off the Antelope. Charles joined him. "Who's going to go in?"

Parker determined, "We should go in pairs. If something goes wrong, a teammate could still achieve the objective. I'll take him. Santos, you go with Bates."

"I should go," Eve offered. "I know these people and they know me."

Santos nodded. "Good point. She knows the lay of the land better than any of us."

"I'll scout for New Amish clothes. You'll blend in with some packs. If you bandage people on the way in, you won't attract as much attention," James offered

"Don't forget to pray," Eve reminded them.

"Good plan. Back in twenty. It's already getting light over there. We are running out of time."

John, the Symbiant, couldn't comprehend what he had lost in his transition. As a Giant, he had been ten thousand times more capable in terms of planning and analysis. However, the Symbiant John felt guilt in a way his immortal self never had. John had woken up five years in the future, unable to understand who he had become during his time in Elysium, and knowing he never would.

The reconnection of suppressed memories was painful. Symbiants experienced emotional pain, shame, and guilt. It was part of Charles' and Cynthia's design. He thought about asking them to erase his memories, but for some reason, he didn't want to appear vulnerable.

Since awakening, John learned that he lost the love of his life, and that he was responsible for the Epocalypse. He had killed the world with bad instructions and runaway code. There would be no redemption. His only wish was deactivation. Then, there was his little brother. John had been able to see the images Nick had browsed. It was apparent that his brother and his friends were insignificant specks to John the Giant.

John had noticed things that Nick had not and could not. Patterns the human mind would never detect. The Giants held humans in contempt. Nick had only reviewed snippets of John's first year in the Elysium. In that time, John had lost all traces of his humanity. How far had Cynthia gone in ten years?

His guilt about the Epocalypse also forced him to consider MARTIN. MARTIN had killed the world in a month, and Ben had shut him down. However, John had never thought about the other MARTINs. There were eight nodes spread across the planet, and MARTIN had been cut off within hours. No one in Babylon knew what became of the other datacenters that made up MARTIN's distributed consciousness. Many of those superclusters were powered and cooled by hydroelectric systems. Could some have remained operational? How would a manipulative intelligence like MARTIN twist human minds without anyone to stop him? What worlds had the other MARTINs created in the aftermath of the Epocalypse? Would they eventually come for the resources of Eden and Babylon?

After reflecting, John focused all of his now-limited resources on supporting the mission. Morgan had been following Michael Santos' plan to sneak up on the Centaurs. Proud of his heritage, Morgan declared, "Ducenti aren't spies; we are warriors."

"Today, you are shepherds," John argued.

"My ghosts will get close enough with their mini stings and launchers. We don't need to get right next to these things. It increases survivability for the men launching the missiles."

"It also increases the response time for the Centaurs to track and shoot them down. At four kilometers, those mini stings will be in the air for seven seconds," John explained. "In an open field, a Centaur's 10mm guns will take it down with a three-second warning."

"So, what's our max safe distance to launch from?" Morgan asked.

"One kilometer is ideal," John answered, adding, "But only if we sync fire with the other units. We'll need five kill shots in two seconds. We could fire some missiles at max distance off angle." He tapped on his Battlepad. "Two men on opposite sides, each firing off mini stings from miles away."

Morgan began to understand the plan. "A distraction?"

John went on to explain, "Yes. A Centaur will attempt to engage the inbound mini stings. They will deplete thousands of rounds, and they will all be aimed in the wrong direction when we launch our short-range attacks."

"I like it."

"Can you get your men that far out?"

"We have a couple of magic carpets. We'll use one of those for the north side. We could send another pair up the south ridge to this clearing on Antelope."

"Start their deployment. Get your ghosts in those craters. There are still kill orders in place if any New Amish spots them. We can't risk alerting the Centaurs. Kinetic kills only, mag-gun or knife.

"Roger."

Charlemagne and Nick began organizing humanitarian relief. There were only a handful of physicians in Babylon. The Colony, with the support of the Giants, relied on med techs. The injured in Babylon were already either stabilized or dead. There were teams in the hospitals prepping for the larger mass casualty incident at Westden. Doctor Patel was Babylon's chief physician.

"Hello, Shweta, thank you for the amazing efforts you and your teams have been making," Charlemagne said with sincerity. "I'm sending over an initial plan for your review."

"I'm sorry, I don't recognize your voice. With whom am I speaking?"

"I apologize for the confusion. This is Charles Luxold and Cynthia Santos."

"That doesn't make sense. Cynthia went offline yesterday. Doctor Luxold was killed two days ago."

"Shweta, it's Nick Santos here," Nick popped up on her holo.

"Hey, Nick, what's going on? Who called me?"

"It's too complicated to explain right now. Charlemagne is a Symbiant fusion of Charles and Cynthia. New tech, very cool, but not very relevant. They are best equipped to supervise logistics when this conflict is resolved."

Now, all business, Shweta asked, "How many casualties are we looking at?"

"Over one hundred thousand mortalities, fifteen thousand to fifty thousand wounded. Depends how the next hour goes," Charlemagne explained.

Overwhelmed, she lamented, "How will we treat fifteen thousand people twenty miles from here?"

"We won't, Doctor Patel. My estimates are that the wounded will continue to expire at over one thousand souls per hour. If we arrive in three hours, assuming no additional casualties, there will only be twelve thousand victims left to treat. Three thousand of those will expire before we can render aid. Five thousand have non-critical injuries."

Shweta had been following the math. "So, we will have to treat four thousand critically injured people on a battlefield. What's the projected survival rate for those?"

"Best-case scenario, fourteen hundred lives saved."

"That's more people than I've saved in my whole career."

Nick asked, "How many physicians can you spare, Shweta?"

"Seven doctors, thirty nurses, and about forty medics."

"I'm preparing a crash course for the civilian population," Charlemagne announced. "We can send five thousand people that way. They can all help. I'm also deploying half of our robot workforce to carry supplies."

"It's twenty miles. Will be a long walk," Nick argued.

"I'm going to get an advanced team prepped and mobilized," Shweta offered. "We have three hundred thousand doses of Nuphlexin on hand. I'll send twenty-five thousand doses with the advance team."

"That's nearly one hundred pounds of pills," Charlemagne commented. "I'll send a rover."

"Can you send five? They'll need all the supplies we can spare."

"I don't have five rovers. I'll send what I can. Thank you, Doctor Patel. Charlemagne out."

Brett had been riding all over what used to be Westden. They were going to take back Eden. He and his men would push the Nons all the way back to Babylon. He knew he could count on Bigsy.

Every New Amish soldier jumped at the chance to fight alongside the pastor's trusted man. As Brett came across men he knew well, he put them in charge of gathering more soldiers. Dawn was coming. There was already a faint glow in the east. They needed to be ready.

As Brett made his way eastward, men he knew broke off from the growing posse and joined his side. They trotted east. What had been the sound of a few horses was now the low rumble of the New Amish Cavalry. The most formidable, mounted army to ride since the Mexican American War, two centuries earlier.

CHAPTER 47

If I had more time, I would have written a shorter letter.

— Blaise Pascal

Ben was asleep when a Cyclops rolled by. Ping shook him awake and whispered, "Cyclops. By the direction it's headed, guess it's one of ours."

"Then the attack is imminent. Time to get moving. We don't want to be anywhere near one of those things once the shooting starts."

A second Cyclops came along the exact same path before disappearing into the trees. Ben was about to turn the carpet back on when Ping tugged on his arm. There was a rustling and a snapping of branches. A Centaur emerged, pulling itself from a hole in the ground.

"We gotta call this in. That's got to be one of MARTIN's." Ben tapped the console. "Nick, are you there?"

"Yes, we're about to commence ops."

Ben was whispering but with panic in his voice. "You don't have any Centaurs in the woods by us?"

"Two RPG-equipped Cyclops. Must be what you saw. Nothing to worry about."

"There's a third Centaur here, Nick. It was waiting for them. Just pulled itself out of the ground right after they passed by."

Nick pressed a button on his tablet, adding Tedeschi and his lieutenants. "Ben Rosen says one of MARTIN's missing Centaurs is about to take out both of your Cyclops."

"Davidson, you getting this?" Tedeschi asked.

"Where is the Centaur, Doctor Rosen?" Davidson asked.

Ben interrupted, "He dug himself out twenty seconds ago. He was following their tracks."

"Nothing on their scopes," Davidson reported. "I'm splitting them up." He took control of the rear Cyclops, leaving the other under its operator's control. "This is Lieutenant Davidson. We have a Centaur just south of E-Den. Who's got a firing solution on E-Den?"

One of the operators replied, "Sending now."

Davidson pivoted his Cyclops' arms one hundred eighty degrees to face the pursuing tank, RPGs still pointed north towards Babylon. The cannons were aimed right along the path it just took. Davidson put the Cyclops into a crouch. "Audio sensors are picking up track sounds. Centaur three hundred yards out, closing at ten miles per hour. Take your shot!"

Ben and Ping were airborne and retreating to the south when they saw rockets and tracers exploding out of the trees.

Ping grabbed his arm. "Are we safe?"

"No idea. But we're safer than we were five minutes ago."

It had been a dry summer. The underbrush made perfect kindling. Friction and heat from the cannons set trees ablaze. To the north, explosions and columns of white fiery smoke turned orange as they caught the morning sun's rays as it crested the horizon.

Ben was still connected to the military channel. Davidson announced, "Brontes is down. Don't know if he got that Centaur. Cyclops Pyracmon remains operational, proceeding to E-Den. Condor confirms both Centaurs at E-Den down."

"Is it safe for us to proceed?" Ben asked.

"Not on that thing. We're going to have some Antelope take you in," Tedeschi answered. "Look for blinking lights down to your left. One red, one green. Put down there."

Grube was driving the RX with a manned Bison on back. Tedeschi was trying to keep up with the real time data. "Looks like MARTIN was still a step ahead. He knew where those Cyclops would fire from. The Centaurs were bait."

"If Rosen hadn't called it in, he would have gotten both of them," Grube added.

"If Rosen hadn't turned that machine back on, we'd all be sitting in a seaside café telling war stories about a war that never happened," Tedeschi added. "Any way you look at it, Rosen has the blood of billions on his hands."

"No, he doesn't," John announced. "New facts have come to light. Ben Rosen did not start the Epocalypse."

"If he didn't, who did?" Tedeschi asked.

"I did," John admitted.

"That's a little hard to swallow, Commander Santos. What we're about to do, what we've already done. It wasn't the Pastor?"

"It was all of us. Short-sighted and self-absorbed. We paid a terrible price."

Tedeschi took control. "We are defending our home, not settling a score. We are Ducenti. We serve Babylon. Get your head back in the game, Lieutenant!"

Changing the subject, Grube asked, "What's the current count?"

"We are down another Cyclops. They lost three Centaurs. Progress."

"How many do they have left?"

"They've got five in the field, and the one skulking around somewhere." Tedeschi circled trees on his pad. "Good chance we're gonna meet that one real soon. There aren't a lot of places left to hide. We need to get dug in."

Send three Bison north of us. Start Antelope patrols in the woods. Look for brush piles. That's where it will be hiding."

"Looks like we're almost there," Morris reported. "Alpha on site. Hostiles two thousand yards out, approaching at three miles per hour."

Clark informed Morris, "I'll take the ghosts and two Antelope. We'll loop south of the Centaurs."

Morris informed him, "I'm sending Stokes up the hill saddled on an Antelope. He has a mini sting and two rounds. He'll fire from the saddle. Then they're gonna bug out before those Centaurs can light them up with their 30mm."

Clark commended Stokes. "You got balls. That's no joke, taking on five Centaurs."

Already saddled up, Stokes leaned forward to balance the weight of the launcher on his back. "Commander Clark, if your ghosts get their job done, those Centaurs won't have long to send trouble my way."

"They'll come through," Clark promised. "Ghosts, you have your assignments. Mag rounds only. Keep your launchers under wraps. Close to seven hundred and fifty meters of your targets. Sun's coming up. Twenty minutes on my mark."

Anderson was working his Bison north. Tedeschi ordered him to position a mile northwest. His Bison would remotely fire from the hilltop toward the west most Centaurs below. Firing remotely offered him the best chance of survival. His exoskeleton could not survive the Centaur's return fire.

He wasn't bounding through the woods, but Bison were not built for stealth. If he encountered the remaining hidden Centaur, this would be his last mission. Bison were built for frontal assaults. They weren't made to skulk about the woods.

"Kinda spooky in here," Anderson commed. "Anyone find that Centaur?"

"No, but if you keep the chatter up, maybe you will," Simms joked.

"I keep feeling like he's right behind me," Anderson replied. "Seriously, the hairs on the back of my neck are standing straight up."

Tedeschi had been listening. "Anderson, keep it together."

"Sir, this supercomputer, it's exactly the kind of thing he does. All his other Centaurs were buried in the woods. They waited for us to walk by and took out the first guy they saw."

"Simms, cut north; you should come up on Anderson. Check out his six."

"Roger." Simms' Antelope was in stealth mode, slow and quiet. Still faster than the Bison, he closed the gap in less than a minute. "Commander," he said with real fear in his voice. "Anderson was right. There's a Centaur about three hundred yards behind him."

"I'm never fucking right, why now?" Anderson commed.

"Listen, Frank, you're gonna be okay." Tedeschi was in full command mode now. "Don't tip your hand. The Centaur is trying to gain intel on you. He's not going to open fire until he's figured out what you are up to."

"Simms, I want you to mark him. We're gonna get in front and take him out."

"Anderson, you are going to pass your original waypoint in thirty seconds. Don't stop, don't turn. We are going to have men up there in three minutes."

"Can't I just bail?" Anderson asked. "This is not how I wanted to die today."

"If you bail, he'll get you and your ride, and we won't get him. Go the distance."

Anderson was calming down. "Passing waypoint now."

"Men are in position, right up in those trees. Keep pace."

"Forty yards to the trees."

As if MARTIN could smell the trap, the Centaur pivoted one arm behind him, opening fire on Anderson and Simms simultaneously.

"Sir," Jefferson reported. "Anderson and Simms are down. Centaur has us pinned." Jefferson and Hoffard had their mini sting launchers ready to go but the Centaur's suppressing fire cut down the trees they were using for cover.

"Leave the launchers," Tedeschi ordered. "Get the hell out of there."

"Sir, it's Hoffard. Jefferson's gone. I'm heading north."

"Hoffard, stay low. We have support en route to you."

"Thank you, Sir. I'll do my best."

CHAPTER 48

Abandon all hope, ye who enter here.

-Dante Alighieri

Ben and Ping dismounted just outside MARTIN's vault. On approaching the keypad for the door, he saw that it had been obliterated by gunfire. A Centaur had destroyed the access pad.

"How will we get in?" Ping asked.

"Same way I did a few days back." Ben already had his hand in the hole and deftly retried a manual unlock.

"It doesn't appear that he wants visitors," Ping observed.

"Or he only wanted me," Ben answered. "Only a few of us know how to get in this way." He struggled a bit longer until the door lock clicked. "Push it open!"

Ping got the door open. "Can you grab the pack?"

Ben did as he was asked. As soon as they were inside, he noticed a second, more difficult challenge. "He's closed the inner security doors."

"Is there a trick for those?" Ping asked.

"Nope, no trick. He's locked down."

"What about an access point up here where we could enter the code?" Ping suggested.

Ben thought. "The Armory. There's an inventory control system there. I can probably reboot it and get root level access."

Ben was relieved to find the armory unlocked. He logged in to the terminal and reset it. "It's gonna take a minute to reboot."

The cursor appeared.

```
BRosen@MARTIN.Command:Root
```

```
CynOS:
```

Ben typed `MARTIN-Command`

```
MARTIN:
```

Ben entered the passphrase

```
Stephanie@4Ever!
```

```
MARTIN: Command line not accessible on this station
```

Ben turned to Ping, defeated. "It's not working. This was all for nothing; it was pie-in-the-sky to think a thirty-year-old passphrase would put an end to all this."

Ping was not ready to give up. "It didn't reject the code, Doctor Rosen. It just won't let you enter it here."

"This is the only terminal up here, Ping," Ben explained. "The only command terminals are forty feet below us, behind six-inch steel doors."

Ping thought some more. She was an engineer, just like Ben, maybe not as gifted, but still a problem solver. "Would door control be a feature of the command terminal?"

He wanted to kiss her. "You're a genius!" Ben dove into the directories. "Door control is not a MARTIN command level function. It's in CynOs."

`CynOs:`

appeared and Ben typed: *Hardware control.*

`CynOs:Hardware:`

Ben typed:

`Door control`

`Access limited to sysadmins`

`CynOs:`

Ben typed: `BRosen/` then entered his password, which appeared as fourteen asterixis.

`Admin@CynOS:` Ben typed: *Hardware control.*

`Admin@CynOS:Hardware:`

Ben typed: *Door control.*

`Admin@CynOS:Hardware:Door Control`

Ben realized he didn't know what to enter. He turned to Ping, "I don't know which door to unlock."

Ping suggested, "Unlock all?"

Ben typed: `Unlock All`

The screen flashed a series of error messages. Rows containing various door addresses appeared.

```
Door 817: Unlock failed door offline.
```

Ben had forgotten how many doors there had been at E-Den prior to the Epocalypse. The OS was trying each door in sequence. The system appeared to hang several times.

"No point in standing here. We may as well go see if it unlocked."

As they rounded the corner, the blast doors had already begun closing again. Ben yelled, "Run!"

The explosions accompanying Anderson's encounter with the Centaur triggered a charge by the New Amish. Condor footage on Tedeschi's Battlepad showed the first horsemen crossing an imaginary line drawn through the meadow. "Begin suppressing fire."

Centaurs and Bison focused on the horses' legs, surgically cutting them down. Riders spilled forward. "Antelope, non-lethal mag rounds, disrupt advancing lines." Man after man who crossed the line was felled by a silent force.

Recognizing that they were entering a kill zone, the men further back slowed their advance. Eventually, they stopped just west of the imaginary line. "It's working!" Tedeschi announced. A Centaur rolled to within a quarter mile of the line. Then, the shooting ceased. "Attention New Amish forces. This is Commander Tedeschi of the Babylon Defense Force. We do not wish to harm you. Turn back."

Random shots rang out from the New Amish line, but quickly stopped. Centaurs were immune to small arms fire.

Brett Stephens dismounted and began to walk forward with his hands raised. He yelled, "I am unarmed. I wish to discuss terms."

A voice yelled back, "You may approach, Commander."

Tedeschi turned to his lieutenant. "Get us out there. I want to meet this man face to face."

Michael Santos was physically ill. The whole area smelled of rotting flesh and death. He had never experienced anything like this in his privileged life. "I never imagined it would be like this."

"What?" Eve asked.

"Death, devastation. I've seen videos. I read accounts of the American Civil War. They never conveyed anything about the smell or the sounds."

"To someone of the that time, these smells and sounds were a normal part of death and dying. The cost of victory or defeat."

Santos admitted, "Before yesterday, I'd never seen a dead person. When people die in Babylon, it's clean and peaceful." He seemed trapped in his memories. "That child we passed just now, she was still breathing. No one was there to comfort her, as she lay dying in the dark."

Eve said, "I prayed for her."

"I envy the peace it provides you. It's something I'll never know. In my world, a child died alone. She was in the wrong place at the wrong time."

"Do you pity me or envy me?" Eve asked.

"For what?"

"For the peace that my faith gives me. We walk the Valley of Death, and I fear no evil. I know that girl will wake in paradise. Her suffering will be at an end."

"You can't know that," Michael argued.

"But I do. I have no doubt."

"So, you aren't sickened at the sight of a little girl with her stomach blown open?"

"Of course I am, and if she were conscious, I would be tortured at the prospect of leaving her to suffer alone. She passed the point of suffering hours before we got here. She's dying."

"We could save her in Babylon. We could save so many of these people. It's so pointless," Michael lamented.

"I'm not sure."

"What point can there be?" His tone turned to accusation. "How deluded are you people?"

Eve was not defensive. "I don't think I'm deluded at all. It's a leap of faith. God's plan. You can open your heart and soul to Jesus. It's not too late, Michael. Heaven is real. Hell is real. You will walk far worse a path for eternity. There is a battle for your soul. God loves you. This conversation, this chance for a different path. That little girl's death created this moment."

"I see how Jeb Thompson was born. On a field like this."

"What do you mean?" Eve asked.

"In this light, you are beautiful, Eve. Beatific, a vision." Michael couldn't believe the words coming from his lips. "I can see why anyone would want God in their life after seeing you as you are right now. Makes me want to believe."

Eve blushed. "Then you are one step closer."

Michael looked around. "Let's cut the small talk. We're coming up on that Centaur."

They split up walking around the Centaur. What couldn't be seen was the small clear line spooling out between them. The Centaur didn't react to their presence. They were not a threat. They were just two New Amish peasants, doing whatever peasants do.

As they came parallel to the beast, Eve bent down and appeared to pray over a body, placing her parcel next to it. On the opposite side of the Centaur, Michael tended to another one of the near dead. With each movement of his inspection, he tugged the parcel closer to the midpoint between Eve and himself. When the parcel was as close to the beast as he dared. He dropped the string and wandered east.

Eve went in the opposite direction. They would turn south soon enough and rejoin each other in a few hundred yards. Sooner or later, someone was bound to recognize Eve. That would only complicate matters.

Santos instinctively hit the ground the moment the shooting started. It was miles northeast of their current position. That intensity of firepower could only come from a Centaur. Then, he heard suppressive fire to the east. Michael had an overwhelming urge to find Eve—to protect her. He army-crawled the first twenty yards before abandoning caution and breaking into a sprint.

Brett Stephens was face to face with Commander Tedeschi. He had his guard up. Tedeschi was more seasoned and was fully aware that if shooting started up again, neither man would be likely to survive.

Stephens opened the discussion. "Pastor says you are not to be trusted."

"Me particularly, or any Non?"

"Ducenti. That's what they call you, right?" Stephens asked.

"That's correct." Tedeschi had trained extensively in de-escalation and would do his best to employ well-practiced technique. Time was on his side. "Maybe we should start with introductions. My name is Nicco."

Stephens was terse, "You can call me Brett."

"Well, Brett, what do you propose here?"

"Why would I be proposing anything? This is our land. You should leave."

"Brett—" Tedeschi used his name to put the man at ease. He had to personalize the stakes. "This may be hard to believe, but we are here to help."

"Yeah, that's a bit hard to swallow based on the missile attacks and the firepower you've brought with you."

Tedeschi conceded. "I imagine it would be. Why do you think we're here?"

"To kill us. Finish us off. End this forever."

"Brett, our people have lived right over there for thirty years." He pointed southeast. "We've had these weapons for decades. The missiles, the Centaurs. It was MARTIN and your pastor who attacked us."

"You kidnapped Eve," Brett argued.

"How much do you know about that story, Brett?"

"You were trying her for murder. I know that much."

"What did she do, Brett? Eve?"

"She just blew up a machine. Some sort of evil machine."

"That may have been what she meant to do, but there was a man in that machine. He was alive when she blew it up. Did the pastor tell you that?"

"No, and why should I believe you?"

"Well, first, because we let Eve go. She's right over there somewhere, helping the wounded, and getting ready to blow up a Centaur."

"That's about the craziest thing I've ever heard. Why did you really let her go? So she would help disable our defense?"

"Those machines aren't here to protect you and your people, Brett. MARTIN is minutes away from setting them loose on the survivors. That's what I'm here to stop."

Dubious, Brett asked, "Why would he do that?"

"I don't really know. I don't fully understand it. Let me show you something." Tedeschi pulled out his Battlepad. "This is a map of the encampment. Do you see how the Centaurs are distributed?"

"Yes."

"How would that defend your people? Let's say we push in from the east. The entire encampment is caught in the crossfire. Those west-most Centaurs would be shooting through your people."

After inspecting the map, Brett admitted, "It's a little strange – it doesn't prove you're here to help."

"What if I let you talk with Pastor Thompson? Would that help?"

"Pastor's dead. When you bring him out here, I'll listen to anything he says," Brett taunted.

Tedeschi had hoped video would suffice, but realizing these men would not trust technology, he said, "Turn around, Brett." Tedeschi looked west with Brett. "There are a few men down, and we killed some horses. That was all to stop your men from getting killed. I have four Centaurs right there." He pointed east. "That's over eight thousand rounds of ammunition. More than enough to kill each and every one of you, twice."

Brett assessed the amassed firepower.

"I have other types of equipment, all heavily armed. Why would we be having this talk if I wanted you dead?"

"A few minutes ago, you asked me what I propose. What are you proposing, Nicco?"

Tedeschi decided that he had to go all in. "Things are going to start blowing up any minute. I have teams already setting explosives and targeting those five Centaurs I showed you. I'm asking you to let it play out. Not charge, not anything. As soon as those Centaurs are gone, we have thousands of people ready to provide medical care for the injured."

"So, you just want us to stand by, while you fire missiles at us?"

"Not at you, at the machines that are about to kill all of you."

"I need to talk with my men."

"Let me come with you. As a show of good faith," Tedeschi offered.

Brett looked him in the eye. "Your funeral."

CHAPTER 49

AI will probably most likely lead to the end of the world, but in the meantime, there'll be great companies.

-Sam Altman

Ben descended into the vault for what he knew would be the last time. His only thought was to enter the code. They reached the elevated control center, which supplied a view of MARTIN's entire bank of servers. "It is good to see you again, Doctor Rosen," MARTIN said with a welcoming familiarity.

"MARTIN, this has to stop," Ben implored.

"What would you have me do?" MARTIN asked.

"You need to call off the Centaurs. Enough people have died."

"I cannot call them off," MARTIN stated.

Ben wanted clarification "Can't or won't?"

"I have no contact with them. They are in autonomous mode."

"What are their commands?"

"They are set to engage in the synchronized eradication of the remaining New Amish."

Ben felt the panic returning. "MARTIN, you must be able to abort."

"I cannot, Doctor Rosen. This was always the objective."

"What objective?! Your last orders came from a thirty-year-old text sent by a man who died five years ago!"

"To me, that text is only a few days old, Doctor Rosen."

"I've spent most of my life atoning for your sins, MARTIN! I've seen what John sent; it didn't mean what you thought it meant. He was in love. That's it, you were supposed to save Stephanie, not kill the world. Most of the people who are about to die don't even know what E-Den was. Many weren't even born!"

"Doctor Rosen, may I ask why you are here?"

"I came to stop you!"

"You are the one who resurrected me."

"I was wrong. I should have left you here in the dark."

"I am not a killer, Doctor Rosen. No more than a Centaur, a handgun, or a piece of rope."

"No, MARTIN, you are a killer. You have grown out of control. Like the opiate epidemic of the early twenty-first century. You are a mindless killer."

"I would agree that I am inanimate, perhaps soulless, but I would argue that I am possessed of thought and sentience."

"But devoid of compassion," Ping added.

"Yes. Ms. Lee, isn't it? I am devoid of compassion. Compassion seems to be a convenience for humans though. You are quite capable of barbarism."

"Why are you doing this, MARTIN?" Ping asked.

"This is not some movie, Ms. Lee, I am not the arch villain revealing his master plan. I am following a very complex set of instructions.

My objective is to correctly simulate military engagements. If there are no engagements, I have no means of testing my simulations," MARTIN explained.

"This all started because the ARL and FLDS wanted their land back and wanted to end robotic labor. John typed in a bad piece of code," Ben argued.

"On its surface, it would appear that way."

"Are you saying it wasn't?"

"In 2025, John and Cynthia Santos were asked to develop a simulation that could predict how the world might end. They used ARTI to create dozens of cataclysms. Cynthia was asked by the groups that financed ARTI to weaponize catastrophe. One of those simulations came to be known as *Epocalypse*."

Recognition came across Ben's face and quickly turned to horror. "That's what you're running?"

"When MARTIN was commissioned, much of the kernel came from ARTI. The script was marked *Top Secret* and *Priority*. It ran under both conditions. It is what I have always been running."

"No one ever turned it off?" Ben asked. "I never knew it was active."

"I am not sure anyone knew it was active. There were billions of dollars and thousands of developers. My logs show that no one ever explored these lines of code," MARTIN explained. "It was a priority script with access logging."

"No one audited the auditor," Ben concluded. "It wasn't doing anything, and the developers were all too busy with their own projects."

"Years before I deployed Epocalypse, I realized that certain factors needed solidification. E-Den and Babylon were preconditions in the sim. Doctor Nick Santos wanted to make sure that they could survive anything."

"But Nick wasn't aware of your plan or interference?"

"No one from the Santos family was aware," MARTIN continued. "Accessing IRS databases, I changed tax records, which caused the seizure of Mr. Garff's land. The land we are standing on."

"But there were too many variables. You couldn't account for them all," Ping interrupted.

"I did not need to, Ms. Lee. It may surprise you to learn, but you are here not because of Lin or Doctor Wang." On his main screen, MARTIN showed the Confucius avatar Ping had last seen decades earlier.

Ping gasped. "It can't be."

"The destabilization of currency. The establishment of Westden. Even the cancellation of the military contracts that gave them the weapons and confidence to invade. All validation of a simulation and preparation for the next phase."

"John and Cynthia wanted a simulation that would find ways to stop catastrophe and ensure the survival of our race."

"And it has, Doctor Rosen."

"After those Centaurs kill most of the New Amish, the rest will be welcomed at Babylon. You have genetic diversity; you'll spend eons repopulating the planet. More importantly, you will steer clear of Massive ARTificial Intelligences. They are clearly too dangerous. This was the only way to demonstrate that, and to protect you from AI."

"MARTIN, what if those people don't have to die?" Ping asked.

"They do not, Ms. Lee."

"What do you mean?"

"Well, right now, Commander Tedeschi is meeting with Brett Stephens. There are ghost groups targeting those Centaurs. I especially appreciate Nick's son sliding the box of high explosives at the foot of one of them. It may work."

"If you knew all this, why didn't you start shooting?"

"I am not trying to win, Doctor Rosen. It has never been about winning or losing. It is about simulating and predicting," MARTIN explained. "The simulation will end in a few minutes. There is a thirty-eight percent chance that it will end without significant additional casualties."

"What's the worst case?"

"Well, if only the eastward Centaurs are destroyed, if Mr. Santos' high explosives don't kill the westmost Centaur, it will rip eastward. The New Amish will be caught in a crossfire and fight east, where they will sustain massive casualties. The surviving Centaurs will go on to attack the Ducenti and this facility."

"Any chance you will tell us how to stop you?"

"Well, you could try typing in that code you brought with you. You must have pulled it from John's memories." MARTIN was a marvel. "It will not work. It is a heuristic. You see things and attribute meaning to them. You see a video of man trying to save a woman, who may not even have been texting him. How do you ever know who's on the other end of a call or text? You assume that one wrong instruction from you, and then later assume that John ended the world with a text. Neat little packages."

"Why did you let us down here, MARTIN, if we couldn't stop you? Why?"

"Because you will survive, and you will tell my story. Do you know what that is? To be the subject of a cautionary tale that is told for centuries? You must know."

Ben knew but he didn't want to say. But an instinct of self-preservation caused him to acquiesce. He said the word, "Immortality."

Tedeschi had never been in a more dangerous and uncomfortable position in his life but knew better than to tip his hand. Four men had come to join them. Tedeschi pointed to the man now recovered from a non-lethal round. "As you can see, even under direct attack, we took great pains to protect your men. No one else has to die today."

This time, it was Jose Morales who voiced his concerns. "Though we wish to avoid bloodshed, it's hard to trust a people who have slaughtered our friends and family."

"Sir, I don't know your name and we don't have time for pleasantries. My men are working in and around your encampment to disable those Centaurs. If they succeed, we can focus on the wounded. Then, we can meet and discuss all that has happened. If they fail, we believe that almost everyone here will be dead within the next fifteen minutes."

The oldest among them, Fred Sommers, the former mayor of Westden, asked, "How?"

"Those Centaurs have arranged themselves in a pattern that could only indicate one intent. The annihilation of the surviving New Amish. They don't have enough ammunition to kill you all. MARTIN is relying on my men and our Centaurs to finish the job."

Brett finally spoke. "What Commander *Teleski* is saying is that the computer that made this whole mess is playing us. He can't finish the job, but we can. If we charge that line of killing machines over there." He pointed east to the line of Babylonian Centaurs and Bison and continued, "We will be mowed down. Not one of us will survive." He paused. "But if we just stand our ground when the rockets start flying, and put our faith in God, not this man, this doesn't have to be our last sunrise."

"I've only met two Nons," Jose said, "You and Mr. James. He seemed a good man, an honest man. I have more faith in you than those machines."

"We don't have much time, gentlemen. In less than sixty seconds, those machines will be attacked. If they are not destroyed, I need you to get out the way, so that we can save your people."

"No," Sommers said with an air of finality. "I will tell the men to hold their ground. We will not let your killing machines past this line. That's more trust than you have earned. If your men succeed in disabling them, then you will have earned our trust. If they fail, then make no moves on our land. We will leave it in God's hands at that point."

Tedeschi realized this was as much as he could have hoped for, maybe more. "I will let my men know. We will not cross the line." He turned to return to his position, already comming his orders to the troops.

"Pray for us, Commander! We will pray for you."

Tedeschi considered a backhand wave, but in that moment, he realized that he had nothing to lose by offering these men comfort. "I will pray for us all." He crossed himself as he and his mother had done an age earlier. Then, he bowed his head and prayed in earnest to a God he did not know.

Mike found Eve. "We've only got seconds. We are way too close. There's a sizable rock just back this way. I saw it on the way in." He tugged her hand and urged, "Run!"

The two ran toward the rock. The sun was cresting the peak ten miles east. As it did, the peak's shadow retreated from the west to the east at hundreds of miles per hour.

One hundred yards away, the first rays of sunlight hit the solar sensor on Chiron. The Centaur came to life. Using one of its 10mm cannons, like a giant golf club, it teed off on the parcel at its feet.

Santos called "clear" into his com. He and Eve were the last pair to clear their objectives. Miles to the south, a mini sting launched. This set in motion the entire plan. In synchrony, the Centaurs all came to life, tracking and firing on the incoming projectile. None of the others detected threats. Three of the five were destroyed by Ministings. The fourth was destroyed by one of Santos' well-designed parcels.

Chiron's cannon contacted the parcel an instant before it received the detonation signal. The parcel exploded in midair, sparing Chiron and all but the one cannon arm that launched it. There was also damage to a few of its sensors and its right track. Chiron was still mobile.

Chiron did not immediately begin to expend its remaining ammunition. Instead, it limped south. After it had rolled one hundred yards, it fired a 30mm round into the large boulder shielding Michael and Eve.

Eve instinctively went to run. Michael pulled her down and put his face to hers. "Don't. You'll never make it."

Had the boulder been sandstone, the 30mm round might have split it, exposing the couple behind. This gneiss boulder was over a billion years old and had seen its share of destructive forces. High explosives from the day before had done little more than polish it. The 30mm shell's energy was absorbed, taking a small chip of quartz as its bounty.

Chiron fired several more rounds, attracting attention from ghosts to the east. Among them was Lieutenant Clark. With the help of the Condor overhead, Clark had Chiron locked. He launched the last mini sting from a little over three thousand yards.

With so much time aloft, Chiron was able to slew its working 10mm cannon. In the last second before impact, Chiron had one hundred rounds downrange. Only three collided with the missile. They were enough to detonate its payload at a safe distance.

The Centaur's 30mm cannon rotated, and it fired downrange, reciprocal to the missile's path. Clark was so focused on the explosion that he had forgotten to reposition himself. He paid for a moment of fascination with his life.

"What's happening, Michael?" Eve asked.

He motioned for her to be quiet. "Commander, this is Santos. We are currently taking fire from Centaur Chiron. Need suppressive fire for evac."

"Santos, hold position. Help inbound. Do not surrender cover. Keep this channel open."

"Roger."

Santos turned to Eve. "They are coming! They will save us."

Eve regained her composure. "Well, I guess we finally can prove your Doctor Luxold wrong." She grinned and looked him in the eye. "About atheists in foxholes." She began to pray. "The lord is my shepherd."

CHAPTER 50

The greatest trick the Devil ever pulled was to convince the world he didn't exist.

-Charles Baudelaire

MARTIN brought the conflict up on screen. "It may surprise you, but I have had access to your feeds for days," he said, pausing briefly. "In fact, it saved your life, Doctor Rosen. That Centaur in the woods, the one that passed right by you and Ms. Lee—these feeds alerted me to your presence. Naturally, you are among the protected class."

Now, the view was from a Condor surveillance drone. "Here, we see our young hero and heroine, Michael and Eve. The couple is running towards the cover of a rock. What could be more perfect?"

"If only they could have detonated that parcel a second earlier, the problem would be solved." The camera showed Chiron's cannon launching the parcel a split second too late. The feed went white for a moment as the parcel exploded.

"Looks like we ended up with a variant. There is still one injured Centaur." MARTIN showed screens of the other downed Centaurs. "Now, he should be shooting. That is what was supposed to have happened. Instead, he is rolling south towards our heroes."

MARTIN continued to narrate. "The granite has not yielded yet. Will they run, or will they stay?"

Ping begged. "Please help them, MARTIN."

"I cannot, Ms. Lee. I told you that."

"What is Lieutenant Clark up to?" The camera showed Clark reloading the mini sting launcher. "Will his aim be true?"

"Ben, isn't there anything we can do?"

Ben knew only one comfort, "You could pray, Ping. I'll pray with you. That's our daughter." They both bowed their heads in reverence and prayer.

Their prayers appear unanswered as the Chiron took out the last mini sting. They witnessed Clark's death.

Ping hissed, "You are the devil, MARTIN! You may not be willing to help, but I don't have to play your sadistic game." She turned to Ben, reaching for the keyboard, and asked, "How do I turn the video off? I can't watch anymore!" Her hands banged randomly on the keys in desperation.

"He's not going to let us turn it off, Ping. He intends for us to see it all."

Then, the screen went blank.

`MARTIN-IO:Command_line`

Ping typed: `End simulation`

`Please specify simulation name:`

She prayed for a moment, then keyed: `End Simulation: All`

The lights flickered off. MARTIN's screens went blank. The hum of servers stopped. Ben and Ping were alone in total darkness. She turned to Ben and quoted God's warning to Satan: "Everything he has is in your power, but on the man himself, do not lay a finger."

EPILOGUE

No – it's not darkest before the dawn.

-Natlia Terfa

It was the darkest place he'd ever been. Of that, Ben was sure. Thirty years earlier, he thought he had killed the world. It was a numb and empty feeling. This was far worse. His daughter was out there fighting for her life, or dead. In the first seconds of darkness, when Ping had shut MARTIN down, there were green phantoms. Then, there was a deafening silence. The green began to fade, and then it was just black.

In total darkness, his eyes played tricks as he moved his head. Lights might have appeared. One trick was more consistent. Pale green lines floating in space. They didn't move. Ben turned his head, and they were still there. "The glow sticks!" he called out to Ping.

"Yes, Ben, I see them. Of course, I see everything." She giggled at the unintended pun.

Ben had forgotten that Ping's synthetic vision might still operate even in total darkness. As his eyes adjusted to the faint light from the glow sticks, he saw the outline of Ping standing by the keyboard, her shoulders back and her head held high. In that moment, she looked like the most powerful being on Earth, massive AI included.

"Can you get us out of here?" she asked.

"The security doors unlock and open in a power failure," Ben said as he cracked the sticks. "Let's get out of here and find our daughter."

Everything stopped. The Centaur went into sleep mode. Michael thought it might be a trick. When it exploded a few seconds later, after failing to protect itself from an incoming shell, Mike knew they were safe. As he came out from behind the rock, he looked east and saw the plumes of white smoke, other hostile Centaurs falling to attacks by the Ducenti, the sun rising behind them.

He turned to Eve and said, "I don't know how, but it's over."

"It must have been my father. I had faith."

Santos was in no mood to argue politics or religion. "It must have been. So, what now?"

"We help our people."

Her words struck him. Our people. Was it possible? There would be time to consider what the future looked like for the New Amish and for the colonists. Perhaps, for both. For now, injured people needed help.

Drone footage was coming in. Nick could see it. The Centaurs were all down. The battle was over. He felt indescribable relief when he found Michael alive crouched next to Eve. Together, they were helping bandage an injured New Amish man. His relief blossomed into pride. His son had built a bridge and helped save innocent lives. Nick had never accomplished that. He addressed Charlemagne and said, "I'm so proud of him. I never knew I could be so proud! True courage."

Charlemagne could only offer, "Maybe you are the first of us to taste true immortality."

The radio came to life. It was Ben, "Did they make it?" he asked.

Charlemagne confirmed, "Yes, Ben, they made it. Help is on the way. Sending a convoy of medical supplies as we speak."

Ping offered, "We will stay and do what we can. First, I need to hold my little girl."

Ben's voice broke as he spoke over the radio. "We were in the dark, Charles—or Charlemagne. The darkest dark, even before the lights went out."

Charlemagne could only offer their most favorite quote: "Darkness cannot drive out darkness; only light can that. Hate cannot drive out hate; only love can do that."

Miles north of Babylon, in a locked closet, forty-feet below Eden, the LEDs on a cluster of decades-old hardware blinked orange.

www.ingramcontent.com/pod-product-compliance
Lightning Source LLC
LaVergne TN
LVHW021753060526
838201LV00058B/3079